About the Author

I was brought up in Buckinghamshire but was born in Devon during the Second World War.

After leaving school I trained as a nurse. Now retired I spend my time writing articles for various magazines. This is my first novel but second book.

I share my life in Exeter Devon with my husband Terry. I have a son – Quinton Winter who lives in Kent with his family.

To Jan
Enjoy
Love Claire.

GW00455894

If Only I'd Listened

Claire Boley

If Only I'd Listened

A CIP catalogue record for this title is available
from the British Library.

This is a work of fiction. Names, characters,
places and incidents originate from the

Dedication to my

grandchildren,

Cal and Mae

Chapter 1

Samantha and I met in the mid 60s when we were pupils at the South East Comprehensive near Deptford, by the age of consent we were having sex regularly, where ever we could, neither of us gave it a thought that the outcome could possibly be a baby, as we hadn't used johnnies. It was not until Sam came over to me when I was stood with my mates in break from class one Friday morning and whispered in my ear that she felt peculiar and that she had missed her period. In fact, it was two periods that she'd missed, this meant that she may be two months' pregnant. My mates stood staring at us both as I had gone so pale and Sam looked so perky.

"What's wrong, Knight? You look like you've seen a ghost," said John, smirking to himself.

"Nothing that concerns you." At that I pulled Sam to one side.

"Looks like she's got a bun in the oven the way you look, hope for your sake she hasn't."

"Mind your own business."

"The way you're speaking to me I bet I'm more right than wrong."

With that I decided to miss the next lesson and take Sam out of school, to have a chat, there was a problem, it was my mock A-level English exam in a couple of hours. At the time, I thought catching the bus to the coffee bar at the bus station in the centre of Lewisham was more important than any exam, so off we went hoping that we would get back before my mock started. We must have been very naive because it didn't enter either of our heads that we would be missed and Mr Down would be asking my mates where I was.

Once outside the school gates I had to put up with tears and tantrums, Sam didn't seem to care who heard her. I knew that it was going to be extremely difficult to calm her down as she had got herself into a terrible state, so I decided that Lewisham was the best place to go, out of sight of anyone that knew us. The bus took ages to arrive, this was due to the fact that it was market day, the queue got longer and longer, while Sam got more and more flushed and agitated. Eventually the bus did arrive and I bought two return tickets to Lewisham bus station, where we sat in the nearest coffee bar to the bus stop, to get back to Deptford and school. We had a long chat and I tried to explain that it was as much my fault as hers, all she was concerned about were her parents and what they would say. I told her that tomorrow she may have her period and all this upset may be for nothing; she wouldn't have any of it, she was quite sure that she was pregnant because of the way she felt which was different.

While sitting in the coffee bar my parents walked past the door, they didn't notice me. The thing was they didn't know that I had a girlfriend, so they didn't know Sam, even if they saw her, they wouldn't be thinking where's Pete if that's Sam sitting in there having a coffee. At this point my life went before me as my parents believed I was at school taking one of the exams that was to mark out my future. If only they knew I was sitting only a few feet from them recovering from the biggest shock I could ever have: my girlfriend may be pregnant. They were expecting me to pass all my exams with flying colours and manage to get into a good university. I just sat still with Sam wondering what was going to happen next, hoping and praying that they didn't decide to come in for a quick coffee like they often did, while they waited for the bus to go home to Blackheath. Luckily for me the bus we needed to catch back to school arrived just as we finished our coffee so we both dashed out of the coffee bar and jumped on the double-decker to Deptford without being spotted.

Once back at the school gates, I hurried off for my mock exam leaving Sam looking very upset and still near to tears.

"Try not to get so upset, we will have to sort something out after my exam. I'll try and see you at lunchtime, remember my exam doesn't finish till one o'clock, if I don't see you then I will meet up with you after school, try and cheer up."

I walked into the classroom and found the master, Mr Down about to start the exam without me. When he saw me arriving late, he looked very annoyed and angry, sternly he told me to sit down at the desk at the back of the room. I normally sat in the front so I immediately thought something was up and wondered what was going to come next. I settled down and tried to focus on the exam. Before I knew it, the mock was over and I was handing in my paper, when Mr Down asked if I would stay behind as he wanted a chat.

After sitting down at the side of Mr Down's desk it came as a complete shock when he informed me that he knew where I'd been and he and most of staff knew that Sam and I had been having sex regularly. He went on to tell me that the subject of Sam and myself had come up in conversation at most staff meetings in the last six months. The most worrying thing to the staff was, what if Sam gets pregnant? When he said this I could feel myself getting hot under the collar and feeling more and more uncomfortable. I honestly didn't know what to reply to this remark. After thinking for a few minutes I decided the best policy was to keep quiet and wait and see what bombshell he was going to throw at me next. I'm sure it was only a few seconds but to me it seemed more like an hour before he came out with the question, asking if what he had been told by the boys before the exam was true.

"Is Sam pregnant?" I went on to explain that Sam and I had been for a chat over a mug of coffee and the answer to his question seemed to be, yes. Mr Down just sat and looked at me over the top of his spectacles, he didn't seem surprised, just bewildered, and sat shaking his head.

After a while of looking and wondering he suddenly came out with a statement.

"Perhaps you should take a long hard look into your future and think about how you are going to go to university and study science with a baby to support. I suggest you go home and sleep on this, tomorrow is another day and things may become clearer. Tell me one thing, what does Samantha think of the position you have both got yourselves in? Pete, the thing is, she hasn't the brain that you have, think of Sam in the C and D streams for most of her subjects while you are in the A stream for all your subjects, she's hardly likely to be considering university. You have to remember that this baby will eventually grow into an adult and will be around for the rest of your lives, whether you like it or not, unless of course you both consider Sam having an abortion." At this point I stood up.

"Mr Down, I'm going, you're giving me a headache. I can't take any more of this, I will have a think about what you have said."

I left the room and wandered outside, hoping to meet Sam before going in for lunch but I didn't. I sat in the dining hall with my mates, wondering if she would come in. That didn't materialize either, where she had gone to eat her lunch I don't know. The afternoon seemed long and drawn out, I could hardly concentrate as I was worried about Sam. Luckily for me, the lessons weren't any of my exam subjects, I had Art for most of the afternoon and then sports/games.

Walking out of the school gates I bumped straight into Sam. She seemed her usual happy self, just as if things had all gone back to normal, no mention of the pregnancy. Together we waited for our different buses, when suddenly out of the blue and in front of everyone that was waiting at the bus stop Sam came out with.

"After leaving you I went to the phone box across the road and phoned mum. I told her of my predicament. She exploded down the phone, 'You and I will have to have a long talk when you get in tonight my girl, what your dad will say I don't know, just hope he's not around when we have our chat!'"

I felt such a fool as I thought she would have had more sense and kept the pregnancy from her mother for a few more days at least, as the situation could and may disappear as quickly as it came. As it was my fault as much as it was Sam's, I made the decision to get on the bus with Sam and go home to meet her parents for the very first time.

It may seem very strange but I had no idea what type of flat or house Sam lived in or exactly where it was. I dreamt that it would be overlooking the river Thames near St Paul's. It came as a complete shock when she told me that we had a ten-minute walk down the Old Kent Road after we had got off the bus outside the Elephant and Castle tube station. First we walked along the New Kent Road pass the Stag's Head pub into the Old Kent Road. The walk seemed endless. Once we got to the turning where the block of flats were situated Sam stood on the curb, then looked to the sky and pointed.

"That's where I live, across the road in that tower block, my flat is on the fifth floor. Can you see those yellow check curtains?"

"Yeah, where the window's open?"

"That's the one, the steps and the lift go up the middle of the block, there are four flats on each landing, as I told you earlier we're on the fifth floor, there's just one problem, the lift has been out of order for a few weeks so we'll have to walk up and down the steps."

I was bewildered and just couldn't believe that a girl I was seeing, let alone may have got pregnant, lives in a block of flats here. After going through the dirty wooden swing doors into the main hall, I had an even a bigger shock: the walls were covered in graffiti and there were used johnnies all over the floor. The smell of both urine and alcohol was horrendous. I'd never been inside a building like this, but I had passed by on the outside and wondered who lived in this type of environment.

I live with my parents and younger sister in a terrace house a short distance from Blackheath railway station. Dad works in the office at the local Woolworths, while mum works as a part time teacher at the local primary school. If they could see me climbing these steps to Sam's flat they would be horrified and wonder what had come over me. The steps were hard work, Sam is used to them and ran up whilst I plodded along behind her.

We reached the door to the flat. This was in a terrible state, grease and black finger marks everywhere, it was in need of a good clean and after being cleaned it ought to be given a couple of coats of paint. The key to the flat was on a length of parcel string; this was tied around Sam's neck, as if it was a necklace, so she couldn't lose it. To unlock the door she had to first untie the string, this was quite a performance as it was tied extra tight.

Eventually we were inside the narrow hallway where we stood on green and brown check lino. This was so sticky that my slip on shoes stuck to the floor making my feet come out of them, while I walked towards the kitchen. The smell in the flat was different from downstairs, here it was of drink and cigarettes.

We both walked solemnly through the kitchen door where we found Sam's mum and dad sitting at the kitchen table with two glasses and a half-empty bottle of whisky. How much they had drunk I am not sure, but it must have been more than one measure. It was obvious to me that they had been there for some time discussing what to say to Sam when she arrived home.

Once they saw the pair of us, Mr Smithson went ballistic, shouting and ranting in between trying to catch his breath. He didn't give either of us a chance to explain ourselves, he was from the old school, no sex before marriage and definitely not before leaving school. He looked at me with a look that I had never seen before. As people often say, if looks could kill, I'd be dead; his eyes seemed to be popping out of his head in temper. I just didn't know what to do, the first thing I thought of was to run but then how could I leave Sam to take her parents temper on her own?

"What the bloody hell do you both think you've been up to? Sex before marriage and even before leaving school, now there's a shitty little bastard on the way. How long has this been going on and where has it been happening? I wouldn't be surprised if you told me it was in the fucking school lavs because it ain't been here. I'm bloody sure you haven't been doing it at your place, if your parents caught you with Sam, I dread to think what would happen, I know damn well they wouldn't like Sam. I fucking know they wouldn't approve of you going with her. I have only one suggestion to make to the pair of you, that is think very hard about what has happened and the fucking position that you've both got your fucking selves in! Perhaps you should consider an abortion. I hope the two of you are listening to me?"

I stood leaning on the kitchen table thinking about what Mr Smithson had just said about where this had been happening. Of course he was right, it was in the girls' toilets, not a cosy love nest. This sounded so disgusting and now there might be a baby on the way. Every time we look at this baby, we will be thinking where it was conceived.

Mr Smithson carried on ranting, while Mrs Smithson sat sideways to the table looking shocked and bewildered with her head in her hands. It seemed as if she had smoked most of the cigarettes as the ashtray was overflowing and an empty pack of Woodbines was by her side. Mrs Smithson's hair looked like it needed a wash, it was lank and grey with creamy yellow areas, caused by nicotine. Her face looked pasty, I guess this was due to not having enough fresh air; her clothes, well, they had seen better days, her top was a pink blouse with a mixture of different coloured buttons. Over the top of this she wore a yellow floral pinafore which had two lengths of string knotted at the back of the main part, these were then tied in a bow around the front to hold the pinafore in position. On her legs she was wearing a pair of navy trousers with an elasticated waist with white ankle socks and filthy pink fluffy slippers on her feet. Sam's dad didn't look any better, in fact his clothes looked even worse, everything appeared to have been bought from the local jumble sale.

"Get out of our flat, go and explain to your parents what has happened, I don't want to see you again. Sam can go with you as she's not welcome to live here, the pair of you is fucking disgusting!" Mr Smithson shouted, in between coughing up sputum into his foul check handkerchief. With that, Sam came round to my side of the table, got hold of my arm and whispered in my ear, "let's go". We turned and walked in a daze out of the kitchen, closing the door behind us, leaving Sam's parents to hopefully calm down and to get over the shock.

We stood in the hallway to think what we should do, but found this difficult as we could hear Sam's parents screaming at each other about the situation we had got ourselves into.

"You shouldn't have told them to get out, Sam is our only daughter, we may never see her again, she may finish up on the streets."

"So what? I don't care if we don't see her again," replied Sam's dad, still coughing well.

"It takes two to tangle," replied Sam's mum.

"I know that, if I give in and see Sam I never want to see him. Mildred, you realise that it's illegal for anyone to have sex before they're sixteen? I'm going to have to stop him from seeing her. I will have to go to the school and the cop shop to sort this out." By this time we could hear Mrs Smithson sobbing and coughing well.

"Oh shut up you crying bitch, you're like a baby, what with that cough as well, you make me feel sick. For God's sake, Mildred, shut up or you can get out as well."

"I'm sorry, Keith, but I can't help getting upset."

Sam and I held each other tight, speculating on what was going to happen in the kitchen next. At the same time wondering what we ought to do, should Sam go into her bedroom and collect a few clothes, or should we just run? There was one big problem: Sam had nothing to put her things in as she didn't have a suitcase and the black plastic bags were in the kitchen cupboard. The only thing she had was a black canvas holdall with a zip and two handles which she carried her books to school in.

"There should be enough room for a few clothes in your bag. I could always carry the few books you have in this bag. It's not very clean but it will do for your school books, let's transfer them over, then you'll have room for your clothes,"

"That's a good idea, I will go into my room and collect my washing things plus clean knickers, etc. You hang on here."

"Don't be long, I don't want him coming out and finding me still here, he frightens me."

"He won't come out, I doubt if he can stand up after drinking the whisky, I'll only be a minute."

Sam was quicker than I thought she'd be. Once back we decided to go as soon as she'd managed to pack her few bits into her black holdall, then she'd come back to collect more clothes and anything else she needed on a day that her parents were at work, down the factory. We went as quietly as possible out of the front door. Once out on the walkway we rushed back down the stairs to the main road, I felt quite relieved to have escaped unscathed.

"Your parents gave me a shock, I never dreamt that they would behave like they did. Mine are quite different. Mum is very friendly and chatty, Dad is very quiet; he never raises his voice to anyone."

"Dad can get very cross especially if he's had a few drinks, it's a wonder he didn't raise his fist at you. He spends a lot of his spare time down the Stag's Head – the pub we passed on the way to here? He hardly ever takes Mum with him, unless she insists, then he usually leaves her sat with her own friends and he goes over and stands at the bar with his mates. I have known him to hit out in the heat of the moment, especially when he returns from the pub. One evening he came back early and supper wasn't ready, because of this he was in such a temper that he tipped the kitchen table upside down, all the plates landed on the floor in pieces, he then demanded that Mum should pay for the new plates out of her own money. That night there was no supper. Dad has never hit me but he has put his fist up to take a blow at Mum, when she has spent too much money or has been out with her girlfriends instead of being at home cooking supper. He has a very short fuse."

"Sounds like it. I couldn't stand that. Anyway, where do you eat your meals? I noticed you haven't a dining room?"

"Oh, in the kitchen around the table Mum and Dad were sitting at. Mum moves some of their rubbish off, to make room for the knives, forks and plates, then the food is left in the saucepans on the table for us to take what we want to eat. I sometimes sit and eat my food on my lap in my bedroom."

My face must have been a picture as I wasn't used to eating or living like this. We carried on talking while walking hand in hand to the tube station, where a serious decision needed to be made, were we going to abscond or go over to Blackheath and explain what has happened to my parents? Once we arrived at the Elephant ticket office we found we only had enough money between us to catch the tube and train to Blackheath station. Like it or not, that was where we had to go. The tube was full all the way to London Bridge where we had to change stations. We sat opposite one another instead of together. I just sat looking over at Sam who looked very pale and tired. I was wondering what she was thinking as we had got ourselves into such a mess; her pregnant at just sixteen and me going to be a father at seventeen and a half, perhaps all and sundry were right when they said that Sam should have an abortion as our lives were going to be ruined before they began.

The tube soon arrived at London Bridge. It was a job to get off due to the number of people trying to get on. Conversation between us was non-existent as we were both worrying about what was going to happen once we got to my home. We found our way to the railway station and got on the train to Blackheath. It seemed to take ages, but it only took fifteen minutes from the Elephant and Castle tube station to Blackheath.

Once we arrived outside my home, I took a deep breath.

"Here goes, Sam." I took the key out of my top pocket and opened the door knowing full well that my parents plus fourteen-year-old sister would be inside waiting for me to return from school to discuss the day's events, over a cup of tea.

"Is that you, Peter?" said Mum from the front room.

"Yeah," I replied from the narrow hallway.

"You're late, where have you been? We were all getting a bit worried as you're normally home by half four and it is now almost six o'clock. We were thinking about going ahead and having supper without you."

Holding on to Sam's hand we walked around the corner into the doorway of the sitting room. There they were, Mum, Dad and Sis; they looked in a state of shock to see me stood in the doorway, holding a girl's hand.

"This is Sam. We have been seeing each other for a while, thought I'd bring her home to meet you all. She goes to school with me, Mum, Dad and Anne."

Mum jumped up out of her chair, trying to make herself presentable by pulling her top down to cover her middle as she had put on a bit of weight since she had bought the jumper, plus the fact it seemed to have shrunk in the wash. Dad as normal just sat in his chair by the window, dressed in his dark grey trousers, grey shirt with a red and white spotted tie, and, over the top, a hand-knitted moss green V-neck pullover, which

Mum had knitted especially for him. As we entered, Dad was reading the newspaper, on seeing the pair of us he dropped it into the paper rack and looked across at Sam and myself. He's a man of few words so he had nothing to say to either of us, although he did manage a smile.

"Come and sit down, it's very nice to meet you. Would you like a cup of tea? It won't take a minute to make one. Perhaps you'd like to stay for supper? I only need to peel a few more spuds, we're having stew. Think about supper while I make your cuppa." Said Mum in such a rush that she could hardly catch her breath.

Sam sat herself down on the sofa next to Anne. I sat on the arm next to Sam as there aren't enough chairs to go around and the sofa is only big enough for two people. I suggested that Sam should put the bag with all her bits on the floor under the side board. Mum returned after a few minutes with the plastic tray and two mugs of tea.

"That's a good place for your bag, it's out of the way. You seem to have quite a lot of things with you, your bag seems extra big, it looks as if you may have left home. Anyway, enough of bags, it's lovely to meet you, Sam, I forgot to ask if you take sugar so I have brought the bowl in with a spoon, I'll put it on the floor by your side. Peter doesn't normally bring friends home so this is quite a surprise, isn't it Ernie?"

"Yeah, I suppose it is."

Then there was a long silence until Mum spoke again.

"Have you decided to stay for supper?" Silence still reigned. "I know, I'll decide for you, the answer is yes. I'll go and peel a couple more spuds, the meal will be in about half an hour. When you've both finished your tea, Pete, you can take Sam into the garden and show her Dad's plants. Have your parents got a garden?"

"No," said Sam sheepishly. "We live on the fifth floor of a tower block, in a flat at the Elephant and Castle, it has a small balcony which looks out over the back into the other flats. Mum says it's no good for growing plants as it's in the shade all day. We can't even dry the washing on the balcony, Dad bought us a clothes dryer to put in the hall. They are quite good, the heater is put on the floor with a type of wooden clothes horse on top, a material cover is put over the top of this, with the clothes underneath, have you seen them, Mrs Knight?"

"No, I've never seen a dryer like the one you are describing, we put our clothes on the line in the garden. If they don't dry completely we have to put them in front of the fire or I lay them out in the airing cupboard." At that, Mum left the room and went out into the kitchen, leaving us to finish our mugs of tea. I could see Sam looking around the room as if she hadn't been in a house like this before. When I visited Sam's flat, I felt strange, so I can imagine how she must be feeling.

Once we had finished we wandered through the kitchen where Mum was still busy peeling the extra spuds. "It's good to get outside while the weather's warm. Pete, take Sam down to the bottom of the garden and show her the plants with the lovely flowers your dad is growing for the flower show."

"Okay I will but you're not very interested in plants are you Sam?"

"As I said just now I don't see many, as I live in a fifth-floor flat with a very small balcony, so I don't know much about them. Mum keeps some indoor plants but she's not very good with them, she forgets to give them water, then they die."

Mum started to laugh. "Lots of people are like that, including me."

Out we went, hoping that we were not being watched from the window and also hoping that Mum couldn't hear our conversation. I showed Sam the dahlias that were being grown for Greenwich Flower Show in August, she seemed impressed.

"This is the first time I've seen dahlias growing in a garden, I love the colours. I sometimes watch gardening programmes on the telly with Mum and Dad, the trouble is our tele is in black and white so we can't see the colours. Hey, fancy you having a greenhouse, what's in it?"

"Nothing much, Mum looks after it, she tries to grow cucumbers and tomatoes, go inside and have a look." Sam slid open the door and went in, giving us a chance to have a chat and discuss if or when we were going to tell Mum and Dad about the pregnancy.

"Shall we tell my parents about our predicament over supper or on another day?"

"I think we should wait a few weeks and tell them when they know me better; then, with a bit of luck, they might take it okay."

"Sam, I think that might be a good idea, as Mum may take it badly; if something upsets her she is prone to vomiting and Dad's not very good at looking after her. If Mum starts to vomit it will really put the cat amongst the pigeons, they may say 'out' like your dad did and then where would we go?" Sam just looked at me.

"I don't want to upset them as they seem to like me, or at least what they have seen of me. Let's try and forget about the pregnancy for the time being and enjoy the evening. I have to think about where I'm going to sleep tonight, Pete."

"Leave it to me. I will think of somewhere, there is always the garden shed, or have you a friend that could put you up for one night?"

"I suppose I have. Mary lives near here and her parents know me, they have a flat above the bookshop that they own near the Blackheath Woolworths, I will give her a call after we've eaten. Her parents often go away to book fairs so she may be at home on her own, if they are away I could probably stay with her for a couple of nights."

"That sounds okay to me."

"Supper's ready!" shouted Mum from the kitchen door.

"We're coming," I called back. Closing the greenhouse door behind us, we plodded through the kitchen into the dining room, where Mum had made an effort by laying the table with the best tablecloth, cutlery and her favourite china. In fact, it was china that she had been given as a wedding present. The tablecloth was one that Mum had embroidered when she was a teenager; she was very proud of it.

"Sit over the other side, Sam, Peter you sit next to Sam. Dad is going to sit at the head of the table while I'm going to sit here, then I can get out to the kitchen easily. Anne, you sit opposite Pete and Sam." After Mum had sorted out the seating arrangements she put the dishes of veg on the table mats. Dad handed them around for us all to take what we wanted. Sam looked very embarrassed as she was used to taking her food straight out of the saucepans on to her plate, if the food needed to be strained it was dished up from the colander.

Watching Sam dishing out her food sent me into a dream, it made me realise that her life was completely different from mine. I was wondering how I could change and go along with her way of thinking, as I was quite sure she couldn't change to be more like me and this was only about cooking and eating, let alone her home life and how she was brought up, with her abusive and drunken dad and a mum that smoked at least thirty plus fags a day.

"You seem to have fallen asleep or at least in a world of your own, Pete, what's up?" asked Mum.

"Oh, I was far away, I'm back with you all now."

Mum looked at me very strangely especially as Sam went red with embarrassment. Dad looked up from his meal and looked at both Sam and myself, but, as usual, said nothing of any consequence.

The conversation was very light over supper without any awkward questions, thank goodness. Sam seemed to enjoy the food, even though she left the fresh veg. The pudding went down a treat – lemon meringue pie.

"Would you like to finish with a mug coffee made in a percolator, Sam?"

"I will say yes, please, I have only ever drunk instant coffee or espresso in a coffee bar."

"I'm sure you will like it, go and sit in the front room as it will take a few minutes to make and then it needs to brew."

Sam got up from the table first, followed by Anne who immediately went upstairs to her room. I followed Sam into the front room. Dad wandered into the kitchen carrying some of the dirty dishes.

"Nice girl, Ernie, what do you think of her?"

"Okay, I suppose, Marg, skirt's a bit short but that's the fashion these days, what with the long white socks, you see girls wearing them on the telly. I will say one thing, she has got a good pair of legs."

"Ernie, shut up, stop it, they will hear you in a minute. I doubt if Pete has noticed her legs as he's always got his head in books."

There was a lot of laughter from both Mum and Dad. Little did they know I could hear them and, yes, I had noticed Sam's legs. In fact, it was the first thing I'd noticed about her, the second was the shape of her neat bum; it was when she was having PE and she was wearing very short tight shorts, it was an amazing sight, the best legs I had seen. In fact, I think they're the best legs and bum in the school.

As it's summer, Sam wears the knee-length white socks on their own, so her bare legs show from the knees up. In the winter she wears tights under these socks to keep both her legs and bum warm. Sam's hair is straight, shoulder length, and is blonde with a fringe. She ties it back in school, out of school she wears it loose, it looks wonderful and feels extra silky, it was a wonder Dad hadn't mentioned her hair as I think he likes blondes. Mum was blonde when she was younger – of course, it's going grey now. Dad often mentions mum having her hair dyed but she won't have any of that nonsense – too expensive, she says.

We made ourselves at home on the sofa while Mum and Dad remained in the kitchen.

"Give me a snog, Sam," I whispered.

Without hesitation, she flung her arms around my neck and gave me a long passionate kiss while I held her tightly around her waist. After a while I opened my eyes only to find Dad standing over us with the mugs of coffee. What a shock we both had!

"What it is to be young! Take your coffee, I will get a couple of small tables for you both; then I'll leave you to it and go and help Mum with the dishes."

"Thanks, we'll be going as soon as we have drunk this, Sam has to ring a friend from the phone box at the end of the street."

"You can use the phone in the hall if you like, Sam."

"No thanks, I would rather phone from the coin box."

Dad stood for a while, looking a bit perplexed, but soon left us to drink our coffee.

"Pete, what are we going to do? The only good thing is that it is Friday so there is no school tomorrow, and Mum and Dad work down the factory until lunchtime so I'll have time to go and get a few more clothes while they're at work. I haven't got any money for the phone or tube, can I borrow some from you?"

"I haven't got money, I'll try and get some off Anne. I know, I'll go upstairs in a moment and ask her if she can help me out, in fact I'll go up now." I ran up the stairs and knocked on Anne's door.

"Come in! Oh, it's you, what the hell do you want? You never come to see me in my room unless you want something."

"I was wondering if I can borrow a couple of bob?"

"You're always asking me for money! If I lend it to you I'll have difficulty getting it back."

"This is urgent, Sam needs some money for the Tube and to make a phone call."

"I can let her have two and six that's all I have, she must let me have it back by the morning."

"Thanks." Anne went over to her purse and got out half a crown.

"If she doesn't give me it back I shall have to tell Mum as this is all the money I have and I want to go out tomorrow. I've arranged to go to the pictures with Margaret." I grabbed the half crown and went back downstairs only to find Sam getting herself organised to go.

"I've managed to get half a crown, that is all the money Anne has and she needs it back tomorrow." Sam just looked at me as if she didn't care, then walked over to the door.

"I had better go and say thanks to your mum and dad, are they still in the kitchen?"

"I think so, I'll call them. Mum, Dad, we're going now." Mum took off her apron and came out of the kitchen, followed by Dad who looked a bit sheepish.

"Shame you're having to go so soon after supper, perhaps you'll come again, what about next Friday?"

"I'll have a chat with Pete, it's up to him. Anyway, thanks for the lovely meal, I must get my bag from the dining room."

"Hope to see you again soon, remember you are welcome to come around anytime."

"Thanks." I opened the front door and followed Sam out on to the path.

"What time can we expect you back, Pete?" asked Dad.

"Oh, not late. Around ten, if not before."

"Okay, see you then, bye."

"Pete, how are we going to get change for the phone?"

"That's quite easy. There's a sweet shop at the end of the road, before the phone box. We can pop in and get a bar of chocolate. They'll give us change."

"Are you sure about that?"

"Course I am, they often give me change."

Chapter 2

We wandered down the road hand in hand to the sweet shop and on to the phone box where there was a queue. Directly in front of us were two Hell's Angels. I recognised them from Deptford. I think they must belong to the East London chapter. One looked quite intimidating in his camouflaged top and trousers with Doc Marten boots, his hair had been shaven of, the other had the same type of clothes but had long hair which was tied back into a pony tail using an elastic band. They were carrying helmets that were a similar style to the ones the Germans wore in the War and both of them had long, scruffy beards. Sam didn't want to stay in the queue as she was frightened about what they might get up to, she suggested that we should go round to Mary's place and knock her up instead of ringing her. We started to walk away when one of the angels shouted at us.

"Where the hell are you two going? Why aren't you staying in the queue? We won't bloody bite!" We looked towards them, then turned and hurried on our way.

"Come on, Sam this is a short cut to the main road and down to the station, give me your bag, I'll carry that."

I put my arm around Sam and took her down the lane that went along the back of the terraced houses. After a few minutes I could hear a bike coming up behind us – it was the intimidating Hell's Angel.

"You two fucking stop when I tell you to, I want to have a chat with you."

We kept walking, pretending not to hear until suddenly the other Hell's Angel descended on us from the other end of the lane also by motorbike.

"Bloody stop when you're told!" he shouted, then to stop us escaping he swung around on his bike so it was placed across the narrow lane. Getting off it, he stood directly in front of us holding a bicycle chain, as if he was going to hit out at the pair of us. I didn't know what to do or say, because at the same time the other Hell's Angel stood behind us holding a different chain. They were both invading our space, and seemed to be preparing to hit out at us.

"Where do you think you're fucking going? I've seen you both before somewhere and I don't like what I see, what do you think you're fucking up to?"

I held on to Sam's hand. By this time we were both standing against a high gate with both of the Hell's Angels' leaning over us. However, luck was on our side; the gate was not locked or on the latch. It was just pushed to, as soon as we leaned on it, it opened. We both fell into the back garden of one of the terraced houses. Once we had picked ourselves up we noticed a couple sat in deck chairs by the back door, having an evening drink.

We ran over, screaming, "Help us, we're being chased by two Hell's Angels."

By this time the Angels were standing inside the garden, swinging their bicycle chains around in the air, obviously looking for a bit more trouble. The couple looked in complete shock, they got up from the deckchairs and ran to the back door. We followed as quickly as we could.

"Come into our kitchen."

Shaking from head to foot the four of us hurried inside, where we watched the Angels out of the side window. They were walking around the garden, swinging their chains, seeing what they could get up to next, having drunk the remainder of the lagers that were left on the garden table. Eventually they came up to the back door and tried the handle. Luckily for us the key was in the door when we entered the kitchen, so the woman managed to lock the door with the key and the mortise bolt.

"Come out you fucking lot, we need you all out here. If you don't come out or let us in, we'll break in; then you'll be for it!" they shouted while trying to kick the door down.

"This is really frightening, what do you think we should do?" asked one of the householders. "Nothing like this has happened to us before. Anyway, you better tell us who you are. Do you live near?"

"I'm Peter and this is my girlfriend Sam. I live just down the road at number 54 with my parents. Sam lives at the Elephant and Castle in a tower block"

"We are Mr and Mrs Snowdon. Call us by our first names: this is Mary and I'm Tom."

"Right, Tom and Mary it'll be."

"What are we going to do, any suggestions? I know, I'll call the police. Before I do I'm going to have a quick peep out of the other window as it has suddenly gone very quiet, perhaps they're sat somewhere thinking about what to get up to next or trying to calm down. I'm sure they haven't left, I bet they've gone into the shed as the door is open. Yeah, that's where they must be. Then again they could have gone down the side path to the front of the house. I'll definitely phone the police, once I've looked out of the other window - they won't think much of that." Tom left the kitchen and went out into the hallway to use the phone and to see if he could see the Angels. Tom spotted them leaning up against the front door trying to see in through the coloured glass. One screamed out at Tom, and at the same time banged his bicycle chain against the wooden door.

"I've told you fucking lot to come out! If you don't there will be trouble, we'll stay here as long as it takes to get you out. If you phone the fucking cops we'll still bloody well get you another day,"

Tom managed to reach the phone and ring 999, of course the Angels could hear the conversation, as the phone didn't have a long enough lead to be taken into the dining room to make the call in private. After Tom had given all the details to the police they promised to come straight round, it seemed ages before they arrived. In the meantime, the Angels continued to try to get in by breaking the glass.

"Here we come, you fucking lot!" shouted one of them just as the glass broke. "Good, you've only got a bloody yale lock on this door! Serves you lot right, we're fucking in, now you are fucking for it!"

Sam stood in the kitchen, holding on to my arm.

"Go behind the kitchen door, Sam, take your bag with you. Mary, you go behind the door with Sam, stay as quiet as possible – in other words, don't breathe or speak." I then went and joined Tom in the hall to confront the Angels, when we could hear the siren from the police car.

"You bastard, you phoned the fucking cops! Here we fucking come!"

With that, they came at us swinging the bicycle chains towards our faces. I managed to jump out of the way but Tom was hit and landed head first against the dresser. He lay unconscious on the floor with blood flowing from the side of his face, but this didn't deter the Angels; they continued to swing their chains around in the air hitting whatever was in the way of them, which included paintings that were on the walls and plants that were positioned in the hall. I stood on the fourth stair shaking and hoping that they had other things on their minds other than me.

"Come on, let's get into the kitchen that'll be fucking fun breaking up the fucking kitchen, bound to be cupboards to empty and chairs to throw around." In they went just as the police arrived through the front door. "Bloody cops, you won't get us!" they shouted, slamming the kitchen door.

Once inside they found Mary and Sam holding on to each other - shaking.

"This is a bloody surprise seeing you two behind this door! The table is the first fucking thing we're going to move, then we're going to fucking get you two! Be prepared, nothing is going fucking stop us! Quick, Gra, hold on to the other end of this table, hurry up, fucking help, put it against the bloody door, bloody thing's heavy! Quick, help me!" Once the table was in position they turned on the girls. "What shall we bloody do with these two Gra, give them a poke?"

Then suddenly, out of the blue, Smithy saw Sam holding on to her bag and shouted,

"Look, Gra, an overnight bag, give it to me girl I wonder what you've got in it?" with that Smithy grabbed it from Sam and immediately looked inside. " Look Gra knickers, glorious knikers."

"Give me my bag back!" screamed Sam as loud as possible.

"No, now we have the bag let's empty it out, Gra!" shouted Smithy, laughing his head off.

"Let's have a look at the knickers, give them here, Smithy. Bit plain for you aren't they, darling, thought you'd wear something a bit fancy – you look like a slapper to me who would wear next to nothing knickers. What else is in there, Smithy?"

"Washing things, sure you're not on the game? Ah, that's what it is, you're on the game!" shouted Smithy, taking everything out of the bag and throwing all the bits around the kitchen.

"Give it back to me now, what's in my bag is nothing to do with you two!" shouted Sam, trying to get hold of the bag without much success, as Smithy was holding it up to the ceiling.

"I know, now we've sorted the bag out, let's tie you both up with our fucking chains against the table. Then, if the fucking cops get in, the table will roll over on to you! What fucking fun!" All the time Smithy was finding this amusing and was laughing away to himself.

"That'll fucking do for a start."

"Here we go ladies, get down on the floor, don't you bloody well shout or you'll be hit like the man in the hall, it served him right he shouldn't have phoned the cops. If you don't behave yourselves and move when I say move. I will fucking pull you over by your hair, then you'll know all about it." They got hold of Sam and Mary, tied their hands behind their backs and then started to pull them one at a time by the arms towards the table.

"That's right, crawl along the bloody floor like animals towards the table, STOP! The table is tight against the door so be prepared, whatever you do don't shout to warn the cops if you do you'll be fucking for it. I know, Smithy find a dish cloth and stuff it in that one's mouth. If there's two put the other in the old woman's mouth; if there's only one get the tart's knickers and stuff them in her mouth. That'll keep them both quiet."

Out in the hall I was still stood on the fourth step when the front door was pushed open by the cops.

"Whatever has been going on? It looks like a bomb has hit this place! He looks in a bad way, phone for an ambulance while we go and see what else is going on. Where are the Hells Angels?"

"In the kitchen, two females are with them."

"Let me try the door. It won't open, there seems to be something jammed up against it."

"Anyone in there?" shouted the other police officer, there was no reply. "Just as I thought; they're up to something. What that is, I don't know but it's definitely not good news. Out the way, boy." The cop pushed me to one side.

"My girlfriend's in the kitchen with them! The thing is, she's eight weeks pregnant!" I shouted, hoping that they would listen.

"Out the way, boy! I can't talk about that now, we've had a 999 call about Hell's Angels being here. We can't be side tracked by your pregnant girlfriend - we must get into the kitchen ASAP!" shouted the exasperated officer.

"She's in the kitchen with the Hell's Angels!" I screamed.

"I did hear what you said, boy." More officers arrived with a couple of ambulance men.

"I've got a job for you, Jim!" called out the officer who appeared to be in charge. "Take the boy into the front room and ask him a few questions about what's been happening. Get him to tell you about the bloke that's on the floor."

The three extra cops tried to push open the door from the hall without success. Inside, the Angels were trying to escape, but found it was impossible to get out via the kitchen door due to the fact that Mary had hidden the door key along with the key to the mortise lock. The only thing left for them was to escape out of the window but that was also locked.

"Here goes!" With that, Gra threw a kitchen chair at the window, glass went everywhere including all over the backs of the girls and into their hair. The Angels managed to clamber up over the kitchen sink and climb out of the broken window, but in the process Gra cut his hand on the glass. "Help me Smithy, I've cut my bloody hand right across the right palm."

"I can't fucking help you, just hurry Gra, jump down and run or we'll get caught and that'll be the fucking end of us." Once down they ran and disappeared into the sunset.

Eventually the cops managed to get the door open into the kitchen but of course once it started to move, the table fell backwards on to Sam and Mary, knocking them unconscious for a few seconds. The table was made of oak and was extremely heavy, it took all three cops to lift it off the girls. Once done, and the chains and mouth gags had been removed, the cops called out to the ambulance men to come and have a look at Sam and Mary to see if either needed to be taken into hospital along with Tom. A decision was made very quickly and it was decided that they should all go to hospital, especially Sam, due to her being pregnant. They were both helped to their feet, then sat down on a couple of chairs to wait while the ambulance men called the local hospital to see if there were any beds available.

"It's Friday, we're in luck, it's the hospital at Vanbrugh Hill who are taking in emergencies and they have three beds available, one male and two female on the medical ward. You have to be taken to casualty first and then you will be transferred across to the ward. Mary, you will only have to stay in overnight. Sam, they may keep you in until Monday as they may feel they need to keep an eye on you over the weekend," said the ambulance driver who seemed to be in charge.

"Sam, we need to know where you live? We have to get hold of your parents and explain to them what has happened," said the youngest of the three police officers.

"They won't be very happy, Pete and I went around after school to tell them that I may be pregnant. They went mad and kicked me out."

"Well, I'm afraid we'll have to see them or at least phone them to let them know you're in the hospital, they're your next of kin."

"Oh, all right. The flat is at the Elephant and Castle just along from the Tube station."

"Well, come on! Give me a phone number or the address for us to get in touch, then we can get you all to the hospital." shouted the oldest copper, who seemed to be getting fed up with the situation.

"I don't feel well. Pete, can you give all my details to the copper? I think I'm going to be sick." With that, Sam started to vomit down the front of her clothes.

"I'm going to go out and get a chair from the ambulance for you, Sam. Mary, I think you can walk, before we go can you tell Pete where he can find a towel to clean Sam up a bit," said the young ambulance assistant. "Yes, Pete you can find a towel at the back of the airing cupboard on the landing? Take care when you open the door as everything may fall out."

"Come on, Pete, give me Sam's phone number now, I'm getting a bit fed up, it's Friday night and we need to hurry and get back on the streets!" screamed the annoyed copper. His screaming made me almost jump out of my skin; so as not to upset him any more I gave him the number without hesitation.

"Now I'll go and get the towel, then I'm going to wait and see you all off to the hospital before going home."

"Oh no son, you're not getting away that easy, I have to have a chat with you about the Hell's Angels and this pregnancy, after that you can go and explain everything to your parents. I mean everything, Sam's pregnancy, the lot."

"Okay," I said very sheepishly. I ran up the stairs and eventually found a towel right at the back of the cupboard. When I returned to the kitchen the assistant had already returned with a wheelchair for Sam and three red cellulose blankets one for each of them.

"Let me clean Sam up a bit before you take her or at least let me put the towel across her lap so she can't see the vomit."

After they were all sorted out I gave Sam a kiss and told her that I would be in to visit her the next day.

"Don't you disappear, son, as I need to take a few details from you about this pregnancy. First things first, do your parents know about it?"

"No," I answered, shaking from head to foot.

"Well I suggest you go home and tell them, then, sometime tomorrow, I'll be sending a police officer to your house to have a chat with you. Hang on a minute, tomorrow is Saturday. No, someone will be around on Monday. You can go home now. Before I leave, I'm going to secure the house. Tomorrow morning, I'll be sending an officer back to dust for fingerprints. Mrs Snowden knows what I'm doing and she's quite happy with me keeping the key. Once I've finished here, I'll be going back to the station to write up a full report."

I was still in a state of shock when I arrived home. The house was in darkness as it was way past midnight – Mum and Dad always go to bed by ten thirty. I tried to be as quiet as possible but of course I had to put the light on to get up the stairs which disturbed my parents, they had left their bedroom door ajar so they knew the time I got in and they could call out to me.

"Is that you, Pete?" said Mum in a distressed tone.

"Yeah it's me."

"Where ever have you been? We've both been laying here waiting for you. I'm going to get up, I'll see you downstairs, go down and put the kettle on so we can have a cup of tea."

I tried to be my normal self and went back down to the kitchen. Mum followed in her thick woolly dressing gown. To my surprise, Dad arrived a few minutes later in his thick winceyette pyjamas – they were showing below his brown check dressing gown. He looked very worried, in fact I had never seen him looking so upset, he hardly ever showed any emotion.

"Right, Pete, where have you been? You look as if you've been in a fight. Why are you shaking, whatever has happened to you?"

I went on to explain what had happened once we had left the house and had gone to the phone box at the end of the road. "I don't know what to say to you," said Mum. "If Sam had used our phone, none of this would have happened. I'm in complete shock, Ernie, instead of us having a cup of tea get a couple of glasses and the bottle of brandy so we can recover from this terrible news." She looked bewildered and shaken.

"That's right, Ernie, put a drop of brandy in each glass. I think Pete ought to have one as well, get another glass." All three of us sat down at the kitchen table, both Mum and Dad looked completely bemused.

"Pete, you have not told us why Sam has to stay in hospital for the weekend, whatever has happened to her?" Dad asked, looking very pale and worried.

"I suppose I better come clean with you both, Sam may be eight weeks' pregnant. We have told her parents, that is why I was late home from school this evening."

"Are you the father?"

"Yeah, and that makes you grandparents in waiting."

There was silence, you could have heard a pin drop. I just waited to hear what was going to come next.

"Well I don't know what to say to you, Ernie, have you anything to say?"

"Not really, I need to get over the shock of this. Yes, I have one thing, what about university? Are you still going if you get good grades or is this the end of that?"

"I keep forgetting about Sam's parents, what do they think about all of this? Has she told them? Pete, are you listening to me?" shouted Mum, looking completely stunned and flushed.

"I told you just now that we went around there after school and her parents were not very happy and thought perhaps Sam should have an abortion. In fact her father went completely mad and told her to leave with me and not return."

"Parents are often like that, but once they calm down everything is usually okay. Tomorrow they'll be wondering what has happened to Sam and they'll be hunting around for her, don't be surprised if they come around here looking for her," said Mum.

"I doubt if they will, because I had a chat with the police and they took her phone number, and they were going to phone her parents to say she was in hospital. Her parents don't know where I live."

"Wait and see. Tomorrow, Pete, is another day, which hospital has she gone to and which ward?"

"They were taking both Mary and Sam to the casualty department in the hospital at Vanbrugh Hill, then they were both being transferred to a ward - they didn't know which. They said something about ward 4 which is a medical ward and it's 'on take', whatever that means."

"Pete, did you just say the other person was called Mary from down the road? Was her surname Snowdon?"

"Yeah, that's right, Mum, Mary and Tom Snowdon, they live at number 100."

"I think I know her at least by sight, she works in the office at school. I believe he's a clerk down at the local bank."

"The police officer said he thought he recognized him from the bank. Well, he was knocked unconscious, but came around before he was taken off in the ambulance."

"All of this is a complete shock to both of us, we never dreamt that you had a girlfriend to begin with, let alone her being pregnant. I don't know what to say about Sam having an abortion as this is going to be our first grandchild. What do you think about it all, Ernie? Come on say something Ern, you must have something to say, do you think Sam should have an abortion?"

"I've no idea, but I do know one thing and that is we should sleep on this, then have another talk in the morning. It costs a fortune to keep a baby, how can you two find the money, first for a deposit to rent a flat and then the monthly rent, along with food and heating? Some flats you have to pay extra money for the rates and they're not cheap. You must remember that we aren't rich so we are unable to help out. Anyway, let's have a quick cup of tea, as we have finished our brandy, and then go up to bed."

Silence descended on the kitchen while I put the kettle on. Mum and Dad just sat looking at one another, dad always looked pasty but he was paler than ever, all of his face plus neck was white with shock. Mum? Well, she had a bright red face just as if her blood pressure had gone through the roof.

"Once you have made the tea, Pete, I'm going up to bed. I will take my tea with me, as I have a terrible headache, I need to lie down, how about you Ernie? You look as white as snow."

I looked at my watch and saw that it was after two. "I'm going to bed now, without a cup of tea, as it's late, in fact it's two o'clock. Night to you both, sleep tight, sorry about all the upset."

I tossed and turned for most of the night worrying about what was going to happen. I could hear Mum and Dad talking. At one point I heard one of them going down the stairs. I never found out why but I guess that it must have been for another cup of tea, they're fond of tea and drink plenty of it, especially when they're worried.

I got up in time for breakfast which was around eight thirty a.m. on a Saturday. When I arrived in the dining room I found Mum looking as if she'd been crying and hadn't had much sleep. Dad, well, he looked the same as usual but they were not talking to each other. Anne came in for her breakfast and straight away asked when I would be paying back the two and six I owed her.

"What is this all about, Pete? Have you borrowed more money from Anne? How do you think you'll be able to pay Anne back?"

"He needed it as his so-called girlfriend had no money. He's promised to pay me back before lunch today, as I'm going out to the pictures with Margaret. If you don't pay me back, I won't be able to go,"

"Mum, can you help me out?"

"No I can't, Dad told you last night about shortness of money. If you can't pay Anne back you shouldn't have borrowed it from her in the first place. I have a suggestion to make and that is get a job, you hang around here every weekend, complaining that you haven't any money and can't go out. Now's your chance, get a job. Anne, did you know that Sam's pregnant?"

"What! No. How disgusting!"

I could feel myself getting embarrassed and feeling more and more stupid while I ate my breakfast as no one was talking to me.

"Once you have had enough to eat, Pete please come out to the kitchen with your dirty dishes," said Mum sounding very annoyed.

"Okay, I won't be long. I don't feel very hungry, in fact I feel sick."

"Perhaps you have made a mistake and it's you that's pregnant," said Anne, laughing at me.

"Don't be so ridiculous Anne, I can assure you that this is not a joke, it's not funny."

"Well, you shouldn't have got her pregnant. I'm glad it's not me pregnant, anyway I wouldn't do such a thing. If you have to do it, haven't you heard of condoms? You buy them at the chemist and they come wrapped in brown paper."

"How do you know that if you've never bought any or been to look for some?"

"Stop it, you two! Pete, hurry up and go and see your mother and leave Anne and me in peace."

Out in the kitchen Mum was about to wash up when I walked In, "Right, Pete, have you decided what you think you should do, or what you're going to do? You take your A levels in a few weeks, then it's the end of the school year. Before you answer Dad and I have had a long chat, we both think Sam should make it up with her parents and go back and live with them. It's impossible for her to live here, don't think about asking because it's out of the question."

"Well I'm going to see her in hospital this afternoon, perhaps her parents will have been in to see her before I get there. I may come back with some news; whether it will be good or not I don't know, we'll have to wait and see."

"Okay, I'll give you till teatime to sort things out, just you remember she can't live here, she can visit but that's it."

"Okay, I do understand what you're saying."

I went upstairs to my room and played my favourite records, lying on my bed and dreaming about my future while listening to *I'm a Loser* by *The Beatles*, I didn't come to any decision except that I had to let Sam know that she would never be able live here, and that Mum suggested that she made it up with her parents. Whatever Sam's parents thought, she should take it on board because parents normally know best.

Time went by very quickly and before I knew it I was walking down the road towards the hospital, hoping that I wouldn't bump into Mr or Mrs Smithson.

I walked in the main door of the hospital and went over to the reception desk where a very attractive young clerk was sitting behind the glass. As I approached, she stood down from her stool, pulling her skirt down towards her knees. She then slid the glass window along and asked if she could help me.

"Yes, I'm wondering which ward my girlfriend is on. Her name is Sam Smithson."

"Oh, let me have look at the list. Here she is on ward 4, it seems as if she is being discharged this afternoon, her parents are coming back for her. I met her parents this morning, they seemed very angry and upset at the same time. How long have you known her?" she said, looking me up and down as if she could eat me up.

"Ages, what's it to do with you?" I replied. "Must go and find her."

I hurried away. Why the receptionist should like the look of me I don't know as she looked at least nineteen and seemed very sophisticated, what with her tight short skirt, low-neck top and stiletto heels. I could see all of this as she pushed the stool away from her desk and stood back from the glass to show off her figure – and there was me in my school shirt and flannels.

Eventually I arrived at ward 4 where I knocked on the door of the sister's office.

"Come in, have you come to see someone?"

"Yeah, Sam Smithson."

"You must be the boyfriend, she's in the left-hand ward sitting by the second bed on the right. She's going home in a few minutes."

"What do you mean going home? She's supposed to be staying until Monday."

"No, her parents are arriving any minute. They're not very happy, but that's nothing to do with the staff. You'll have to have a chat with Sam and her parents."

"What! They don't want anything to do with me!"

"I'm sorry about that but it's your problem, we can't get involved."

"I'll go and find Sam, see what she has to say."

I left the sister sat at her desk looking at me. I wandered into the ward and found Sam sitting there, reading the newspaper. She was wearing a light green towelling dressing gown and looked very pale. She gave me slight smile but didn't volunteer a kiss.

"I'm pleased you have come to see me, but I'm glad Mum and Dad aren't here; they're supposed to be coming in any minute to take me home. What time is it?"

"About half past two."

"They don't want to see you, they've told me straight that they never want to see you again. I've had to promise them that I'll avoid you at school. I'd better tell you that I'm going back to school on Monday and will be staying until the end of term. What I'm going to do then I don't know, one thing's for sure I'm going to keep this baby. Have you anything to say, Pete?"

"No, only that my parents are not happy either, you can't come and live with us. Mum will be pleased that you have made it up with your mum and dad. Let me give you a kiss."

with that, Sam looked up at me in a way that encouraged me to lean over and kiss her on the mouth.

Sam smiled. "It feels wonderful to have a kiss, you make me feel that life is worth living. I'll be a school on Monday if I can't see you before. I'll meet you as usual at the gate at quarter to nine."

"That's fine, as soon as your parents turn up I'll go. I don't want a fuss, it was bad enough the other evening at the flat."

"The food here is awful. I'll be glad to get home and have decent meal, Mum's food is not up to much but it's better than hospital food. For lunch we had mutton stew, the gravy was like water and rice pudding was for afters. The rice pudding didn't even have any sugar as they give it to diabetics. I asked the nurse to sweeten it up but she couldn't, apparently they don't have sugar only sweeteners on this ward, so that was that."

"I couldn't eat it, I'm not very keen on rice pudding, I guess it is easy to make, and is cheap and cheerful"

"Oh, here's Mum, she won't like seeing you here."

"What the hell's going on Sam? You promised me that you wouldn't ever see him again. Go, before I lose my temper and Sam's dad arrives."

I just looked at them both and went over to kiss Sam when her mum shouted:

"Don't you dare start that nonsense here, kissing Sam in the middle of the ward! We've had enough of you and all your shenanigans. Sam has told us both what has been going on; go now!"

"Bye Sam, see you Monday."

"She won't see you if I have anything to do with it."

I stood at the bottom of the bed and replied, "I can't see how you can stop me from seeing Sam, as we go to the same school. We might not be in the same class but there are plenty of hours in a day, with time off to see one another between lessons."

"I can see Sam's dad will have to come and have a chat with your dad if you continue to cause upset."

I left feeling ashamed. On the way out I bumped straight into Mr Smithson in the corridor.

"Hi, have you just been to see my daughter?"

I pretended I didn't know who he was. "Are you talking to me? Should I know you?"

"Yes, I'm talking to you, and yes I think you should know me; you have been to see Sam Smithson, haven't you?"

"Yeah, what about it?"

"I'm her dad if you can't remember. I have a suggestion to make and that is for you to keep away from Sam – if you don't, your life won't be worth living. See this, I'm good at using it." By this time he was stood a mere foot away from me, staring into my eyes with his fist ready to punch out at me.

"It's all right, I get the message, no need to hit out at me, I'm a peaceful bloke, I'm not into the fighting game."

"Right, you've got the message! Now go, before I have more to say."

I was so hot and bothered that I didn't know what to do or where to go for a minute. Then I decided that perhaps I should go for a walk around the shops or over to the park, to try and clear my head, before going home.

Chapter 3

I was so fed up with tossing and turning all of Sunday night. I must have seen every hour, so once it was six thirty and almost daylight, I decided to get up and face the day ahead. Mum and Dad hardly ever got up before seven thirty so I had an hour to sort myself out before they descended on me, or at least I thought I had.

"Whatever's up, Pete? It's only quarter to seven!" called Mum from their bedroom.

"Oh, I've decided to get up. I haven't slept a wink all night, I've seen every hour."

"I'll get up and make us all a cup of tea."

"I'll do that, once I've washed and dressed I'll bring one up for you both."

I quickly got ready and went down to the kitchen only to find that we had a flood. I'm glad that I wasn't the last to go to bed, someone had left the cold water tap running with the plug in position all night and water was everywhere. I immediately turned the tap off and pulled the plug out before going back upstairs. The thing was, the overflow has been blocked for ages due to it costing such a lot of money to get it unblocked. The last person to bed was supposed to check that the back door's locked; if they had checked, they would have noticed that the tap was running.

Once inside Mum and Dad's bedroom, I took a deep breath and shouted, "We have a flood in the kitchen! There's water everywhere, I don't know who was supposed to check the back door last night but whoever it was, didn't." They looked at each other and Dad admitted that it must have been him.

"With all the upset I forgot. I'll get up straight away and come down and help to clear it up. Pete, you can help, Mum is not feeling too good and is going to have a lie in and hopefully get some extra sleep, she doesn't have to go to work until lunchtime."

"Oh, my first lesson is at ten thirty. I must catch the bus at ten from the station, it gets me to school by 10.20. The thing is I have planned to meet Sam at eight forty-five at the school gates, I was going in early."

"Sam, Sam, bloody Sam! I am fed up with her name being mentioned in this house, I went to bed on that name and have woken up to it! I'm just fed up with hearing her name. Go down stairs and start to clean up the mess. I'll be down once I'm dressed."

"Okay, but I must get my books and things together or I'll be late."

I went into my room and got my things together before going to find a mop and hopefully a bucket. The kitchen floor was in a terrible state; most of the water had gone under the vinyl. With every step I took the water came up the sides of the flooring. Dad soon arrived, wondering what to do first.

"Well Pete this is the last thing I expected to come down to this morning. The last thirty-six hours or so have been a living hell for your mother and me. Whatever you do, don't mention the name Sam or I'll show you the door."

I'd never seen Dad like this so I decided the best policy was to say nothing and get on with mopping up the water.

"Once you've finished the mopping we'll have to remove the vinyl and see what it's like underneath, hurry up we haven't got all day. I'll see if I can find another mop in the garden shed - we used to have two."

Dad disappeared into the garden. He seemed to have been gone for ages when the front door bell went. I crept out into the hall and into the front room and had a look out through the net curtains from the corner window and saw a police officer. I quickly and quietly went back into the kitchen and closed the door to the hall, hoping that he would go on his way thinking we were all still in bed. Thank goodness luck was on my side, I didn't hear the doorbell again.

Dad came back in with a small mop. "This is all I can find in the shed, I haven't been out there for quite a few weeks and it's in some state. Looks as though someone has been sleeping rough out there. The thing is, I don't lock the door at night and I wouldn't be surprised if a tramp hadn't been sleeping in the shed. Behind the door was a two-foot piece of wood; it looked like part of a broom handle. Do you know anything about it?"

"No, nothing to do with me, I never go in there."

"I have a feeling that the person must have put it there to use if someone walked in and disturbed them. After cleaning up this mess I'll have to spend the rest of the morning sorting out the shed and then try and find a lock, get a move on, Pete or we'll never finish."

"I can't work any quicker. By the way, a police officer came to the front door while you were out the back, I didn't go to the door, I just looked out the window, then I came back in here. I don't think he saw me."

"I can't take much more of this, we've never had police at our door before,"

"I expect it's my fault; all I can say is sorry."

"Get on with mopping the floor, once it's been cleaned up we'll have to take up the vinyl. What's under the vinyl, God only knows, it's been down for years."

Silence reigned in the kitchen until it was time to pull up the vinyl.

"You go over there to the right-hand side and try and pull it up by the hall door and I'll pull from over here."

"This is hard work it seems to be stuck down."

"Well it's been down for at least five years and I have a feeling that it's glued down along the sides."

"How on earth are we going to get it up, Dad?"

"I don't know, I think it will have to be brute force and ignorance."

"Well, here goes." I pulled extra hard and the vinyl came away, but, in the process, I fell back against a cupboard.

"Not that hard, Pete! I'd forgotten there's lino under the vinyl and they're stuck together. We'll have to get both lots up before you go to school."

"What? I have to catch the ten o'clock bus from the station! I need to have breakfast before I go."

"Well, we'll have to get a move on as it's nine o'clock already. It has to be done."

"Come on, then. Pull from over there, Dad. Are you listening? You seem to have gone into a world of your own again."

"I'm listening, but at the same time I'm thinking about the best way to get rid of this lot," replied Dad, nodding at the floor.

"Dad, don't think for too long or I'll be leaving to go to school."

"I know what I'll do: I'll cut it all up into strips and then throw it out in the garden. Pass me the Stanley knife."

"Do you need me for anything else or can I get ready for school? I'm sorry about all the upheaval I've caused for everyone, what with poor Mum having to stay in bed."

"You go and get ready. I'll finish here. Whatever happens, you need to get on with your studies and pass your exams. I can't open the back door, so I'm going to lay the flooring back down before cutting it into strips. At least there isn't any more vinyl to pull."

"I'll go to the bus stop and have a chocolate bar on the way instead of having breakfast."

"Oh, Pete, I'd forgotten about breakfast! Let's see if I can open the fridge door to get some milk so you can have some cereal."

"Thanks, Dad. Do you want some?"

"Yes, I suppose I do. Let's eat in the dining room as it stinks in here. The quicker I get the floor up, the better, but I must eat something."

It didn't take Dad long to get the fridge door open and we were eating our cereal at the dining room table. Once it was eaten, I went on my way to the station to catch the bus.

Chapter 4

I arrived at school just in time for my first lesson, which was English. Over the weekend I had managed to do my homework, so at least everything was up to date. Hopefully I would not be in any more trouble. Having got Sam pregnant and knowing through Mr Hall that every member of the staff knew about our relationship, I saw Mr Thomas in a new light. I could feel myself getting more and more embarrassed as I entered the room. Mr Thomas was sat at his desk when he looked over towards me.

"Morning Pete, how are you this bright and sunny morning?" I must have looked very surprised as he had never spoken to me like this before, obviously he knew everything that had been going on.

"Okay, in fact, great." I thought this was the best thing to say, he appeared to be smirking to himself and this made me feel more embarrassed than ever. There were only five of us taking A-level English and only two had turned up and they were the girls, where the boys were I don't know. I usually sat with the boys behind the girls, but, as the boys hadn't turned up, I sat alongside the girls. They cringed at me sitting next to them, I could think for no reason other than they had found out about Sam being pregnant.

The lesson seemed to be going well when suddenly, out of the blue, Mr Thomas shouted, "What is the matter with you, Knight? You look like you are asleep! Wake up!"

I immediately opened my eyes. I thought I was listening to him talking but obviously I was asleep and dreaming. The girls started to snicker, I felt stupid.

"Hope you've done all the homework I set you last week. Let me have a look at your books; if you haven't done it, you'll be in more trouble."

Thank goodness I had managed to do it in between the upset.

"Knight, you've been asleep for most of this lesson. I'm not going over the lesson again specially for you, it's your own fault, you should go to bed earlier then you would stay awake. I'm going to give you all some old exam papers to work through at home. You can give your answers in next Monday, then we can go through the papers together. Has anyone got any questions before I go through the timetable for the exam?"

No one answered and I couldn't think of any questions as my mind was on other things.

"Right, you haven't any questions. The exam is the first Monday in May at ten o'clock, it lasts for two hours, let's work it out, three weeks to go, not long."

Then suddenly one of the girls seemed to come to and ask where the exam was being held. "In the main hall, you need to be in your seats fifteen minutes before the start, Mr Hall has volunteered to sit in on it for me. If he's busy I will have to get someone in from another school; I am not allowed to sit in for him, as you are my students. It is eleven thirty, time to go. See you all on Wednesday, girls. If you see the boys perhaps you can let them know what we have been doing today and suggest they come and get the old papers to work on."

With that I wandered out of the classroom, oblivious to what was going on around me.

"Pete, what's the matter with you, didn't you see me waiting outside your classroom? I have been standing here for at least ten minutes."

"Sorry, Sam, I was far away dreaming, I thought you were in class until twelve. Anyway it is great to see you, how are you feeling?"

"Not too bad. At least I haven't been sick today, it makes a change to keep my food down. How are you?"

"Okay, I guess. I didn't sleep last night, I'm so worried about everything. We had a flood at home this morning, the kitchen seems to be ruined, and I hurt my shoulder while helping dad to move the lino. My English lesson was a disaster, I fell asleep." Sam found this funny and laughed her head off at the thought of me sleeping in Mr Thomas's lesson.

"What did he have to say about that?"

"Not a lot, it was obvious to me that he knows you're pregnant. He wouldn't go over any of the work he was teaching while I was asleep, he yelled to wake me up. The girls in the class thought it was a joke and sat laughing at me. I have got to settle down to my work as I need good exam results, my first exam is only three weeks away. You must try and look after yourself; at the moment, I can't think of any way of helping unless I pass my A-levels. My parents and I can't have the worry. I left Mum in bed this morning as she is not feeling great. Dad is worried sick,
he doesn't seem to be able to think straight." At
that Sam burst into tears.

"Well, what am I supposed to say, Sam? We don't have any money between us, and both Mum and Dad have told me straight that they can't help out in any way as they only have just enough money to get by on. What about your parents? I doubt if they can help, it costs a lot to keep a baby, and looking at the bigger picture perhaps it would be a good idea for you to have an abortion and we call it a day. I am very sorry because I'm very fond of you but at this moment everything in my life is going wrong and I need to sort myself out and get good exam results. Sorry if I sound callous, but that is how it is."

Sam just stood looking at me with tears streaming down her face.

"Have you got a handkerchief that I can use?"

"No, but I can let you have a couple of tissues. I suggest you go and have a think on your own about what I have just said. Don't take too long about deciding whether or not to have an abortion. I can have another chat with you on Thursday to hear what you have decided. Sorry, but bye for now. Try not to keep crying."

I went on my way. As the sun was shining down on the world and I had a couple of hours to spare, I decided to go for a walk to the local park and sit on my favourite bench.

On the way I visited the sandwich bar and bought a couple of sandwiches and a Mars bar plus a can of Coke. I often visit the park as it is quiet and it gives me time to sit and reflect on my life and also watch the people exercising their dogs. I settled down on the bench to eat my sandwiches when, out of the blue, came a voice.

"Hi, how are you doing?" I looked up and who should it be but the receptionist, dressed to kill.

"Hi I'm fine, but what are you doing here? I've never seen you here before, no work today?"

"Oh I only work part time, I never work on a Monday. I didn't expect to bump into you, where's your girlfriend?"

"Back at school. Take a seat, I'm eating my lunch, fancy a sandwich? I have two and I'm not feeling hungry, have this one, its prawn."

"Thanks."

I carried on eating with my newfound acquaintance. Out of the corner of my eye I could see her watching me. After I finished my sandwich I decided the time had come to have a chat and ask a few questions, it seemed as though she didn't have much to say for herself, perhaps she's shy, just thick, or she could be starstruck.

"Tell me a bit about yourself, do you live around here?"

"Yeah, I live with my parents. I used to be married but it finished and I'm back home. We live in a very small rented flat above one of the shops across the road from here. Mum and Dad have been trying to get a council flat but they are in short supply, they thought they would like to live near the river but at the moment that's impossible. Where do you live?"

"Blackheath in a terrace house with my parents and sis."

"It's nice to bump into you, I saw you from over by the tree and decided that I should come over to you. I haven't got a boyfriend."

"It's no good looking in my direction; I have Sam. She's up the duff, also I am trying to sort myself out, so I have no time to get involved with anyone else."

"That's a shame. I feel we would get on well together, having said that I must be a few years older than you. How old are you?" "Just seventeen."

"Oh, I am nineteen, going on twenty. Yes, I think you are a bit young for me, I like my men more mature. That doesn't mean we can't be friends, I shouldn't say it but I really fancy you."

"If we are going to be friends I better introduce myself. I'm Pete from Blackheath and you are?"

"Jackie from Deptford; everyone calls me Jack."

We shook hands and kissed each other on the cheek.

"Friends it is then, nothing more, no good fancying me."

"Okay."

"I will have to move now as time is passing by and I have to get back to school."

"Can I walk over the road with you?"

"If you like, but I'm in a hurry so I can't dawdle. I walk fast, I don't know how you will manage to keep up with me in those shoes, they can't be very good for walking or for your feet."

"I suppose they aren't, but they are the fashion. I'm into fashion. If I had a lot of money I would spend most of it on clothes. Have you ever been to Carnaby Street? I bought these shoes up there the other Saturday. We could go up there together one Saturday."

"I told you that I am a bit young for you. I don't even care or want to know where Carnaby Street is and I definitely don't want to go there with you."

"That's a pity. Anyway, I'll tell you where it is, it's off Regents Street, up the West End. Lots to see and do there."

"I've never been up the West End. If we meet again, and if I have the time to have a chat, you can tell me all about it, but not now."

Jackie suddenly held on to my left arm and put her head on my shoulder.

"I'm sure you can find time to come with me one Saturday, you don't know what you are missing."

"I've just said, no! I also said friends only, that means if we bump into each other, we can have a chat – nothing else! Anyway, I haven't any money so I can't take you out even if I wanted to; it is best for both of us that we part company now."

I pushed Jackie away and got up off the bench. After putting all my empty paper bags into my haversack, I ran towards the gate, leaving Jackie still sat on the bench.

"What's the rush? I have something to say to you!" she screamed after me. "Wait, I'm coming."

I kept running, hoping that she wouldn't be able to catch up, but luck wasn't on my side: she had taken her shoes off and came running after me, shouting as loud as she could.

"Wait, Pete, don't leave me!" It seemed like everyone in the park could hear her and were watching. Most of the people along the side path were stood staring towards me. Jackie made it appear that she was my girlfriend by the noise and fuss she was making about me leaving her. To me the best thing was to wait for her to catch up.

"You listen to me, we have only just met and you mean nothing to me, don't embarrass me by shouting across the park. I am a peaceful bloke and don't like your behaviour! Go home!" With that she tried to put her arms around my neck. I pulled her arms down and held them tightly by her side.

"I told you back on the bench that I'm not interested in you so please go and leave me alone. I have to go back to school for two o'clock and its now ten minutes to two by my watch. Go!"

I pushed her aside and ran out of the park gate, on to the path by the main road. In the distance and coming towards me I could see the elderly lady who was always in the park with her dog. Once I caught up with her she seemed a little agitated and wanted to talk to me.

"Hello to you. I saw you in the park talking to that young lady. Take a bit of advice from me, I wouldn't have anything to do with her, she is always causing trouble. She is a right little madam."

"I don't know her, she isn't a friend. I met her at the reception desk at the local hospital the other day."

"Oh yes, she works there some days. She is always trying to get off with different men, just watch it. Jack tells most people that she has been married but that is not true, she was sent to a mental institution for about three years, just after leaving school, something was wrong with her mind. She left school in the July and by the Christmas she was locked up, she was a perfect nuisance pestering men. She's a lot better now than she was three years ago, at least I don't think she goes around asking for sex and inviting men to look at her bits. I understand the doctors have put her on very strong medication. My advice to you is not to tell her where you live or where you spend your time, avoid her like the plague or you may find her outside your home, shouting the odds at you."

"Thanks for your advice. I hope I don't meet her again, any way I don't live near here thank goodness. I must hurry, bye and thank you."

I hurried on my way wondering what else could possibly happen to me on my journey through life.

Chapter 5

The afternoon went peacefully, with Mrs Dobson taking six of us for Biology. The class finished at half three just in time for me to catch the bus. I wandered out into the grounds where I immediately bumped into some of my mates. As we all chatted and walked towards the school gates I could see a familiar face.

"John, help me. See that bird at the gate? She's waiting for me."

"What, her in the tight skirt and the stilettos?"

"Yeah."

"How the hell do you know her?"

"Oh, it is a long story, I haven't time to tell you. I only want you lot to know she's the local nuisance and seems to have taken a shine to me."

"What a laugh! I can't believe what I'm hearing, her fancying you! If it had been me she fancied, I would understand it! You know, she's not a bad bit of stuff, different from Sam. Before we go any further, have you or haven't you? Where is Sam? Does she know about her?"

"Come on, don't change the subject to Sam, help me out, you're supposed to be my mate."

"Hold your hair on Pete, keep your head down and carry on walking and talking to me. You lot walk along with us making sure Pete is in between us all, don't laugh, just help Pete."

As we got closer to the gate Jackie walked into the entrance and stood in our way, making it difficult for any of us to get out without having to ask her to move.

"Excuse me, please can you move out of our way so we can all get out to catch our buses? Move over, please, and be careful

– there are cars behind you trying to get in," said John, pretending not to notice anything amiss about her.

"I don't care about that, I have come to meet Pete, he asked me to come to the school gates."

My mates started to snigger, this made me feel extremely embarrassed, at the same time I was fuming and thinking what a fool I had made of myself. Thank goodness the woman with the dog had told me all about her, if she hadn't I would have appeared pleased and proud to see her as, deep down, I fancied Jackie and wouldn't mind giving her a quickie.

"Get out of our way now, let us all come through!" shouted John.

"Pete what's the matter with you?" screamed Jackie. "You asked me to come and meet you; I thought we were friends?"

Suddenly, out of the blue, Mr Hall came around the corner from one of the buses. "What is all this noise, what is going on Knight? Who is this girl? Surely you are not involved with her?"

"Yes he is involved with me, he told me that he liked me and wanted to be friends, he gave me a kiss in the park."

"What are you thinking about, Knight?"

"This is nothing to do with you, Mr Hall. We are not friends, we are only acquaintances. I bumped into her when I went to the hospital to visit Sam, she works at the reception desk."

"What! She works on reception at the hospital? I can't believe what I'm hearing. Is this some kind of joke, Knight? Someone that looks like her has a job as a receptionist at the local hospital."

"I love my job, I meet lots of people, all the men like me and how I look," said Jack, trying to look coy.

"I bet they do. Get off the school premises now before I call the police."

"Sometimes I wonder about you Knight, whatever are you thinking, have you taken leave of your senses?"

It suddenly dawned on me that she must be on the game. I felt daft and wished the floor would open and swallow me up. My mates just stood looking at me and sniggering. Jackie, thank goodness, did what Mr Hall asked and went or least out of the school gate and out of sight of Mr Hall.

"Right, Knight, go and get on your bus before you cause any more trouble. I and most of the staff have had enough of you this week."

Mr Hall stood in the entrance looking furious as we all walked towards the double-decker buses. Before running up the stairs and sitting on the back seat I glanced over my shoulder and noticed that Jackie was going on her way, thank goodness. John followed me on to the bus and sat down next to me. My other mates wandered up the stairs and just stood looking on and listening into our conversation.

"I am going to come on the bus with you this afternoon, Pete, as I want to know all the details about this girl and you. Perhaps I can take over from where you left off," said John, laughing. "You don't live in my direction."

"I know that but I must find out all the nitty gritty, then I can catch another bus back home from your place as they run every few minutes. Is anyone else coming with me to get the gossip?"

"I'm coming, no one is at home till half five so I have plenty of time. You lot had better get off, as the bus is starting up," said Dave, as he pushed past the others and plonked himself down on the seat in front of John and myself.

"I haven't much to tell you as nothing has happened – not yet, anyway."

"Oh, you are thinking about it then," said John rubbing his hands. "You need to watch your step as you don't want the pox. You better pluck up courage and go to the chemist and buy some johnnies. That will cost you! Of course, you have never bought any; if you had, you wouldn't have got Sam up the duff. When you go to buy some you have to ask for a pack of three. Just to let you know they come wrapped in brown paper so no one knows what you are buying, unless of course they are standing close to you when you ask the young assistant for them," laughed John with Dave's encouragement. "You can buy them when you go to the gents, in a machine for a florin or at the barbers. I find it more fun to buy them at the chemist as you usually get served by a young female assistant and they always get embarrassed. I have known people to ask for a bottle of shampoo because they've been too shy to ask for a pack of three once they've plucked up the courage to go to the counter. Thinking about it, it would be better for you to go to the machine in the lavs."

"Yeah, I think so as well," said Dave, still laughing out loud.

"Now we're settled down and we have sorted out where you are going to get some johnnies, let's have all the nitty gritty,. Come on, Pete!"

"I haven't much to tell you. Anyway, the bus is not the place to talk about anything like this, when we get off we can always go into the station and have a chat in the coffee bar."

"That's a deal, on the way you can tell us her name and where she lives."

"Who's going to pay for my coffee? I haven't any money. It's going to be a very expensive gossip for you two!"

"John, can we buy poor old Pete a coffee?"

"I think we can, I found a bob in the kitchen drawer this morning, so I took it. When we get to the coffee bar I will give you some money, you can go and get the coffee, are you listening to me, Dave?"

"Yeah, course I'm listening."

"It is you two who want the gossip, so it is only right that you two should pay for my coffee. Here goes: her name is Jackie, she likes to be called Jack. She lives across the road from the local park at Deptford in a flat above a shop. Apparently if you want to see her you have to ring the bell, next to the shop bell, this rings upstairs. She also told me that her parents are elderly so she always answers the door, that's if she is in, if she's out no one will answer."

The bus soon arrived at Blackheath station. The three of us clambered down the stairs and hurried into the coffee bar where we found an empty table.

"Come on, John, hand over some money to help with Pete's drink. I'm feeling a bit flush so does anyone fancy a Wagon Wheel or a Penguin? I'm going to have one."

"No thanks, I will be having supper as soon as I get in."

"What about you, John?"

"Oh, I fancy a Penguin, if that's okay? Here's some change to go towards Pete's coffee."

"I will ask if they have any Penguins, thanks for the money." With that, Dave went up and ordered the expressos.

"John, they only have Wagon Wheels? Do you want one of them?"

"Yeah, that will do."

Eventually we all settled down and I told them the story of Jackie and how I met her.

"I'm going to find an excuse for going to the reception at the hospital, perhaps I will call in Saturday afternoon because that is when you met her. Before I go I will make sure that I get some johnnies, you never know, my luck might be in. I can always see if she is willing to visit the bogs with me."

"You be careful John, whatever you do don't tell her where I live; I don't want her turning up on my doorstep. I am in enough trouble without any of her nonsense. Remember what the woman with the dog told me: Jackie is a pest and once she finds things out about you she won't leave you alone, she is like a dog with a bone."

"I will try and remember, but the thing is, Pete, I am not a goody goody like you."

"John, perhaps you and I can meet up, and we could go together, then we can see which one of us she fancies? I haven't much on Saturday afternoon. Pete, how about you coming with us? You could introduce her to us," said Dave, rubbing his hands. "I don't think that's a good idea. Anyway, I may be seeing Sam."

"Come on, Pete, don't be such a spoilsport; perhaps we can have a gang bang!"

"Both of you listen to me: it is ages till Saturday, it's only Monday and I will be seeing you most days this week. By Friday I should know what is happening on Saturday."

"Leave it until Friday afternoon. I know, just before we get on our different buses we could have a meeting."

"That's a good idea, I really need to leave you two and go home. Look at the time, it's almost five o'clock! Must go!"

With that, I picked up my haversack and hurried home to be greeted by my parents who were sitting in the front room, as usual. This particular afternoon they didn't look at all happy; in fact, they looked very sad. I plonked myself down on the sofa,

"What's up with you two? Is it the kitchen?"

"Well, yes and no," answered Mum, looking straight into my eyes. "First things first: the police came back after lunch looking for you, they said that it was very important that you should contact them as soon as you got in. The thing is, Pete, you are late; we told them you would be in touch before five o'clock and its now five thirty and they've been on the phone asking if you have arrived home."

This made me change from being calm into a person with a very short fuse, which I didn't realise I had.

"I am nearly seventeen years old, surely I am entitled to a life? The thing is, Mum, you shouldn't have told them the time you were expecting me home!" I shouted.

"Hang on a minute! Behave yourself, Peter! Don't speak to your mother in that tone, you are enough to send us both to the drink. In fact, I think I will have a G and T now. I know it's a bit early, but would you like one, Marg?"

"I think I would, perhaps it will calm my nerves. While we get ourselves a drink, Pete, go and phone the police."

"I will when I'm ready, I need to visit the toilet."

"Well hurry up, Pete."

"I will take as long as it takes."

"Pete, don't speak to us like that! I don't know what has come over you this last week."

"I do, Sam being pregnant plus my exams and trying to decide whether to go to university or not."

"Well, I can decide that for you, you have the brains to go to university so that is where your mother and I would like you to go."

"There you go again trying to sort out my life. I am going to decide for myself. Dad, at the moment Thursday is D-day for me. I am meeting up with Sam to hear if she's keeping this baby or if she is going to dispose of it."

60

"That sounds awful, 'dispose of the baby'. Please remember that this is our first grandchild."

"I will try to, but if you continue to speak to me like you are, I will not keep you informed of procedures."

"Go and phone the police before I get really cross with you, I just cannot understand what has come over you."

After leaving the toilet, I rang the police, only to hear that they would like me to go down to the station to have a chat – they wouldn't tell me what about.

"Well, I have made the phone call, the police want me down the station straight away. I can only guess that it is about Sam and this damn pregnancy, or it could be about the girl that was on the game in the park."

"What are you talking about Pete? It sounds like a load of rubbish, you will make your mother and I ill in a minute, just go and when you come back I hope you talk more sense than you are at the moment."

"I forgot to ask, what has happened about the kitchen floor? I see you have got the lino up and out in the garden, but what a stink! I could even smell it in the bog."

"We will have a chat about that once you've returned from the police station, going there is more important than any kitchen floor."

Once I arrived at the station I was taken by the duty sergeant to the interviewing room, where I sat at the table to wait for a police officer.

Once he arrived, he introduced himself and asked, "Have you any idea why you have been asked to come and report to us?"

"No."

"Well, it's about you getting Sam Smithson pregnant. Sam's parents have asked us to have a chat with you. They have reason to think that you have been having underage sex with their daughter, they're not happy."

"What do you mean? She is sixteen and a half years old, she was sixteen on 18th November and it is now the beginning of May, and she's only eight weeks' pregnant."

"I have had a talk to your headmaster and he has seen you giving Sam a quick kiss, but that was only once when he was looking out of the staff room window. He doesn't think you have been having underage sex."

"I can assure you that Sam and I have only been doing it since Christmas. This time last year I only knew Sam to look at, then a mate caught me looking at her and told me her name. At the Christmas school disco I went over and asked her for a dance, it has all happened since that first dance."

"That's not what I've been led to believe from Mr Smithson."

"Well, what I have said is the truth. You should realise that Mr Smithson is not a very nice man, he would make up anything to get me into trouble."

"We can only believe what we are told until we know different. Mr Smithson came in here and made a statement so we had to follow it up. The thing is the age you can legally have sex is sixteen. A boy who has sex with a girl under sixteen is breaking the law even if she agrees. If she's between thirteen and fifteen the boy can go to prison for two years, if the girl is under thirteen the boy can go to prison for life."

"You are frightening me, I can assure you officer that Sam was definitely sixteen before we had sex and she was quite willing, so what happens now?"

"I will be having another chat with your headmaster, then I will be seeing Mr Smithson with Sam sitting in on the meeting, at their flat, this will all take place late tomorrow afternoon. I will come and see you first thing Saturday, nine thirty will be the time, you should be up and running by then. I'll put it in my diary. You can go home now."

"I'm sorry, for causing all this trouble." At
that we both got up from the chairs.

"Go home before I change my mind and decide to keep you here."

I was in a complete daze when I left the station, I felt as if everyone was looking at me while I walked along the road, but of course they weren't. I unlocked the front door and went into the sitting room where Mum and Dad were still sat. Mum got up from her chair and picked up the dirty glasses.

"I will go and get dinner now you've arrived, tell your dad what has happened, he can repeat it to me later. I hope it's not more bad news, your sister is upstairs doing her homework so please try not to make too much noise, I don't want her upset."

Once Mum had left the room, I told Dad exactly what the police wanted and explained that an officer would be coming around here on Saturday morning.

"What! They're coming around here on Saturday? That means we all have to be up dressed and dusted by nine thirty?"

"Yeah, that's right; sorry and all that."

"Well, Pete, we will try and put all this to one side until Saturday, as your Mum and I are fed up with the same old record. Perhaps this will make you realise that you are in the wrong and what a terrible thing you have been doing; you're lucky that

you're not in a cell and they have thrown away the key."

Chapter 6

Thursday arrived and my alarm went off at quarter to eight; if I hadn't set it, I think I would have slept until lunch time. This particular morning my parents were very agreeable, they didn't ask why I was so quiet and not eating as much as I normally did for breakfast. Even sis was quiet, thank goodness; she normally chatted for England at breakfast. After packing my haversack with my books and schoolwork, and having given Mum a peck on the check, I made for the front door.

"Good luck, Pete!" they all shouted from the dining room.

"Thanks."

I wandered down the road to catch the bus. It was a lovely sunny day, which cheered me up no end. Long may it last! If everything went well with Sam, it would be a wonderful day, the best day for weeks. I arrived at the school gate thinking that Sam may be waiting for me, but she wasn't.

My school day went as normal, I tried to keep my head down and get on with my work and not think about where Sam may be. Lunchtime came and went. I finished my studies at half two and was about to go home when I bumped into Sam sitting on the stone bench in the playground. "What the hell are you doing here? I thought you had lessons all day?"

"I have, I'm not feeling to good so I have come out for a breath of fresh air."

"Perhaps we can have our chat now? Any more thoughts about an abortion?"

"No, I am going with Mum to see the doctor this evening. Mum and Dad think I should get rid of the baby, but I want to keep it."

"Well, I think I should be able to have a say about this. I am

64

the father, aren't I?"

"Course you are, I was a virgin until I met you."

"Deep down I would like you to keep this baby but it will be very difficult for us both, to start with we have no idea how we will get on living together. Anyway, Sam, you are getting quite big, when did you say it's due? Before you answer that, I'd better tell you I've been to the police station as your father reported you being pregnant to the police. They are sending a police officer around to my place on Saturday to have another chat, they also said something about seeing you and your father at your flat late this afternoon."

"Dad didn't tell me he'd been to a police station. I know he was off his head the other night and threatened me with going down the station in the Old Kent Road. Getting back to your question about when this baby is due, I'm not sure of the date but it is sometime in November."

"You go with your mum to the doctor's, then let us continue with school and see each other as we have been until the end of term. The thing is, Sam, I must get my exams even if I don't go to university. I need good results to get a job to keep all of us, remember a baby is not cheap to keep."

"What type of job are you thinking of getting, Pete?"

"I'm not sure, perhaps one in an insurance office or bank."

"Have you any idea about where we can live?"

"No idea at all, you can have a think about that. I am going home, I will get a newspaper on the way. I will see you tomorrow, if you want to phone after seeing the doctor feel free, you know the number. Mum and Dad are interested in the baby and would like to get to know you better, as I have said before you can't live with us. When you go to the doctor, don't be surprised if he asks when you started having sex, as it's not legal until you are sixteen even if you agreed, if you were between thirteen and fifteen the boy can be sent to prison for two years."

"What, is that right?"

"Yeah, afraid so."

"I will be careful what I say, I shouldn't have to ask but can we have a kiss?"

"Of course we can."

After a quick snog and arranging to meet up the next morning we parted company and I caught the bus home to Blackheath, where I went into the paper shop and bought the local rag to look up the price of rented flats in the area. I was not surprised to see that the rents were beyond our means. They started at seven pounds ten shillings a week with one month's rent in advance, this was sharing a bathroom with other tenants.

Once I arrived home, I left the local paper on the hall table and I went straight up to my room as my parents and sis were still out. Mum usually got back from work at around half four, unless she had to call into the grocery shop. Dad got home at half five but this depended on the time the last customer left the shop. The official time for dad to come home was around five but he had to lock up and then take the keys around to the caretaker who went back later to give the shop a clean. Sis normally got in at the same time as me, we often bumped into each other at the bus stop, then walked home together, but on Thursdays I'm usually early. After unpacking my books, I took my empty lunch box down to the kitchen where I put it on the draining board. This was the first time I had been in the kitchen since the flood and the lino had been taken up. I stood in the doorway and had a good look at the floor. It was awful; thank goodness it was Dad and not me that had forgotten to go and check that the back door was locked before going to bed. If it had been me, I am sure I wouldn't be around anymore.

I quickly heated up the electric kettle and made a mug of instant coffee. It had to be black as there wasn't any milk, why this was I don't know, as Dad and sis didn't take milk and Mum only had it in tea. Eventually I went up to my room to concentrate on my homework.

The next thing I heard was someone opening the front door. I went and looked over the banisters; it was mum.

"Hello, Pete, I'm worn out. On the way home I had to get milk from Sainsbury's we seem to be drinking an awful lot. I'm going to sit in the front room and wait for you to come down. I see you've bought the local rag, I will have a read while I wait; that's if I don't fall asleep over the paper."

66

Eventually I joined Mum for a chat. "I see you have been looking at the flats, Pete, you have put pen marks against some of them. What are you up to? Surely you're not thinking of leaving us; you are a real worry to me and your father."

"I was just looking to see how much the rent would be for a one-bedroom flat or bedsitter around here. What else am I supposed to do? You and Dad won't let Sam come and live with us, so I have no other choice. Anyway, Mum, I won't be moving out until both of us have left school and I have a job. Sam's going to the doctor's this evening so we will know more about the pregnancy later tonight, that's if she is allowed to use the phone at the flat. It is a real worry; Sam wants to keep this baby and doesn't want to go for an abortion. How she thinks she can keep it, I don't know. I can see why you and Dad are so upset with me. The only thing I can keep saying is sorry. I will go and make us a cuppa then you must tell me what is happening about the kitchen floor."

"I can tell you that now, son, it won't take a minute; the answer is nothing. Dad didn't pay any of the insurance premiums, apparently the bank forgot to write and let him know that there wasn't any money in our account after paying the other bills, so that is that. Whatever you do, don't mention it to your father, he says that he will sort it, it's one thing on top of another."

"I don't know what to say, I'll go and make a pot of tea."

Chapter 7

The phone rang at around ten thirty.

Mum answered and then called up the stairs to me. "Pete, can you hear me? Telephone for you!"

I opened the bathroom door. "Yeah, I can hear you, I am in the bathroom, who is it?"

"I have a feeling it's Sam, whoever it is she doesn't sound very happy. I think she may be crying or has a cold, she's speaking very quietly." I put on my brown check dressing gown and went out on to the landing.

"Thanks, I'll come down and have a chat." I went downstairs and took the phone. "Hello?" I asked.

"Pete, it's me, Sam. Mum and Dad have gone to bed, so I have crept out of my room to ring, if the line goes dead it's because I have got caught and I have to put the receiver down. I've been to the doctor's; Mum came into the surgery with me. I have to have a think about our future and go back and see him at the end of the week, must go." The receiver went bang.

I stood in the hall thinking about the call before going into the sitting room to see Mum.

"Well, who was it?"

"Sam."

"She didn't stay long on the phone, hasn't she got much to say? I thought she was seeing her doctor this evening?"

"Yeah, the thing is, she is not allowed to contact me, her mum and dad had gone to bed so she crept out of her room and rang me, her parents heard her so she had to put the phone down."

"Whatever next am I going to hear? You're the father of this baby and Sam who is the mother mustn't contact you, I have never heard the likes of it."

"Sam's dad is up in arms, that is why I had to go to the police station; he reported us for having sex under the age of sixteen, the thing is we didn't have underage sex."

"I do try to believe you Pete but some of things you say are very hard to take in or believe."

"I can hardly believe some of the things myself."

"We must try and forget about it until Saturday morning, that's when the police officer is coming around, your dad has told me all about it, he says that he will stay in the room with you when he comes."

"The officer is coming at nine thirty. I am pleased Dad will be there, I would hate it if I was on my own."

"Dad is in bed already as he has a headache. I must go and join him, have you finished in the bathroom?"

"Yeah."

"Night then, see you in the morning; don't forget to switch the telly off at the wall." With that, Mum patted me on the head and went up to bed leaving me sitting in the front room alone with my thoughts. When I came around from my daydream and looked at my watch I noticed a couple of hours had past, so I quickly sorted things out and ran up the stairs to bed. I slept quite well, considering the upheaval.

Friday was a quiet day for me at school, I didn't need to get in until after lunch, the only subject I had was with Mr Down at two o'clock. I arrived in his room only to find that he was nowhere to be seen, the other boys in my group were sat waiting for him.

"Now we are sat here waiting for old Down, Pete, you can tell us what exactly is going on with you and Sam. The gossip is that you have been down the police station and Sam is up the duff," said Jason, leaning forward on his desk, at the same time rubbing his hands and grinning all over his face.

"Yeah, that's right, but I can't talk about it."

"Oh well we will have to get hold of Sam and see if she will tell us what is happening."

"Don't upset her. She has enough to put up with, without you upsetting her."

"We notice she's getting quite big tits and big around the middle. How many months has she had a bun in the oven? You can tell us that."

"About three months."

"Six months to go then Knight and you will be a dad!" shouted Mr Down as he walked through the door. "You won't know what has hit you once this baby pops out. Remember, it doesn't pop back in again," smirked Mr Down, while the boys laughed out loud.

"That's enough, boys, we have had our laugh!" shouted Mr Down, banging all our books down on his desk. He made me feel awful I just sat with my head in my hands trying to compose myself.

"Only two more weeks before the big day, hope you have been studying hard. I have good news for all of you, your exam results were a success, you can all give yourselves a pat on the back. I will hand out your papers at the end of this lesson then you can have a read."

The lesson went very smoothly, and was over before I could think, which was quite a relief, "Don't forget to take your mock exam papers with you, read them at your leisure and take note of all my remarks, if you have any queries about them please come and see me, then I will go over them with you."

With that, we all left the room. I hurriedly went to catch my bus as it was nearly quarter to four. I could hear footsteps coming up behind me as I was walking along the main path.

"Pete!" shouted a female, I looked behind and there was Sam's best friend, Celia.

"Yeah, do you want something? I'm in a hurry; my bus leaves in a minute."

"Sam was very upset this morning, she thought you were going to meet her at the gate and you didn't turn up. She was so upset she had to go home."

"I forgot it was Friday, and I didn't have a class till two o'clock, so I stayed at home to study as my exams start in two weeks. Sam should have phoned me then I would have had a chat and may have come in early. Anyway, Celia, she did know that I was not coming in until two."

"Well, she has gone home."

"Thanks." I went on my way and just managed to get on the bus, it was so full I had to stand holding on for grim death all the way to Blackheath. It seemed to take ages what with the traffic and the stopping and starting at the lights and the people getting off and on at the bus stops. Eventually the bus arrived at the railway station, I jumped off only to be confronted by Sam and her mother, who were standing waiting for me.

"Caught you! We need to have a chat, we can have it here in the street, over a coffee at the railway station or we can all go around to your place, what's it going to be?" shouted Sam's mum. She seemed to be able to get as cross as Sam's dad; I guess they wouldn't be together if they were not two of a kind. She made me feel terrible; I started to sweat from head to toe, seeing them was the last thing on my mind.

"I'm not sure, I haven't any money so it can't be a coffee, I'm not in the habit of having arguments in the street and before you start shouting again I'm a peaceful bloke, I'm not used to this type of thing."

"You should have thought of that before getting Sam in the family way. You see the thing is we have been to see the doctor and Sam is definitely three months' pregnant, going on four. Sam's dad and me want to know your intentions. Sam had to come home from school today as you didn't turn up to see her."

"Calm down, that's the first thing to do."

"What, me calm down? What a nerve you have, telling me to calm down after all you have done," Mrs Smithson looked so flushed that her blood pressure must have been right up in the sky.

"Mrs Smithson, please speak to me quietly and calmly. Someone will come over in a minute and they will be asking what's up."

"I don't care if they come over or stay away… oh, I must sit down; I have come over all dizzy."

"See, this is what happens when anyone gets themselves into such a state. There's a bench inside the station on the left; hold on to my arm and I will help you to it."

"If you think I need your help I don't. Come on Sam you hold my arm, take me to the bench."

"I can't hold you up if you faint, I'll just have to let you go down on the ground, but I'll have a go. Are you going to come with us to the bench, Pete? If she faints I won't know what to do as she is too heavy for me to hold up."

"Okay, but I can only stay a few minutes. Once your mum has sat down, I'll have to go."

Sam tried to stand her mum up and walk her into the station, I followed close behind hoping that she didn't fall backwards.

"While you two sit here, I will go and get you a glass of water, then I must go."

When I returned they were both sat on the bench and seemed perfectly happy chatting away to each other as if nothing was wrong. "Thanks, Pete," said Mrs Smithson in a quiet voice.

"Here you are, drink this, I must go home now."

Immediately Mrs Smithson's tune changed back to her aggressive manner. "No you don't, you don't get away that easy, we still haven't had our little chat."

"Mrs Smithson I think you should try and calm down and perhaps see me sometime next week after I have sorted things out in my own mind. I understand that Sam intends to keep this baby come what may, so it doesn't matter if we don't chat today. Let me have a think. I'm seeing the police tomorrow morning, that's Saturday. What about Tuesday here at the same time as today, but you have to promise that there will be no shouting?" "I can't promise anything where you're concerned."

"Please try and calm down or you will be down the hospital. Think of Sam, all this shouting is not helping her; she will finish up being ill. I can see you both in bed next to one another if you don't calm down."

"Go away, we will meet you here on Tuesday. You better think about what is going to happen."

"Okay, bye. See you at school on Monday, Sam. You know my number if you want to phone."

"Bye."

As I walked out of the station I looked over my shoulder and saw Sam sat next to her mum, with her arm around her shoulder, both of them looking upset, in fact they both looked near to tears. I turned away and kept walking until I reached home. I unlocked the door and went in only to find Mr Smithson sat in the front room with Mum, having a cup of tea. I just could not believe my eyes.

"What is happening here?"

"Oh, Pete, I think you have met Sam's dad, he has come to have a few words with me about you and Sam."

"I have just left Sam with her Mum at the station. Mr Smithson, I have nothing to say to you except your wife is at the station sat on a bench with Sam, she seems to have got herself into some state. I suggest you leave that cup of tea and go to see her."

"Do you always let him speak to you like that? I wouldn't let Sam boss me around. I'm in charge in my house, both Sam and the Mrs have to do as I say or there's trouble."

"Go, like Pete has said. Go now. Leave your cup of tea and go. Show Mr Smithson out, please, Pete."

Mr Smithson looked furious – he put the cup down without drinking any of the tea.

"Follow me." We walked out into the hall and, while I was looking for the door keys, he had a few more words to say.

"You remember, boy, this is not the last you have heard or seen of me."

I didn't reply, I just opened the front door. Luckily for me he walked straight out on to the pavement without uttering another word or causing any more upset. I quickly shut the door behind him.

When I turned around, Mum was stood looking at me.

"I'll make a fresh pot of tea and bring it into the front room, then we can have a chat about what Mr Smithson had to say. You get one of the small coffee tables out while I put the kettle on. I'll only be a minute."

Mum was quicker than I thought she would be, as well as the pot of tea she brought in two cream horns. "I bought these on the way home from work, I thought you might like one and being
Friday we could celebrate the beginning of the weekend."

"Thanks, Mum, they are one of my favourite cakes."

"There are two more in the kitchen, one for Anne and the other for your dad."

"What time did Mr Smithson arrive?"

"About three o'clock. It was funny really, I was walking back from the bus and I felt some one was walking close behind me.
Ever had the feeling that someone is following you?"

"Yeah."

"Well, first of all I thought it must be my imagination so I just kept walking. Once I arrived at the front door and got the key out, he was stood by my side."

"Whatever did you say to him?"

"'Is something wrong? I don't know you.' He said, 'There is plenty wrong. I'm Sam's dad and I have come to have a chat; that's if you are who you are supposed to be. Are you Mrs Knight?' Of course, my answer was 'Yes' and then it went from there."

"Mum, he could have been anyone; luckily for you he was who he said he was. You shouldn't have let him in, especially you being here on your own."

"He seemed okay. That was until you arrived, then he started behaving differently. I can honestly say I wouldn't like to cross him."

"You can say that again. Anyway, what did he have to say?"

"First it was about you having sex before Sam was sixteen and how he had gone to the police, he wondered if we realised that you could be taken to court if it could be proved to be true, plus how were you going to provide for this baby as they had no money. I explained that we only had the house and there was no money in our bank account to help out."

"What did he say to that?"

"You walked in then, so that was that. Between us, we got rid of him."

"Thank goodness."

"Anyway, Pete, at work this morning the girl that works in the school office asked what the matter was with me as she didn't think I looked my normal self. Of course I do realise that I don't, so I went on to tell her about the baby. I do know that you won't be very happy about me talking about you to her. I have lots to tell you, it seems that she had a baby a couple of years ago out of wedlock."

"That's right, I'm not happy about you telling a stranger my business; you don't know who she may tell. Anyway, I am willing to listen to what she had to say. Come on, Mum, give me all the news, talk away."

"Well, Marjorie had a daughter and her parents were not happy about the pregnancy as you can imagine. She was given two choices by them. One: to go to a mother and baby home or a private nursing home, then, at ten days' old, the baby would be taken away to a foster home then put up for adoption, once it had been examined by a doctor to see if it was fit enough to be adopted. Or two: Marjorie could be sent to a Magdalen Home, this is a convent run by nuns for what they call 'fallen women'. After the birth the baby is taken away from the mother and adopted by a wealthy couple who would give a donation to the convent. The birth mothers are then put to work in the laundries and are named 'lifers' as they never go home, unless of course their parents come and take them home, but they rarely do."

"Mum, you're telling me that these places still exist in the '60s?"

"Yes, very common. Anyway, Marjorie was sent to a mother and baby home in Luton, her baby girl was adopted from there, she thinks about her daughter every day. The only thing Marjorie has to remind her of the baby is a photo of her a few days' old. Apparently once she got pregnant the father didn't want to know her or anything about the baby. Your dad or I don't want this to happen to Sam's baby, the thing is it's our grandchild, I don't think I could cope."

"Mum, I'm not going to let Sam or the baby down. The child is the innocent party and has not asked to be born, the baby deserves to be loved by its birth mother. It shouldn't be sent away, it wouldn't be right."

"Pete I am so pleased you feel like this, let me give you a hug. Marjorie did mention that she could keep the baby if she left the area, but, as she said, how would she have managed? I know some get a bedsitter and go on from there, how they feed and water a baby, God only knows."

"Well I am going to stand by Sam, so I have to think of a way to do it."

"Tomorrow, Pete, I am going to get up early and give the downstairs a good vacuum. I don't think I have cleaned anywhere for at least two weeks, I don't want the officer to see how dirty our home is. I hope he doesn't smell the kitchen floor."

Chapter 8

Saturday arrived, and we all got up earlier than normal. Mum was up by seven and was first in the bathroom followed by Dad and then me. Anne had a lie-in until after the officer had arrived, once up she spent the morning in the kitchen, complaining to Mum about the smell that was lingering.

"How can you expect me to eat in here with this smell, it stinks. This is all Pete's fault, if he hadn't got Sam up the duff the police wouldn't be here and I would be able to eat in the dining room."

Once dressed, Mum came into the front room looking as if she was to entertain the Queen, knee-length floral dress with stiletto heels, not her normal skirt and jumper with fur slippers. I hadn't seen her with so much make-up on her face for years, she normally looked pale, but today it was bright red lipstick with rouge on her cheeks, even her hair looked as if it had been to the early morning hairdressers. Dad had put on his weekend gear, pale blue jeans with a brown polo shirt, on his feet he wore his suede slip-ons. I wore my usual, grey flannels and my white shirt, with slippers. After a morning hello, the three of us went into the dining room to eat our breakfast. It must have been the quietest breakfast we'd had for a long time, all deep in our own thoughts. It didn't seem long before the front doorbell rang. Mum jumped up from her seat as if her best friend had arrived.

"Which one of you is going to the door? I'm going to disappear once the officer is in and settled."

"Marg, that's fine, I will go to the door. Pete, you come with me. Take a deep breath, son, here we go."

Dad opened the door, only to find two people: one plainclothed woman and a police officer in uniform.

"Good morning, sir, I am PC Jones and this is Mavis Swift, a police cadet. I believe you are expecting me. Please may we both come in?"

"Of course." At that they both walked into the hall and we all shook hands with one another before going into the front room where Mum was waiting.

"Mavis has come to listen in to what I have to say, and also to take notes for me."

"Before I disappear and leave you all to it, would you like a cup of coffee?"

"No thanks," replied the officer, looking very serious. Mum went on her way, closing the door behind her. I have a feeling that she went upstairs to her bedroom.

"Sit down then," said Dad, looking very embarrassed. "I will sit in this chair; it's where I usually sit, the chair suits my bum. Pete, you sit over there, where your mother normally sits, then if you would both like to sit on the sofa that would be great."

"Thanks," said the cadet, "do you think I could have one of those tables then I can put my papers down on it to write my notes?"

"Of course you can, you can get it, Pete."

"Now you both know why we are here. Last night as promised we went around to the flat to see Sam with her mum and dad, we had a long chat and Mavis took down a lot of notes, in a moment she will read some of them out to you. Later on today we will be going back again, to put them completely in the picture."

Mavis picked up her notes and read a few lines to herself before telling us what the Smithsons had to say. "As you both know full well, Mr and Mrs Smithson are not at all happy about the situation. In fact, he is furious and blames everything on you, Pete, as Sam's dad feels you must have led her on. Sam tried to explain to her father that it was her fault as she agreed to have sex with you and if she had not agreed you couldn't have done anything about it, unless of course you raped her and you didn't. Mrs Smithson was very quiet as she didn't feel too good, in fact, she was only there in person and had nothing to say. Mr Smithson keeps thinking that you must have had sex with Sam before she was sixteen, we tried to explain that you can get pregnant by just having sex the once and that you had sex for the first time at the end of March. As well as seeing the Smithsons we have had to go to your school and see what the staff had to say. You are very lucky Pete because the head said he didn't know anything about a relationship between you and Sam, he did say he saw you give Sam a quick kiss on one occasion but he didn't think anything untoward had been happening, even though some of the staff had mentioned it. Do you have anything to say, Pete?"

"Yeah. I am telling the truth, we did not have sex until Sam was sixteen, the first time was in March this year. I didn't know her at Christmas, I didn't even know her name, she's not in my class for any subject. One day I asked one of the boys in her form what she was called so I could go and say hello. I know now that I should have kept clear of her and got on with my work, but it's too late. I had a chat with Mum yesterday and told her that I was going to stand by Sam as she wanted to keep the baby and I would help her to do this by not going to university but by getting a job after I have finished my A-levels."

"What on earth are you talking about, Pete? Your mother and I have worked very hard to keep you at school and are prepared to help you through university, you have got the brain to go far. One mistake doesn't mean you have to give up on your ambitions and get a local job."

"Surely it is up to me."

"It is no good having an argument at this stage, we have to think of this baby and how Sam is going to manage," said the police officer, looking over at the cadet.

"It's time for me to take notes. Pete, you are telling the officer and myself that you didn't have sex with Sam until she was sixteen?"

"That's right."

"Let me get my pen out and write down the question you have asked, and also write down Pete's reply."

"Can you tell us where the act took place?"

"I wish I didn't have to tell you, but I must say the truth and I am afraid it was in the girls' toilets at school."

79

"Pete, I am disgusted with you. Whatever happens don't let your mother know it will break her heart and make her ill, she will never be able forgive you."

"Calm down, Mr Knight, we mustn't get too emotional, please try and stay calm."

"I understand."

"After we leave here we are going back to see Sam and her family, they want an answer to this question: are you definitely going to look after this baby with Sam?"

"I am going to try to. The plan is to get a job after I leave school at the end of May, beginning of June. Before all this happened I had planned to go to university, but the pregnancy has put a stop to that."

"What sort of job are hoping to get?"

"I am thinking of an office job, bank or insurance. Depends what's around when I finish my exams."

Both the police officer and the cadet looked at me in such a way that they seemed to be believing what I was saying, thank goodness. Dad, well, he just sat there, what he was thinking I have no idea, except he didn't seem to approve of any of what was being talked about.

"I am going to suggest that I go and make us all a cup of tea, do you both take milk and sugar?"

"I would just like a glass of cold water," said Mavis smiling to herself.

"What would you like, police officer?"

"A cup of tea will do fine."

"Pete, I guess you would like your usual coffee?"

"Yeah, thanks, Dad."

Dad was back quicker than any of us expected as Mum was sat in the kitchen, having a chat with Anne.

"My wife is going to make the drinks for us, she will come in with the tray."

"That's good because we would like to explain to her what is going on and see what she thinks of everything, as she may have something to add."

"Okay, but she hasn't a very strong constitution. The slightest thing upsets her stomach which will mean she will be staying in bed for a couple of days if she is upset."

"Oh dear, we'll be careful what we say and how we say it," replied the officer, looking very sympathetic towards Dad and myself.

It was not long before Mum arrived with the tray of drinks, the officer stood up when she came into the room.

"Please don't stand on ceremony for me, but while you are standing please can you pass over one of the small side tables to put this on? They are behind Ernie's chair, then I will leave you all to it."

"Coming over, Mrs Knight. Do you think you can stay for a few minutes? Perhaps you could sit down next to Mavis, I will stand over here."

"I don't understand why you need me here, I thought you were getting on well on your own," answered Mum while she made herself comfortable on the sofa. Mum's dress was a bit short so she had to keep pulling it down to cover her knees. The thing is, Mum hadn't heard of tights and the tops of her stockings showed along with her suspenders, so all the time she was on the sofa she kept having to stand up to pull her dress down. The officer looked shocked when he looked towards Mum, I don't think he could believe his eyes.

"We just need to let you know what is going on and see if you have anything to add to any of our questions."

It was not long before Mum became pale and agitated. "I can't cope with any more of your questions, I will have to go and lie down."

"We will leave you all to it in just a minute. One more thing, what do you think of Pete giving up going to university because of this baby and Sam?"

"Pete and I had a chat yesterday, I feel for the baby's sake getting a job is the right thing to do, I wouldn't like to think the baby would eventually have to go for adoption because of Sam not being able to cope. Both Ernie and I have to remember that this baby is our first grandchild, we will do all we can to help, I expect Ern has told you both that we are not well off, all the money we have has been earned, no handouts in this home."

"I will write that down so we don't forget to tell the Smithsons."

"We will be on our way now. Pete, I doubt if we will need to come around again, if we do we will phone first and give you plenty of notice, back at the station I will type up the notes into a report and put them on file."

At that we all got up, the officer shook hands with all of us while Mavis picked up all her notes, then both the officer and the cadet made their way out into the hall to the front door. It was quite a relief when I closed the door behind them.

"I must have a sit down, that was one of the most terrible mornings I have ever had." I looked at my watch and noticed that it was only quarter to eleven, it seemed like they had been here longer than an hour and a quarter.

"I think you got away with it lightly, don't you Marg?"

"Yes I do."

"I hope we can try and get our lives back to normal and tonight have a good night's sleep; in other words, early bed. What do you think, Marg?"

"That sounds good to me, let's say lights out by ten thirty."

The three of us went back into the front room, Mum collected up the dirty mugs then went out into the kitchen while Dad and I sorted out the small tables and put them back behind what we all called Dad's chair.

"I'm completely exhausted, Pete, you must feel worn out; if I were you I would have a quiet day."

"I am expecting a phone call from two of my mates later this morning; we have sort of arranged to go out for the afternoon."

"I have never known you to go out with your mates, especially on a Saturday, where ever are you going?"

"They are deciding that, then they are going to phone and let me know the time and place. They did say something about going for a walk in Blackheath, they are thinking of coming over on the bus from Deptford."

"I can only say I hope you don't get yourself into any more trouble."

"I hope not as well."

"If you think trouble is in store I should stay in, I'm sure you have a lot of revising to do."

"I have quite a bit, it's Sunday tomorrow nothing is on, so I'm thinking about doing it then."

"It's up to you, Pete, but don't bring any more trouble home here, your Mum or I can't cope with any more. We're staying in today, this afternoon I may have a sleep in my chair."

"I think I will go to my room and have a lie down and hopefully have a sleep; if anyone phones perhaps you can take a message and phone number, then I will ring back."

"Yes, okay, Pete."

"Thanks, Dad."

Chapter 9

I managed to have a sleep but was woken by Mum knocking at my door. "Pete, can you hear me?"

"Yeah what is it now? I was asleep."

"Sorry to wake you. One of your mates, I think he called himself John, phoned and said he and Dave would meet you in the coffee bar at the station at half past one, the thing is it's one o'clock, if you are going you better get up."

"Okay, thanks, Mum, I will lay here and have a think. Did he leave a phone number?"

"No, I told him you were asleep and that I would wake you at one. They mentioned something about calling around here if you
didn't turn up at the station by two."

"Oh, I will get up and go."

"Do you want something for lunch?"

"Yeah, I'd better,"

"I have some tongue in the fridge, I will make you a sandwich."

"Thanks."

By the time I got up and sorted myself out, it was almost half past one before I got downstairs.

"The sandwich looks nice, thanks, Mum."

"I wonder what you are going to get up to?"

"I have no idea, I won't be able to do anything much as I have only got a few pennies."

"There you go again, as I have said to you before, you ought to get a Saturday job. Have a look in the window of the paper shop in the high street, they sometimes have jobs advertised, also butchers sometimes need boys to deliver meat, they provide the bike to ride around on. I am sure that they might take you on, even if it's only every other Saturday."

"I'll have a look, can you let me have a bob or two?"

"Pete, you know the answer to that; it's no."

"Mum please, just a bob so I can have a coffee."

"Pete, this is the last time, your pocket money should be enough to last a week. The bob I give you will be taken out of next week's money."

"Thanks, Mum, love you."

I quickly ate the sandwich then drank a full glass of water down in one go. This of course gave me hiccups so I had to sit and recover in the dining room before going back upstairs to comb my hair into the DA style, with the help of Dad's brylcream. Once ready I looked in the landing mirror and thought I looked quite swish in my black drainpipe jeans, lime-green florescent socks with black winkle pickers, white shirt with a black bootlace tie. Thank goodness it was a sunny afternoon as I have no idea what coat I would have put on, as I only have an anorak. After admiring myself I crept down the stairs hoping to get out before Mum spotted me with my new image.

"What have you done to your hair? I must admit, Pete, it does suit you, but what has come over you to go out looking like you do?"

"Well, as it is Saturday I have decided that I should dress myself up, as you all keep telling me I am sixteen going on seventeen. I thought perhaps if I dressed like this I may find a Saturday job, you and Dad bought me these clothes or at least you gave me the money for them and I went with Sam to get them. I had these clothes on when I was eating my sandwich – the hair, well, I've only combed it a different way and used Dad's brylcream on it, the style is called DA."

"I can't believe what I am seeing. I can tell you one thing, your hair, it needs cutting."

"I am not having it cut, this is the latest style. I'm going, goodbye. I'll be back some time."

At that I walked out of the front door, banging it shut behind me.

I met up with John and Dave as planned outside the station before going into the coffee bar, where we sat at a table behind some girls. "My God, you look different, where did you get all that gear? You have even got a pair of winkles. The hair, well it looks good, whatever has happened to you, Pete?"

"I thought I would give you both a shock, you both look a bit plain compared to me, I feel a bit like the odd one out. The thing is I believe if you want to get off with a nineteen-year-old you have to dress up and give them something to look at," I replied, smirking.

"What are we going to do John? We look stupid, dressed like we are, how can we try and get off with the receptionist?"

"We'll manage, have confidence. If Pete can chat her up, I'm sure we can."

"I've got a brain wave."

"Whatever can that be Dave, your brain doesn't work quick at the best of times, what bright idea have you got?"

"Once we have drunk our coffee let's go to the chemist and buy some brylcream and a comb, then visit the gents where we can change our hair styles to look the same as Pete's. I'm sure our hair is longer than yours, Pete, and you have managed to get yours into a DA."

"My goodness what has come over you, Dave, but it sounds good to me."

"I hope you have got some money, as I only have a bob, just enough for my coffee. I'm going to look for a Saturday job, Mum said that they put adverts in the paper shop window, you know the shop next to the chemist. I will have a look at the board while you both go into the chemist. Hope you have some johnnies If you haven't, you better buy them as well, just in case you get lucky."

"John, have you brought some johnnies with you?" asked Dave.

"Yeah course I have. I always carry some with me, they're in my wallet, I have one pack of three. I will give you one each, let me get my wallet out." With that, John went into his back pocket to get his wallet then discreetly tried to get the johnnies out and pass them around the table until there was laughter from one of the girls at the other table.

"See what they are doing, girls? Those boys are passing around johnnies!" shouted the most brazen.

At that, and in the excitement of the moment, John turned around to have a look at the girls and dropped the johnnies on the floor. The three of us felt completely stupid as one of us had to pick them up. I picked the short straw and had to get down on my hands and knees, by this time most of the people in the café were watching and tut-tutting us.

"Time for you three to go, you on the floor, hurry up, get up and get out, you three haven't even bought a drink, don't bother to return, we can't do with time wasters in here."

At that I got up with the johnnies in my hand, with our heads down we walked out of the café and went in the direction of the chemist shop.

It took us quite a while to get to the chemist as we were busy admiring all the girls that walked past in miniskirts. They also seemed to find the three of us interesting and were looking back over their shoulders.

"What do you think of them, Dave? It is no good us asking Pete what he thinks because he has Sam with a bun in her oven."

"Hang on you, just because I have a girlfriend who's up the duff, I can still have an opinion. They are not bad for Blackheath, I have seen a lot worse."

"As Pete says they are not bad for around here," replied Dave.

"Shall we follow them?" asked John. "Or shall we continue on our mission to the chemist, then to the hospital to see the receptionist? What did you say her name is, Pete?"

"Jackie, she likes to be called Jack."

"John I think we should go and see this Jackie, our luck may be in with her," said Dave, rubbing his hands.

"It's a long walk up to the hospital, but you don't have to walk back down; there's a bus every half-hour and I have a feeling that it goes to Deptford. Before we set off you must remember that
I'm not sure if Jackie will be there, we'll have to chance it."

"That's okay with us, isn't it, Dave?"

"Yeah, let's go and get the brylcream, do you know where there is a lav with a mirror, Pete?"

"Yeah, there is one on the way to the hospital. As you go along the path, it's on the right, if it's locked we can always use the one in the hospital. We can either go past the reception to the lavs or we can go in the back entrance to the hospital and the lavs are on the left-hand side, just inside the door. I think if you are going to change your hairstyles we should go in the back way and then walk through the corridors to the reception."

"That sounds fine, we'll go in the back door."

"I'm going to look at this noticeboard while you two go in the chemist. Don't take too long, its three thirty already and it will take about a quarter of an hour to walk to the hospital."

"We will hurry," said John, pushing open the chemist's door.

The noticeboard was quite interesting but there were not many Saturday jobs available for boys. Female and male models were needed for a photographer in the West End, the problem was that they had to be over eighteen.

"We have the brylcream, found anything, Pete?"

"Not really, a thirteen-year-old boy is needed for a paper round, a photographer needs male and female models in the West End but they have to be over eighteen, slim and tall."

"What, I'd enjoy that, I'm sure they would take me for eighteen, it would be fun, I'm tall and handsome! Is there a phone number?"

"Yeah, but Dave, you are short and quite fat."

"Stop that nonsense, Pete, you are not much taller than me and you are not skinny, remember, they can't see me on the phone so if I get an appointment and I go for an interview that is when they will see my size, they will either like what they see or kick me out."

"You two just shut up! Have you got a pen, Dave? Then I can write the number down so I can ring and see how much they pay."

"I'm not having anything to do with this, I've been in enough trouble, in a minute I will go and leave you two to it."

"Spoil sport, Pete! Come on, Dave, give me your pen, then I can write the number down on my hand."

"Oh, here you are," said Dave passing the pen to John.

"Come on you two, hurry up, let's get going or we will never get to the hospital! I have a feeling Jackie finishes work at four."

After John had written the number down we got going; the walk that should have taken a quarter of an hour only took about five minutes, as we decided to run most of the way. When we got to the back entrance of the hospital we managed to push open the large wooden door and went straight into the mens'. Luckily for us the lavs were empty. The mirror on the wall was small like a shaving mirror, only big enough for one head to look in it at a time.

"The mirror's a bit small. Anyway, Dave, let's have the brylcream, what have you done with the comb?"

"I thought you picked that up, John."

"No I didn't, Pete have you got a comb?"

"Yeah, somewhere, here it is, give me it back when you've finished. I must have a wee while you two are sorting yourselves out."

"What about this then boys?" said John after he had smothered his hair in brylcream with his hands and then combed it into position.

"That looks okay. Let me have the comb, then I can sort my hair out," said Dave, putting his fingers into the brylcream pot.

"Well, what a difference a hairstyle can make, you two look completely different. Get a move on, give me my comb back, Dave."

"I thought you'd let us keep it."

"No, it's mine."

At that I grabbed the comb from Dave. "Eh, you can keep it, I don't want it in my pocket now you have used it and covered it in brylcream – here you are." Dave grabbed it back and put it straight into his back pocket. "Are you ready?" shouted John "Yeah," replied Dave.

"Here we go then, left, right, left, right." Out
we marched into the long corridor.

"Which way now Pete?"

"We need to walk right down to the end, then turn right, the reception desk is on the left. With luck, Jackie should be sat there."

We arrived at the reception only to find an elderly man sat on the stool behind the glass screen reading his newspaper, which he had laid out on top of the desk. He looked like he was the hospital porter, but it turned out that he was the relief receptionist. We could only see the top half of him, from where we were stood. His stomach seemed so big that it was coming out over the top of his trousers on to the desk; whether he ate a lot or he drank a lot of beer, I don't know but he did look large. Of course it could have been the black V-neck jumper he was wearing over his green and white check shirt that made him look big, as it seemed extra tight. He must have been at least forty with a balding head and side burns down to his chin.

As I was the one that knew Jackie I went over. The man pulled open the glass screen.

"What can I do for you three?"

"We have come to see Jack," I replied timidly.

"Jackie? She's not here today, can I help you?"

"No, it's Jack we want," said John.

I was wishing the floor would swallow us all up.

"Well, it's her day off; she'll be back in tomorrow, unless she gets a better offer, ha, ha, ha."

"Thanks."

"Before you go, I wouldn't have thought she would be interested in you three, you are all a bit young for her, she likes the more mature and experienced man, like me, unless of course she is going to give you a lesson in the act of lovemaking."

The colour of our faces went from being pale white to bright red.

"I know, I will let her know that you have called to see her. What are your names, have you a telephone number so she can ring you? Jack is very good at phoning men, she spends most of her time on the phone, ringing round or answering the phone to men."

The three of us looked at one another. "What do you want to do? Hurry up, I want to get back to my newspaper, I'm looking at the page-three girl."

"It's Pete that she knows, yes, tell her Pete called with two mates," laughed John.

"I'm not interested in her, it's my mates who are interested, I've bought them along to introduce them, they are called Dave and John, they come from Deptford."

"You have come all the way from Deptford to see dear old Jack? She will be chuffed to bits when I tell her. I have a notepad somewhere, to write down messages for our Jackie. I will write down your names and phone numbers if you give them to me, once I've found the pad."

"We don't have phones where we come from. Come on, you two, let's get out of here."

We turned and quickly went out of the main door to wait for the Deptford bus.

"Once you two get on the bus, I'm going."

"What do you mean, you are going?"

"I mean I'm going home, I've had enough for one Saturday."

I turned around only to see the man from the reception desk stood behind us. Gosh he was big, very broad and at least six feet tall.

"I've come out to have another chat with you three and to have a fag at the same time, it's quite busy in that office. I have to answer the phone for the hospital, you see the switchboard is in reception. Before I chat any more I must tell you that I've written down your names on the pad for Jack."

What a mess he looked. Below the waist he wore black trousers, these were covered in white paint and dust, even his trouser zip was half undone, they had definitely seen better days. His shoes looked like ones that had been worn on a building site. We all stood starring at him. "Are you sure you are the receptionist? You look more like a builder's mate to me."

"Course I am, I told you I'm the relief receptionist."

"You're telling us that you are employed by the hospital dressed like you are as a receptionist?"

"Well yeah, its Saturday today so I can wear casual gear."

"You are a joke, no one works in a hospital dressed like you," laughed Dave.

"Before we go, we want the truth, where is Jackie?"

"No idea. The thing is, she has been taken back inside as an inpatient. They couldn't get anyone to work the switchboard at short notice so they asked me, I'm usually on maintenance, I'm the odd job man. I hang out in the reception when they don't need me to do odd jobs; I enjoy looking at Jack's legs and of course her tits. See, the thing is, she enjoys my company."

"I'm fed up with all this rubbish, I'm off. John, Dave, are you going to wait for the bus or walk back to the high street with me? If you aren't coming I'm going to take a short cut to home."

"Oh, we'll come with you, Pete. Anything to keep the peace."

At that we said cheerio to the so-called receptionist and left him watching us with his fag hanging out of his mouth.

We soon arrived back in the high street. "I'm going to find a phone box and make a call to the photographer fellow," said John, laughing out loud.

"The nearest phone box is at the post office, I think there are three outside, the only trouble is that there is normally a queue, before now I have had to wait as long as half an hour to use a phone. Now, mates, once I've shown you the post office I'm going to leave you to it."

"What, you are going to go home? It's a Saturday and it's early, John and I thought we would pick up a couple of birds that were up for it and go to the flicks."

"I'm in enough trouble without getting into any more. See that blue car parked about a quarter a mile up the road on the left, the one behind the red van?"

"Yeah, what about it?"

"Well, that is where the phone boxes are, the bus stop is outside the next block of houses so you can catch the bus back to Deptford or Lewisham from there. Bye, see you Monday." With that, I turned and went on my way before I could get involved in anything else.

"Bye, spoilsport!" my mates shouted after me.

I arrived home just in time for the fish and chip supper. Mum, Dad and Anne had just sat down at the table when I walked in through the front door; my meal had been put in the oven.

"Thank goodness you have come home on time, I've only just put your meal in the oven. You'll have to be very careful when getting it out as the plate will be hot, I've covered your food over with another plate so take care, Pete, the oven glove is on the side."

"I will."

Anne started yapping as soon as I walked in with my meal.

"Well, let's hear all your gossip, Pete, where have you been? What are your mates like? You need to look in the mirror at your stupid hairstyle and your strange clothes."

"I don't think it's anything to do with you, Anne, my hair, my clothes, where I have been with my mates. You remember what I am about to say, they wouldn't fancy you, they like the more mature girls not ones that are still wearing ankle socks, so you can forget about them fancying you."

"Stop it you two, let's have supper in peace. Pete, for once, is right, it's nothing to do with any of us where he has been, unless he wants to tell us," said Dad banging his hand down on the table and making us all jump.

"Yes be quiet, shut up!" shouted Mum.

We all sat quietly and got on with eating. All anyone would have heard if they were listening in was the noise of the knives and forks. I think Anne was shocked to think both Mum and Dad stuck up for me.

"Pudding for all of you?" asked Mum in a quiet voice.

"What is it?"

"The usual apple crumble, with custard or ice cream."

"Can I just have custard?" asked Anne sheepishly.

"No Anne, apples are good for you, every Saturday we have a fuss with you, and I am fed up with the same old question."

"That is that then, no pudding thanks, I don't understand why we can't have a crumble with a different fruit."

"Because apples are cheap," answered Dad for Mum.

"I will have some please with custard and some ice cream," I said.

"Pig!" shouted Anne.

"I shall get really cross with you two in a minute, at least Pete is having pudding, not like you, Anne. I hope I don't catch you in the kitchen pinching the biscuits later this evening because that will be last straw." shouted Dad.

"I'm going to my room!" shouted Anne as she got up from her chair, going out of the dining room she banged the door closed behind her.

"I don't know what has come over you two; when you were younger you got on so well. I guess it is because you are teenagers now."

"That's it, we are teenagers, once I have eaten my pudding I am going to my room to read the results of my mocks."

"Pete, you've heard – sorry, with all the upset I have forgotten all about them."

"Well, to let you both know, I have done okay; Mr Hall said we all deserve a pat on the back. I'm going to read everything through, to see if Mr Hall needs to help me with anything. I enjoyed the crumble, Mum."

"Thanks, Pete."

"I've got room for a bit more if there is some."

"Of course there is, Pete, would you like more, Ernie?"

"Yes I think I would, it tastes better than normal. Perhaps you have used different apples?"

"I've used the Bramleys that you stored in the shed, this is the last of them."

Mum went out to the kitchen to fetch what was left.

"There's quite a bit, it has to be eaten up today as we have a surprise pudding tomorrow so any left over from seconds will be thrown out. I don't want any more, pass your plate please Ern and you, Pete."

After eating seconds, I left the table and went upstairs, as planned. The results were good, not too many mistakes.

Chapter 10

I spent most of Sunday in my room, studying in between listening to Radio Caroline. I only went downstairs when Mum called me for lunch, which was the usual roast beef and Yorkshire pudding, followed by jam tart. I enjoyed Sunday afternoon tea as Mum always managed to bake a couple of cakes, usually a Victoria sponge and a fruit cake. Both were favourites of mine, and tasted delicious.

Monday soon arrived; before I knew it, I was sitting on the low wall next to the school gates waiting for Sam. She hadn't phoned over the weekend; I can only guess that this must have been because she was busy sorting herself out with her parents.

I looked very boring compared to Saturday. Being in the sixth form meant that none of us needed to wear the school uniform, but I always wear grey flannels and white shirt, the other boys turning up in check shirts with jeans if they can get away with it. For school, I combed my hair back into its normal style, it was getting quite long especially in the front where it was down over my eyes. I could definitely see better when I smothered it all in brylcream and combed it into a DA, but the head didn't agree to any of us using brylcream or having a DA.

Sam soon arrived. "I'm pleased you're here, I have lots to tell you."

"You look wonderful, great to see your legs, like the bump, let's have a snog and a cuddle." I immediately pulled her towards me so she was standing between my legs. As she lay against my body I could feel our baby kicking. "You are getting quite large out the front, with my baby in your tum makes me feel good. I felt that, our baby doesn't half kick!"

"Yeah, it's been kicking most of the night, I don't think it likes to go to sleep anymore."

At that we had a long passionate kiss, until suddenly from the other side of the drive Dave shouted, "Look at you two so early in the morning!"

He made us both jump. "Go away leave us alone!" I shouted back.

Then came the wolf whistling from every direction, all the kids seemed to be watching us. I immediately jumped down from the wall while still holding on to Sam's hands, I started to walk her towards the main door.

"Come on, Sam, let's go and find somewhere private where we won't be disturbed."

"If that means going to the girls' lavatories, the answer to that is no, I am not going there."

"Don't be stupid, you're pregnant now, we can have sex as often as we like, you can't get pregnant on top of being pregnant."

"It is not that, the staff may be looking out for us now the police have told them where we have been having sex."

"That is that then, what are we supposed to do? Visit the park after dark and perform on a bench? If you think that is a better idea, I know of a way in when the gates are locked."

"What, Pete? I didn't think you'd know how to get into the park."

"Lots of things you don't know about me, you haven't even asked what I've been up to over the weekend. I can tell you one thing I haven't been doing and that is sitting at home twiddling my fingers waiting for the phone to ring."

"You trying to tell me something, have you been with someone else?"

"Not exactly."

"What has been happening, Pete?"

"I met up with my mates and the three of us went out looking for Jack, she fancies me," I said, laughing in Sam's face

"You are telling me that you would have had sex with her given half the chance?"

"Sort of, my mates were thinking of a gang bang. Don't worry she wasn't around, the thing is Sam once you have had sex especially if you are a bloke, you can't live without it, so

96

everyone I've talked to tells me, that includes the police, and I'm desperate, so when are we going to have it again?"

"You're teasing me."

"Why should I do that?"

"I don't know, but I'm not going to the girls' lavs or anywhere else with you."

"You'd better think about it, Sam, I'm going to my first lesson of the day, see you later alligator, bye for now." I went off smiling to myself and leaving Sam with a lot to think about. Lunchtime came and for once Sam came over to where I was sat and ate her packed lunch with me instead of sitting with her best mate, Celia.

"What has come over you? Not sitting with Celia today? You hardly ever sit and eat lunch with me."

"Celia is not here today, she's not well. I don't want you going off with someone else so I've come to sit with you. I love you, Pete, and I'm pregnant. If you haven't noticed, I'm getting bigger by the minute."

"So you should be getting bigger by the minute. I would think something was wrong if you were getting smaller."

"Stop being so…"

"So what?"

"Oh, at times you are sarcastic and you tease me both at the same time. I'm beginning to think you don't care about me."

"You know that's not true, the thing is, I don't know what to do or say about the position we're in. I don't even know what your parents think, the only thing I do know is that they are very angry with me. You see I couldn't have sex with you unless you agreed and, boy, you agreed all right. Having sex with you is amazing, even though we have only had quickies in the girls' lavs; every time it's been great."

"Stop it, Pete, do you love me?"

"Is sex love? If it is I do love you."

Sam just looked at me, her eyes filling with tears once again.

"Sam stop getting upset, of course I love you. If I didn't I wouldn't be thinking of living in sin with you, once you have the baby."

"We aren't going to live together before then?"

"No, it's best that you stay with your parents and go to a mother and baby home for the birth."

"You really mean what you are saying."

"Course I do, I wouldn't say it if I could think of a better idea." Sniff, sniff went Sam, with tears pouring down her cheeks.

"You realise that it's Tuesday tomorrow and you are going to see my mum again at the station after school?"

"I had forgotten all about that, but I will be there, you will be with her won't you?"

"Yeah, and Dad."

"What! Your dad is coming for coffee at the station?"

"Yeah."

"I can't believe what you're saying, perhaps we should think of somewhere else to meet. I don't want trouble in that coffee bar, the man behind the bar knows me. I can see your father causing trouble and me being banned, then I will have nowhere to go with my mates."

"Well, you had better think of somewhere else because I don't know anywhere and it's tomorrow."

"I will have a think. What about if we meet at my home, that's if my parents agree, then I will also have someone on my side, it won't be so one-sided."

"I don't know about that."

"What do you mean, whose side are you on? It doesn't sound like it's mine."

"Course I'm on your side, but Mum and Dad have agreed to let me stay at the flat with them so I have to stand up for them a bit, or they may let me down. Then I will be on the streets."

"I'm going to ask my parents tonight about you all coming around to my home. I will give you the answer in the morning, then you can ring your mum and dad during the day to say where we'll meet."

"That sounds all right."

"Well, Sam, I'm going on my way, I want to have a chat with my mates before my next lesson."

"You telling me to get lost?"

"Something like that."

"Pete, can't we go and sit on the lawn at the back of the sixth form together?"

"You are saying that you want to come to meet my mates. I don't think so, you will not enjoy what we will be talking about. Why don't you go and have a chat with your girlfriends and get all their gossip? Perhaps one of them is up the duff, then you can get some tips about where they perform and how they perform."

"You don't seem to want my company, Pete."

"That's it, Sam, you have got it right at last. I don't, at least not at the moment. I will see you after school." With that, I just walked away, leaving Sam standing outside the canteen, wondering what to do next.

I arrived at the sixth form hut, where my mates were sitting on the lawn enjoying the sun while admiring the girls that were lying out on the lawn, with their skirts pulled up showing all of their bare legs. The blouses they wore were undone so we could see their boobs through their Mary Quant see-through bras.

"This is good isn't it Pete? Sat here having a look at this lot," remarked John with his eyes nearly popping out of his head.

"Not bad, not bad at all."

"What have you been up to Pete?"

"Not a lot, I've been spending my time studying."

"Like a goody, goody."

"Well I've got to try and get good grades, whether I go to university or not I need them. What have you lot been up to?"

"Same as usual, eyeing up the girls, not studying."

"You will be in trouble if you don't do any work."

"Here you go again, goody, goody."

"Have you lot decided what you are going to do when you leave this dump?"

"Well, Pete, let us have a think. I have made my mind up about one thing, I'm going to definitely buy johnnies so I don't get any girl up the duff." At that, all my mates burst out laughing.

"You lot think it's funny what's happened to me, I wish you all felt sorry for me."

"Why should we? You got yourself into this position so you have to get yourself out of it."

"It is not as easy as it seems, you lot are supposed to be mates of mine."

"We will tell you one thing; we wouldn't have got Sam of all people up the duff, she is the type of girl you give a good poke, not a baby, for goodness sake."

"Shut up you lot, we have known each other for years ever since we came to this school when we were eleven, surely one of you can feel sorry for me."

"No, I don't think so, hands up who feels for Pete?" No one put their hands up.

"We told you that you should have tried to get her to have an abortion, they are free, but it's a bit late now, she looks a good five months."

"She is four months," I replied. "Anyway, I'm fed up with hearing all this, I'm going to lay down over on the bank for a while and enjoy the sights."

"You are still on the lookout, then?"

"I am not going to answer that question, just leave it."

With that, I went over to the grass bank and laid down on my own until the bell rang for afternoon lessons. The afternoon went well, before I knew it the bell was ringing again to say it was three thirty and time to go home.

I walked out of the main door and as usual Sam was stood waiting for me, but this time she had Margaret with her. I went over to say a quick hello and, out of the blue, Margaret started to rant and shout at me.

"Pete why are you being so horrible to Sam? You have upset her so much that she can't concentrate on her lessons, this afternoon she was crying through most of history."

"I don't have to explain myself to you, Margaret, it is private between Sam and myself. She knows what the matter is; if she doesn't want to tell you that is that, I'm not going to tell you."

"She has told me that you want her to make love in the lavs! I will tell you something, I wouldn't go in there with anyone let alone you, so I don't blame her when she said no to sex in the lavatories."

"Right then madam Margaret, where would you make love or have sex whatever you want to call it?"

"Let me have a think, I know if the sun was out I may go in the evening to the local park. I realise that the gates close at around eight but you can always get in through the fence, someone has made an opening along the back path, it opens up into some bushes very cosy, anything is better than the girls lavatories."

"Thanks for your advice, I will remember that; when I decide to ask Sam for a bit and she says yes I will take her there."

"I wish you would stop being horrible to me, I'm sure I don't deserve it,"

"Right, Sam, I will be nice to you from now on no teasing, no sly remarks, no asking for a quickie. Does that sound okay to you both? Yes or no? Well, answer me, I'm in a hurry."

"It sounds okay to me," said Margaret looking as if she should have been minding her own business.

"Stop keeping on at me Pete, I'm a human being and don't deserve any of these comments."

"Come here give me a hug, poor old you, who can't take a joke."

Margaret put her nose in the air and walked off leaving us to our own devices.

"I love you Pete and I can't cope with you keeping on at me."

"Let us walk towards the entrance, my bus will come soon then I can get on it and leave you in peace. Sam I am very fond of you and if I didn't think it would work out with you I would still be thinking of going to university and I'm not, I'm thinking of a way to live with you, without much money. Have I made that clear or do I need to repeat what I've said in a simple language?" "Yeah I understand."

The bus arrived and parked up; it was full due to other passengers having got on in Lewisham. It stayed outside school for about a quarter of an hour to wait for all the kids to get on.

"Pete, I don't want to go home. Can I come home for supper with you?"

"I'm not sure about that, let me have a think."

"Oh, please Pete."

"Yeah okay then, that is if you have some money to get back to the Elephant and Castle later tonight as I haven't any money."

"Yeah, I've got a note but it is supposed to last to the end of the week."

"I can't borrow any more from Anne and the thing is you can't stay the night, Mum has made that quite clear. I'm sure they will be pleased to see you and will give you supper. Come on, Sam, get on the bus, we don't want to have to stand all the way to Blackheath especially with you in your condition."

"Pete, please don't keep on at me, I feel bad enough without you keeping on. My clothes are so tight that I feel very uncomfortable especially in this heat."

"Sorry, I will keep my mouth shut."

"Good."

We got on the bus and sat on the two empty side seats just inside the door. It was quite a squash as the lady sitting on the third seat alongside of us was large, also she had a trolley basket that took up a lot of room. She made it difficult for the other passengers to get past to go to the front of the bus and for the passengers that were standing in the aisle. I could see that Sam had the fidgets and was feeling very uncomfortable. I didn't like to say anything to her as her hormones were playing up so much that whatever I said seemed to make her burst out crying and I didn't fancy her crying in front of all the other passengers; the best policy was for me was to keep quiet and that is what I did. The bus seemed to take ages to get to Blackheath. Every time it stopped I hoped that the woman with the trolley would get off, as she seemed to think it was still winter not the beginning of summer. She was wearing a long tweed skirt with a silky blouse with a thick cardigan over the top, this was as long as her skirt. On her feet she wore thick brown stockings with black flat laceup shoes, these were also more suitable to the winter season, all had seen better days. On top of this I don't think she had seen a bath or shower for a while, which of course made her smell quite high. Sam asked me if she could borrow a handkerchief from me.

"Have you got a cold?" I asked.

"Yeah, I have the start of one. It's urgent Pete, please can I borrow your handkerchief before I sneeze all over you?"

"I've told you before I use tissues; here you are."

Sam grabbed the tissue and straight away held it up to her nose and that is where it stayed for the duration of the trip to Blackheath.

Once off the bus we thought we could both speak freely so Sam immediately said, "Pete, I must say thanks for that tissue, it saved my life, the smell coming from that old woman and being pregnant made me feel sick."

I looked behind me and who should have got off the bus after us but the woman with the trolley.

I spoke quietly to Sam. "That's okay. Careful what you say, she is stood behind us. I wondered why you needed a tissue as I hadn't noticed that you had a cold."

"I'm stood behind you two and I'm not deaf, I've just heard what you said, girl."

We looked over our shoulders and saw the woman looking very sternly towards us.

"You two should mind what you say and how you say it. It also seems you should mind what you get up to, I can't imagine that's a cushion in there."

"I think you should be careful what you say, old woman."

"Old? I'm not old."

"You are to us."

"Any more of your cheek, I will have to go to your school and report both of you for being so rude to a very upstanding lady. I am a 'lady'; I am the right honourable Annabelle Johnson, you must have heard of me."

"No," we both replied.

"Well I am one of the governors at your school, so watch out." "Come on, Sam, let's go before we get into real trouble."

With that, I got hold of Sam's hand and we both walked quickly along the pavement in the direction of my home. Once out of sight of the woman we stopped to catch our breath.

"At least she doesn't know our names, Pete. I will have to sit down on this wall for a bit as I have a pain down here. God, this baby is kicking so hard!"

"Let me have a feel of your tum, perhaps I will be able to feel it kicking." I put the palm of my hand on Sam's abdomen.

"Gosh, it is kicking! Well, I'm going to be a dad! Can everyone hear me? I'm going to be a dad!" I shouted as loud as I could. Sam just sat looking up at me, dancing around the path.

"At last you realise I have a baby inside me and it's yours."

"Yeah, it's great, isn't it great?" By this time everyone seemed to be watching me but no one seemed to be happy for us, all the pedestrians looked very grumpy and hurried on their way.

"I suppose so, it's not you who has to get bigger and bigger before it pops out and says hello to the world."

"Sam, listen to me, I'm going to stand by you; once I have passed my A-levels, I am going to get a job."

"Pete! I do listen to you but you change your mind so often, you are like the wind!" Sam screamed.

"I do mean it, I'm going to look after you."

"Oh, the pain down here is awful, I don't know whether I can walk to your house. Pete, what are we going to do? Please sit down with me, perhaps the pain will go in a few minutes."

"Okay, just sit where you are and have a rest." I sat down next to Sam and put my arm around her shoulder. Sam was in such pain that she held on to my thigh as if it was the end of her world.

"If the pain doesn't go, I will go and find a phone and ring for an ambulance. I will give you five more minutes, try and calm down."

We were both sitting on the wall of a semi-detached house looking into space when, out of the blue, Mum appeared from around the corner carrying two heavy bags full of the weekly vegetables.

"Whatever is the matter with you two?"

"Sam's not feeling too good, she was coming home with me and suddenly she had pain in her abdomen."

"You look very pale, I think we should get the ambulance. I will go to that house and see if I can use the phone; you stay with Sam, Pete." Mum left her shopping and went up to the nearest front door. Luck was on our side: the house keeper answered and allowed her in to use the phone. She soon returned.

"They said the ambulance should be here in about ten minutes. I will sit and wait with you both; once the ambulance has arrived and the ambulance men have organised Sam, I will leave you to it."

"Thanks, Mum."

We all sat on the wall and tried to wait patiently, it was one of the longest ten minutes of my life. Eventually we heard the siren and saw the ambulance come speeding around the corner. Once the ambulance had parked up the two assistants got out, both of whom looked familiar.

"Hello, this is Reg and I am Tom, can you tell me your name and what the matter is?"

"My name is Sam Smithson, I'm not feeling too good. I have a pain down here," said Sam, feeling her abdomen.

"How long have you had the pain? Hang on a minute I think I have seen you before."

"I have had this pain for the last half hour. You may have seen me before, I had to be taken to hospital a few weeks ago."

"That's right I've seen you both before; you were having trouble with some Hell's Angels."

"Stop your talking and get a move on! Can't you see Sam is pregnant and needs to go to hospital?" said Mum, sounding very annoyed.

"Who are you?"

"I'm Pete's mum, that makes me the grandmother of this baby."

"Your son is the father?"

"Yeah that's right."

"Bit young to get someone pregnant."

"I don't think that is any of your business, you are supposed to take them to hospital to find out what the matter is."

"Before we take you can you tell us how many weeks pregnant you are."

"I'm not sure, it's due some time in November."

"So that makes you about four months, you are quite large for four months."

"Don't keep on about Sam's size and dates she needs to be taken into hospital to be checked over."

"Okay, keep your hair on. I will get a chair from the ambulance." Reg went into the back of the ambulance and collected a wicker chair.

"Which one of you is coming with Sam?"

"I am, Mum's going home."

"Well, Mum, we are taking Sam to the hospital down the road."

"Try not to worry about a thing, Sam, I have your parents' phone number so I will ring and let them know where you are once I get home."

"Thanks, Mrs Knight."

After Sam was made comfortable in the ambulance I climbed in and sat alongside her. The younger of the two ambulance men sat opposite us.

Arriving at the hospital we were taken straight into the casualty department where Sam was examined immediately by the senior house officer, who explained that she needed to be taken to the same ward as before where she would be seen by another doctor. We had to wait in the corridor for a hospital porter, who eventually pushed Sam in the wheelchair up to the ward, where the sister was waiting.

"Hello, Sam, sorry to see you back in here again, I'm going to put you on the bed so the doctor can examine you. Pete, I suggest that you go and sit out in the passage while I get Sam organised. You can come back in once the doctor has examined her."

I wandered out into the main corridor where I found a seat. I must have been there for a good hour dreaming and watching the nurses going about their duties, when out of the blue a doctor in a white coat was stood in front of me. "Are you Pete?"

"That's me," I replied.

"About Sam, she's going to have to stay in for a few days. First thing is her blood pressure – it's up. The second is that she's very constipated; that's the reason for the pain in her abdomen. I suggest that you go and have a few words with her then go home so she can have a rest."

I went back into the ward, where I sat on the edge of Sam's bed. "How are you feeling? The doctor has told me all about your problems."

"I have awful pain in my abdomen and my head is spinning, this is caused by high blood pressure."

"The doctor has asked me to leave you in peace, so I will give you a kiss cheerio and go home."

"Yeah, I feel like I need a sleep."

"If Mum has not phoned your mum, I will ring her, then perhaps she'll come and see you tomorrow. I'm going to go and get on with my revision, only a couple of weeks to go before Alevels."

"Pete, I'm sorry for all the trouble I have caused, deep down I wish I was not pregnant."

"Sam, it's a bit late to say that, you could have had an abortion, but you didn't want one. Try and calm down, have a rest, then you will feel better, try not to worry about anything, worrying can cause high blood pressure."

"Okay, will you be in tomorrow?"

"Yeah, after school."

"I crave a bit of chocolate, do you think you could buy me some? The nurse told me that there's a shop in the main hall that sells sweets and things."

"I will see what I can do, if I don't come back it's because the shop's closed. I will try and get some at the paper shop in my

street and I'll bring it in tomorrow."

"Thanks Pete, you are so sweet, I love you."

With that, I gave Sam a kiss and wandered out of the ward and down the long corridor to the entrance hall, where I found the shop closed. Directly opposite the shop was the reception desk. I glanced across and there was Jackie sat in the window, filing her nails. Luckily for me, she was looking down at her hands. I looked at my watch – it was almost half five. Jackie normally finished work at this time, then she caught the bus to Deptford from outside the hospital. I was fortunate as, just as I got outside, the bus came along so I jumped on without being caught by Jackie.

I arrived home just in time for supper. Of course my parents plus Anne were sitting in the front room waiting for me to return with all the news from the hospital.

"What has happened? Where is Sam? I rang her mum as soon as I got in, she was not very happy. They both blame everything on you. Her mum was talking about Sam having to go to a mother and baby home from the middle of October, do you know anything about this?"

"No, Sam has not mentioned it, I think it's all getting her down. I have left her in hospital with a headache caused by high blood pressure and she's constipated, that's why her abdomen was so painful. She has to stay in until her blood pressure comes down and she has been to the toilet,"

"That could take ages."

"I know, the ward sister seemed quite worried, I hope her parents don't go in and upset her."

"It's no wonder she has high blood pressure with parents like hers. At this rate, Marg, you will be ill again, we must all try and keep you calm. Anne please can you help your mother with supper tonight, you are old enough to understand the situation. I really don't want any nonsense from either of you, please try and get on with one another," said Dad, looking very perturbed.

"I will try and be good as long as Pete promises to behave and not tease me, he still owes me some money."

"Please stop it, Anne," said Mum while getting up out of her chair. "Anne come and help me, you can lay the dining room table, supper will be ready in about ten minutes, I've just got to dish it up."

"Okay, I'm coming," said Anne as if she was going into another strop.

Dad just stayed sitting in his chair looking across at me. "I can't imagine what the outcome is going to be with you, Sam and the baby. Did you hear what your mum said about Sam's parents wanting her to go to a mother and baby home? I don't know anything about places like that, I don't even know if you have to pay. The thing is Pete, we haven't much money, all the money we earn is used up every week, it costs a lot to keep a house going what with food, electric, rates etc. How you two will manage I've no idea. I am very worried for you both, I daren't mention my concerns to your mother, it would make her ill."

"All I can say is that I am very sorry. I am working very hard to try and get good A-level results, then perhaps I will be able to get a job in an office, maybe in the City."

"That sounds very grand, I hope it comes true, and life settles down; it will never be like it was before you got Sam pregnant that's for sure. Both your mum and I are pleased that Sam is keeping the baby and you are standing by her. If she gave the baby up for adoption your mother would worry about what was happening to the baby every day, we would both be in a terrible state wondering about the type of home it was living in. We both think you are doing the right thing."

Chapter 11

Tuesday morning soon arrived, after a good night's sleep I was ready for my day at school. Mum and Dad seemed a lot more relaxed, so over all it seemed as if it was going to be a good day.

I caught the bus to the school gates where John was standing, talking to Celia.

"Hi, Pete, what has been going on? Celia says that Sam's in hospital."

"Yeah that's right, don't ask me why because it's private."

"Oh Celia has told me all about it."

"You're not a very good friend, fancy telling John all about Sam."

"The thing is, Pete, her mum phoned me and told me all about it and how cross they both are with you. They even said that they thought that if you had to have sex that you would have bought some johnnies and you didn't. If you had used johnnies and they had split it would have been a different story altogether and they wouldn't have been so cross, even though they didn't approve of you or of you having sex with Sam."

"Have you anything else to tell my mates, Celia? I can tell you one thing, and that's that Sam will not be very happy. I didn't think you would be a gossip, especially as you are supposed to be Sam's best friend. Best friends normally tell each other secrets and then they keep the secrets to themselves. That is why they are called best friends."

Celia just stood looking at her feet and going bright red in the face.

"Pete, you are making me feel like a naughty school girl, I've only told your mate things that Mrs Smithson said to me over the phone, I haven't added anything to what Sam's mum told me." "Celia, I guess I should have told you to shut up but I didn't, now I know all the nitty gritty," said John.

"You are a naughty school girl! I'm not happy with you Celia, I hope for your sake that my mates don't come up to me and say they have been told all about Sam."

"I'm promising you Pete that I won't be repeating what Celia has told me."

"Thank you, John, I'm going on my way to class before I lose my temper with you, Celia."

I left them looking at each other. I went to my first lesson which was English with Mr Thomas, in room five. This was quite a walk to this particular room as it was on the second floor at the end of the building. The lesson started at nine thirty and Mr Thomas was in full flow when I arrived at least ten minutes late.

"Late again, Knight, you seem to have lost any interest in school and your exams, it must be something to do with getting a young lady up the duff. Sit down, whatever happens today please try and stay awake. After the lesson I would like to have a chat with you in private."

I sat down on the chair next to the boys. The girls were sitting in the front row so I didn't have the embarrassment of them looking across at me and sniggering while I was trying to concentrate. The lesson soon finished and I stayed in my seat to have the chat to old Thomas. Mr Thomas was almost as strange as Mr Hall, in a different way. Instead of having sideburns he had his shaved off, so he didn't have any hair down the front of his ears; this made the hair growing out from inside his ears visible to the world. Everything he wore matched, not like Mr Hall who looked a complete mess. Thomas looked very prim, if a man can look prim.

"Right, Peter Knight, come and sit at my desk so we can have a quiet chat." I moved myself and all my belongings over to old Thomas's desk. "Last evening we had our weekly staff meeting and the main subject on the agenda again was you and your future. As I am head of the sixth form I have been asked by the headmaster to have a chat and find out what is going on." I just sat looking stupid.

"What do you want to know? Fire your questions at me then I will see if I can answer them."

"You used to be such a polite boy and now you seem to have the cheek of Old Nick."

"Sorry, but I am fed up with people keeping on at me and asking so many questions about things that I don't think have anything to do with them."

"The thing is, Knight, I and all of the staff have tried to educate you and I think we have succeeded in getting you to a standard that deserves you going to a good university. Now you seem to be blowing it away."

"I do realise what has happened and now know that I should not have got involved with Sam. I also know that we should have used condoms and we didn't."

"Right, at least you realise that. Me and all the staff are wondering what you are going to do about this baby. Sam Smithson is beginning to show and we all feel she is very embarrassed. The other afternoon in class she sat at the back and cried for most of the lesson, she was getting in some state. After the lesson Mrs Dobson had a chat with her and Sam told her that you keep teasing and she feels that you don't care."

"Yes, I suppose that's true, I do tease her. The fact is I don't really know what to do or say. I am giving up the idea of going to university and I have told both Sam and my parents I'm going to try and get a job in a bank or insurance office. Before doing this I am trying hard to study and get good grades at A-level."

"What about Sam? Is she going to a mother and baby home or what? Are you considering marrying her? How are you going to keep this baby? I know Mr Hall had a chat with you back along and asked if you were thinking about Sam having an abortion, but you didn't get back to him."

"Like I have told my parents I am standing by Sam. Where she's going to have this baby I have no idea. I don't know whether she is staying at the flat with her mum and dad or going into one of the mother and baby homes. I expect you know she's in hospital with high blood pressure and is having to stay in until it comes down."

"Yes, Knight, I did hear something about that, it seems to be the latest gossip around school."

"I wish I could turn the clock back and I also wish the gossip would stop. It was Celia that started it, I caught her telling John Bradbury about a phone call she received from Sam's mother. He promised not to repeat what Celia told him but obviously he has been telling everyone or perhaps she has told more people. Have you any idea what it feels like to have people gossiping about you?"

"Gossip is awful. I will have a chat to Celia Wilson and also John Bradbury. I know, if you see them ask them to come here after school. I will be in this room until five as I have books to mark and I find it easier to mark them here. Go on your way, perhaps we can have another chat in a few days."

"If I bump into them I will ask them to come and see you. Thanks."

I went and joined my so-called friends in the canteen where I bought a mug of coffee out of the vending machine. Over in the corner I could see Celia with a few of her and Sam's friends deep in conversation.

"Well fancy seeing you again Celia, you seem very popular today, I have never seen you surrounded by so many mates. Can I join in the fun? Can I hear all your news? Celia, it must be very interesting."

The girls looked stunned to see it was me who was stood behind them, listening in.

"I've got to go," said Celia.

"Oh no, you are not going anywhere until I've heard what you have been talking about. Which one of you is going to tell me about your conversation? Come on, Margaret, you are good at spilling the beans, what has Celia been talking about? Hurry up one of you tell me." Silence reigned.

"Well if no one is going to tell me I am going to guess, then perhaps one of you will admit what Celia has been talking about. Has Celia been telling you all about Sam and why she is in hospital? You over there, you look the most embarrassed, what has Celia been saying? Come on I haven't got all day."

"I don't know what to say but, yes."

"That is it Celia, I've been to see Mr Thomas and he has told me that someone is gossiping about Sam. I thought it must be you, he would like to see you in his room after school, he will be in the sixth form until around five this evening."

"What, you want me to go and see the head of the sixth form about me talking about Sam?"

"Yeah that's what I said, he is expecting you. I hope I don't catch any of you chatting about what Celia has just told you, remember everything to do with Sam and myself is private. I'm going now to have a chat with John Bradbury, has anyone seen him?" No one answered so I went on my way and found John with one of the girls by the bike shed at the back of the school. "John, what's going on here? Mary, you of all people a friend of Sam's with John. It must be catching, hope you have some johnnies in your back pocket, John."

"Why have you got to come around here to disturb us?"

"I'm here to ask you to go and see Thomas in the sixth form after school, he is expecting you. I will go on my way now. I suggest that you go to the girls' lavs, it is more comfortable in there and warmer, especially the forth one along. Good luck, John."

"We are only having a snog, I'm not like you and Sam, sex in the lavs and a bun in the oven. I'm still a virgin and I would need a cosy bed to lose my virginity, not the girls' lavs."

I burst out laughing after hearing what Mary had to say. "I will see you later, John." I turned to go.

"I only came for a kiss and cuddle!" Mary shouted at John. "I've had enough, I'm going."

"What about me, Mary? I've been waiting weeks for you to touch me up and I planned to give you a quick poke!" shouted John.

"Well what about you? I've just told you I've had enough, I'm going," said an annoyed Mary.

"That will teach you, you didn't get that right," I said, laughing at John as I walked away.

"Oh well, there is always someone else game. Are you coming to the disco on Friday?"

"I will have to wait and see what's happening, Sam may still be in hospital."

"It's always Sam, Sam, Sam, with you Pete, why can't you change the record for one day in your life?"

"Don't keep on at me, John. You have to go to see old Thomas in his room after school. Don't forget because he'll be waiting for you."

"Okay, I will see you later in the week and hopefully you will come to the disco. Most of the girls are coming and some are really up for it, you should come and get your mind off Sam and enjoy another girl's company. Perhaps you will manage to give at least one of them a quickie; remember to bring your johnnies."

"I'm not listening to you and your rubbish, I'm going to my next lesson. Bye."

"Cheers Pete, I will try and remember to go and see Thomas." "You better see him, or you won't be popular with me."

After school I caught the bus to Blackheath. Instead of going straight home I went to the hospital to see Sam. Once in the main hall I passed the reception desk then over to the hospital shop where I bought the promised bar of chocolate and also a *Honey* magazine. I was waiting in the queue to pay up when I was tapped on the shoulder. I turned around and who should be stood directly behind me and looking down at me, but the man I met at the reception desk the other week end.

"Back again then?" he said.

"Yeah," I said hoping to get away without having to explain what I was up to.

"Jack came back to work on Sunday, I told her that you and your mates were here to see her. She asked me to keep an eye open for you and, if I saw you or one of your mates, to ask you all to call around next Saturday afternoon as she would definitely be here then."

"Get this straight, I am not interested in her, it's my mates that want to meet her. All I was doing was introducing them to her."

"Can I tell Jack that you will all come up on Saturday?"

"We may or they may, I might be too busy. You see, I may as well tell you, I have a girlfriend. That is why I'm up here, she is a patient on one of the wards."

"Which ward is she on then?"

"Oh, I can't tell you that, once I've paid for this I'm going." Luckily for me I was next in the queue but he carried on chatting and asking questions. "You must tell me her name, then I can look her up on the patients list so I can see which ward she's on."

"No, I'm not going to tell you her name, everything about her is private."

"I can find out all about her if I want to, I can guess her age, it must be around sixteen because you are about seventeen, I can look down the list of patients' names for all the wards, I will soon find her. I will have a look when I go back over to reception, it won't take me long." I looked in complete shock.

"Why do you look so surprised?"

"Well it's none of your business, you shouldn't be able to look up details of patients."

"Jack looks up details about the patients in between answering the phone."

"I don't think that should be allowed."

"That caught you out boy, we can only find out the name of the ward that anyone is on, not what the matter is with them. We can only guess that by the type of the ward they are on," he said looking at me as he laughed to himself.

"I'm going. I hope that I never bump into you again." Before I disappeared, the man had the last word.

"I will never forget you and your friends and how your friends want to meet Jack. it makes me laugh as I think she is far too old for any of you lot, remember she is nineteen and very experienced in the way of the world."

I hurried on my way hoping that the man didn't watch and see which direction I went to the ward. Thank goodness, luck was on my side: when I went around the corner into the long corridor, he was still standing at the counter and I managed to turn into the ward without him watching me.

Sam was sitting up in bed as if she was waiting for a visitor; hopefully it was me she was expecting and not her parents. "Hi Pete, great to see you."

I gave her a kiss on the forehead.

"What about a kiss on the lips? Come and sit on my bed, let's have a snog."

I sat on the bed and held Sam close and gave her a long lingering kiss.

"You look a lot better. In fact, you look and seem quite perky, it must be all the rest you are having. Here's the chocolate you wanted and a magazine that I think you may enjoy, it's called *Honey*. It has only been out a couple of months."

"I've never heard of it but I will read it. Thanks. Yeah, I'm not allowed out of bed, the nurse came around just now and took my blood pressure, she said I may be able to get out of bed on Thursday and go home on Friday, that's if my blood pressure stays down. Mum and Dad have to stay away for a few days as the doctors think they are the cause of it being so high."

"What is going to happen when you go home, especially if your parents are the cause of your high blood pressure? I am quite sure it will go up again, living with your parents won't help it to stay down. You will be in the same state as you are now, but staying in bed at the flat."

"The doctor is trying to arrange for me to go to a mother and baby home, from the middle of October. The trouble is the local homes are all booked up from mid-October, so they are thinking about sending me to a home in Luton or Aylesbury."

"I want to find out from you about this discharge on Friday, if you go back to the flat your blood pressure will most probably go up again. You can't guarantee your mum or dad won't lose their temper and upset you, then up it will go, so what is going to happen, Sam?"

"I don't know. I have a feeling the doctor wants to have a chat with you. When he came around this morning, he asked when you were coming in."

"Well Sam, I'm here now so where is the doctor?"

"I don't know."

117

"I think you will have to go to the sister's office and ask to see him."

"No way am I going to do that, I wouldn't know what to say."

"Caught you," said a male voice from behind me. In shock I turned around and nearly fell off the edge of the bed. "I'm Dr Jameson, I'm the doctor that is looking after Sam. You must be the boyfriend, I want to see you."

I introduced myself and shook his hand.

"Stay where you are, I will find myself a chair and then we can have a chat." At that he left his notes at the bottom of the bed and wandered out of the ward to fetch a chair.

"Sam, I wonder what he wants?"

"I think he wants to know your intentions. They told me this morning that the most important thing was this baby and they had to find out from you whether we were going to get married or what."

"Sam, we are too young to get married."

"Well, what are we going to do about this baby? He will be back in a second and he will want answers to his questions."

"Do you want to go to a mother and baby home?"

"No I don't, that is another thing we have to have a talk about."

"Sam, you know what my mum said; you can't come and live with us, there is not enough room or enough money to feed you as well."

"Let's have a chat with the doc, see what he has to say."

I stayed sitting on the bed holding on to Sam's hand when the doctor returned, dragging a chair behind him. He picked up Sam's notes and, at the same time, started to pull the curtains around her bed.

"I'm pulling the curtains around so we can have a chat in private. Before we discuss where Sam is going, I have to tell you that she has recovered from the constipation and the ward sister has had a talk to her about diet and how much fluid she should drink a day if she doesn't want to end up constipated again. At the moment her blood pressure is normal but that could go up again at any time, especially if she has any stress.

Have you any thoughts about where Sam should go on Friday if we are able discharge her?"

"No."

"What do you mean no? It's your baby she's having and apparently you are standing by her, so you'd better start thinking unless you are leaving her in the lurch."

"I'm not trying to get out of the responsibility but I don't know where she should or can go. Both Mum and Dad have said she can't live with us in Blackheath as we have only enough money to feed our family; my parents would find it difficult to feed an extra person full time."

"At this rate it is going to be a mother and baby home whether you like it or not. Sam's parents are not very suitable for her to live with, what with his temper along with both of them drinking, plus both of them smoking. None of these things help with Sam's condition. Sam has been telling us about how kind your parents are, perhaps they should come in and have a chat." At that I put my head in my hands and sat thinking for quite a few minutes.

"I'm sorry about this, I haven't got an answer but I will have a chat with Mum and Dad again when I get home. I may be able to give you an answer tomorrow."

"What time will you be in tomorrow?"

"I'm not sure, most probably the same time as today as I need to go to school."

"Tomorrow's Wednesday, I really need to know first thing in the morning as it is the consultant's round at ten o'clock, he will be asking what is going to happen to Sam."

"I will see what I can do. Perhaps Mum will come in instead of me in the morning. The thing is, I have exams coming up in the next few days."

"What exams are they?"

"A-levels."

"You are taking A levels? Are you going to university? If you are, you seem to have got yourself in a bit of a mess."

"I know, I was planning before all this happened to go to Oxford or Cambridge to study science."

"I'm just Sam's doctor, I can't get involved in all of this, I can only think of Sam and the baby. I have other patients to see so I will go on my way and hope to have some news from you in the morning."

"If Mum doesn't come in she will most probably phone into the ward."

At that the doctor pulled the curtains back, tapped me on the shoulder and said cheers.

"Well Pete, what do you honestly think we should do?"

"I have no idea, I will have a chat with Mum and Dad this evening, once Anne has gone to her room. I will sit them both down and see what they have to say. Sam, do you know anything about these mother and baby homes?"

"No, the only thing they have told me is that they are free or I don't have to pay very much. Apparently I will have to do housework while I live there, also the mothers can only have visitors at weekends."

"What, is that right?"

"Yeah."

"If you are right about you having to go to Aylesbury or Luton, to a mother and baby home, I don't know where I will get money for the train fare to visit you. Aylesbury is miles from here. Luton, well that is not so far, but it will cost a bit."

"Pete, please don't worry me or I will never get out of here, my blood pressure will go up again. When I was in here before the food was awful, it hasn't improved, the quicker I can get out the better. I don't think they will let me go home to the flat, Mum and Dad came in and caused trouble last night. Dad was drunk, he'd been down to the Bricklayers Arms before coming in. Mum was sober thank goodness. The doctor and the ward sister came in to see them. Dad was swearing and carrying on, so after a while the ward sister had to phone for the hospital porter to come and show them the door as nothing either of them said made sense, and he was getting angrier and angrier. The doctor told them not to come in until at least Thursday afternoon. Whether they understood the situation, I don't know."

"Poor old you, let's have a cuddle. I'll have to get going soon, the ward clock says it is six o'clock. I promise I will have a chat with Mum and Dad tonight and see what they can come up with."

"Pete, please stay a bit longer, the trolley with supper should come in any minute, then you can see what I am having to eat, also you can have a mouthful to see what you think of it. Breakfast is the best meal of the day, it's even better than what I get at home, but then at home we only have toast and marmalade, here I have cereal, bacon and tomatoes with one piece of toast and that is wholemeal. They do have white bread, but they won't let me eat that."

"It seems that you will have to change your diet once you are out of here, I expect they will give you a diet sheet? I remember when Mum was taken into hospital with abdominal pains, they discovered that she was suffering from constipation, they gave her a diet sheet and she also had to see a dietician."

"Well they said something about someone coming from the kitchen to have a chat about food. At home we eat an awful lot of bread, they said that if I had to eat bread it needed be wholemeal, they told me that I must eat fruit and drink plenty of water."

"Mum eats wholemeal bread, I'm not very keen on it, I must admit that when I do eat it I manage to go the lav easier. Mum always makes sure that we have fruit in the house and usually we have a pudding which includes fruit most days."

"My mum never buys fruit; she says she can't afford it. You see, the thing is, Dad spends most of the spare cash down the pub, he doesn't give Mum housekeeping money, what she earns in the factory she has to use for food. That's why she looks a bit worse for wear."

"Sam, I'm really sorry to hear all of this but it does not help either of us. My dad hands over housekeeping every week on a Friday, they only have an alcoholic drink in the house once in a while. I have never known Dad to leave Mum at home and go out with his mates, if he goes out he takes Mum and they normally go and visit friends over in Greenwich. They usually return home by nine o'clock."

"That is completely different to mine, I've been left on my own since I was eight years old while they have both gone down the pub on a Saturday night. When I was younger, Mum used to go into the flat next door and ask them to keep an eye and ear open for me. I often woke up and got out of bed and found them missing, I couldn't get out of the flat because they locked the door and gave the spare key to Marjorie, she would hear me crying and would come in. She doesn't live next door any more, her husband is still there, he works down the factory with Dad,"

"What has happened to Marjorie?"

"She died a couple of years ago. You see, she smoked herself to death, when she came in to see to me she always had a fag hanging out of her mouth. Dad said something about Stan, that's the husband, he smokes, and apparently he is going the same way."

"What a carry on. I think you will be best out of it. I will definitely have a chat with Mum and Dad tonight and see if they can put you up. Most probably they will say yes, I can give up my bed for you and I will sleep downstairs on the floor. I don't mind, anything for you, Sam."

"The floor's a bit hard."

"I know that but what else can we do? I can always get the cushions from the sofa and cover them with a sheet and use that as the mattress, we have plenty of spare sheets and blankets so making it into a bed is not a problem."

"That sounds quite a good idea."

"Here comes the kitchen porter with the trolley."

"Who dishes the food out?"

"Either the staff nurse or the ward sister, it depends which one is on duty. A nursing auxiliary brings the food over to my bed on a tray, at breakfast time we are all given a menu to fill in for the meals we would like to have for the next twenty-four hours. I tick which food I fancy and if I'm lucky I get something that I like."

The kitchen porter turned out to be the man who sat at the reception desk.

"Why is the porter coming over to my bed? He's smiling as if he knows me, do you know him Pete?"

"At last I have found you. Is this the girlfriend I've heard so much about?"

"Yes, this is my girlfriend, but you don't know anything about her."

"Are you going to introduce me?"

"No."

"I'm sorry about that, I will introduce myself then. I'm Alf, Pete and I have met before, he came up to the hospital to see the receptionist with his mates the other Saturday."

"Shut up and go before you get yourself and me into a lot of trouble."

"If you want to know more about the receptionist and Pete call in and see me, I'm often at the reception desk, in fact I'm there later today, cheers."

Thank goodness he walked away, leaving Sam and I with our own thoughts.

"What the hell was he on about, Pete?"

"Rubbish."

"If he is talking a lot of rubbish why did he come over to my bed? You may as well tell me what has been going on."

"I think it is best that you don't know."

"Well I can find out by going to the reception desk."

"There's nothing to find out, my mates fancied the receptionist, I took them to meet her and she was off sick."

"You know her then?"

"Sort of."

"Come on, Pete, you may as well tell me because if you don't

I can find out."

"I don't want to upset you, try and forget what he said."

"I think I will find that a job. Here comes my supper, see what you think of it."

At that, the auxiliary put the tray of food on the bed table.

"It looks okay to me, its boiled ham, peas and boiled potatoes and that dreaded rice pudding."

"Yeah, try some, Pete."

I took the fork and tried the main course, which was not too bad, but the rice pudding tasted awful.

"The main course is okay, but that pudding! Whatever made you ask for that? It's dreadful, there isn't any sugar in it."

"Now you know what I'm having to eat."

"Well I liked the main course, even the sauce was quite nice, I think you should try and eat it all or you will be hungry."

"I will try."

"Now, Sam, I am going to go and leave you to eat it. I promise that I will have a chat with Mum and Dad and will see you

tomorrow at the same time as today."

"Okay then, bye."

We blew each other a kiss and I hurried on my way.

Chapter 12

I arrived home at around seven p.m. Mum, Dad and Anne had finished their supper, Anne had already gone to her room to do her homework, at least I thought she had, so I didn't need to worry about what I said to Mum or Dad as she was not around to make sly remarks. As soon as I put the key in the door, Mum came rushing into the hall from the sitting room, rubbing her hands.

"Hi Pete, we are pleased to see you. Your dad and I can't wait to hear how you got on at the hospital and to find out how Sam is. We have both been sitting here on tenterhooks ever since we got in from work."

"Everything went okay, I guess, once I've eaten my supper I will tell you and Dad all my news."

"I've put your cutlery in the sitting room, we thought you may like to sit with us instead of on your own in the dining room. I'll get your supper from the oven." The supper looked great, liver, bacon and onions with mashed potatoes and cabbage, pudding was plums and custard.

"Thanks for keeping it warm, looks nice."

"Once you've finished it, I will put the kettle on and make you a cup of coffee. Dad and I are going to have our usual cup of tea."

"I get fed up with coffee, I'll have a cup of tea."

"Okay then."

I sat down on the sofa. I could see that Mum was quite excited and could hardly wait to hear what I had to say. Dad, as usual, sat in his arm chair reading the paper.

"Now you are eating your pudding I will go and put the kettle on." With that, Mum wandered out to the kitchen. Dad remained silent with his head in the *Evening Standard*.

Eventually, he looked up. "I was just looking at the flats to rent. Mum has been telling me that you bought the *Standard* the other night to see the price of renting a flat or bed sitter."

"Yeah, that's right, what a price the rents are in Blackheath! I have a feeling we will have to go and live in North London, where the rents seem cheaper, unless you have a better idea, Dad?"

"I had a chat with your mother but we didn't come up with anything. I think you should get your exams out of the way, then go from there."

"That's my plan. I know I need to pass my A-levels with good grades, I'm trying to study in between all this upset."

"Here I am with a nice pot of tea for the three of us, can you get me a small table, Ernie?"

"Of course I can, my dear."

Dad got up and moved the smallest table over for Mum to put the brown teapot on along with the tea cups that they had got free with the Embassy cigarette coupons. Both Dad and Mum used to smoke Embassy fags, they gave them up about six months ago after Dad got a very bad cough. He had to go and see the doctor as the cough kept them both awake at night. The doctor told Dad that it was the fags that caused him to cough and that it would be a good idea if they both tried to give up smoking.

After they had a chat together they got hold of their last pack of fags and threw it in the dustbin. The house and their clothes used to smell quite strong of fags. They wouldn't have it, but I think between them they smoked something like thirty to forty a day. The only thing remaining to do with fags are the fancy ash trays, which are still in the fire place, and the stained walls, ceilings and doors – all of these are a dirty cream due to the smoke. We all have to put up with this as they can't afford to get anyone in to give the rooms a coat of paint and they don't feel strong enough to paint anything themselves.

Once we all settled down, I explained what the doctor had told me at the hospital and what he advised.

"Well, Pete, as usual I don't know what to say to all of this. What do you think should happen, Marg?"

"I have no idea, Ernie. Have you any bright suggestions, Pete?"

"I have had a think and I thought perhaps I should give up my bed for Sam and I could sleep in here, on the floor."

"Well I can tell you the answer to that now it is no. Ernie, have you anything to say?"

"The same as you, Marg: no."

"If you are saying no to my suggestion, you must have a better idea."

They both sat looking at each other across the room.

"I can tell you now that your mother and I are not going to allow Sam to come and live here. One, we can't afford to keep her. Two, you have to concentrate on your exams and you need a good night's sleep and you won't get that sleeping on the floor. And three, Sam should go and live with her parents; it isn't as if she hasn't got parents or a home to go to."

"I understand what you are saying, but, as I have told you, a hundred times before, the doctor doesn't advise that she should go and live at the flat."

"Well, Pete, I can only say one thing and that is that you shouldn't have got involved with Sam. Between you, you have upset all our lives and made a complete mess of your own."

"I keep saying sorry, how many more times have I got to say sorry to you both?"

"As many times as you like, but it won't make us change our mind, especially about Sam living here. She needs to try and sort herself out with her mum and dad; perhaps she should have a talk to the hospital almoner."

"Who the hell is that?"

"I think they are called social workers these days, they should be able to help Sam, they try to sort out patients' problems.

Hasn't the doctor suggested that she has a chat to one?"

"Sam hasn't mentioned anything about seeing one."

"The woman I was telling you about at work who had a baby had to see a social worker before she went to the mother and baby home."

"What! Mum, it seems to me that you are hell bent on Sam going to one of these homes!"

"Perhaps I am, I think it would be a good idea, at least she would be looked after. She may have to do house work but that would keep her out of mischief. The staff apparently are very kind."

"That is a different story from what I have been told. They are supposed to be very strict and the girls have to sleep in dormitories. The worst thing about it all is that the relatives and friends of the girls can only visit at weekends."

"Pete, I'm getting really fed up with all of this, it seems to me that you both want your cake and eat it. If you had both thought about the outcome, then if you still needed to have sex, or make love whatever you call it these days, you could have saved some of your pocket money and gone and spent it on condoms," said Dad, looking very annoyed and getting quite red in the face.

"For goodness sake, Pete, stop upsetting us, you can see your dad is getting in quite a state. You do realise that both Dad and I have had to go to see our doctor."

"No, you haven't told me about that."

"Well we didn't want you to have that worry on top of everything else."

"What is wrong with you both?"

127

"We both have high blood pressure caused by all this stress. The doctor has put us both on blood pressure tablets, we have to take them once a day. The thing is, we both have been having awful headaches and your dad has been feeling dizzy."

"Again I can only say sorry."

"Look at me, Pete, I'm all flushed, the doctor has told us both to take it easy. Your mother hasn't told you it all, she has been vomiting as well and has also lost half a stone in weight in the last week."

"I don't want you both to become ill, so I'm going to sort it out myself and not mention it to you again, or not until I know exactly what has been decided."

"Thanks, Pete."

"I'm going to finish my cup of tea then go up to my room. My first exam is Thursday afternoon."

"What subject is that?"

"English, next Monday is Biology and next Wednesday it is Chemistry. Then it is all over, I finish school next Friday."

"With all this upset, the exams and your last day at school as a pupil has crept up on us so quickly. I guess you will be applying for a job? I see in the *Evening Standard* that banks are looking for school leavers, do you fancy working in a bank? The prospects are very good."

"I can't think about jobs at this moment. Let me go up and do some revision, then perhaps I can come down later and read the ads. Also, I may be able to have another chat with you both."

"Once your mum has finished the dishes we are both going to try and have a quiet evening, you can come down and collect the paper then read it in your room. Sorry, but we need peace."

"Yeah, that's right, before we do the dishes I want to watch *Coronation Street*. It is on in a mo so please can you lean over and turn the telly on for me, Ern?"

"Of course I can, my dear."

"I'm going; I will come down later for the paper."

"Okay."

I went upstairs hoping to get a bit of peace, but instead Anne was in her room laughing and chatting with a friend. Neither

Mum nor Dad had told me that Anne had a friend over for the evening. How they thought I was going to do some studying I don't know, as I could hear everything they were saying through the wall. Both of them are only fourteen but they were having a good old talk and a laugh about boys and what they had got up to behind the bike shed at their school. If Mum or Dad could hear them they would have been horrified. I thought Anne was an innocent school girl in ankle socks, but she's not. After about ten minutes of listening in I knocked on her door.

"Can you two shut up? I'm trying to study, all I can hear is you both talking about your love lives and what you get up to behind the bike shed. Anne, you talk about me, but you are just as bad, if not worse."

There was silence. Then suddenly, out of the blue, the bedroom door opened and there stood Anne with her friend, who seemed very embarrassed.

"Well, Mum didn't say we had a guest in the house. Anne introduce me, what is your name?"

"Sheila."

"Sheila what?"

"Sheila Stone."

"I have a mate at school with that surname. Is he your brother or is he a cousin? His first name is Dave."

"I don't know him, he is nothing to do with me. I haven't got a brother and he isn't a cousin."

"You two ought to watch it talking behind closed doors loud enough for someone to hear next door. I'm surprised at the pair of you, having a quick poke behind the bike shed."

"Please don't say anything to Dave as he may tell Mum and I will be in awful trouble."

"Bit late, you should always think before you speak; you never know who's listening in."

"Pete, stop it, don't say anything! Sheila will be in awful trouble; her dad's a vicar."

"That's a joke! I guess you go to church every Sunday behaving as if you are a goody goody and butter won't melt in your mouth."

"Stop it, for God's sake, stop it, Pete!"

129

"What's going on up there?" shouted Dad from the bottom of the stairs.

"Nothing. I'm just having a chat with these innocent little girls."

"Are you upsetting them, Pete?"

"No, they are telling me what they have been getting up to at school. Dad, did you know that they have bike sheds at their school and they go behind them with boys?"

"Stop it, Pete! Don't listen to him, Dad, he is making it up!"

Dad started to walk up the stairs looking harassed.

"Pete, I have told you that we have had enough of your silly nonsense. Whatever you say about the girls, your mother and I will not believe you."

With that, Dad turned and went back down, leaving the girls pulling faces at me.

"You two just watch it, I will get you. In fact, I quite fancy you, Sheila. The only trouble is, you are a bit young, what with your ankle socks. Perhaps in a couple of years I will take a closer look at you, that is, if I am not hitched up with Samantha." "Anne has been telling me all about her and the baby. I call it disgusting I won't be going out with you! In fact, everything Anne and I have been talking about is lies."

"Well fancy that, I'm not surprised, who would want to take either of you behind any shed? I think it is time that both of you change your ankle socks for either stockings or tights. Always remember that tights are a bit difficult to remove, men prefer stockings as they can stay in position when they give anyone a quick poke."

"You are disgusting!" shouted both the girls in unity.

"Right, girls, on a serious note, please can you be quiet so I can do some studying?"

"We will try as long as you keep your big mouth shut." At that they walked through Anne's bedroom door, slamming it behind them.

I went back into my room and tried to concentrate on my work for a couple of hours, but all I could think about was Sam and having quickies with her in the girls' lavs. Nine o'clock soon arrived and I decided to call it a day and go back downstairs and have another chat with Mum and Dad. I found them still sat in the sitting room, looking half asleep.

"You made me jump," said Mum, looking a bit startled. Dad still had his eyes closed but I could tell that he was awake as they kept flickering. "You okay, Ern?" called out Mum.

"Yes I suppose so, I was far away thinking about what Pete was going to do for a job and where he was going to live."

"Open your eyes, then you can have a chat to him; he has just come into the room."

"Did you really mean it when you said that Sam couldn't come and live here?"

"Yes we did, don't mention it again."

"Oh well, I will have to have a think as I have to let the doctor know by tomorrow morning about what we are going to do. I hope I manage to sleep tonight."

"What, you are worrying about sleeping? What about your dad and me? We haven't had a good night's sleep in weeks!"

"I've had enough of you two, I try and be nice to you both and tell you what is going on, but you always stay so negative about me and Sam. Whatever you think the outcome is going to be, we are going to live together. I didn't say that we are going to get married, I wouldn't be that daft, I'm only seventeen."

"At least you realise that you are bit young for that sort of commitment."

"Even if we were thinking of marrying we couldn't afford to.
I hope you two are listening to me."

"Yes we are."

By this time I was sat on the sofa wondering what great statement they were going to make, if any. My head was in my hands and I just sat looking into the fireplace.

"It is no good sitting there with your head in your hands, Peter, the three of us need to have a serious chat, both your mother and I think Sam should go back to her parents' flat, she is used to living with them and she is used to their behavior. Once the end of September comes she will only have a few weeks to go before she needs to go to a mother and baby home."

"Here you go again, I had a feeling this was coming. All this is to do with that woman you met at work, Mum. Do you both really want your first grandchild to be born in one of those places?"

"No but what else do you suggest, Pete?" asked Dad, looking more and more flushed.

"Dad, our conversation seems to go around and around in circles and you in particular seem to like to follow one question with another, anyway I have no idea. I haven't an answer to your questions but I do think that it should be first things first. I must pass my exams and then try and get a job, then when the baby is born find a flat in North London. Let me have the paper. I'm going to take it up to my room and read it in peace."

"Sense at last, son. I suggest that you phone the ward and tell them we think Sam should go home to the flat, and go to a mother and baby home from there," said Dad, looking exasperated.

"I'm going to sleep on this, but before I do, what do you think,
Mum?"

"I'm going to agree with your father as he is usually right."

"You haven't got a mind of your own then, Mum?"

"Stop it now, Pete. As we told you earlier, your mum and I don't feel too good."

"My head is spinning, I can't take much more of this. I'm going to bed now; perhaps I will feel better in the morning. If I don't, I'll have to go to the doctor's again. Are you going to come up now or are you going to read a bit more of your book, Ern?"

"I will make my way up in a few minutes. I just want to finish the chapter; that's if Pete does not keep on disturbing my brain."

"I'll go to bed now; I know I will find it difficult to get to sleep as I have a lot on my mind."

"Do shut up, Pete. Go up to your room and leave your mother and I in peace. We have had enough; we told you earlier that we can't take much more. Here's the paper."

"Thanks. Night, then. Oh, before I go, has Sheila gone home?"

"How the hell do we know? We haven't been up to Anne's room and we haven't heard the front door bang shut."

"I will knock on Anne's door when I go up and let her know we are all going to bed early and tell Anne that Sheila should be getting ready to go."

"Sometimes, Pete you can be quite kind and helpful; other times, well, you exhaust us."

At that I went upstairs, little did they realise that I wanted to have another look at Sheila.

I knocked on the door and wandered in only to find the pair of them sat crossed-leg on the floor playing Monopoly.

"Mum and Dad are off to bed in a few minutes so they have asked me to come in and ask when Sheila is going home."

"Well, Pete, we want to finish this game. Why don't you join in?"

"I'm not sure if I should," I said as if I was shy.

"The thing is my dad is going to pick me up after he has finished playing darts at the pub. That will be at about eleven o'clock."

"Which pub's that?"

"The one by the station, I think it's called the Kings Arms?"

"If you like, Sheila I could walk you down to it, I need some fresh air."

"Pete, we are playing this game and we want to finish it."

"You can always leave it on the side and finish it another night. As I said just now, Mum and Dad want to go to bed."

"Well we want to finish our game."

"So you don't want me to walk you to the pub, Sheila?"

"Anne, if everyone is going to bed, perhaps I should go and come around again tomorrow night, we can always finish the game then. I think it is a good idea if Pete walks me to the pub, it would save Dad having to come around here also he may wake everyone up when he rings the bell, then I wouldn't be very popular with your parents."

"You must think of Mum and Dad; they are exhausted, Anne."

"Well, that is all to do with you and Sam not me and the man in the moon!" shouted Anne, sounding very annoyed.

"Don't you start, Anne."

"Start what? All this upset is to do with you not buying any johnnies from the chemist and then having sex in the girls' toilets without using anything."

"You are a good one to talk, Anne, having a quick grope at the back of the bike sheds. That can lead to full-blown sex, then what would you do? I bet neither of you have ever gone and bought johnnies."

"So what if we have or haven't? It is a boy's place to go and buy them."

"Do you two always go on like this? Just shut up a minute and let me tell you that I'm going to go now. Pete, you can walk me to the pub."

"You just watch it, Sheila, you never know what Pete might suggest."

"I wouldn't suggest anything with a girl in ankle socks, think yourself lucky you are far too young for me."

"That's good because I don't fancy you. I'm only going to let you walk me to the pub because I don't like the dark."

"That will teach you, Pete."

"Sheila, go and get your coat and I will go to my room and put my shoes on. I'll see you downstairs in the hall."

At that I wandered into my room to find my shoes. Afterwards, I went into the bathroom and found Dad's Old Spice aftershave; I put a little on my cheeks. Downstairs, I found the girls sat in the front room, having a chat with Mum and Dad.

"What a smell! Whatever have you put on?" asked Anne, laughing out loud.

"It smells like my aftershave. Am I right, Pete?"

"Yeah."

"Whatever have you used that for?"

I felt completely and utterly stupid. All four of them were sat looking up at me, making me more and more embarrassed by the minute.

"No need to look so embarrassed, Pete, I don't mind you using it but I would like you to ask first," said Dad.

"Sorry."

"Now you have put it on, Pete, where are you going?"

"Oh, I told Sheila that I would walk her to the King's Arms where her dad is playing darts."

"That is very kind of you, I'm sure that did not warrant using my aftershave."

Anne just burst out laughing. "Perhaps he has put it on because it is quicker than washing, I have a good nose for smells and he honks sometimes."

"Anne just stop it, if you can't you had better say good night to Sheila right now and go to your room. I can't smell Pete, I have never known him to honk, as you call it."

"I have."

"I just told you to shut up or go to your room."

"Good night, Sheila. I am being treated like a child, I will see you in school tomorrow." Anne left the room but not before putting her tongue out at me.

"I saw that, Anne, just go," said Dad looking extremely annoyed.

Mum looked as if she was about to burst into tears. "I feel so awful that I am going to go up to bed, so good night to you all, See you in a while, Ernie."

"Good night my dear, as soon as Sheila has gone I will come up, I should only be a few minutes."

"We will go now, Dad."

"Yes, I must go I don't want to keep you all up," said Sheila. "I might be back again tomorrow if that is okay with you, Mr Knight? Anne and I have been playing Monopoly, but we haven't finished the game."

"Of course you can come around again tomorrow."

"Well, I will walk Sheila to the pub; it won't take me long. I'll try and be quiet when I come in."

"You'd better try too, your mother is not feeling too good. I'm hoping she will feel better in the morning, if she gets a good night's sleep."

We went out into the hall and out of the front door on to the pavement.

"What is the matter with your mum?"

"Oh, Mum has not been feeling too good for a few weeks, she is suffering from headaches caused by me upsetting her with all my problems."

"Anne told me this evening that you have got this girl pregnant."

"She is not just this girl, she is Sam and she is my girlfriend – we are planning to live together after the birth of our baby."

"Anne didn't tell me her name, but one of the boys at our school has been seeing a girl called Sam that lives at the Elephant and Castle, which is a long way from here. Someone told me she went to South East Comp."

"What! That sounds like Sam!"

"When you said her name, I thought it could be the girl that I had heard about at school."

"Well, I can tell you straight: I am her boyfriend and I got her pregnant. Whatever this boy has been saying about Sam, it can't be true; she was a virgin when I met her and she has not been with anyone else, or at least that is what she told me. Now you are putting doubts into my head."

"I didn't mean to upset you. Anyway, Pete, you and I should not be talking about your girlfriend." With that, Sheila held on to my hand.

"What do you think you're doing, holding on to my hand? Bit forward, isn't it?"

"It's dark and I don't like the dark, so I have to hold on to someone or something. You should remember, Pete, it doesn't mean anything holding on to your hand, it doesn't mean I've fallen in love with you or anything daft like that."

"That's okay then, as long as it doesn't mean anything to you because it doesn't mean a damn thing to me."

We carried on walking down the road, with me asking quite a few questions. "Is it true your dad is a holy father?"

"You mean a vicar?"

"Yeah."

"Yes he is and I go to church with him and Mum every Sunday."

"I'm a bit surprised about him going to the pub, I didn't think vicars went to the pub and I never dreamt that they played darts let alone have a pint of beer."

"Well they do, Dad formed a darts team with some of his parishioners, Dad's the captain."

"Do they always play at this pub?"

"Yeah, once a week, every Tuesday."

"Sheila where do you live?"

"Our house is in Shooters Hill, it's quite large."

"How the hell do your parents afford to live there?"

"Oh, it is the vicarage so we don't pay rent."

"Being the vicar must be great, time off in the week, no rent, part of your holidays paid for by some of the parishioners. I do realise that vicars don't earn much money, so they should be helped out by someone."

"How do you know so much about vicars and their holidays being paid for by well off parishioners?"

"Oh, Mum. Ages ago, she used to be friends with a vicar, in fact she went to church every Sunday until she met Dad, then she gave up religion and married Dad in the registry office. I always think Mum wishes that she had remained friends with the vicar or perhaps married him. At night, Mum always kneels by her bed to say her prayers."

"I never kneel by my bed, I think Mum and Dad would like to think I did. I go to church to keep the peace. Eventually, when I leave home, I doubt if I will ever go into a church again."

"I have never been inside a church."

"What, never? You haven't missed much, it's very boring, you could always come with me one Sunday, we could meet outside then go in together, what about this Sunday coming? Have a think about it."

"It's only Tuesday, Sunday is a long way off. You said something about coming around to see Anne again tomorrow night so I could let you know then."

"Yeah, that's right."

"Well I will have a think and let you know tomorrow night."

"Okay, I will wait to hear what you think, here's the pub."

"Sheila, are you sure that your dad is in this pub? This one has a bad reputation, I thought we were going to the one around the corner."

"Yeah this is the one, are you going to come in and meet Dad?"

"That is another thing, I've never been in a pub."

"Pete, there is always a first time for everything so come in with me."

We went into the bar through the side entrance. It was very dark and dingy, with quite a few men sat around on wooden stools. There was a very strong smell of beer and fags.

"Hi, Sheila, found yourself a boyfriend?" shouted one of the men.

"No, he is Anne's brother."

"Thank goodness for that, we'd hate to think you had started courting at your tender age," shouted one of the others.

"Elsie, where's Dad?" called Sheila to the barmaid.

"They are playing darts in the back room tonight, you can both go through if you like."

"Thanks."

At that we wandered back out into the corridor, passing the doors to the ladies' and gents' lavs. Eventually, we arrived at the back room which was closed. Everything seemed very quiet. Sheila seemed used to going into this room and, without bothering to knock, she opened the door only to find her dad sat on one of the benches, having a chat to a group of youngsters. I did not recognize any of them.

"Hi, Sheila, come and sit down; I will get you a soft drink. Who's your friend?"

"This is Anne's brother; he walked me here from Anne's house."

"That was kind of you son, come and sit down. Introduce me to him, Sheila, then I will get you both a drink."

"Pete, this is Dad; Dad, this is Pete."

We shook hands and then I sat down on the bench next to a couple of the lads that Sheila seemed to know.

"Nice to meet you Pete, now what would you like to drink? Coke, or maybe a shandy?"

"A Coke would go down well, as I am very thirsty, thanks, Rev."

"Oh do call me John; everyone does."

"That's okay then. Reverent John,"

"No, just John, please, Pete."

"Okay, John."

Once John had gone over to the bar, the lad who was sitting alongside of me looked me up and down very strangely. "How do you know Sheila? You don't come to our school."

"No, I go to the South East Comprehensive,"

"Not as posh as us, we go to the same school as your sister and Sheila."

"What makes you so sure that I am not as posh as you lot?"

"The way you talk and the way you look. We could never go to our school with hair looking like yours, down around your shoulders. As you can see we have to have short back and sides. Like your sister, we all go to the grammar school, just down the road from here."

"Just because I speak with a London accent, not like you lot with a plum in your mouth, and my hair is longer than yours, doesn't mean I don't have brains like you lot because I do. I am hoping to go to university. The thing is you have to remember that not all grammar school kids get to university. I actually know someone who became a postman having been to a grammar school. It doesn't mean because you pass your Eleven Plus that you will go further up the ladder than someone who went to secondary modern or comprehensive school. I have to let you know that I chose not to take my Eleven Plus. When I was younger I used to get very nervous about exams, and Mum and Dad suggested that I went to South East Comprehensive. That's why I am at the comp, not because I am thick. I am in the A stream for every subject and hoping to go to a university to study science."

"What? That's amazing!"

"Yeah, I think it is as well."

John then returned from the bar carrying our drinks. "What's amazing?"

"Oh, we are having a chat to Pete. He's telling us about his school and how he is hoping to go university and also how he is in the A stream for every subject."

"Well done, Pete, which school do you go to?"

"South East Secondary Modern. Now it's a comprehensive; it changed over last summer,"

"I don't know much about that school."

"There isn't much to know, it's the same as any other school."

"Pete, why are you at a comprehensive instead of a grammar school? I would have thought you would have passed your Eleven Plus quite easily as you are doing so well."

"The thing is, John, I used to get very nervous when it came to exams. Both Mum and Dad thought it better that I went to a school where I didn't need to take an exam to get in."

"Sheila's mum and I are very pleased with the grammar school and how Sheila has turned out. Both the boys and the girls in her year are doing very well. Having said that, I do remember you coming home and saying something about one of the boys in your year getting someone pregnant at the South East comp."

"Yeah, that is right, Dad, but I don't know whether it's true or not."

I could feel myself getting very embarrassed and feeling stupid.

"What is the matter, Pete? You've gone bright red, has John said something that hit a sore spot?"

"No not really, I must drink up quickly and go home; my parents will be wondering what has happened to me."

I just sat and drank my Coke as quick as I dare without appearing rude. John was sitting on the bench directly opposite me, and while drinking his pint he was looking over the top of his specs into my eyes. What he was thinking I could only guess, because he didn't say anything.

"Thanks for the Coke, John, I have to go." I got up and said cheers to everyone but, in the rush to get out of the situation, I tripped over my feet and almost landed in a heap on the floor.

"Are you okay?" said Sheila who came to the rescue and held on to my arm.

"Yeah I'm okay. I've got to go." I took Sheila's hand from my arm and put it down by her side, then hurried out of the bar and into the corridor. I tried to calm myself down by standing against the wall and holding my head in my hands before I walked out into the unlit court yard and headed home.

Chapter 13

Wednesday morning my alarm clock went off as usual at seven a.m. I'd placed the clock on the other side of the room so I had to get out of bed to turn the alarm off. This particular morning I was not looking forward to getting up, so the alarm continued to ring until dad came in and shouted at me before he angrily switched off the alarm and pulled back my bedclothes. "Get up you lazy what's it, Pete! You have disturbed your mum and I with this damn alarm, you could have the sense to get up and turn it off."

"Sorry."

"I would think so too, your mum and I thought we'd have a lie-in as we don't need to go into work until mid-morning."

"I will get myself up, I'm quite able to organise myself. I will sit quietly and have breakfast with Anne. Before I go to school I will ring the hospital to tell the ward sister what has been arranged for Sam."

"Well as far as your mother and I are concerned she needs to go home to the flat."

"Yeah, I have decided you are right, that is the best place for her."

"Three cheers, your mum will be pleased."

"I will phone at eight o'clock, that's the time the day staff take over. If the sister isn't there I will leave a message with the staff nurse, then I'll go into see Sam after school."

"Okay then, we will see you late afternoon."

"Before you go back to bed, Dad, how's Mum this morning?"

"I asked her just now and she said she did not feel too bad – apparently she had a good sleep."

"That's good."

With that, Dad left and went back to bed. I got myself up and down the stairs to the dining room where Anne was already sitting, eating her breakfast.

"Well, how did you get on with Sheila? She told me that she fancied you and was hoping you would kiss her goodnight."

"Well, I didn't kiss her goodnight, so that's that, she is far too young for me. Like I told you both, I'm not interested in girls in ankle socks."

"Bet she held on to your arm; she told me that she was going to try to."

"Yes, she did, I told her straight that I am not interested in her, as I have Sam. Talking about Sam, I must phone the ward."

"What is going to happen? Mum said you wanted her to live here with us."

"If Mum has told you that I can tell you that she is not going to live here, the three of us think she should go back to her flat."

"What will she think about that?"

"I don't know and also I don't really care, I just feel it is the best thing for her. I've got to do my exams next week and I have got to pass so I get a good job,"

"You have changed your tune, Pete."

"I'm allowed to change my mind. I must go and phone the hospital."

"I bet you have changed your mind because of what I told you about the boy at my school who told me he was seeing someone from your school. Her name's Sam and she may be pregnant by him," said Anne, laughing all over her face.

"I don't want to enter into any of this with you, Sheila's dad said something about someone getting pregnant. I have made a decision and that is to cool it with Sam for a while."

"Well done Pete," laughed Anne while clapping her hands.

At that I went out into the hall, closing the door behind me hoping that Anne couldn't hear my conversation. "Good morning, please can I speak to the ward sister?"

"Who is speaking?"

"Pete, the boyfriend of Sam Smithson."

"Just a moment."

"Sister speaking."

"Hi, this is Pete Knight, Sam's boyfriend, I said that I would phone in this morning to let you know whether Sam can come and live with me and my parents, and I'm afraid the answer is no. My parents are not at all well and also we can't afford to keep her, I suggest that it is arranged for her to go and live at her parents' flat until she goes to a mother and baby home from there. Please can you tell Sam that I will come in to see her after my exam."

"I think Sam will be very disappointed. I will have a chat with her when I go around with the medication."

"Thanks. Please send her my love."

"Yeah, will do, bye."

I put the phone down and went back into the dining room where Anne was still sitting, looking a bit shifty. "Well what did they say?"

"I'm not going to tell you. I can tell by the colour of your face that you were listening through the wall."

Anne immediately got up. "Oh I'm going, I'll see what gossip I can find out at school. Sheila will tell me what she knows from you, hope you haven't told her any of your business as she will repeat it around our school, she is a little gossip. No one tells her anything unless of course they want everyone else to know."

"No I did not tell her anything important. Mind you, she kept asking questions, but I wasn't game."

"Thank goodness for that, I'm going. I'll see you later, Pete."

"Yeah, see you later alligator."

"What the hell are you saying to me?"

"You are supposed to answer 'in while crocodile'."

"Never heard that before."

"I doubt if you would have, it is something they used to say in the fifties. Mum and dad said it to one another when I was young, I don't know where it came from, it could have been the telly."

Anne went on her merry way while I stayed behind to compose myself before going to catch the bus.

144

For a change my day at school went quite well. All my mates kept quiet about Sam, Dave was the only one who mentioned her name and that was only with a question about the Friday night disco, on the way to catch the bus home.

"Pete, are you coming with us to the disco? Or are you going to come with Sam? Or maybe you aren't coming at all?"

"I haven't thought about it. I doubt if Sam will want to come, she is quite large now and feels quite uncomfortable. Anyway she will be back home at the flat, her dad won't let her out of his sight. I may come with you lot."

"What, Pete, you're coming out with us, you devil."

"I feel that I should try and have a life of my own."

"We have all been telling you that for months."

"Well I think you lot may be right."

"Three cheers to you, Pete."

I got on the bus and sat just inside the door. By the time the bus arrived at the hospital I was in some state, worrying in case the ward sister had phoned Sam's parents and arranged for them to visit this afternoon, to have a chat about Sam going home to live with them.

I pushed open the ward door and bumped straight into the ward sister who was coming out of her office. "I'm glad you've arrived. I was about to give up on you and go home."

"What's up?"

"I need to have a chat with you before you go into see Sam. Come into my office and take a seat this side of my desk." The sister went around and sat on the chair that faced the door and also the corridor. I guess she sat looking this way so she could see what was going on, she did not seem to miss a trick.

"Now, Pete, we have had a chat with Sam and explained to her that she can't live at your place and that she will have to go home to the flat, until she goes to the mother and baby home in October. Sam did not take it very well, in fact it upset her so much that she is having to stay put for a few more days. Tomorrow I am going to phone her parents and try and explain to them that they have to try and stay calm for Sam and the baby's sake when she goes home."

"I don't know how they will take that, all they seem to want to do is go down the pub or go to work. I wish they would give up the fags and the drink, especially if Sam is going to live with them."

"I didn't realise that they smoked. I will have to get a doctor to have a word with them when they come in, the thing is smoking in front of a baby or a pregnant mother is not a good idea."

"I don't want to see them, if I see them coming I shall run. You do know that I am going to try and stand by Sam, if I pass my A levels and get a good job we are going to get a flat together. I do realise that getting a flat with a baby will be difficult, but I am determined to try and make it work."

"I'm pleased about that, it would be awful if the baby had to be given up for adoption."

"I don't want that to happen. Mum and Dad would never get over their first grandchild being given away."

"Now you go along and see Sam, she hasn't had any visitors today but then she has only had you visiting her any day. I forgot to say that the social worker came in earlier and had a chat with her."

"Do you know what she had to say?"

"No, that is between Sam and the social worker. Sam may tell you but it is nothing to do with the nursing staff. I did notice that
she took quite a few notes while chatting with Sam."

"I will go and see her and see what she has to tell me."

I wandered out into the corridor and along to the ward where Sam was sat hanging her legs over the side of her bed, looking very miserable. A lady from the next bed sat looking towards Sam. They seemed to be having a chat but whatever she was talking about didn't seem to be cheering Sam up. Once I got to Sam's bed I put my arms out to give her a kiss and cuddle, but Sam wasn't having any of it.

The woman sat staring towards me, then, out of the blue, she informed me about Sam. "She is not happy; in fact she's very miserable. She has been telling me all about you and how you are expecting her to go back to her parents' flat."

"She has a name which is Sam, and where Sam is having to go and live is nothing to do with you."

"Pete, please don't be so horrible. This lady wants to help me, she got pregnant at sixteen and was kicked out with nowhere to go."

"Yeah that's right, I'm married now to the bloke that gave me a bun in the oven and we are very happy with two more children. Let me introduce myself, I'm Mary and I'm pleased to meet you."

I shook her hand. "I'm also pleased to meet you, I'm Pete the dad of Sam's baby." With that, I sat down in the armchair next to Sam's bed.

"Sam has been telling me all about you and how you met at school. Everything about you two seems to be very similar to me and my bloke."

"We have got ourselves in a complete mess. Mum and Dad won't let Sam come and stay with me at our house. The thing is, there is not enough room, plus we can't afford to feed her. Has Sam told you about her mum and dad and how they have virtually disowned her?"

"Yeah, she has told me it all. I have a plan but it has to be arranged, also I need to ask my old man before it can be put into practice. Sam, would you like to come and live with me and Derek? We have a spare room. If Derek agrees, you would be able to stay with us until the baby's born. We live in Blackheath, so you two would be able to meet up without any problems."

"That sounds okay; can I have a think about it and also have a private chat to Pete?"

"Yeah, of course you can. I'm going to go out on the balcony and have a fag." Mary picked up her fags and matches from her locker and wandered down to the end of the ward through the door to the balcony.

"Now Mary has gone for her fag, give me a cuddle. It seems that things are sorting themselves out, thank goodness."

"Yeah, Mary seems very nice; the only problem I can see is the fags."

"Pete, before talking about Mary I have to have a chat with you about the social worker and what she had to say to me."

"Surely she doesn't have to be involved if you go and stay with Mary?"

"I don't know, because this is the first I've heard about Mary letting me stay with her."

"It is kind of Mary, but we must remember that she has to have a talk with Derek before anything can be decided. Also, have you met him?"

"Yeah, I met him last night he makes me laugh. Mary has told me all about her kids and of course him."

"Now, Sam, whether your parents want you to live with them or not they are your next of kin, this means they have the last word about where you live, as you are under twenty-one."

"What! I can't believe what I'm hearing," shouted Sam, getting down from the side of her bed and stomping around on the floor.

"Sam, try and calm down, you are upsetting the other women. I know, let us ask the ward sister and see if I'm right. Yeah, she is the best person to ask, also she is very understanding. I had a chat with her before I came into see you."

"Let's go and see her now then, come on Pete I'm off to see her."

I followed Sam along to the office where we found the sister still sitting where I had left her, but now a relative of another patient was sitting on the chair that I had been sitting on. Sam didn't knock on the door, she just stormed in without even thinking how rude she was being,

"Mary, who is in the bed next to me, has said I can go and live with her. Pete says I can't unless I get permission from Mum and Dad, is that right?"

"Calm down Sam, I am having a chat with this lady, I can't talk to you at the same time."

"This is urgent, I need to know now."

"Sorry, Sam, go back to the ward and wait until I have finished here. Please try and calm down, remember your blood pressure. Getting in this sort of state will not help your health, you need to try and stay calm."

Sam was getting more and more flushed as she tried to get the attention of the ward sister.

"No, I am going to stay here until you tell me if what Pete has told me is true."

"Sorry, Sam, you must leave my office at once. If you won't go quietly I will have to call security for help. Pete, please can you take Sam back to the ward? I will come and see you both when I have finished here."

"Sam, come back to the ward with me; if you don't, you will be in more trouble."

Sam just looked at me and stormed out of the office, pushing me to one side as if I was a stranger and nothing to do with her. Once Sam got back to her bed she lay with her head under her top pillow and her hands over her ears so she could not hear what I had to say. After a few minutes she came out from under the pillow, but only to ask me why I was still here as she had nothing to say to me.

"If you are not going to let me live with you and your parents and I can't go and stay with Mary, you may as well go home and let me sort myself out on my own."

"Sam please try and calm down. I do care, if I didn't I wouldn't bother to come and visit you."

"Go! For goodness sake, go, Pete!" Sam screamed.

"All right, I'll go. I won't be coming in to see you again for a few days; perhaps by the time I come in again you will have come to your senses and sorted yourself out. Goodbye. Before I go please try and remember that you need to live in a calm environment for the sake of our baby."

With that I left Sam's bedside and immediately bumped into the ward sister and the senior houseman coming into the ward to see Sam.

"Hi, are you going home?"

"Yeah, Sam is in a very funny mood; I think it is best that I go."

"We would like you to be with Sam when we have a chat, please come back to Sam's bedside."

"Okay, but don't expect to get much joy from her. I have never known her to get cross."

"Most probably it is her hormones," said the sister, smiling towards me.

"You lot always say it's her hormones, I'm not so sure."

The three of us wandered into the ward, only to find Sam sitting up on her bed, chatting and smiling with Mary. Once she saw us arriving at her bedside, she looked very annoyed.

"We have come to have a word with you, Sam. I'll pull the curtains around your bed so we can have a chat in private," said the ward sister.

"I don't know why you need to do that because Mary can join in the conversation. I have decided that I am going to go and live with her until I am able to go to the mother and baby home."

"It's not that easy. Pete has told you your parents are your next of kin and they have the last say, even if they don't want you to live with them they have to agree to where you live. I am going to pull the curtains around your bed."

Sam immediately went back under her pillow and put her hands over her ears. The three of us looked at one another. The ward sister looked exasperated.

"Sam, act your age and come out from under that pillow, we all need to have a talk about your future."

We were sure that she could hear what we were saying, so the doctor started the conversation by telling her what a difficult position she had got herself in and how worried I was. After a few minutes she came out from under the pillow and said she did not want anything to do with me as I was not any help to her.

"Sam, you are talking a load of rubbish, you know very well that I want to help you."

"The best thing you can do is go home to your wonderful parents and never return."

"Stop it, Sam," said the doctor trying to remain calm. "You know you don't mean that."

"Yes I do."

I just did not know what to do or say, my head was spinning.

"Sam don't be so horrible, you know I want to help you."

"I have two words to say to you Pete: *get out.*"

"Okay, if that is how you want to talk to me, I'm going."

I turned and walked away from Sam's bed. I was followed by the ward sister.

"I'm sorry but I have to go."

"We understand. I'm going to go back. As soon as we have got some sense into Sam, I will ring you at your home, we have your phone number."

"Yeah you have, I will wait for you to ring. I feel awful, I have a terrible headache. Once I'm home I may go to bed but Mum and Dad will be there; one of them will take a message for me."

"I will speak to you later."

At that I went out into the grounds to wait for the bus to take me back down to the main street. While waiting, the hospital receptionist descended on me. "Hi, Pete! You look awful! Whatever is the matter?"

"Oh hello, Jackie. It is nothing to do with you. Since you have asked, though, I'm having a terrible time with Sam; she is up the duff and is in hospital."

"Are you sure you're the father?"

"Yeah, I'm afraid so, Jackie."

"I can't believe what you are saying, I thought you were a free agent and honestly I did not think you would have a girlfriend with a bun in the oven."

"I was a free agent when you bumped into me in the park, things have changed very quickly."

"They must have, it was only a few weeks ago that you and your mates came looking for me."

"Oh, I knew then that Sam had a bun in the oven. I was hoping that she might have an abortion, but she wouldn't. I was only looking for you with my mates as they wanted to meet you, I told them all about you and that got them interested. Anyway, they have moved on since then – they're interested in someone else, so you've missed out."

"That's life! Here's the bus. Where are you getting off, Pete? Do you fancy going for a coffee to have a chat?"

"No I can't do that, I'm in a hurry, I want to get home and have a sleep, I'm exhausted. Sam is driving me to distraction, I have left her in a terrible state. The ward sister and the doctor are having a chat with her, I hope she listens to what they have to say."

We got on the double-decker and luckily managed to get a seat together downstairs, about halfway along on the left-hand side. I let Jackie walk in front of me so I could admire her legs and bum, today she's wearing a white skinny rib sleeveless poloneck top with a red leather miniskirt. Her legs were bare, whilst on her feet she had a pair of black patent leather shoes with threeinch heels. She sat herself down by the window. After I settled down beside her I began to think that it was not such a good idea to have let her sit with me, let alone on the inside, as she sat with her miniskirt right up around her bum. If Jackie had sat on the outside with a bit of luck she may have pulled her skirt down, but she began rubbing her bare right leg along my left thigh. I could feel myself getting embarrassed at the same time as getting excited, I just couldn't wait to get off the bus.

"Whatever is the matter, Pete? You look as if you have suddenly got a temperature!"

I turned towards Jackie and whispered in her ear, "So would you have a temperature if someone was doing to you what you are doing to me, especially on the local bus."

"I'm only trying to be friendly, you are obviously enjoying it," she replied in a loud voice so that most of the bus could hear her.

"Jackie, shut up and behave yourself."

With that the woman sat in front of us turned around and told us both to be quiet.

"For goodness sake, you two, be quiet, and you, girl, pull your skirt down – I can see your knickers."

Jackie seemed to find this a joke and burst out laughing.

"Good job I've got them on, I don't wear them very often."

By this time most of the passengers that were sitting close to us were having a peep at Jackie's legs.

"Have a good look all of you, I may pull my skirt down in a mo. Before I do, you may as well have a look at my legs and of course my knickers."

I felt my world was falling apart, everyone was looking at Jackie first and then me. Thank goodness the bus came to a halt at the next set of traffic lights. I managed to get up and hurry along the isle and jump off before the bus moved on again and Jackie realised I had left her.

"Don't look at me as if she's my girlfriend because she ain't!" I shouted from the platform to any of the passengers that wished to hear me. It was such a relief to get off and leave Jackie to her own devices, showing her bits and pieces to the other passengers.

I hurried home hoping that I could have a cup of tea before the ward sister phoned to give me what I hoped was going to be good news. I put the key in the door and I could hear Mum chatting to someone.

"Here's Pete now, you'd better talk to him about Sam."

"Whoever is it? I have only just opened the door."

"It's the ward sister."

"Can't you take a message? I need to go to the lav."

"No I can't, this is your problem, so you have to talk to her."

"Give me the phone then," I said, snatching it out of Mum's hand. I wished that I had opened the door a few minutes later, then I might have missed the call and Mum would have had to take the message. Instead of going to the sitting room, Mum stood behind me, trying to listen into the conversation. This made me more annoyed than ever. I just answered 'yes' and 'no', depending on what questions the ward sister asked me. When I put the phone down, Mum stood waiting to hear what I had to say.

"Well, what news have you? What did she have to say?"

"Can you give me a chance to get my shoes off?"

"Your dad and I can't wait until you have done that, we have been waiting a couple of hours already for your news."

"Well, you will have to wait a bit longer."

"Stop your cheek, Pete."

"Why should I? Just now you were getting so annoyed with me for no reason, so it is my turn now."

"Stop it, Pete!"

"No, I won't!"

"Yes, you will."

"You will both have to wait as I am not going to tell you until I have been to the lav and taken my shoes off."

Mum gave a large sigh as if she was completely and utterly fed up, then walked out of the hall into the kitchen where Dad was making a pot of tea.

"I'm completely fed up with that boy, Ernie," said Mum, forgetting that I was standing behind her.

"Mum, I am standing behind you, listening to you talking to Dad."

"Well I am fed up with you."

"I didn't say I wouldn't tell you what the sister said. I said I wanted time to go to the lav, take my shoes off then sit down for a few minutes before telling you both, surely that is not much to ask?"

"Come on, Marg, give the boy a chance to get in the door before starting on him."

"You are standing up for him now? It was a different story before he came home, telling me how fed up you were with him and Sam."

"Yeah, that is true, but I still think you should give him a chance to get in the door, I'm making a pot of tea for the three of us. Both of you calm down and go into the sitting room and wait for me to bring in the tea."

We did what Dad said; I followed Mum into the front room, she sat in her normal chair and I sat facing the fireplace on the sofa. Mum didn't say a word, she just sat down looking into space. Dad soon arrived with the tea, looking a bit anxious.

"Pete, surely you could have got one of the small tables out for me to put the tray on without me having to ask you?"

"Course I could, but calm down; it is not the end of the world, me not getting the table out."

"Shut up, Pete, why can't you just do as you are asked without causing an upset?"

154

"Well if you spoke to me in the way you want me to speak to you, things would be better." Silence reigned for a few minutes while Mum poured the tea.

Dad sat in his normal chair, with his back to the window, and he was looking a bit flushed.

"Now we have our tea. Let's hear your news, Pete; good or bad, we would like to hear it all."

"It's like this: the doctor doesn't want Sam to go back to the flat to live. Sam has made friends with a woman in the bed next to her and she wants to go and live at her place with her and her husband. I am not sure that this is a good idea, the only good thing about it is that they live in Blackheath and we would be able to see each other as frequently as we wanted to."

"Have you met this couple?" asked Mum, looking a bit worried.

"I've met her, she was going out for a fag when I got to the ward this afternoon. I don't like the idea of Sam living with people that smoke, apparently they have a couple of teenage sons and an older son that this woman had when she was sixteen." "Who's the father of that one?" asked Dad.

"The husband. They met at school like Sam and I; they have been together ever since."

"I suppose that's something. I wonder where they live in Blackheath and what type of jobs they have."

"I have no idea, I don't even know what they are called, but the woman seems to have befriended Sam."

"What does the ward sister think about Sam going to live with this couple?"

"She says Sam's parents need to agree."

"Who is going to ask her parents?"

"The ward sister is going to ring them and try and arrange for them to go into the ward and have a chat with her and Sam's doctor. She mentioned something about phoning them this evening and getting them to visit in the morning, it has to be organised as soon as possible as they need Sam's bed for someone else."

"So we have to wait until tomorrow to hear what's going to happen?"

"That's about it."

"Now, Pete, has anyone asked Sam where she is going to have the baby?"

"There are three mother and baby homes that she is thinking about, one in Aylesbury, another in Luton and a third in Weymouth."

"Has she got a favourite? The woman I met at work went to the one in Luton, she said they were very kind to her."

"Sam really doesn't want to go to one of these places, but she doesn't seem to have a choice. She did mention that she thought Aylesbury would be a good place to go as I would be able to visit her easier than at any of the other homes. You see, if I get a flat in North London I could live there while Sam's at the home and I could easily get the tube to Finchley Road then catch the Aylesbury train out to see her at the weekends."

"You seem to have it all organised Pete, I hope you haven't been thinking about this instead of your exams."

"Mum, I'm bound to think about it."

"Well, have you thought about what part of North London?" asked Dad.

"It is early days but I did see a one-bedroom flat in the paper near Willesden Green tube station for seven pound ten shillings a week. That included the rates, but the electric and gas would be extra."

"That is quite a lot of money, Pete. I wonder if they will let you live there with a baby."

"I have no idea, I've only read about it in the *Evening Standard*, I haven't phoned up and asked for details. The thing is, I won't be moving out into a flat until I have a job. The job is my first priority. As you both know I haven't got any money, so, before I can move out, I have to save for a deposit, unless of course someone helps me out."

"Yeah, the job has to come first, Sam and the baby have to come after the job," said Dad, ignoring my comment about being helped out with the deposit.

"If I can't get a job we won't be able to rent any flat, then Sam will be up the creek. Also the social worker may try to get her to have the baby fostered with view to adoption."

"Oh, Pete, don't think about that! I couldn't bear to think my first grandchild was going to be taken into care."

"We have talked about this enough for the moment, Pete, try not to upset your mother."

"I don't want to upset either of you, I just think the three of us have to have a think about what I have said."

"I know that but enough is enough for tonight, tomorrow is your first exam. What time do you have to get to school?" asked Mum.

"The exam starts at nine thirty. It goes on for two hours, then I am free until next Monday when I take Biology. I think that starts at two o'clock."

"I should try and get to bed early, even if you can't sleep at least you're resting."

"Yeah, I was thinking about getting to bed by ten."
"That is a good idea – I have noticed your light still on after twelve most nights. That is far too late for anyone taking exams."

"Before you go up to your room I better let you know that Sheila isn't upstairs with Anne so you should have a quiet evening. Anne said something about Sheila's dad not letting her come around midweek, so most probably she will be around on Friday."

"I'm going out Friday night, there is a disco at school so I'm going with my mates."

"What about Sam?"

"I forgot to tell you that she is not going back to school as she feels too embarrassed about her size. Also, she feels too uncomfortable, so she won't be going."

"Why are you going to the dance? It seems very strange to me, I thought the reason for anyone going to a disco was to find a girlfriend or at least find a girl to dance with and they are usually girls that you like."

"I guess you are right, but my reason for going is to go out with my mates. This might be the last time that I will be able to go out with them, due to me living with Sam and having a baby to look after."

"I suppose you are right. Marg, what do you think about Pete going to the disco?" said Dad, looking a bit down in the dumps.

"Same as you, Ern, a bit surprised."

"Well you agree with me going, even though you are surprised?"

"At least it is the day after your English A-level exam."

"So you are saying that I can go? Because as usual I need to borrow some money for the ticket."

"That is all you ever seem to ask for money, money and more money! How much will you need?"

"The ticket is five bob and I will need a bit more to buy a Coke."

"So altogether you will need ten shillings. How are you going to get there? If it is on the bus you will need the bus fare. It is going to be an expensive night out for us and we aren't going anywhere."

"Oh, Ern, don't be so mean, I think perhaps we should pay up as this may be the last school dance that Pete will ever go to." "Yeah, you could be right, Mum. There has not been any mention of an end-of-term dance."

"Well, if we pay for this dance, don't bother to ask us again if there is an end of term one. We can't afford to keep paying out."

"Thanks to you both, I won't ask again. At least, not in a rush."

"You hadn't better."

"I'm going to go to my room and have a look through my books."

"I doubt if we will see you again tonight, so night, Pete, see you in the morning."

"Night."

I went quietly up the stairs hoping not to disturb Anne. All was quiet on the Western Front. I settled myself down when out of the blue came loud music from Anne's room, it sounded as if she had put her wireless on full blast to listen to Radio Luxembourg. It was so loud that it was impossible to understand the song she was listening to. I got down from my bed and went and banged on her door. It opened quicker than I ever thought it would.

"Yes, what do you want?"

"I've come to ask you to turn that noise down."

"Isn't there a word that you've forgotten?"

"No."

"I know there is."

"What is it then?"

"Please."

"Blow you, Anne, why should I say please to you when it is you that is disturbing me with that awful din."

"You two having a row again?" shouted Mum from the bottom of the stairs.

"Pete does not like my music."

"Well your dad and I don't like it either, having your music on so loud will make you deaf."

"That's a laugh."

"Well it is the truth, Anne, now turn the music down like Pete has asked, please."

"All right!" Anne shouted out before going back into her room and banging her bedroom door shut. The bang was so loud that it was a wonder the wall didn't crack or the door didn't come off its hinges.

I went back into my room and continued reading my book.

Chapter 14

When I woke on Thursday morning I couldn't believe that I had slept all night without waking. In fact, I found that I was in the same position on my bed but with my book on the floor, as I was at nine o'clock last evening. I hadn't even put my pyjamas on. I must have been tired. I jumped off my bed in a rush as it was half past seven and my exam was at half nine. I hurried out on to the landing hoping that I could go straight into the bathroom for a strip wash only to find that Anne was in no hurry to come out of the bathroom.

"Anne, I'm late, hurry up please, I need to catch the eight fifteen bus to school. My English exam is at nine thirty, I can't afford to wait for a later bus."

"Well, you will have to wait!" shouted Anne from the other side of the door.

"Please try and hurry."

"Give me five minutes."

"Whatever is going on, why are you two shouting at one another again? Your mother can't put up with much more of this," shouted Dad from their bedroom door.

"Sorry but I overslept."

"Lucky you, your mother and I have been awake most of the night."

"Surely you are not going to blame me for you two not sleeping again?"

"No."

At that, Anne came out of the bathroom, holding her nose when she saw me already dressed.

"Fancy dressing before having a wash! Dad, I told you the other day that Pete honks, now you know why: he sleeps with his clothes on."

"No I don't."

"Why have you got your school clothes on then?"

"Shut up, you two! Peter, can you tell me this is not true. The thing is I have not got a good sense of smell."

"Last night I fell asleep with my clothes on and I did not wake up until this morning."

"You had better change all your clothes, we will be getting a letter from the school saying that they don't think you wash because you honk, as Anne calls it."

"I'm waiting to go into the bathroom for a strip wash, I'm in a hurry. The problem is the bus goes at eight fifteen from the station."

"Well hurry up, chop, chop," said Dad, clapping his hands as if I was a child.

Once in the bathroom, I stripped off only to find that Anne had used all the hot water and she, or our parents, had turned the immersion off so I had to have a wash in cold water. Anne had already eaten her breakfast by the time I'd got downstairs.

"How was the water?" said Anne, laughing in my face.

"Cold, did you turn the immersion off?"

"Why should I do that?"

"I don't know, I can't see Dad or Mum turning the water off unless they are so hard up."

Anne was still laughing. "I will admit it was me. Just thought I would let you see what it could be like once you are living in a flat with no money to put in the meter for hot water."

"Stop being so cruel, Anne, both your dad and I have had to use cold water. None of us have time to wait for the water to warm up," said Mum as she walked through the dining room door in her flimsy cream dressing gown with her pale pink night dress showing below her gown. "The thing is, Anne, men need hot water to have a decent shave. Your father will have to go to work having had half a decent shave. The customers, plus the boss will wonder what has happened to him as he always tries to look smart."

Anne looked very sheepish. "Sorry."

"I should think so too, go and get your things together and go on your way." Anne left the table to collect her packed lunch.

"I'm off, see you all later. Bye."

"I don't know what we are going to do with you two," said Mum, looking quite harassed.

"One thing is for sure, I won't be here for much longer, that's if Sam and I live in North London. You and Dad will have to phone before you visit, as it is too far away for you to just pop in. I hope we have the use of a phone, I doubt if we will be able to afford one of our own straight away. I imagine they are quite expensive. You never know, we may have one in the hallway that all the tenants can use."

"We will miss you, Pete, we might get fed up with you two arguing but we love you both and wouldn't be without you."

"Thanks." I gave Mum a hug and a kiss on the cheek. "I must be going or I will miss the bus."

"What time does your exam finish?"

"Around eleven thirty. Before I forget, can you let me have five bob to buy the ticket for the disco tomorrow night?"

"I expect so, you'll have to wait while I go upstairs to get my bag, you know I keep it under the bed at night. Not that there is much in it, I will just go up and get it."

I waited for what seemed to be an eternity.

"Sorry to take so long, I got upstairs and needed to go to the toilet, I'm always having to go in a rush, there seems to be something wrong with me. The doctor seems to think it could be my nerves upsetting my stomach."

"Has he given you anything for it?"

"No, he wants me to go back again to see him next Monday. Dad told you the other day that I have lost a lot of weight."

"Yeah he did, I did not realise that it was as bad as it seems to be."

"You go on your way, Pete, or you will miss the bus and that will never do."

"After my exam, I am going to go back up to the hospital to see how Sam is. I hope she is in a better mood than yesterday."

"Pete, try and be patient with her; it is most probably her hormones."

"Everyone I speak says it's her hormones. I never get cross with her, it is her that seems to get cross. Perhaps she is not good news, perhaps she takes after her dad. Her mum tries hard to be calm but she finds it difficult at times."

"Don't think about that side of things, you have enough on your plate today. Good luck, Pete, we will see you at your normal time. Bye."

"Bye, Mum, say cheers to Dad for me."

"Yes I will."

Out of the front door I went, then down the road.

Thank goodness the bus arrived on time. More often than not it is late, then everyone is complaining and most of the men are late for work, which does not suit as they have to stay on to make up their hours. I managed to get the second seat down the aisle on the right-hand side. I find the nearer I can sit to the door the better on the way to school, as it is easier to get off the bus as it only stops for a few minutes outside the school gates. If I sit down the front it sometimes moves away before I manage to get up the aisle and jump off. This particular morning a very large woman sat down next to me, making my journey very uncomfortable. Half her body was across the aisle, while the other half was on the seat with her top half touching the seat in front of her.

"Son, do you think you could move over a bit? I haven't got enough room," said the woman, who appeared very breathless.

"I will be out the window in a minute if I move over any further."

"Don't be so cheeky."

"What, me cheeky? I don't think so, it's you, you are far too big and I am the one that hasn't got enough room! Please can you move back towards the aisle? I can hardly breathe, you are almost sat on top of me."

"Well if I move back towards the aisle the clippie won't have room to come along the aisle to collect the fares."

"I'm sorry to have to say it but perhaps you should get up and go and stand on the platform and give everyone more room."

"You have got a nerve, boy. I always thought schoolboys gave up their seats for older people, so why don't you go and stand on the platform to give me more room?"

"The answer to that is no, I am not going to. Why should you take up two seats and pay for one, and me stand and pay for the privilege of standing? If you do what I suggest one of these other ladies that are standing can sit with me."

"You really have a nerve, boy."

"Well, I think he is right," said a man who was standing along from our seat.

"What am I supposed to do? I can't get up and out into the aisle now the bus has started to move. Also there isn't enough room without the bus stopping and the clippie getting you lot to get off the bus to allow me to move along the aisle to the platform."

"Well, there you go, you need to go on a diet," said the man laughing to himself. "If you stay where you're sat, how do you expect the boy to get off the bus?"

"I don't know," said the woman, beginning to look very sheepish and stupid. "Yes I do, how about you and I swapping seats?"

"How are we going to do that? You have just said to this man that there isn't enough room for you to walk along the aisle to the platform without us all getting off the bus first, so how can we change seats?"

"You can always stand on your seat and jump across me then I will move over to your seat."

"That sounds okay in theory, but I notice that your stomach almost touches the back of the seat that is in front of you."

"Oh, for goodness sake! Come on, have a go!"

I stood up and, with difficulty, stood on the seat and tried to put my left leg across the woman's chest. "This isn't going to work, you are too big, my legs are not long enough, how can you move across on to my side of the seat?"

"What are you up to, boy?" shouted the clippie from the platform.

"We are trying to swap seats," I called back to him. "I'm finding it a bit difficult as this woman is enormous."

"How dare you say that about me!"

"Well, it's the truth."

"Get yourself up off the seat and swap places in the normal way! You, boy, get your feet down off that seat! Someone else has to sit there after you've finished with it."

I slipped myself down on to the seat, feeling very foolish.

"The trouble is, clippie, I need more room and this boy will not move up."

"How can he move over?" asked the man who joined in the conversation earlier.

"I have a suggestion. Turn yourself towards the aisle then perhaps I can squeeze between your shoulder and the back of that seat."

"I will try," the woman said, picking up her wicker basket, which she had between her legs and feet, and turning towards the aisle. With great difficulty I squeezed past her and stood waiting patiently for her to move across to the window seat. Once she settled herself down, I sat, only to find that I could only sit on one half of my buttocks; the other was halfway across the aisle.

"That is much better," said the woman. "This is very comfortable."

"It might be for you, it is not for me. It seems as if it is my turn to disturb the other passengers. Thank God I am getting off at the next stop. I hope I don't meet you on this bus again."

"I expect you will. I am using this particular bus every day for the next month."

"Well, I will only have to suffer you until next Friday. If I see you, I will turn and go to another seat, I'm not going to get involved with you and your fat body."

"I have never met anyone as rude as you, boy."

"They always say it takes one to know one; also, there is a first time for everything. By the way, I have never met anyone as fat as you."

At that I got up and walked to the platform where the clippie told me that I should learn to behave myself and be polite to my elders.

I just looked at him. "If you expect me to be polite to someone like her you have another thing coming."

"If I were you, boy, I would get off this bus before I ask for your name so I can report you."

"I can tell you my name: it's Mickey Mouse."

"Go, before I lose my temper and report you to your head."

I jumped off the bus and hurried on my way to the exam. I was the last one to arrive. When I walked into the room everyone seemed to have settled themselves down and were on their marks, ready to turn the papers over.

"Late as usual, Knight. You will be late for your own funeral one day,"

"Sorry, it was the bus it was late, then it had to go extra slow due to an extra-large woman that sat next to me. The bus couldn't go faster than twenty miles per hour – her weight, well, she was like a ten-ton Tessy."

"Shut up, Knight, and sit down, we are waiting for you."

I sat down as ordered to and got my pens out of my bag, only to find that my biro had run out of ink.

"Mr Down?"

"Yes?"

"My pen has run out of ink."

"Well, fancy that, Knight! I wouldn't be surprised if you didn't say I've run out of brains." All the other students started sniggering.

"Settle down you lot before I completely lose my cool. Here is a pen; catch it, Knight."

"Thanks, sir."

Before I blinked it seemed time to hand the papers in and walk out of the room. Where the time had gone I don't know, but at least the two hours had not dragged. I must have had something to write down and hopefully it was correct. I wandered around to the sixth form common room for a coffee and to pay for the dance ticket. What had happened I had no idea, but the girls were sat in one corner and the boys were over in the far corner and no one was talking. It took ages to find out what was wrong with them as no one wanted to be the first to spill the beans. Eventually, but not until I had walked around to try and have a chat with one of my mates that had lost his tongue, did I get told.

166

"What the hell is the matter with you lot?" I asked.

Dave put his finger up to his mouth as if to say be quiet, then, out of the blue, Dorothy who was sat in the other corner and could never resist speaking up if there was a problem, came out with:

"We have stopped talking to the boys."

"What have they been up to, Dot?"

"Not a lot."

"You may as well tell me what the matter is."

"We are fed up! It's to do with this dance on Friday; we, meaning us girls, came in and found the boys sat in the corner, discussing which of us girls they were going to try and poke at the dance."

"That's dreadful, you boys should know better, talking about things like that. I would never dream about doing anything like that, never, let alone discuss it."

"Pete, you trying to make out you are so good in front of the girls? I can assure you, girls, he is just like us, if not worse."

Nobody answered; they just looked over at me. Then, out of the blue, one of the girls decided to make a statement.

"In a minute we will all decide not to go to this stupid dance, then you lot will all look ridiculous stood around, all boys together, wondering which one of you has the nerve to play with themselves first."

"Sometimes you girls are quite disgusting. You are worse than the boys, especially the way you talk."

"What are you going to do about the way we talk then, Knight?"

"I'm not going to do anything. I'm not interested in any of you as I have Sam."

Suddenly the door in the corner opened and out came Mr Thomas, head of sixth form. He had been sitting behind his office door, listening in to our conversation.

"I don't know what to say to you lot, except I have listened to everything you have been talking about and I think you are all as bad as one another. You should make it up and be friends then go along to the dance and enjoy yourselves, this may be the last school dance you will ever go to. In a few days you will all part company and may never spend any time with one another again, unless of course you go to university together or get a job at the same firm. Come to your senses, then organise yourselves to come into my office to get your tickets."

We all looked at each other. I felt such a fool as I had only come into the sixth form at the end of the conversation, so I shouldn't have made any comment.

"Let's be goody-goodies and line up and get the tickets. Who is going to be first in the queue?" said James, who never behaved himself.

Mary Anne, who always tried to be in charge, shouted, "The girls!"

The girls walked ahead while the boys stood back looking at the shape of their legs plus their boobs, James directed them from the sidelines.

"Left right, left right, that's right girls stand up straight, heads back, tits out, in you all go."

"Shut up!" shouted Mary Anne. "We will all walk in the opposite direction if you don't shut up, James, none of us care whether we go to this stupid dance or not, so shut up or there won't be any girls at the dance. That'll teach you all a lesson, it will be one person's fault, James Wilkinson. You will have a lot to answer for!"

It only took a few minutes for the girls to buy their tickets, then it was the boys' turn to line up, so, one at a time, we went into the office. I was last in the queue. Mr Thomas looked as if he was ready to fire questions at me after I had exchanged my money for the dance ticket.

"Celia did come to see me the other afternoon, I hope after our little chat she won't continue to gossip about you and Sam. She did say she was sorry, if that's any consolation. Anyway, Knight, how are you? I've noticed that Sam is not at school."

"Sam is still in hospital, I doubt if she will be coming to school again as she is getting quite large. In fact, some people have asked her if she is having twins, thank goodness the answer to that is no. I finish school next Friday, then I'm going to look for a job. Hopefully, then I can get a flat for Sam and myself."

"Well, good luck to you both."

I left the office and went and had a quick coffee before catching the bus back to Blackheath and home. Once at home I phoned the hospital to see if Sam had calmed down and also to see if she would like me to visit. The answer to both was yes, so I organised myself and went on my way to the hospital. On arrival I found Sam sat as usual on the bed, chatting to her neighbour.

"Pleased to see you, Pete, sorry about my behaviour yesterday." I gave her a kiss on the forehead, then went on to talk to her about our future together.

"Mum and Dad came in this morning to have a chat about where I'm going to live before having our baby. They have agreed with me living in Blackheath with Mary and Derek."

"You are telling me that your parents have agreed with you living with strangers?"

"Pete, they are not strangers to me. Mary has told me all about where she lives and about her husband and children."

"Yes, I have told her everything she needs to know. Sam will have a small bedroom of her own on the top floor of our house, you see we have two small rooms in the roof space and one will be hers. The other is where my eldest son sleeps."

"Don't I as the father of this baby have any say in where you live?"

"No, Pete, you must remember that I can't live with you at your place, so if I live with Mary you will be able to visit me whenever you want. If I go back to live with Mum and Dad, I wouldn't be able to see you at my place, we would have to stand and meet out in the street."

"I couldn't cope with that. I agree that it would be better living with Mary than living at the Elephant and Castle with your parents. Sam, can we go out on to the balcony and have a chat in private?"

"Come on, then."

We wandered down the ward onto the balcony where we managed to find two chairs in the far corner.

"Now, Sam, I am worried. I have only met Mary once for a few minutes and I don't know her husband at all. Do you know what he does for a living?"

"Yeah I do, he's a road sweeper. Mary says he collects the dustbins two days a week and the other three days he sweeps the pavements outside Blackheath station."

"What does she do?"

"Nothing."

"How on earth are they going to keep you?"

"Don't know."

"Before you agree to go and live with them I think you should find out how they can afford to feed and water you. Also, you need to ask if they are expecting you to pay for your keep?"

"Pete, I will ask her as soon as we go back into the ward."

"I know you should ask because if you don't you may get yourself in a terrible pickle. Find out what type of place they live in. It sounds to me as if it is a three-storey house rented from the council. If Mary doesn't go to work it must be the council. I know I mustn't forget that you come from a council flat. The thing is you and I come from different environments. You come from a working-class home and live in a tower block and I come from lower middle-class family and live in a terrace house, the difference is quite considerable. I'm very sorry that you can't come and live at our place but Mum and Dad can't afford to keep you as well as Anne and me. They both have to go to work to keep the roof over their heads, they own the house or at least they will own it once they've finished paying the mortgage off. At the end of the day there is not much money left over; some days, Sam, we only eat small portions due to bills that have to be paid."

"Let's go back to my bed; please stay with me while I ask Mary all these questions."

"Yeah, I will stay with you. Mum and Dad are very worried about both of us even though they can't afford to help us out. The questions I have asked you about Mary and Derek came from Mum and Dad. I think they are quite sensible things to think about and ask. Anyway, let's go back to your bed."

Sam looked quite worried about having to ask the questions, in fact she looked as if her blood pressure was going to go up again.

"Sam I think you should have a lie-down and I will ask Mary the questions for you."

"Thanks." Once back in the ward we could see Mary at a distance sat by her bed, she looked as if she was in a dream world.

"Is everything okay, Pete? You don't look too good, Sam – has he upset you again?"

"No, I have not upset Sam, she is going to get into bed and have a rest."

"Sam you don't look too good."

"I'm okay. Pete has some questions for you."

"What questions are they then, boy?"

"Once Sam is settled in her bed I need to have a chat with you. I need you to answer my questions truthfully."

"Course I will answer truthfully, fire away, I never make things up."

"How are you going to afford to feed and water Sam, I understand that you don't go to work?"

"No I don't as such, sometimes I go to the pub and work behind the bar for five shillings an hour."

"Which pub is that?"

"The Queen's Head, it is down the road from the Kings Head."

"Do you work there every night or just once in a blue moon?"

"It just depends. If the regular bar maid doesn't turn up they ring me to go in for a couple of hours."

"Well, tell me how you think you can feed Sam as I promise you that her mum and dad won't give you any money for food."

"They told me they would."

"That's a laugh! I can tell you they may not, as they like to spend all their spare money down the pub or on fags, isn't that right, Sam?"

"Yeah."

"Are you going to wash Sam's clothes? She is not used to washing them, her mother normally washes everything including Sam's bits in the kitchen sink. If you aren't going to do the washing for her, it is going to be difficult for Sam as she hasn't any money to go to the launderette."

"Well that is where I do my washing – in the kitchen sink. I hadn't thought about having to wash Sam's clothes. I can see there's more to her coming to live at our place than I thought there was."

"Are you changing your mind, Mary?"

"Yeah, I am having second thoughts about this. I better have another chat with Derek, he's coming in a bit later." We changed the subject to my exams, then the staff nurse came through the swing door.

"What is the matter, Sam? Back in bed again, you ought to try and stay up in the chair, you look a bit flushed."

"I'm not feeling too good."

"Have you upset Sam again, Pete?"

"Not intentionally, we have been talking about how Mary and her husband can afford to keep Sam."

"We have all been wondering that. The thing is, Mary, your husband is a dustman and he doesn't earn much money."

"We make do, we don't starve. We always have food on the table, how dare you all start saying we can't afford to keep Sam."

"The first thing she needs is a good diet, Sam being pregnant and you feeding her pie and chips is no good, it isn't even good enough for you. Sam needs daily fruit and vegetables. I doubt very much that you have that on a daily basis."

"You are right there, staff nurse, we have that about once a month or when we all get bunged up and can't go to the lav."

"Well, there you go. I think you should think hard before agreeing to take Sam in, it is a shame your parents can't have Sam living with you Pete. The thing is, she would only need to be with you for a few weeks as she will be going to a mother and baby home, so before you know it she would be moving out again,"

"Have you agreed to go to one of these homes?"

"Yeah, the social worker had a chat with me and I have agreed to go to one. I'm not sure which."

"Sam, you haven't told me this has been arranged."

"I didn't think I needed to tell you. Social came in to see me the other afternoon and we had a long chat. I'm thinking about going to Aylesbury at the beginning of October if not before."

"Sam, you mean you have arranged this without me knowing anything about it?"

"'Fraid so."

"I'm going to go home now and have a chat with Mum and Dad, and see whether they will change their minds. Sam, please don't arrange things without me being around, you know very well I'm standing by you. Once I have taken my exams I am going to get a job and then get a flat for the pair of us with our baby. Do you realise I leave school the end of next week?"

"Sam, I hope you are listening to Pete," said the staff nurse as she went on her way.

"Pete, I am sorry, I didn't know when you finished school, I just thought it was at the end of term."

"Well now you know. Before I go, Mary, can I ask you to mind your own business as it's obvious to me that you can't possibly have Sam living with you?"

With that, Mary got up out of her chair and leaned over to me.

"I was only trying to help. I'm going out for a fag, perhaps when I return you will have gone home and Sam and I can have some peace."

She went down the ward towards the balcony. On the way I saw her stop to have a chat with another patient.

"Who's Mary talking to Sam?"

"Oh, that's someone she knows, apparently she lives near her. They went to school together, Mary told me that she has known her since she was in junior school in Blackheath,"

"I hope she doesn't gossip to that woman about us."

"She told me that she had a chat to her about my pregnancy and high blood pressure. I think that is all she has talked about."

"Keep your fingers crossed and try and keep smiling you have a lovely smile. I'm going to go on my way and I will have a chat with my parents again. I doubt if they will let you come to live with us until after my exams, that is if they even agree. My last exam is next Wednesday, and it's Wednesday today so there is a week to go. Perhaps the ward sister will let you stay here until next Wednesday evening. Remember, I do love you Sam. I'm going to walk home from here as I have a lot to think about before chatting to Mum and Dad."

"It will take you ages to walk home."

"That's okay, it's a lovely evening. I will see you tomorrow at the same time as today." I kissed Sam goodbye. It took longer than I thought to walk home, by the time I got to our street my feet were aching like they had never ached before. I unlocked the front door only to find the back door wide open as Mum and Dad were in the back garden, cutting the grass.

"We thought you would have been home earlier than this so you could help us with this lawn and the watering," said Mum looking a bit fed up and exhausted from the heat.

"I walked home from the hospital as I had a lot to think about, perhaps when you have finished the lawn we can have a serious talk."

"Not again, Pete, we have told you before that we have had enough, we can't take any more. I hope you're not going to upset your mother, she said earlier today that she felt a lot better now that somewhere has been arranged for Sam to live."

"Well, that is what I want to talk to you both about, Sam can't possibly live with this woman as she doesn't go to work and her husband is a dustman and a road sweeper; they can't afford to keep Sam, they haven't any money."

"Are you telling us that this girlfriend of yours was arranging to stay with people who sweep the road? This gets worse by the minute, Pete!"

"I know it does."

"We really expected you to be going out with someone with brains and from a decent family. Look what's happened, you've finished up getting Sam pregnant and she comes from a tower block down from the Elephant and Castle. We both realise that she can't help where she comes from, so we are trying our hardest to come to terms with the situation."

"I think you should try a bit harder and think about Sam coming to live here."

"Well, we have told you that she can't. You have got to get good grades, if that is possible with all this upset. Anyway, we can't talk about it out here, the neighbours may be listening in, you never know who they may talk to."

"Let's go inside, as I have to talk to you now."

Both Mum and Dad looked annoyed. "We've got to finish the watering."

"Oh well, I will carry on talking here. I can't try much harder for my exams, I study every night, anyway it's all over after next week. Then I will be staying home, all day and every day looking through newspapers for a job and also a flat, that's if I can get enough money together to put a deposit down. Then I won't be under your feet. You will only have Anne to worry about, but you do realise that she's not as innocent as she tries to make out, don't you? You two ought to listen outside her door when she has her friend around, you would be in for a shock."

"Shut up, Pete, don't add more disruption to our lives. We will both be lying in bed worrying what she's been up to. You are determined to upset us both!"

"I won't say another word about Anne."

"No don't, keep your mouth shut, keep it zipped."

"That is a bit harsh coming from you, Dad."

"It may be, there's plenty more where that has just come from, if you don't start behaving yourself. Go indoors, before I lose my temper completely."

I left them to it and I went inside, banging the kitchen door behind me. I could smell my supper in the oven, but, as I was so fed up, I went straight up to my room without either looking at or eating my supper. I was hungry but I felt I didn't deserve any. I lay on my bed, daydreaming, when suddenly, out of the blue, my door opened and Dad was stood there, looking as if he was going to kill me.

"Pete, you are determined to upset your mother and I. Your mother has left your supper in the oven – surely you could smell it? We have come in from the garden only to find you haven't taken your supper out and it's now burnt to a cinder."

"Sorry."

"If we hadn't come in when we did the oven would have been ruined. I am now going to go downstairs and try and clean the shelves with wire wool and see what damage there is."

"I will come down and try and help."

"Don't you bother, your mother is so upset, and now there isn't any food for you. It's best you stay put, stay up here, keep out the way."

"I'm starving, you both must remember that I have only had my packed lunch since breakfast. If there isn't any food for me, it will mean that I will not have eaten for about twenty hours by breakfast tomorrow."

"It's not our fault, it was in the oven waiting for you. I think you should have gone to the hospital after having supper, at least you wouldn't have been hungry when you returned with the bad news."

At that moment, the phone rang.

"I will go down and answer that," said Dad, rushing down the stairs to the hall. It was as if the call was from a secret admirer – mind you, I can't imagine anyone fancying dear old Dad except Mum.

"Hello, is that Mr Knight?"

"Yes it is, who am I speaking to?"

"It's Mr Smithson, Sam's dad. I want to have a chat to you or your wife about Sam."

"What about her?"

"You know she's in hospital. We want to know if you are going to put her up at your place once she comes out, as we can't have her back here."

"Why can't you? She's your daughter and she is your responsibility. Mr Smithson, you sound as if you have had a few drinks – have you been down the pub again and had one too many?"

"That's none of your bloody business whether I have or not. Back to Sam; we can't have her here, we don't want her back. If you can't put her up she will be out on the streets. We are disgusted with that boy of yours getting Sam pregnant in the schools lavs."

"Mr Smithson, you are talking about your daughter, you needn't think we are very happy about the situation either, it has made my wife and I ill. I'm going to ask you again, have you been drinking? Has it taken you dutch courage to phone? Anyway, about Sam, we haven't room to have her here and also we can't afford to feed another mouth. One thing is for sure we haven't taken to the bottle, like you seem to have."

"Well how do you think we can afford to feed her?" he replied, ignoring the statement about the drink.

"Well, she is your daughter, not mine, and you have managed to bring her up and look after her until now so we think you should continue to look after her. You will have to give up the drink and the fags if you find it hard without much money."

"I can fucking well tell you, I am not giving up the drink or anything else to look after Sam. My old woman and I have made our bloody minds up."

"Have you had a chat with Sam and explained that you won't have her living with you?"

"Not yet."

"Well it's about time you did. If I were you, I would go into the hospital and have a chat with Sam along with her social worker."

"A social worker? Who the bloody hell is he or she when they are at home?"

"They help to sort out problems for people like you."

"We don't need to be sorted out, we bloody well know exactly what we want."

"Well, Sam can't live here, we know that Sam would be better living with you and her mum until she goes to the mother and baby home as she is used to living at the flat with you two. You do realise that Pete is going to find a flat to live in with Sam once the baby is born? He finishes at school next Friday, then he is going to get a job."

"Good luck to him finding a job with enough money to keep Sam, baby and himself. We won't be helping out with anything, the missus and I have decided we don't want anything to do with this fucking baby." With that, the phone went dead, as if he had tripped over the phone wire and dropped the receiver.

"Oh well, that's that, Pete; he put the phone down on me. He is not a happy man, in fact he is extremely unhappy. He seems to think we should take responsibility for Sam."

"That's him, that's about right."

"He sounded as if he was drunk out of his mind. If I could smell the alcohol down the phone, I would have passed out. I wonder what he drinks? Not that I'm interested, just curious…"

"Sam told me once that it was chasers."

"Whatever are they?"

"Beer followed by a whisky."

"I've never had a whisky in my life. I do remember a boy in my class at school many, many years ago drinking whisky, apparently he drank it straight down in one go and nearly passed out,"

"I thought you sipped it? Dad, where did he get it from? It's difficult to buy drink from off licenses these days if you are under age?"

"He told me that he got it out of the sideboard at his home, when his mum and dad were out. He only managed to pinch a couple of tots as his dad noticed the whisky was going down in the bottle – his father used a biro to put a line on the bottle so he could see if any more had been taken. The boy got into quite a bit of trouble over it. In those days, dads gave sons the belt or the slipper if they did anything bad, I have a feeling that this boy got the belt."

"You're joking, Dad."

"No, I'm not. If you had got Sam pregnant in those days, you would have been in real trouble. You both would have been out on your necks living on the streets or in a barn far away from here, think yourself lucky boy."

"I do think I'm lucky, it doesn't make things any easier. What do you think Mr Smithson is going to do now?"

"I don't know. As I've said before, I don't really care. Your mother and I care about you and Sam but that does not mean we will take Sam in. Her dad can ring every night, but he won't make us change our minds."

"When I go into see Sam tomorrow I will mention to her about her dad phoning here and how he tried to persuade you and mum to allow her to live here. What she will say about it, I don't know, I do know for sure that it will upset her."

"Well don't tell her. If you don't tell her she can't get upset, unless of course her parents visit her and tell her what they have been up to."

"I don't like to keep things from her. On this occasion I'm going to agree with you dad and I'm not going to tell her."

"I think that is the best way to go son, keep quiet. If she eventually finds out about the phone calls admit you knew about them and make up an excuse for why you didn't tell her."

"I will have to keep a reason at the back of my mind, I will have a think."

"That is the best way. Now, let's forget about it Pete; she may never find out about the call. I'm going into the kitchen to try and clean the oven."

Chapter 15

As my Biology A-level was not until Monday I stayed in bed until ten o'clock on Friday, dreaming about my life and worrying about how Sam and I were going to manage. Once up and dressed, I had a look through Thursday night's *Evening Standard* at the job vacancies and to see if there were any cheap flats available to rent. Dad had left the paper on the side for me with a note explaining how he had looked all the way through the ads and had put a cross next to the jobs that he thought may be of interest to me. He had also looked through the flats but

179

had only found a couple of bedsitters in Willesden Green and Cricklewood that he thought were suitable. They seemed expensive to me, four pounds ten shillings a week but this included the rates, which was something. They wanted a deposit of a month's rent, which would be refundable when we left. All of this made me realise that I had to get a decent job and this was more important than a flat in the first instance, as most properly I could stay living here with Mum and Dad, while I saved up the deposit. I spent a couple of hours reading through the job adverts in between drinking mugs of coffee, not one of the jobs seemed interesting enough for me to phone up to get details.

After I had eaten a sandwich for lunch, I spent the afternoon at the hospital. Luckily for me, Sam seemed in a good mood. I told her what I had been doing and then out of the blue her face changed from smiling to sober. "Mum and Dad came in this morning, they aren't very happy with you lot."

"What do you mean by that?"

"Dad told me he phoned your house and asked your dad if you lot are going to put me up. They are both very cross and don't see why they should take me back to live with them."

"You give me a good reason why my Mum and Dad should take you in. To start with we haven't even got a bed for you to sleep on, let alone a bedroom. Anyway, Sam, how are you going to go for your monthly check-up at the doctor's from my home? Soon you will have to go to the doctor's every week."

"I don't know, I hadn't thought about going to the surgery."

"It is about time you did. I'm beginning to think that you let me get you pregnant so you could leave home and live with me in luxury with my parents. I'm sorry, Sam, but this is not going to happen. You will have to go back to the flat until you go to the mother and baby home."

"I can't go back there, they don't want me."

"Well for the next week I'm too busy with exams to worry about where you are going to live. The thing is, Sam, you have your own room at the flat, that is where you should be."

"The doctor doesn't want me to go back to it."

"That is just too bad. The doctor will have to think of somewhere for you to live, if he doesn't want you going back to the flat. I don't know whether the doctor told you that you may be able to go to the mother and baby home early. Mum knows a girl that went to Luton and stayed about two months before the baby was born. She didn't like it much, but that is life, as Mum said."

"You have upset me with your mum this and your mum that, it's a pity you came in this afternoon."

"If that is how you feel you can sort it out yourself, it's not as if you have not got parents. I'm going." I just got up off Sam's bed and made my way to the ward door and out into the sunshine.

It was about five o'clock by the time I got home and Mum was making supper. "John from school phoned just as I got in, he was wondering whether you were going to meet up with him and

the others before going to the disco."

"Has he left his phone number?"

"No, I forgot to ask for it."

"Well how do you expect me to get in touch with him?"

"I thought you would have his number."

"Well, Mum, I haven't."

"Pete, stop being so obnoxious."

"That is a big word for you, Mum."

"Behave yourself, Pete, I will give you a clip around the ear in a moment to bring you to your senses. Something is definitely the matter with you! Can you tell me what it is?"

"If you really need to know, it is Sam; her parents have been to see her and they won't have her back living with them."

"Both Dad and I have told you about a hundred times before that we can't put her up; we have not got enough money to keep her along with Anne and you."

"I do know that and I also know how much it would cost to feed an extra mouth."

"Well then drop the subject."

With that the phone rang.

"I expect that's for you, Pete."

181

"Yeah, I will answer it."

It was John. "Pete, are we going to meet up before the disco?" "Okay, where?"

"What about the coffee bar where we met the other Saturday?"

"I don't know whether I dare go in there, the man behind the counter banned us because we didn't buy any coffee and also for handing around the johnnies."

"Oh yeah, I remember that. I did look in there the other day, he wasn't anywhere to be seen, perhaps he's left. Anyway, to play it safe, we better go elsewhere."

"What about that pub by the station? We are all over sixteen, so we can go in and have a coke or a shandy."

"That sounds okay to me, what's it called?"

"It is either The King's Head or the Queen's Head. Let's meet at the King's Head; if we don't fancy the place when we get there, we can always leave and go to the Queen's Head. Does that sound okay, John?"

"Yeah that sounds great. Half seven in the King's Head, bye."

Bang went the phone at the other end. I turned around only to find Mum as usual stood behind me listening in to my conversation once again, instead of leaving me in the hall to get on with my phone call.

"Pete, I am not deaf and I also know what johnnies are."

"So?"

"What have you been up too, being banned from a coffee bar? Whatever next am I going to hear."

"You never know what you'll hear, especially if you listen into my calls. Whatever it is it will be quite exciting as you and Dad live a very boring life compared to what I hope to have with Sam."

"Peter, I am completely fed up with you! The quicker you, one, get your exams, two, find a job, after that a flat, the better," said Mum holding up three fingers and looking as if the end of her world had come once again.

"I will remember what you have just said and get a move on with all three things. I am going up to my room and get ready for the night's events."

"What about your supper?"

"I must get used to not eating very much as I won't have enough money when I move out to eat properly, so I don't need your supper tonight."

"Don't be so damn stupid Peter, you can't go out to a disco on an empty stomach."

"You just watch me."

I turned and ran up the stairs, leaving Mum behind wondering what was going to happen next. Once I was ready to go to the disco I went downstairs and into the sitting room to say goodbye.

"I doubt if you two will be up when I get back, so I will say bye for now and see you in the morning."

"You go carefully. Make sure you catch the bus home and, if it is the last one, make sure you don't miss it; we can't afford to pay for a taxi. Are you listening to me, Pete?" said Dad, getting more and more annoyed.

"Of course I'm listening to you, I will see you in the morning." With that, I hurried on my way to the King's Head where I found John and Dave sitting alone in the corner of the bar, waiting for me.

"At last you've arrived, we have been waiting to get our first drink in. There are no customers; also, Pete, the bar maid is very young."

"So?"

"Dave and I were wondering if we could persuade her to sell us alcohol, what do you think?"

"We can always ask her?"

"Pete, you go up and ask."

"No I won't. One of you will have to, I always seem to pull the short straw. Dave, you go up; you might find that she fancies you, then she will definitely sell you alcohol."

"She doesn't seem to be around. I will have to ring the bell. You two decide what you want to drink while I go and ring."

Dave rang the bell while we sorted out what we wanted long before the barmaid arrived from upstairs. It was as if she had been up to no good, she looked very flushed.

"What can I do for you three?"

"Can we have two pints of Whitbread and one pint of brown split?"

"Are you three old enough to drink alcohol?"

"Of course we are, darling, we are at least as old as you and you sell it so we must be old enough to drink it."

She looked at the three of us very strangely, but went ahead and poured us our drinks. Dave paid up and came back to the table. I was the stupid one that asked for the brown split. I enjoyed it so much that I decided to try and get another pint, and I succeeded, before a very large man came down the stairs grinning at the barmaid. He didn't have much to say except 'hi' and 'how quiet it is tonight'. We finished our drinks. John and Dave had had a pint and half each to my two pints.

"I fancy another," said John.

"I wouldn't mind another," said Dave.

"You can go up this time, Pete, I'm sure you must have a taste for brown splits by now. The barmaid may sell you another pint." "I haven't the money to buy you two a drink."

"What, you allowed us to buy you a couple knowing that you couldn't buy us one back? You owe us one each!"

"Well, I will have to buy you one another night."

"Are we coming out again, Pete?" said John rubbing his hands with glee.

"Maybe, the thing is I've taken a liking to this brown split," I said, hiccupping in between chatting.

"I'll pay up for Dave and myself, you will have to pay for your own Pete," said John, sounding annoyed.

"I will pay for my own, give me the money for your two."

John paid up and I asked the bar maid for the drinks while the large man watched us all with suspicion. However, he didn't make any comment. Once I was halfway through my third pint my world started to go around. I thought the large man, who was now sat at the bar on a stool, had a familiar face. He looked similar to the maintenance man at the hospital; in fact, he could have been taken for his twin brother. Thinking about it, Jackie had said that he had a brother, but I never dreamt that we would bump into him in a pub in Blackheath.

"Pete, that bloke looks like the maintenance man at the hospital."

"I was thinking that myself, Dave. Jack told me he had a brother."

"You over there, have you got a brother?" shouted John.

"Yeah, I also have a name. It's Bob, not 'You over there'."

"I just asked you if you have got a brother," said John.

"Yes, I've just said I have. What is it to you three whether I have or I haven't?"

"We think we have seen him at the hospital. The man we saw up there could be your twin."

"Guess what, boys? He works up there in the maintenance department; if you have been up to the hospital, you may have seen him, as he often wastes his time in reception."

"Are you the boss of this joint or a customer?"

"Why?"

"We were just wondering."

"My wife is the boss here, I just come down and drink the profits."

"Now we know."

"If you think Annie will sell you alcohol - she won't, she is not that daft. If she dared to, she would be sacked."

He must have been half asleep when we bought our drinks, because he didn't say a word to Annie.

"We better go, boys, before his wife arrives," I said, trying to stand up without appearing to be tiddly.

"What have you had in those glasses?"

I stood holding on to the table while John and Dave remained sitting on the bench. We looked at one another as if we had done something terribly wrong.

"You may as well tell me what you have been drinking."

"Why should we? You are not the boss, so it's not any of your business," I said, laughing and hiccupping at the same time.

"Well, boys, it is obvious to me that you all have been drinking alcohol, but you who is stood up must have had the most. Perhaps you had some before you left home; I think if you let go of that table, you will fall over."

"No I won't."

"Let go then and walk across the room without help."

I let go and immediately sat down on the stone floor.

"I thought as much. You boys should not be in here. You two pick your mate up and get out."

Dave and John looked very sheepish, all I could do was laugh. With difficulty they managed to pick me up and drag me out of the bar as my legs wouldn't hold me up. Once outside in the car park they sat me down on the floor against the fence to try and get me to come to my senses. Dave and John just stood looking down at me wondering what was going to happen next.

"I don't feel too great."

"Pete, did you have any supper before you came out?"

"No."

"Why ever not?"

"I was in too much of a hurry, I haven't had a proper meal for two days."

"Pete, whatever is the matter with you? Not eating! I'm sure your mum feeds you! Anyway, how can we go to the school disco with you in this state?"

With that I spewed up all over John's shoes.

"What the hell are you doing spewing up all over my new shoes? If you don't come to your senses in a minute we'll leave you here to sort yourself out."

Suddenly the door that we had come out of opened and there stood Bob's wife with her hands on her hips as if she meant business.

"You three have five minutes to get off my premises, if you don't go the police will be called."

"We will go as soon as I can get up."

"I will help you up by throwing a bucket of cold water over you if you don't get a move on. I'm going to prepare myself by getting the bucket from the shed, I hope the three of you will have gone before I get back. First I need to get a key to unlock the shed so you have a few extra minutes to be on your way."

John and Dave managed to hold me up and attempted to walk me across the car park to the council path and sit me on a low wall, where I immediately fell backwards and landed on my back in the pub garden. I remained there while my mates decided what to do with me.

"I am sorry, Pete, but we will have to leave you here."

"What, you can't leave me here!"

"Have you any other suggestions about what we should do with you?"

"I know, we will try and get you back up and sitting on the wall again, then we will go and phone for a taxi to take you home," said John looking very annoyed. "Up you get, Pete, hold on to my left shoulder and Dave's right."

"Be careful you two, my head is going around and around. Hang on a moment, I can't move my right arm so I can't hold on to Dave's shoulder."

"You will have to, you are so heavy we can't take all your weight. If you were a girl, I would call you ten-tonne Tessy. One, two, three – up you get, Pete!" shouted John as they managed with great difficulty to pull me back up and sit me on the wall.

"What a state you're in Pete, your shirt is covered in dirt all the way down the back! The only place you can go is home."

"Will you two come home with me? I can't face Mum and Dad on my own."

"We'll go and phone for a taxi and have a think about that while you sit here."

"Don't get a taxi; I can't afford that and I know Mum and Dad won't pay for one."

"What do you think we should do, carry you home?"

"If you come with me I'll try and walk."

"Let's all of us sit on the wall and have a think and see if you can sober up a bit," said Dave, laughing at me. We must have sat there for a good twenty minutes contemplating about my predicament.

"Pete, try and stand up and walk a few steps."

I put my left hand down on the wall to steady myself and stood bolt upright. "Three cheers, I'm stood up."

"Walk a few steps."

"Okay, here goes." I put my right foot forward and fell head first on to the concrete. Dave and John just sat and laughed, but they were kind enough to get me back on my feet. The only thing was that they would not let me sit down on the wall again as they didn't feel they could get me up again if I fell backwards into the garden.

"You are in a bad way, Pete! Next time, remember to eat your supper before coming out."

"Your home is not that far from here. If you try to be sensible we may be able to walk you to your front door, but I'm not staying to see your parents. What do you think, Dave?"

"I agree with you, John, but I am definitely not staying to face your mum and dad, Pete."

"I don't know what my parents will say. I know they won't be very happy, I wish you could stay and wait for them to open the door."

"You must be joking if you think we are going to meet them with you in this state! Anyway, the first thing we need to do is get you to walk a few steps. Come on, Pete."

I was standing in between John and Dave.

"Put your right arm around my left shoulder."

"I told you two just now that I have hurt my right arm; I can't move it, so I can't hold on to your shoulder, John."

"Well, I will have to put my arm around your waist. Now put your left arm around Dave's right shoulder – surely you can do that?"

"Yeah."

I managed to do as John asked, but my right arm was aching so much that I could hardly lift it up.

"This right arm of mine is aching like mad, I'm wondering if I have broken it."

"What! You must be joking. Pete, can you move your fingers?"

I tried, but they wouldn't move.

"It seems you may have broken something. Anyway, Pete, try and forget about that – we must get you home," said Dave.

With difficulty, the three of us started to walk along the path. We were swaying from side to side; at one point we walked into the road and a car just missed us. It seemed to take an hour to get to the end of my road, let alone to my front door.

"You two, do you know the time?"

"Let's see. it's nearly ten o'clock."

"What, Mum and Dad will be going up to bed in a minute."

"What is that to do with anything, Pete?"

"Just that they will still be up and will wonder what is happening. When we knock on the door, they may not even answer."

"A big boy like you must have a key."

"Yeah, it should be in my trouser pocket. Yeah, it's definitely in my right pocket. I can't get it out, my hand and arm are so sore."

"I will get it out, then we can let you in and run before your mum or dad catch us."

"I'm going to be sick again," and at that I spewed up all over the front door.

"What are we going to do now, Pete? If we unlock the door all the vomit will go inside the house. Tell me, Pete, before we unlock the door, does it open into the hallway or straight into a lounge?"

"Oh, we do have a hallway, we are posh enough to have that." "That is good, now is their lino on the floor or carpet?"

"Why all these stupid questions? Just open up the bloody door and let me go in!"

At that moment, the door opened from inside and there was Dad standing in the door way in his pyjamas; behind him stood Mum in her dressing gown. "What the bloody hell is going on here?" shouted Dad, looking in complete shock.

I put my foot upon the doorstep to walk into the hallway.

"Pete, what the hell do you think you are doing trying to walk into the hall after vomiting down the door? Look at the mess you have made on the floor! Just don't walk in here – stay put!" "Sorry, Dad and Mum," I said, still hiccupping well. "Who are you two?"

"We are school mates – I'm Dave and this is John."

"Right, how did you manage to get Pete in this state?"

"We didn't get him in this state; he bought his own drink after not having any supper."

"That is right, Dad," I said, falling backwards down the two steps towards the public path. Dave just managed to save me from landing on the path by holding on to my right arm, but this of course made me scream out.

"Why the hell are you screaming? You'll wake the neighbours in a minute."

"He has hurt his right arm."

"When we left the pub Pete fell backwards into the pub garden. You see, Mr Knight, we sat Pete on the garden wall, then he fell backwards into the garden. We did manage to get him back up, that was when he hurt his arm,"

"Look at the back of your shirt, Pete, have you seen it?" said Mum, looking embarrassed

"I can't see my back, my head does not swivel round – if it did, I wouldn't miss a thing."

"Stop being so cheeky, Pete."

"Well, it is true, Mum. I would have seen you stood listening into my phone calls if my head swivelled."

"Pete, we have had enough of your nonsense! Just be quiet while I talk to your mates. Now, you two, tell me what Pete has been drinking? In fact, what have you two had? You must have joined in – you can't tell me that you have been drinking Coke and Pete has had alcohol!"

"Pete has been drinking pints of brown split and we have had a couple of pints of Whitbread."

"I've never heard of a brown split."

"Brown split is half of bitter and a bottle of brown ale."

"It sounds awful, it must have tasted terrible. I can't understand how you could get like this drinking something that sounds so awful. Anyway, how many did you have?"

"Oh, three pints. They tasted great. We are going back for more another night, aren't we, boys?"

"Not if we have anything to do with it. Anyway, which one of you is going to help clean up this mess? We are not going to; we will provide the bucket and mop but that is the only contribution we are making to clearing this mess."

"Go and get the bucket and mop, Dad, and I will try and clean up the hall."

"I look forward to watching this. Don't you three move from the door step – I'll only be a few minutes but I have to go out to the shed."

Mum looked so upset that she disappeared upstairs. Dad soon returned with a bucket full of soapy water in one hand and a mop in the other.

"Here you are Pete, one bucket with soapy water and a mop, let us see how you get on."

I took the bucket in my left hand, but of course I could not stand up very well and started to sway.

"Dad, I'm sorry but I can't hold the mop in my right hand, I'm going to fall over again. Someone help me."

"Don't try and be completely stupid, Pete, use your left hand for mopping the floor. You don't need to hold the bucket, just put it down on the floor. Be careful, Pete, don't put it in the way of the door or your mates may trip over it."

"Keep your hair on, Dad."

Both John and Dave stood behind me smirking.

"If you can't clean it up, Pete, you better get help from your mates. I'm sure they'll be capable of mopping.Which one of you is going to help?"

"Give me the mop, Pete, I'll have a go. Get out the way, all of you," said, John looking as annoyed as Dad. He took the mop out of my hand. "Move out the way, let me get to the bucket."

"Pete, I think you and Dave ought to try and come into the back of the hallway before we get in more of a mess and you can't get in."

Luckily for us we could just about get in without slipping and sliding on my vomit of brown split. How Dad expected one of us to clean the glass panel on the door, I don't know, but he had made his mind up that he was not going to help us.

"I'm the supervisor here, don't expect me to help. Every bit of Pete's vomit has to be cleaned up by you three, even the glass on the door has to be washed down. The only thing I'm prepared to do is to change the water in the bucket."

John started to use the mop but it was very difficult as the vomit was extra slimy. Every time John moved the mop along the hall he slid along with it, making the vomit go further into the house. Thank goodness the floor had lino on it with a rug on the top, which Dad had already removed, not wooden floor boards or a fitted carpet like in some hall ways.

It seemed to take John ages to mop up the floor, let alone clean the glass. Dad seemed to get more and more exasperated with the three of us.

"I'm going to go and sit down and try to have a sleep in the front room. Once you have finished one of you come and wake me so I can inspect the floor and the glass."

Dave and I remained at the far end of the hall, holding on to the banisters, but the drink suddenly seemed to be taking its toll on both John and Dave.

"I don't feel too good, the smell of this vomit is terrible – it will make me spew up in a minute! Have you got a lavatory down here, Pete? I think I better go to it. If you have"

"Yeah, it is through the kitchen door, out the back door, then it's the second door on the left"

"One of you take the mop. Hurry up or there will be another mess to clean up."

"While you go out there, I will try and carry on with the mopping, but I don't feel too good, perhaps the beer was off," said Dave, looking very pale.

A few minutes later, John returned looking extremely guilty.

"What has gone wrong, John?"

"Pete, I am sorry but I thought you said first on the left and I opened the door and vomited all over the coal."

"What? They will kill me!"

"If you don't mention it, they won't know anything about it. It's summer, so they may not go in there until the autumn."

"I suppose you may be right, the only trouble is Mum hangs the bag for collecting the runner beans behind the door, so she will be going in. When she opens the door I hope I'm not around. If she doesn't open the door till the autumn I definitely won't be around as I'm looking for a flat in North London for Sam and me."

"Oh, you are still going down that old road."

"Yes I am, I haven't much choice."

"Well you can always disappear off the face of the earth."

"I can't carry on mopping. Pete, do you think your dad will mind if we take a rest? We could sit on the stairs for half an hour or so."

"He won't realise we are not working as he is asleep. When John went to the lav I looked in through the crack in the door."

"Pete, I must go to the lav, second door on the left?"

"Yeah second door, just try and be quiet; we don't want to wake Dad."

By the time Dave got back from the lav, John and I were sat on the bottom step looking at the floor. "I feel a bit better I'm sure that beer was off. Let me get past you two, then I can sit on a step behind you."

"Hang on a mo, Dave. I will move out of the way for you to get past." I attempted to get up but I was still a bit wobbly. "Dave, can you hold on to me? I can't hold on to the banister; it's on the right-hand side. I can't use my right arm, as I keep telling you all, but you don't listen."

"I will try and hold you up." Dave leant over to pull me up.

"Your mouth stinks of vomit, Dave. Can you look the other way so I can't smell it? Hurry up!"

"I'm trying my best, Pete, but I'm not feeling too good and I'm also a bit wobbly. The only difference between you and I is that I haven't hurt my arm. Your mouth stinks of vomit and booze, like mine. In a mo, I may have to go back to the lav."

"Well, go back to the lav before you sit down on the stairs or we will all have to move again. We all know what could happen and I for one don't want vomit down my back."

"Eh, the thought of vomit down my back makes me feel sick," said John, sounding half asleep.

"I'm off." Dave wobbled back through the kitchen to the lav.

"I think it's going to be my turn next, John."

"Go and join Dave, there should be enough room for the two of you."

"I will never make it down there on my own."

"Well, you will have to try to."

I got up with difficulty and managed to hobble over to the far wall, where I steadied myself before trying to walk towards the kitchen and out to the lav. After a lot of starts and stops I arrived at the lav door, only to find that Dave had locked it from the inside.

"Open the door, I need to come in! If you don't open it, I shall spew up out here, then there will be more trouble."

"Hang on a minute while I try to get up off the floor." It seemed ages before the door opened, but it could have only been a few minutes. "Welcome to the lav, one of the poshest lavs I've ever been in," said Dave, directing me in as if he was an attendant at the local lavatory.

"Be quiet you, silly twit, you will wake my dad in a minute."

"So what? He will have to wake up sometime. Now, let's get down to business; have you come to spew or to wee? If you have come to wee, remember to lift the seat; if you are going to spew, leave the seat down – then you can rest your chin on the seat while you are kneeling at the lavatory, spewing."

"Shut up you silly bugger and let me have a think, I'm going to spew up."

"Well, come over to the lavatory, let me help you kneel down."

"Shut up, go and leave me to it or I will lose my cool."

"Dear oh dear, Peter is going to lose his cool."

"Yes I am, just go before I spew up over you."

At that, Dave disappeared, slamming the door behind him and leaving me kneeling on the floor at the side of the lav. The next thing I can remember is Dad standing over me.

"Pete, I've had enough of you and your mates! You haven't finished cleaning the floor and you haven't even started on the door."

"Sorry," I said, looking up from the floor. "Can you help me up?"

"As usual, Pete, you have forgotten the most important word."

"Whatever can that possibly be?"

"Enough of your cheek, the word is 'please'."

"Oh yeah; please, Daddy, can you help me up?"

Dad leant down and shouted in my ear, "Get up now! If you don't, I will completely lose my rag!"

"I can't get up."

"There is no such word as 'can't'. Give me your arm." He got hold of my right arm and pulled extra hard; at least I arrived on my feet, even though I was screaming out in pain.

"Now go and sort your mates out, either get them up on their feet to help you with the cleaning or send them packing. Whichever you decide, get a move on, because I have had enough of the three of you."

"I don't know how I can get back to the hall."

"Pete, the same way as you got here."

"Oh right, that must have been crawling because I couldn't have walked."

"Well, whichever way you got here, get a move on and get back to the hall."

I managed with difficulty to get into the kitchen and, holding on to the sink, I shouted, "You two out there! Forget about
cleaning the floor, just get up and go!"

"Why?"

"Dad is on the warpath. You two must have seen him come out of the front room."

"I was sat here with my head in my hands so I didn't see him," said John.

"He must have passed me as I tried to come back in to the hall. When I think about it, I did bump into a man that said a few words – I thought he was a lodger. It must have been the drink I've had because he didn't look like your dad to me."

"Well, it was and he is not a very happy man, so I suggest you both leave. Go! Now!"

"Still here?" Dad demanded as he reappeared on the scene. "Either go this minute or start to clean up this mess. While you are deciding which it is going to be, who went into the coal hole?" "Why?"

"Pete, your mates must have told you that one of them had vomited all over the coal."

"How do you know they have?"

"Well they left the door ajar after spewing up, I'm not blind and my sense of smell is very good."

"It could have been me."

"Yeah, it could have been you. If it was, you are in trouble big time – you will be staying in all the weekend, Pete. If your mates admit to spewing up over the coal they have to go now and never return, and you will be sorting out the coal hole."

"Mr Knight, it was me, I'm really sorry, I thought Pete said the lav was the first door on the left. That is where I went by mistake. The thing is, I was desperate and I opened the door and spewed up. I'm sorry."

"Sorry is not good enough, the coal is ruined. Over the summer it may dry out but what will happen when we put it in the grate and light it? I don't fancy sitting down in the front room with that in the fireplace, the thought makes me feel sick. When Pete's mum looks in the coal hole and sees the vomit I dread to think what will happen. I suggest you two go – go home, now."

"Dad, how can you send them packing? It's past midnight!"

"What do you suggest then, clever clogs?"

"They could stay the night."

"You must be joking, Pete, they are not staying here longer than a few more minutes. I'm going to ring for a taxi."

"We can't afford that."

"Well you should have thought about the consequences before going to the pub and having an alcoholic drink. You are supposed to be intelligent human beings. I know, instead of me ringing for a taxi just go now and pick up a black cab on the way back to where ever you live, I will open the front door for you both."

"Dad, I didn't think you could be so mean. Surely they can stay over? They can sleep on the floor in my room, there is room for the three of us."

"If I give in, before going to bed the three of you have to clean up the mess, including the coal hole. I don't care if it takes you till the morning, it has to be done."

"Thank you, Mr Knight, we will clean it up."

"I'm going to leave you three to it. If it's not cleaned by the morning, watch out."

With that, Dad went up to bed and left us to it.

"Before we seriously start to clean up, would you both like a coffee? I feel a bit better, thank God."

"You look very pale."

"So do you two. I've just asked if you want a coffee."

"Yes, please," said John.

"What about you, Dave?"

"Yeah, but make it a black one, with no sugar."

We were all standing in the kitchen, when Dad came halfway down the stairs and put his head over the banisters.

"Pete, don't think because I have given into you that you can go out over this weekend. You can't – you are grounded." I just looked stupid and carried on making the coffee. "I hope you heard what I said."

"Yes I did."

"Night then, try and be as quiet as possible."

"Night!" we all called up the stairs.

After drinking the coffee, we got on with the cleaning. We didn't get up to my room until two o'clock and then we had to put together makeshift beds on the floor. These consisted of just blankets and a couple of pillows which I found in the back of the airing cupboard. Eventually the three of us settled down to try and have a sleep when the phone rang. "Can that be anything to do with you two?" "What?" said John.

"Can't you two hear the phone ringing?"

"Yeah, I can hear it but why should it be anything to do with us? I expect it is a wrong number," laughed John.

"I'm not expecting a call in the middle of the night," answered Dave.

John sat up looking very embarrassed but didn't make any attempt to stand up.

"Is it something to do with you, John? You are sat looking as if you may know something about this call. Before I go and answer it, tell me."

"I gave my mum your number so she could get hold of me if she needed to."

"You two will get me hung if this call wakes up my parents."

I crept down the stairs and quietly asked who was on the end of the line and explained that it was too late to ring anyone unless you are ringing the police.

"This is John Wilson's mum."

"So?"

"I'm wondering if you have seen John."

"Why?"

"Well, he has not come home."

"I thought he was a big boy and he could stay out all night."

"He is not that big, have you seen him?"

"Yes I have. He is upstairs in my room; we all got drunk and came back here to sleep it off."

"So you are telling me that John is there and has spent my hard-earned cash on alcohol?"

"Yeah, he is here and, yes, I suppose he has spent your cash on drink. If you gave him money, that is what he's spent it on. He will be on his way as soon as we get up."

"I need to speak to him now, can I have a chat to him?" "I will have to wake him," I said, lying through my teeth.

I went back upstairs. "John it's your mum – she wants to talk to you."

"I'll go and see what the hell she wants."

John soon returned, looking very sheepish.

"Mum got Dad to have a word with me. They are not very happy. They have both been up waiting for me to return from the disco. You see, I was supposed to be home on the last bus. Dave, your mum phoned my parents at midnight as they are also worried."

"What?"

"Pete, it is not just you that is in trouble; we should not have met in the pub, it was a great temptation to ask for a beer. I didn't expect the barmaid to serve us alcohol – I thought she would have refused, then we would have had a Coke or shandy and gone on our way."

"If you really want to know, that is what I thought, but there you go, she did, and what a night we have had! Three naughty boys together."

"You three be quiet – your dad and I have had enough! Just shut up and go to sleep, the three of you." "Sorry, Mum, we will be quiet."

Chapter 16

Saturday morning arrived. "Come on you two, get up. You ought to be on your way before my parents are up and about."

"What's the time?"

"About seven o'clock."

"It's early."

"I don't care about the time, just get up and get going."

"Yes, sir," said Dave, saluting me as if we were in the army.

"Well, hurry up both of you."

"Give us time, we are not in the army. It's Saturday morning and I'm used to having a lie-in. I don't normally get up until at least ten," said John, staying put on the floor,

"There can't be a lie-in here. Just hurry up, both of you."

"Yes, sergeant."

"The two of you just shut up and stop being so annoying, I have a headache."

"What do you think we have, a pain in our dicks? I can assure you we haven't, but we do have a funny pain in our heads."

"Right, here we go! One, two, three, up we get!" shouted Dave.

"Don't make so much noise."

"Any other complaints, sergeant?"

"Just get a move on and stop being so stupid."

"I need to go to the bog before I leave," said John, holding on to his trousers as if he was going to wet himself.

"Well, go, but don't make a noise. After you've been, don't come back in here, as we will be downstairs."

"Yes, boss."

"Why can't you just shut up and get a move on?"

Dave and I went down to the kitchen to wait for John. He took ages.

"Feel better now, it must have been the beer. Don't go in the bog upstairs for a while; it stinks like I've let off a stink bomb."

"I'm going to go in the lav down here then."

"Just hurry up, I can't stand much more of you two. Dad will be down making a cup of tea in a minute."

"Can we have breakfast before you kick us out?"

"No, hurry up, Dave, or John will be out in the street waiting for you."

Dave didn't seem to take so long. "That feels a lot better, but I think the flush in the lav has broken – it won't work. Thank God I was not the last to use it last night."

"Come on, Dave, we have got to go before we end up in more trouble."

"Yeah, get out, you know the way to the bus stop."

"Cheers, sergeant," they both said while saluting me.

I opened the front door and let them both out onto the path. Once out, I shut the door behind them before they could cause any more upset. I immediately went to the downstairs lav to see if Dave was telling the truth about the flush or if he was making it up for a joke. Thank goodness, it was one of his stupid jokes.

Arriving back in the kitchen I found both Dad and Mum standing there, waiting for the kettle to boil.

"What were you doing out there? I thought you were still in bed."

"No, I've been up quite a while, I was just having a look around."

"Where are your mates? Have they gone?"

"Afraid so, I got them to go before you got up."

"Pete, I never had a chance to meet them properly," said Mum, with Dad looking on as if Mum had had a funny turn.

"Marg, after what you said last night about all three of them, I never thought you would have wanted to meet them."

"Sober, I expect they are really nice boys."

"That's right, Mum, they are very nice boys; they are my mates."

"I thought they might have said goodbye to us," said Dad.

"Well, Dad, you know what thought did."

"For one day, just try and behave! Your mum and I are fed up with your sarcasm!"

"Okay, I will try, but it will be difficult."

"It shouldn't be. Anyway, would you like a cup of tea?"

"I would like a black coffee, my head's spinning."

"Well that serves you right. Remember, you are grounded until at least Monday. It is no good thinking you can go and see Sam because you can't."

"Sam will miss me, I'm her only visitor."

"She will have to miss you, as you are grounded so that is that."

"Let me have my coffee, I'm going back to bed."

"Now you are up, you may as well stay up."

"What the hell am I going to do down here for the rest of the day?" I picked up my mug of coffee and went up to my room to bed before Mum or Dad could think of something else to say. I remained in bed until late morning. By the time I arrived downstairs again, Anne was up and about, and Mum must have spilled the beans to her about last night as she was sat in Dad's arm chair, sniggering to herself.

"I've heard all about it."

"About what?"

"Last night."

"What was that, then, clever clogs?"

"About getting drunk and spewing up in the hall, I can smell the drink in the hall now," said Anne, holding on to her nose.

"No, you can't."

"Yes, I can."

"Can you two stop having a shouting match with one another, I can hear you in the kitchen? Just try and stop shouting. Now you are up, you can help your father in the garden, Pete."

"Mum, why did you have to tell Anne what happened here last night? It is none of her business. By the way, it was Anne that started shouting at me."

"Just shut up, Pete, and go help your dad."

"I will think about it,"

"Don't think for too long or you will be grounded for longer." "I only know about what happened last night, Pete, because I was woken by all the noise you were making down here. When Mum came up to bed I asked her what was going on. It's as simple as that; Mum told me."

"That is exactly right, now you know. Pete, please be quiet and go out into the garden."

"No, I'm going back upstairs."

"Good, best place for you," said Anne.

I picked up the books that I intended reading and went back to my room. Mum wouldn't let it rest, she followed me up the stairs. "You needn't think you are too big to be told off because you're not. Get yourself back down those stairs and into the garden; your father is waiting for you."

"Give me a good reason for why I should help in the garden?"

"Pete, we need your help, your father would like you to dig up the potatoes and put them on a sack to dry."

"I will go down when I get around to it. I'm going to sit here until I feel fit enough to help."

"Whatever do you mean? You're not ill."

"My head is spinning, it's going round and around. I'm in an awful state."

"So will I be if you don't get back down those stairs and help your father."

"I've just told you I'll go down as soon as I feel better."

"Pete, in a minute I will have to go and lie down; my blood pressure will go up again with all this upheaval."

"I thought you were on tablets to keep it down."

"Yes I am, but I can still feel ill. I'm going to go and lie on the bed for a while."

"Go and do that, it won't make me go down and help Dad any quicker."

"Pete, you are the end."

With that, Mum walked straight out of my room and in to her bed room. An hour or so later, my door was knocked.

"Yes, do come in; I won't bite."

It was Dad, red with rage. "I've been waiting for you to come out into the garden to help dig the potatoes!"

"So? I told Mum I can't come out until I feel better. That might be tomorrow or late this afternoon; my head is spinning."

"Pete, that won't do! The potatoes need to be dug up before it rains."

"Well, dig them up yourself; it won't kill you to dig."

"Any more of your cheek and you'll be leaving home as soon as your last exam is over on Wednesday. I can assure you that I won't care where you go and live, I've had enough and so has your mother."

"I'll come down. Give me a few minutes, I need to go to the lav."

"Hurry up, you haven't even attempted to get off your bed."

"Okay, I'm coming."

"This is your last chance. If you don't come down and help me, you will be out on your neck, next Wednesday evening." With that, Dad went back down the stairs and out into the garden. I sat and watched him for a while from my window, then hurriedly went to the lav and down over the stairs to attempt to help.

"Thank goodness you have arrived. How you think a poor old thing like me can dig up all these spuds without any help, I don't know."

"Well, I'm here now. What do you want me to do?"

"I've told you! Dig up the bloody spuds!" Dad shouted at me.

"You want me to dig up all these spuds with my head spinning?"

"Yes I do, get a move on."

"This is hard work, it's like slave labour."

"That's why I need your help, I can't dig them up on my own."

"Where do you want me to start?"

"Over there, by the gooseberry bushes."

"I will get scratched to death."

"Well, that is what I need you to do; here is the fork."

"Where shall I put them?"

"Pete, are you so thick, or are you just trying to be awkward? They have to be put on that sack which is laying on the ground."

"Oh, I wondered what the sack was for."

"Now you know. Get a move on, we have to keep our fingers crossed and hope that it doesn't rain."

"Where are you going to dig, Dad?"

"I'm not, I'm going to see how your mother is, then I will bring you a mug of tea - that's if you want one."

"Yes, please, but I'd prefer coffee."

"I'll be back in a while. When you have finished digging the spuds I've another job for you. I'm able to keep you busy all weekend." Dad went on his way laughing to himself, as if everything was funny, especially me having to dig up the potatoes with a sore head. Eventually he returned. "You're a bit slow."

"This is hard work, I'm not used to it."

"Well it's time you got used to it. Once you are out in the big wide world, you'll have to get used to hard work. In no more than a couple of weeks, Pete, you will be calling yourself a man, not a school boy." I must have looked a bit shocked, as Dad continued, "In a few months from now, you'll have a little one calling you Dad."

"I don't need you to remind me of that, it's a worrying situation."

"As your mother has told you, once this baby pops out it won't go back inside again. You better get used to it as you'll be a dad for life."

"I'm aware of that, and I also realise that I shouldn't have got involved with Sam."

"A bit late thinking like that. Your mates might have got drunk last night along with you, but at least they have not got anyone up the duff or is it called having a *bun in the oven* these days?"

"Bun in the oven."

"Pete, this is man to man, Keep your head down and study hard to get good exam results, then try and get a good job before worrying about Sam. I know I keep saying this, but it is the best advice I can give you."

"Dad, can I stay and live here till I save up for a flat? The thing is, I have to find the deposit which is a month's rent and also I will need to buy a suit if I manage to get a job in a bank or insurance office. When I was down the street the other afternoon I had a look in Burton's, how I'm going to find the money for a suit I don't know, they're expensive."

"Your mother and I have been wondering how you thought you were going to manage. Life is not easy once you have left school."

"I'm beginning to think that you don't want to answer my question about me staying here for a while."

"Well, Pete, you'll have to turn over a new leaf if we allow that. I can't say yes and I can't say no at the moment, it depends how this weekend goes. Your mother and I have to get over last night. If the weekend goes okay, the three of us will have to have a serious chat. if it doesn't go well, you'll be given your marching orders. Now you know."

Chapter 17

After Dad had his long chat with me he seemed a lot happier, and the weekend went quite well, even though I was given jobs to do by both Mum and Dad and I was grounded. I didn't hear a word from Sam, I just guessed that no news was good news as far as she was concerned. Monday came around quicker than I expected and, before I knew it, I was on the bus to school for my human biology A-level exam. The bus was full so I had to stand in the aisle.

The woman who had a problem with me on the bus the other week was sitting on an inside seat next to a woman who looked almost as big as her. In fact they could have been taken for sisters or even twins as they looked so alike, with the same hairstyle, identical dresses but in different colours. The cardigans they were wearing were both the same colour, a bright pink – these clashed well with their dresses. The only thing was they didn't talk to each other; the one I had met before was sat staring out of the window. When she got up to get off the bus she didn't even say excuse me, let alone goodbye, to the other woman. With great difficulty, she just pushed past her. Once she saw me standing at the back of the bus, her face changed to thunder and she started yelling at the top of her voice.

"Out the way, boy! Let me get by, I'm in a hurry."

"You again! Say 'please', then I will move over."

"Me say 'please' to you!"

"Yeah, say 'please'."

"I'm not going to say 'please' to someone as rude as you, boy."

"Me, rude? I'm never rude; you're the rude one."

"You were rude when I saw you last week. Get out of my way."

"I will when you have said 'please.'"

"If you don't move for me to get off this bus, it will start up again and I'll be late for work."

"Good."

"What's the matter?" shouted the clippie.

"This boy won't move out the way for me to get past."

"I'm not going to move until she says 'please'."

"I remember you, boy, from last week; I told you then to behave yourself. Let the poor soul get past."

"When she says 'please', I'll move."

"The boy is right, every time you come on this bus you cause a problem, I'm standing up for the boy!" shouted one of the passengers.

"Good," called a few more.

"PLEASE!" said the woman, looking all hot and bothered.

"Now you have said 'please', I'll step out of your way, madam. Then you can squeeze past me."

"You have got a lot of cheek."

"Not as much as you."

The woman eventually past with her extra-large shopping bag. What she had in it I have no idea, it was so large that she couldn't see where she was putting her feet and they landed on mine.

"Take care, that was my foot you just walked over! That hurt!

"What did?"

"Your feet hurt mine."

"Serves you right! You should have moved when I asked you to get out of my way, then I would have taken care."

"I hope I don't ever meet you again."

"That depends."

"Depends on what?"

"Whether you get on this bus, as I'm going to be on it most days. I told you all this rubbish the other week!" she shouted in my face.

208

At that, the woman was helped down on to the platform and out on to the pavement by the clippie, still holding her large shopping bag out in front with both hands she walked down the road. She seemed to have great difficulty putting one foot in front of the other. This must have been because she had swollen feet and ankles and was wearing wooden Dr Scholl's sandals. It was no wonder my feet hurt after she landed on them. Suddenly she stopped walking and turned towards a terrace house; leaving her bag on the pavement and holding on to a rail, she slowly climbed up the couple of steps to the front door, where she rang the bell. The bus moved off so I couldn't see whether anyone answered the door or not; what she was up to is anyone's guess, but I don't think she was going to work at the house unless it was as a cleaner.

The bus soon arrived at the school gates. I jumped off and hurried through the main door and along corridors to the classroom.

"Early today, Knight? Makes a change," said the master who was sitting in on the exam.

"I've come here to take my exam not to cause any trouble or to get myself into a state before I take it. You might not think it, but this exam is very important to me."

"Whatever has come over you?"

"Just let me sit here quietly so I can get myself in the right frame of mind for the exam."

"This is definitely a turn up for the books, Knight, it doesn't sound like you."

I put my elbows on the desk and put my head in my hands to have a few minutes' peace, before being disturbed by the other pupils. By nine fifteen, the others had arrived and we were all in position for the exam.

The papers were handed out and the exam started at around nine thirty and finished at eleven thirty. I was the only boy taking human biology so, once the exam was over, I went on my way. As the sun was out and I had my packed lunch in my bag, I went and sat on the wall by the main gate to eat and to wait for the bus.

"I thought I might catch you here, Pete."

I looked up and found it was Celia. "What do you want?"

"I heard from Sam this morning."

"So?"

"She told me she's leaving hospital this afternoon, her parents went in to see her yesterday and had a long chat with the social worker."

"It was Sunday yesterday; social workers don't work on Sundays unless there is an emergency."

"There was an emergency all right – they needed Sam's bed. Her parents were told that they had to have her back living with them. Sam's not happy – apparently they've been trying to get hold of you all weekend, but your phone's not working."

"I wondered why I hadn't heard from her."

"You could have tried your phone, then you would have guessed. Sam said it seemed to be engaged all weekend."

"Well I didn't try it. Someone must have taken the receiver off the hook. I'm not very popular at home at the moment."

"What have you been up to? I understand from some of my mates that you have an eye on your sister's friend."

"Who's that then?"

"Sheila."

"The vicar's daughter?"

"Yeah."

"What rubbish have they been telling you? Anyway, how do you know her? She doesn't come to this school."

"I have two mates that go to the grammar school and they have been telling me all about you and her."

"There's nothing for them to tell you, I've only met her once."

"That was it, she said you walked her to the pub and held her hand."

"There is nothing wrong with holding someone's hand, especially in the dark."

"You admit you held her hand?"

"Well, yeah."

"And the rest?"

"What's the rest?"

"Snogging behind the shed before going into the pub."

"That's not true."

"They've been telling everyone about you feeling Sheila's tits and you having a hard."

"That's all lies. None of it's true."

"Well, they're enjoying telling the lies to Sheila's friends."

"Have you told Sam all this rubbish?"

"Of course, she's my best mate."

"Celia, I'm fed up with hearing all of this rubbish. I'm going to go up to the hospital once I've finished these sandwiches to see what really is going on."

"I've told you, I think she is going home at half past two."

With that I got up and pushed the remainder of my sandwiches in my bag. I left Celia standing by the wall, while I walked across to the bus stop.

I arrived at the hospital and found Sam up and dressed with her suitcase packed. "What the hell have you come for?"

"To see you."

"I don't know why you've bothered."

"What do you mean?"

"I've been trying to ring you from the patients' phone and the office phone all the weekend and your phone has been engaged all the time."

"I wondered why you hadn't phoned me."

"You could have picked up your phone to see if it was working."

"It never entered my head that something was wrong with it. You see, I have had other things on my mind."

"Anything to do with a girl called Sheila?"

"Who's she?"

"You know damn well who she is, she's a friend of your sister."

"Oh, her."

"Celia has told me all about you and this Sheila."

"Whatever Celia has told you, it's not true."

"She said you walked her to a pub."

"That part's true."

"What about snogging behind the shed?"

"Lies, complete lies. I've just seen Celia and she told me all this stupid rubbish that Sheila and her mates have been spreading round. It's all lies. Believe me, it's lies."

"I'll try to believe you but I find it very difficult. Anyway, let's get back to me. I'm going home at half past two; Dad and Mum are coming to fetch me."

"You're telling me that you're going back to that flat and your parents?"

"Yeah, Mum and Dad came in and had a chat with the social, she has arranged for someone to come and visit me at the flat regularly to make sure I'm okay. You see, I have no alternative, I'm going to stay there until I go to the mum and baby home in Aylesbury. The baby is due the middle of November, the social think I may be able to go there at the beginning of October or before. It seems that I got pregnant the first time we had sex in March."

"I can't believe what you're telling me – the flat is the last place I thought you would be going. Anyway, if you're happy with that, I'm pleased as well. I have given up thinking about when and where you got pregnant, it's more important when it's due. So you're saying it's the middle of November?"

"Yeah that's right, the middle of November. I've been thinking about what you and your parents said about me going back to the flat and all of you are right. Anyway, changing the subject, what do you think of my new dress, new to me I mean? The social gave it to me, as I haven't any clothes of my own that fit. I hate it, I think it smells."

"I can't smell anything. Stand up and give me a twirl, it looks okay to me. The only thing is the colour, I'm not sure if yellow suits you."

"I like the colour but the rest of it I hate. It's the only thing I have to wear that fits. I'll be staying in bed when it goes for a wash."

"I don't know what to say as I haven't any money to buy you any clothes. When you get out of here you can always look in the local rag for jumble sales, especially the ones held around the Elephant and Castle area. If you go along you may be able to buy some clothes, then take them home and put them in the washing machine. More often than not they come up looking like new."

"We haven't got a washing machine; I'll have to go to the launderette."

"Sorry, I forgot your mum hasn't one. You'll have to get some money then go to the launderette; yeah, that is what you'll have to do. Anyway Sam, I leave school the end of this week, then I'll be looking for a job. I'm going to spend my first week's money on a suit, then I'm saving up for the deposit on a flat for the pair of us."

"It'll be strange seeing you in a suit, I never thought I would be going out with a bloke that wore a suit to work. I assumed I would be seeing someone from the local factory where I would be working on the production line."

"I'll have to wear one if I'm going to get a job in an office or somewhere similar."

"I won't be able to go to work."

"I realise that, you're going to look after our baby. I'm hoping to get us a flat in North London then get a job in a bank or insurance office at Finchley Road. I've been looking in the *Evening Standard* for flats, they seem to be cheaper over there, also office jobs are available in that area."

"That sounds okay."

"While you're in Aylesbury I'll be able to visit you at weekends. I think there is an hourly train service to Aylesbury from Baker Street and it goes through Finchley Road, so if I manage to get a job plus flat around there it'll be easy for me to catch a train."

"You have been thinking about me and you! But what about a bed and other things like knives and forks for the flat?"

"Hopefully, Sam, the flat will be furnished and that will include knives and forks being provided."

"What are we going to do about food?"

"We'll have to buy food, times will be very hard. Mum said she would buy everything for the baby such as a cot and sheets. Perhaps your mum could buy the nappies? Mum told me that we need two packs: one pack of thick and one of thin, twenty-four nappies altogether."

"Pete, I don't know much about bringing a baby into the world and looking after it."

"You should have thought about that before you agreed to keep it. You'll have to learn as you look after it, perhaps your mum will help you. Probably the social worker will give you a few tips, but it won't be easy for either of us. The thing is I won't be there in the daytime as I'll need to go to work to pay the rent. I'm prepared to give it a go with you."

"I'll be on my own all day with our baby."

"Yeah afraid so, you'll be able to go out and about. If I manage to get a flat at Willesden Green I understand there's a park that you can walk to. The first thing for me to do is to get a job."

"I've got to tell you, Mum and Dad won't allow you around at our flat, but we can meet up. The social has explained to them that they can't stop me from meeting you."

"That's okay, you can always come over to my place, the only thing is you can't live there with me." I looked at my watch. "Sam, it's quarter past two, they'll be here in a few minutes."

"Don't run away, the social is coming to make sure they behave as Dad keeps shouting off."

We carried on chatting for a few more minutes discussing things like when and where we're going to meet up. First to arrive was the social worker thank God.

"I'm pleased you're here, Pete. I'm Miss Collins, Sam's social worker. I'm going to be looking after Sam until she goes to the mother and baby home. Sam's mum and dad will be here soon, so, before they arrive, I want to explain my plan for Sam." She went on to tell me what had been arranged. Everything she told me I agreed with, that made both Sam and the social worker happy.

Sam's parents eventually arrived. Her mum looked exhausted and her dad looked as if he had been drinking; he was flushed and not walking in a straight line. In fact, he looked as if he had been pulled through a hedge backwards.

"You two are a bit late."

"We don't have to come on time for you," replied Mr Smithson.

"The thing is, I have other patients to look after and have meetings to go to."

"That's your problem, not mine."

"When we had our chat yesterday afternoon you promised me that you would try and behave for the sake of Sam and her baby." "I'm trying to behave."

"Miss Collins, he's always like this. To him, this is his best behaviour," said Sam's mum, almost in tears.

"Mind what you say woman, don't you start telling yarns about me!"

"Do you always talk like that to your wife?"

"I can talk to her how I bloody well like, it's is none of your fucking business!"

"I'm afraid it is my business; if Sam is going to live with you, it's my business."

I looked across at Sam. She looked upset and about to burst into tears once again. "Shut up the pair of you, I can't put up with you drinking and upsetting Mum. The only reason I'm coming to live at the flat is because I have nowhere else to live, you promised me that you would both behave and you, Dad, would not get drunk."

"Dear, darling Sam you know I can't keep a fucking promise. I've had the day off work to come and fetch you, so I'm bound to go down the fucking pub. You know I always go to the pub if I have a day off, I was so bored sat at home this morning with your mother that I went to see my mates and guess what? I had a few fucking drinks to help me through my fucking day."

"Mr Smithson, please don't swear."

"If I want to fucking swear, I will fucking swear."

"You'll have to leave the ward then, we don't have swearing here."

"You must be fucking joking!"

"I'm not joking, please leave."

"Keith, do as you are told."

"Mildred, mind your own fucking business."

"Mr Smithson please leave the ward. If you don't go, I'll have to call the porter to escort you to the main door."

"You must be having a fucking laugh, a porter won't be able to chuck me out!"

"Well, if you don't go quietly it'll be the police; it's up to you."

"I'll go. Come on, Mildred, you have to come with me, we'll both fucking go." He held on to Mrs Smithson's arm and pushed her past Sam. Walking backwards down the ward he held two fingers in the air at the social worker and at anyone else who could see him.

"Well, he showed his true colours," said the social worker.

"I'm so sorry," sniffed Sam, wiping her eyes with her fingers. I put my arm around Sam's shoulder.

"I'll try and sort something out."

"How on earth do you think you can do that, Pete? Your parents have both said that Sam can't stay at your house and you are still at school."

"I don't know what I can do, but I can have a think. By the way, I leave school on Friday – my last exam is on Wednesday."

"I didn't realise that, I thought you would be staying at school until the end of term."

"No, Friday. Anyway, the end of term is only a few weeks away."

"With your father behaving like he did just then means you can't go back to the flat, especially with you being pregnant."

"What am I going to do? I have nowhere else to go."

"I'll have a chat with the ward sister and your doctor, perhaps there's a bed on another ward for you. The thing is, this bed is needed," At that the nursing auxiliary arrived with sheets on a trolley.

"I've come to wash your bed and change the sheets for the new patient. I'll just go and get the skip from the sluice to put your dirty linen in."

"Hang on a minute, I might not be going."

"What do you mean, not going home?"

"I can't send Sam home to the flat."

"Well, sister says we're expecting a new patient within an hour, I've been sent to sort the bed out."

"I'll go and see the sister, just don't strip the bed till I get back."

"Okay, Miss Collins, I have other things to do. I'll leave the trolley here until I know what's happening." The auxiliary wandered off.

"I'll go to sister's office and have a chat with her and try and sort the situation out. See you both in a minute."

"Okay," we said in harmony.

We both sat looking at each other wondering what was going too happen next, nothing seemed to run smoothly for us. Out of the blue the swing doors opened and who should come rushing through them but Mrs Smithson.

"Dad's gone home, I've come back to say sorry for his behaviour."

"What good is that, Mum? Miss Collins won't let me come home to the flat, especially with me being pregnant. I'm going to be homeless! This is all because of dad and his drink problem."

"He hasn't got a problem."

"What do you call it then?"

Mrs Smithson looked stupid. "I'm not sure, he just enjoys a drink, like I do."

"Mrs Smithson, how many pints does your husband drink a week?" I asked.

"I have no idea! Anyway, it is none of your bloody business!"

"Well, there you go. Mum, you have no idea and you expect to say sorry and all is forgiven."

"Yeah."

"It is not that easy, Mrs Smithson, as well as the drinking both your husband and yourself smoke cigarettes, I could smell the fags on you when you were here just now," said Miss Collins, who had returned from the office and came in on the tail end of the conversation.

"You're telling me that we have to give up smoking now as well as our booze?"

"Yes, I'm afraid so, especially if Sam's going to live with you. I told you yesterday about having to give up smoking and cutting down on the drinking."

"My old man will never give up drinking."

"You do agree with the three of us that he has a problem?"
There was silence, then Mrs Smithson agreed. "I suppose so."

"You must have a good idea about how much he drinks, Mrs Smithson."

"I only go to the pub with him once a week."

"Well, how much does he drink when you're there?"

"I don't know, I drink about three pints of bitter, then I have a mother's ruin. You know what that is, a gin and tonic to finish off the night."

"You must have some idea. If you have three pints, he must have that and the rest, whatever that is. Anyway, Mrs Smithson, you have far too much to drink for a woman."

Ignoring that statement Sam went on to say, "Mum, I thought
Dad drank whisky chasers?"

"Yeah, Sam, he does some nights."

"Mrs Smithson, you are saying that he drinks at least three pints and each one is followed by a chaser of some sort?"

"Yeah that's right, it's usually a whisky chaser but some nights it's beer followed by vodka."

"When he buys you a gin and tonic does he have one on top of the beer and whisky chasers?"

"Not very often, he usually buys another beer and whisky chaser."

"I'm sorry, Mrs Smithson, but I am afraid your husband has a drink problem which needs sorting out if Sam's to go home with you. Also, your drinking habit isn't too good either. The thought of what you drink makes me feel sick."

"So she can't come home to live with me?"

"You have got that right, Mum, I can't go home with you."

"I must ask you, Mrs Smithson, does your husband get aggressive when he has one too many?"

"No, never."

"That's not true, Mum, you know he gets cross with you. I remember when he hit you about and you could not go to work due to a bloodshot eye he gave you when he returned from the pub one lunchtime."

"Mrs Smithson, is this true? Did you have to go to see the doctor?"

"Yeah, I jolly well did. The doctor made me stay home from work for two weeks, it made us very short of money."

"I remember it like yesterday, Mum. I couldn't take sandwiches for school lunch as you had no money for bread, let alone a filling for them. The teachers felt sorry for me and I was given free meals, they said something about billing you but luckily they never did."

"Now you mention it, I remember being very worried in case a bill arrived. It didn't, thank God."

"Mum, can you remember when I came to the pub with you and Dad? This particular time, Dad sat at the table with us. After a few drinks, he got cross with a man sitting at our table, who was eyeing you up and down. He went to hit him and was pulled back by one of the other customers. The barman came over and sent dad packing, I think he was banned for a couple of weeks."

"That was a few years ago now. He promised me that it wouldn't happen again, but of course it has. Only the other week the barman from that particular pub phoned and told me that he had hit out at another customer while he was stood at the bar."

"Something has to happen to improve matters," said the exasperated social worker.

"Any suggestions?"

"Yes, I think he should join AA."

"Whatever is that when it's at home?"

"Mrs Smithson, it is a fellowship for people with drink problems. It stands for Alcoholics Anonymous. You could go with him."

"I've never heard of it," said Sam, looking shocked.

"I doubt if you would have, people don't admit to going to AA, they find it too embarrassing. If your dad and mum decide to go along to a meeting their identity won't be disclosed. Some of the meetings are open to visitors and others are only for people with a drink problem."

"How long are the meetings?"

"Usually about ninety minutes. They're held at different times throughout the day in different areas of London and in towns outside London. You don't have to pay to go along, a hat is passed around after the meeting for anyone who wishes to give a donation, it's purely voluntary."

"I think it would be a good idea if Dad went along, Mum. If we could get him off the booze, he would have more money for other things."

"Sam, if you're thinking about him helping you two out with money, I know that he won't."

"Mrs Smithson, he may be a completely different man if he gives up the alcohol and he might even feel like helping Sam and
Pete with a few bits for your first grandchild."

"Mum, do you realise I have never known Dad not to go to the pub most nights, then come back having had one too many. It would be nice to see him sober, if only for one day."

"If that happened, it would be a flipping miracle."

"Well, miracles do happen, Mrs Smithson."

"If you say so."

"First things first, we have to sort out Sam and see where she can live. I've had a chat with the ward sister and she definitely needs this bed, within the next hour. The ward upstairs has an empty bed, the only trouble is the ward is for female geriatrics."

"Miss Collins, what does a geriatric mean?"

"It is a ward for females past retirement age."

"I can't go there!"

"Ward sister is looking into it for us, they may be able to put you in a single room and take the patient out of the single room and put her in a bed on the ward."

"You mean, I would be in a room on my own?"

"Yes, that's right, but you'll only be able to stay there until I find somewhere else for you to go and live, outside of the hospital."

"Mum, please, have you any suggestions?"

"No, I haven't."

"What about your mum? My gran, I haven't seen her very often but she may put me up."

"Can you tell me a bit about her, Mrs Smithson?"

"Only that she's my mum; I don't have much to do with her. In fact, I don't have anything to do with her; you see, she doesn't drink alcohol so she doesn't like my husband, never has done. The three of us had a row one afternoon over booze, I haven't seen her since. She always sends Sam five bob for her birthday and Christmas."

"I've never received that."

"We always give it to you."

"That is not true, it must have been spent by you two."

"Stop arguing. Do you think your mum would put Sam up?"

"I have no idea, she doesn't even know she's pregnant."

"Where does she live? And has she got a phone?"

"She lives down the other end of the Old Kent on the right hand side. She has a phone but I don't know the number."

"Mum, she might put me up for a few weeks, I would like that and I would get to know her. I haven't seen her since I was about three years old."

"She lives a different sort of life to any of us, church on Sundays. Someone told me the other week that she belongs to the local Women's Institute."

"You're telling me that you know people that know her?"

"Yeah, I've always lived around here, when I was a child I went to school down the road from the flat we live in, an old school friend tells me what she's up to."

"How old is Gran?"

"She's getting on a bit, she must be fifty-something next year. I'm thirty-six, I had Sam when I was twenty."

"She is not so old that Sam couldn't stay with her. Do you think you could look for her phone number so I can ring and then arrange to go and see her?"

"That'll take me a while but I'll try. Where I'll start to look, I have no idea."

"Pete, you're quiet. Have you anything to say?"

"I'm recovering from the shock that Sam has a gran who lives down the road from Sam's parents' flat. I think if your gran can take you in for a few weeks, it would be marvellous."

"You would think that, to save your family from looking after Sam."

"Mrs Smithson, for goodness sake try and be kind to Pete, he is this baby's dad."

"I know that, but surely his mum and dad should be helping out. I can't see them sat here with us lot."

"Mrs Smithson, have you given any thought to the fact that they may be at work, trying to earn a crust?"

"That's right, Miss Collins. Mum is at school and Dad is down at Woolworth's."

"Mum, I think you should keep your mouth shut."

"Sam, don't you speak to me like that, I'll have to have words with your dad about you."

"What can he do about what I say to you?"

"You would be surprised, the first thing he'll do is get you to wash your mouth out with soap."

"If I'm not allowed to live with you two drunken twits, neither of you will see me to be able to say or do much."

"The pair of you, please stop quarrelling," said Miss Collins, looking more exasperated than ever.

"I may as well go home and see what my bloody husband is up to."

"Yeah, Mum, go home and have look for Gran's phone number."

"Before you go, Mrs Smithson, once you have found that number please can you ring into the ward and give it to the ward sister? The quicker you can find it the sooner I can get Sam organised."

"I'll see what I can do, I doubt if it will be today. I've got to sort the old man out first, he is my first priority."

"Go along then, I'll wait for your call."

Mrs Smithson went and left the three of us sat looking at one another in despair.

"I'm going to go and see how sister is getting on with finding you a bed. At the same time, I'll see if I can get you a cup of tea – I think you both need one."

We were both mentally and emotionally exhausted. Sam fell asleep in the arm chair while I sat on the edge of the bed, daydreaming.

Miss Collins soon returned with a pot of tea for the two of us. "Sister has arranged a bed for you upstairs. Once you've finished your cup of tea you can go and introduce yourselves to the sister on your new ward."

Chapter 18

I helped carry Sam's tatty suitcase up the stairs to York ward. There was a lift that we could have taken, but Sam insisted that she would rather walk as she didn't like enclosed spaces. The ward sister was sat in her office.

"Pleased to meet the pair of you, I'm Sister Dickson. I'll take the pair of you along to the room that is going to be yours, Sam, for the next few days."

Sister Dickson was the complete opposite to Sister Turner, who was very tall and thin, with dark-rimmed spectacles and short greyish hair that had been permed. Sister Dickson was short and fat with a large chest that made her dress look as if the buttons were going to pop undone at any minute. She was getting on in years like Sister Turner, but, instead of allowing her hair to go grey, she had it dyed bright ginger and it was straight. It looked to me as if she had been along to Vidal Sassoon's to have latest geometric hairstyle, but being a nurse she had to pin the front back out of her eyes. She seemed very bubbly, not like Sister Turner who found it difficult to even smile, let alone laugh.

"This is your room, Sam, it should be very quiet and private, it has a wash basin but I'm afraid you will have to go down the corridor to the toilet. The locker has been cleaned out so you can use it for your bits and bobs. See the window in the door?"

"Yeah, what about it?"

"Well you can pull the small curtain across it so you can't be seen from the corridor when you are having a wash."

"That's good, I wouldn't want anyone to see me naked, especially the size I am." We all laughed.

"Sam, at least you will be thin again in a few months, not like me, I can't lose weight, I seem to get fatter and fatter, whatever I eat I put on weight," said sister Dickson, looking down at her dress and making sure that none of the buttons had popped undone.

"I hope and pray I get thin again, I couldn't cope with being fat."

"I can assure you, it is not fun. Not many men like fat women. Every man that I have met has told me to lose weight, and I can't so I don't have a man and I'm never likely to," said the sister, looking very sad.

"You're so bubbly and seem to be full of fun, you deserve a man."

"Thanks, Pete, that's kind of you."

"There must be a man out there that would enjoy your company whether you are fat or thin. If Sam remains fat after having the baby, I would still want to be with her."

"Thank you, Pete," said Sam, looking very surprised.

"You two are young, not like me. You may not think it but I'm in my early forties and there are not many single men of my age about. Lots of married men pretend to be single and try and persuade females to have quickies. Anyway, that's enough about me, I shouldn't be talking to you two about my love life. Let me show you where the toilets are, Sam, then I'll go and get on with my work."

Sister Dickson and Sam went down the corridor chatting away to each other as if they had known each other for years. Sam soon returned.

"Sister is very nice, Pete, different from the one downstairs. The loos aren't special, they are very basic. You go into a large room that has four doors off the room. Three doors go into separate loos, the fourth door goes into the bath room which has a very old-fashioned bath in the middle of it. Sister told me all about the bath and how the elderly patients are lifted in and out of it. To get a patient into the bath is quite a performance, the temperature of the water has to be checked first with a bath thermometer. Once the water is at the right temperature the patient is lifted in by two nurses holding an arm and a leg each. To get the patient out of the bath, the water has to be emptied out first, then two nurses take an arm and a leg each and lift the patient out on to the chair."

"That must be hard work."

"That's what I said to sister, she told me that many nurses hurt their backs and are off work because of it. Some apparently give up nursing because of the lifting."

"I'm not surprised."

"She also told me that they were hoping to have a hoist set up in the bathroom in the next month or two. It sounded as if it was a crane that was arriving, but she assured me it was called a hoist for lifting elderly patients in and out of the bath. Once I thought I would like to be a nurse but not anymore, I've seen enough in hospitals to put me off nursing for life. Anyway, I haven't passed any exams so I would only be able to train to be a State Enrolled Nurse, or work as a nursing auxiliary. To become a State Registered Nurse, I would need O-levels."

"Sam, don't bother to think about any of that, you are going to be busy enough looking after our baby. You won't have time to go to work, let alone train to be a nurse."

"I suppose you are right."

"I know I am, you need to rest and wait and see if your gran comes to see you to arrange for you to go and stay with her."

"I hope Mum finds her phone number; if she doesn't I don't know what will happen to me."

"We will worry about that when she can't find the number, surely you know your gran's address?"

"Yeah, but I've never been there. Gran kicked Mum out when she got involved with Dad. When I was very young, Mum used to take me in my pushchair to meet Gran for a coffee, but we never went to her flat. I haven't seen her since my third birthday."

"Well, she will have a surprise when she's told you have a bun in the oven."

"I don't know what she will say. Mum always said that Gran's very posh and never approved of my dad. I don't think she knows that we live where we do; where we live can't be more than a mile from Gran's flat. I know Mum never told Dad that we met up with Gran; Mum always said Dad would kill her if he knew, so I never told him."

"It's not your fault that your mum married your dad, so your gran may come to your rescue and take you in, if you prayed I would tell you to say your prayers but as you don't, just hope."

"Yeah, okay, I'll just hope."

We both burst out laughing and threw our arms around each other. Things seemed to be a lot brighter, it was great to see Sam laughing, long may it last. Before going home, I helped Sam to unpack her case and put the few clothes she had into her locker.

"You don't seem to have much."

"I told you earlier that I haven't many clothes that fit, I'll be pleased when this baby pops out and hopefully my body will go back to its normal size – thin. It will be three cheers to my body."

We both laughed so loud that the ward sister came into my room.

"I like hearing people laugh, can I be nosy and ask what you are laughing at?"

"Yeah course you can, we were just talking about my body, and how I'm looking forward to being thin again."

"I've never had a baby, but I can imagine when the time for having the baby gets nearer, you wish for a thin body and normal clothes."

"You can say that again! Nothing fits properly, even my knickers are tight."

The sister looked me up and down. "I had the day off yesterday and I went shopping for knickers for myself, the ones I bought I'm sure would be ideal for you. I haven't taken them out of the packet. I know, I will bring them in tomorrow and give them to you as a present, I just can't imagine wearing tight knickers in your condition."

"Thanks, sister, that's kind of you. I look forward to seeing you in the morning."

"I'm pleased to be of service to a young lady in waiting. I will go and get on with my work." She went on her way humming to herself as if she hadn't a care in the world.

"She's so happy, Pete, she is always laughing. I wish I could be as happy."

"Well, once you have had this baby and we have a home of our own, we should always be laughing. As I said earlier, hope for a better life."

"I will."

"Let me have a feel of your bump and see if I can feel our baby kicking."

"I'll sit down on the bed and make myself comfortable, you sit next to me."

"Okay."

"Let me hold your hand and then I can put it where you can feel the baby kicking."

"Gosh, it doesn't half kick! I'm going to call it kicker."

"That is a good name for it, I wonder if it is a girl or a boy?"

"I guess it is most probably a boy the way it kicks, perhaps it will be a footballer, he may play for our country."

"You never know, Pete, but what shall we call it? Have you any ideas? I thought if it was a girl I would call her Pamela Anne; if he is a boy Stewart John. What do you think?"

"If they are the names you like, they are okay with me. Pam is short for Pamela and Stew is short for Stewart."

"They will do, I don't want this baby to have any fancy names."

"Sam, I'm not into fancy either."

"That's it, then. Pam if it's a girl and Stew if it's a boy. It doesn't half kick! I think it wants to come out. Don't think you can come into this world early, because you can't! We are not ready for you yet."

"You tell it, Sam! We are not ready. We haven't even got a pram for it to sleep in, let alone a flat to live in, and I have to find a job."

"I feel exhausted. I am going to have a sleep if this little kicker will let me. I don't want you to go, but I must have a sleep."

"Before I go, let's have a snog. It's great you having a room to yourself, no one can see or hear what we are up to."

"Come here, Pete, come and have a lie down on my bed; there is no need for you to just sit there, wondering what to do next."

It didn't take me long to put my legs up and cuddle in with Sam.

"We will be able to cuddle like this every night once we have our own flat. The only thing is, we will have to make sure that we keep johnnies available or before we know it you will have another bun in the oven. At the moment we don't need to use a johnny as you can't get pregnant on top of being pregnant."

"I thought I could."

I burst out laughing thinking Sam was joking but she wasn't. She meant it. She looked so stupid that she hid her head in the pillow. After about five minutes she looked out.

"I've never had a sex lesson in my life, the week they had one at school I was off sick. I didn't know that I needed to buy johnnies. Pete, I have never seen a Johnny; what do they look like?"

"First I can tell you another word for a johnny is a rubber, because they are made of rubber. They look a bit like a sausage skin, you will be seeing a sausage in a new light and think of a sausage as a dick, as long as you don't think of sticking the sausage up your fanny and use it as a dick. Mind you, it wouldn't get you pregnant. Bet you didn't know some girls use cucumbers for a dick."

228

"What? No, I didn't know that. Some cucumbers are a bit prickly, perhaps they peel it before putting it up the you-knowwhat."

"Well, they do use them; you've got a lot to learn, I thought I was innocent one around here. A couple of years ago my granddad died and Mum and Dad had to clear out his flat. I went around and found them both laughing away to themselves. I asked them what the joke was and, with a lot of embarrassment, they handed me a small cardboard box similar in size to a spectacle case. I looked inside and there was a washable johnny laying out flat, having been powdered to stop the thick rubber sticking together."

Sam looked shocked but she did laugh along with me. "You are saying it was reusable and washable, eh?"

"Yeah. How old it was, we never discovered. Dad thought about giving it to a museum but in the end I think he threw it away."

"Forget about that, I want to go to sleep. Why don't you stay and have a sleep with me?"

"I will stay until you go to sleep, then I must go. If you wake and find me gone, just remember that I love you and I will be back tomorrow afternoon. I have forgotten to tell you that mylast exam is Wednesday afternoon."

Sam closed her eyes. As soon as I thought she was asleep I pulled my arm out from under her, then managed to get down from the bed without disturbing her. I went on my way after saying bye to the ward sister, who was sat in her office, writing up her notes.

I arrived home in time to sit down and have supper. Mum and Dad seemed quite happy, but Anne was in a very bad mood. She didn't even say hello to me.

"What is the matter with you, sis?"

"Nothing, should there be?"

"Well, you don't seem very happy, you haven't even said hello to me."

"Why should I?"

"I'm your brother, you normally speak to me, even if you say something sarcastic."

229

"The truth is I'd rather keep my mouth shut. I've heard so much rubbish at school today about Sam."

"It's better that you tell me than I find out from my mates."

"Don't you two start causing an upset, your mother has been feeling a bit better the last couple of days."

"When you go up to your room, I will follow you up; then you can tell me your gossip."

"Don't you come up straight away as I have things to put away."

"How long will it take you to put your things away?"

"About ten minutes. I know, I will knock on your door to let you know when you can come to my bedroom."

"Now you have sorted yourselves out let's have our supper in peace," said Mum, looking as if she had aged five years in five minutes. Silence reigned, but Anne sat opposite me smirking to herself, all the time she was eating. Someone had amused Anne so much that, out of the blue, she started to laugh out loud.

"I told you just now, Anne, not to upset your mother with your silly nonsense. I suggest you take your supper up to your room and finish eating there."

"I don't know why I should do that, the joke is about Pete. I'm not laughing at you two."

"You hadn't better be laughing at your mum and I. If you want to stay eating down here, you can tell us this silly joke of yours."

"You have asked for it, Dad, so here goes. The boys at my school are laughing about Pete. They think the black boy in the fifth year got Sam pregnant, not Pete; they can't wait to know the colour of this baby."

"You are not growing into a very nice person. Being my sister, I would have thought you would have stood up for me, not laughed at me. Sam has promised me she was a virgin when she had sex for the first time with me."

"I wish that you two would behave and not upset your mother and I with all this stupid gossip. Now we are going to worry about the colour of this baby's skin; then again, we don't believe you and your silly friends, Anne."

"We will all have to wait and see. The boys at my school are having a bet about its colour."

"I've had enough. Sam is a lot happier than she was and now you are determined to make me unhappy by saying all these stupid things."

"I don't think they're stupid."

"For goodness sake, Anne, shut up, or I will tell our parents about you and the bike shed at your school."

"What is all that about, Pete?"

"I will tell you when I feel like it."

"We would like to get it all out in the open now, so come on – tell your mum and I."

"Don't tell them, Pete."

"I am going to, then perhaps you will all treat me a bit better and Mum and Dad won't think of you as a wonderful goody goody. Anne has been going behind the bike shed with a boy from her class – apparently he has been touching her up. At least I am sixteen, going on seventeen, not fourteen and looking twelve in ankle socks."

"For goodness sake the pair of you shut up, you take your supper up to your room young lady and stay there until we call you down."

Anne left the table quietly and quickly and without any fuss. Mum and Dad remained sitting at the table, looking at each other, then at me without saying a word.

After about ten minutes of staring at one another, Dad shouted at me, "How the hell did you find out about Anne and this bike shed?"

"I heard her laughing in her room with her friend, Sheila about how she had a so-called boyfriend and how they spent the other Monday lunchtime behind the bike shed. Apparently, there was another couple with them; the boyfriend of the other girl offered Anne's boyfriend a Johnny, but he refused it, saying he was not going that far."

"One thing I'm going to say in her defence is you shouldn't have listened into her conversation. Having said that, if you hadn't, we wouldn't have known what she was up to," said Mum, looking very embarrassed.

231

"Now, Pete, what is this nonsense about Sam being pregnant by a black boy and not you?"

"I have no idea. We will have to wait and see the colour of this baby when it pops out. I hope after all this performance that it's mine."

"I'm not saying another word about that, I'm just going to hope like you that it is our grandchild. Please, Ern, come and help me with the dishes in the kitchen."

Chapter 19

After that upheaval, the rest of the evening was quiet. When Mum and Dad came back into the sitting room they didn't have much to say to each other, let alone to me, so I disappeared up to my bedroom where I read a book until I fell asleep. My parents left Anne to her own devices. She wasn't seen again until Tuesday morning when we all hoped that she had had a good night's sleep and had calmed down.

I decided it was best to get up at my usual time of half past seven even though I was not going into school. I didn't want to cause any more upset and I thought it was a good idea to be down for breakfast at the same time as Anne, so she couldn't tell the parents any more rubbish about me and, if she tried to, I would be there to defend myself.

"I have had a chat with Anne about her going behind the bike shed with her boyfriend. She says it's not true."

"Why did you say all those things then, Anne?"

"It was not me talking, it was Sheila. I was listening to what she had been up to. I'm too good to do anything, like you have been telling Mum and Dad."

"I don't know what to say, then, except sorry."

"PETE, YOU SHOULDN'T STAND OUTSIDE MY DOOR LISTENING!" screamed Anne down my ear.

"There is no need to shout like that, Anne, it's not very ladylike."

"I don't care if it is ladylike or not, Mum, he shouldn't listen outside my door."

"I know that, Anne, but Pete did, and he heard what he heard and he has said sorry. You should try and stop upsetting each other, before we know it, Pete may be living the other side of London with Sam and the baby," replied Mum, looking extra flushed.

"Good! I will be pleased to see him go!" said Anne, putting her tongue out at me.

"Have you ever thought that I may be pleased to see the back of you, Anne?"

"For goodness sake the pair of you, stop shouting at one another, please, please, be quiet and try and get on with one another," said Dad, sounding annoyed. "I'm going to go to the kitchen to pick up my sandwiches and go to work, when I come home tonight I hope we can all eat supper in peace."

"Well, as usual, I better say sorry for all the upset."

"Thank you, Pete. I'm going to be late if I don't go now as it is almost quarter to nine."

"Well, hurry up," said Anne, laughing to herself.

Soon everyone had gone on their way when, out of the blue, the phone rang.

"Pete, is that you?"

"Yeah, who is it?"

"Sam's social worker, with more good news for you. Sam's gran has been contacted and she is willing to come to the ward to see Sam and she would also like to meet you. Could you come in
later this morning, say eleven thirty?"

"Yeah, I can get up to the ward by then."

"I will try and be there for when you arrive. Sam's gran seems to think she can get up here by about quarter to twelve. See you just before then, bye."

Bang went the phone. It was as if the social worker was in such a hurry that she didn't have time to say goodbye properly, let alone put the phone down quietly.

I intended to have a peaceful morning but instead I now had to hurry and get myself together. While organizing myself I went into a daydream wondering what Sam's gran would look like. I could picture her as a little old lady that wore a long brown tweed coat, on her head I imagined she had a dull-coloured hat with a feather to one side. On her feet I could see thick grey stockings with brown court shoes. Instead of carrying a handbag, she had a large black shopping bag that doubled up for everything she needed to carry in her handbag, plus shopping. Under her coat I thought she might wear an apron to keep her jumper and skirt clean. Then again, she could be very glamorous, wearing a fur coat with everything that goes with it. One thing for sure is that she doesn't drink unless it is a sweet sherry for medicinal purposes.

As I had got up early I was ready to go to the hospital by ten o'clock, so I decided that I would walk and enjoy the sunshine. I arrived outside the main entrance at around quarter past eleven when I bumped straight into an elderly lady who was trying to walk in the same direction as myself. She was having a job opening the swing door into the main hall.

"Can I help? You seem to be having difficulty."

"I am, I can't open the door very easily with either hand, but my right arm and fingers are extremely painful today. The thing is boy, I have arthritis in both hands along with my right arm. I can't push open any door easily. As well as having arthritis I had a stroke back along, so my left side isn't up to much. Thank goodness I can walk, slowly but surely."

I pushed open the door and let the lady walk in front of me into the main hall. I watched from behind and noticed that she had great difficulty walking just a few steps at a time without a walking stick.

"You seem to be having terrible trouble walking. I think perhaps you need to sit in one those wheelchairs that are over there against the wall. If you sit and wait, a porter may come along and help by taking you in the wheelchair to where you need to go."

"I'm all right. I don't want to use a wheelchair, that will make me appear really old. I have a walking stick at home but I don't like people to see me using it. I try to be independent, also I'm vain, the stick is not very fashionable. The physiotherapist from this hospital gave it to me, she said I should use it every time I walk out of my flat. It's the colour of a tin can, that is the problem. I think I would use it if someone painted it for me."

"I would have thought that was easy enough, haven't you got any relatives or friends that are handy with a paint brush?"

"No. I'm coming over all dizzy, I must sit down before I fall down." I rushed over and fetched a wheelchair.

"Sit down in this chair."

"Thank you, it's kind of you to bother with an old lady like me."

"I'm going to go on my way. If you stay sat where you are a porter may come along and sort you out. If I see one, I will mention you to him."

"You are so kind. Before you rush away I've got something else to say to you."

"I can't waste any more of my time chatting to you. I'm in a hurry, I have an appointment in ten minutes."

"That's strange, I've also got an appointment in ten minutes, please stay and help me."

I started to walk away. "I have to go, look after yourself, someone should come along in a few minutes."

I hurried on my way, arriving at the ward just before quarter to twelve. Sam seemed quite happy chatting with her social worker.

"I'm pleased you managed to get here on time, Pete," said the social worker, looking at her watch. "I'm wondering where Sam's gran is. You haven't past an old lady on your way, have you?"

"No."

"This is strange as she suggested the time."

"I had a chat to a lady in the main hall, I doubt if it was her as she was having difficulty walking, I had to put her in a wheelchair. The thing is, none of us know what Sam's gran looks like. It couldn't have been her as this woman couldn't even open the door without help."

"You're right there, Pete. Sam's gran must be healthy or she wouldn't have wanted to meet you both, let alone be thinking about you staying with her. Unless, of course, she wants someone to look after her. What do you think, Sam?"

"Mum did say once to me that Gran suffered from arthritis in her knees and Mum was worried in case she eventually got arthritis. Pete, if it was her that you met, I couldn't help to look after her in my state."

"We would not expect you to," said the social worker, butting in.

"Sam, we must keep our fingers crossed that it was not her. She may be late because of the buses, you know very well what they are like – they're never on time."

The three of us sat watching the clock without saying a word. Before we knew it, the clock said twelve fifteen.

"Well, another half an hour has gone by. They will be bringing in your lunch soon, Sam, so I'm going to go and have mine. If your gran should arrive before I get back, ask the ward sister to ring me, then I will come straight up."

"Leave it with me, I will go and see sister for Sam."

At that the social worker went on her way. We sat patiently on the edge of the bed waiting for Sam's lunch. I sat wondering if the woman downstairs really was Sam's gran. Lunch soon arrived, I was offered some but I refused it saying I didn't like stew, as it didn't look anything like Mum's.

"While you are eating, I'm going to go back down to the hall and see if the woman that I met there is still in the hall. I'm going to ask her if she is your gran. Can you tell me her name?"

"Yeah, it's Mrs Mable Spencer."

"Right, I will go and look for Mrs Mabel Spencer."

"Don't be long, Pete."

"I will be as quick as possible."

I hurried down the stairs as if I hadn't got a minute to spare. Once in the main hall I stood in the entrance and stared. The woman whom I thought may have been Mrs Spencer had disappeared, so that was that. Instead of going straight back to the ward I decided to sit down on a bench and watch the different types of people coming and going. After about ten minutes of daydreaming I wandered back to see how Sam was getting on with the stew. Once at the top of the stairs I could hear talking coming from her room. I took a deep breath and entered – there, sat in the same wheelchair, was the woman whom I had met in the hall an hour or so ago.

"Pete, this is Gran. Gran, this is Pete."

"We met earlier down in the hall, I put you in that wheelchair. I have just been down to the hall again to ask you if you are Mrs
Spencer and obviously you are."

"Yeah, that's me. Please call me Gran."

"Okay, Gran, I'm pleased to meet you."

"I expect you are. It seems to me that you have both got yourselves in a bit of a pickle."

"Afraid so."

"Sam has been telling me all about the baby and how she needs somewhere to live for a few weeks. I'm going to have a think very seriously about her living with me. The thing is, Pete, I don't know whether Sam and I will get on. If she's anything like her mother, we won't."

"Please don't think for too long as Sam has to be out of this room by the end of the week, then she may be homeless unless you take her in."

"Don't you try and blackmail me, my boy."

"I'm not, I'm just saying how it is."

"I like living a peaceful life with my cat. If I take you in, Sam, I don't want your mum and dad visiting and causing a row and upsetting my life. The thing is, I don't drink alcohol and I have never known your dad sober. Before he married your mother he used to turn up to take her out having had one too many."

"His drinking is the reason I can't go back to their flat to live. The social won't allow me to. She wants me to live somewhere peaceful for the sake of this baby."

"Well, if I have my way it will be very peaceful living with me, because your mum and dad are not going to come around to my flat and cause chaos. I have friends that often see him worse for wear trying to walk in a straight line down the Old Kent, I often ask the friends if your mum is with him in the same state, they never seem to see her. Has she given up the bottle? Before she met him she was tea total. The thing is, I kicked her out after she came back from the pub drunk out of her mind."

"She does have a drink occasionally, but I have never seen her drunk. Dad normally goes to the pub on his own. If Mum goes with him they finish up having a row as he leaves her sat with her girlfriends and he stands at the bar with his mates."

"That's about right, nothing's changed."

"I promised the social worker that I would let the sister know when you arrived. I will go now and let her know you're here, unless you've told her already, Sam?"

"No, Gran arrived just before you got back, I forgot about seeing the ward sister."

"I'll go and see her now."

"Thanks, Pete."

I found sister in the medicine room sorting out the drugs that had to be returned to the pharmacy.

"This is a job and a half, Pete. Anyway, what can I do for you?"

"I've come to let you know that Sam's gran is here."

"Right, I will give Miss Collins a call. Come with me to the office then I can give you the knickers I promised Sam."

"Thanks, it's very kind of you to let her have them."

I went back to Sam's room where I stood at the bottom of her bed and tossed the brown paper bag that the sister gave me across to Sam.

"What's that?" asked Sam.

"Have a look."

"Knickers, glorious knickers," said Sam, taking them all out of the bag. "I didn't expect her to give me this many! There are ten pairs!"

"Why have you been given knickers, Sam?" asked Gran, looking a bit surprised.

"The ones I have are far too tight. Everything I wear is tight. My bras... well, if my tits get any bigger, I won't be able to wear a bra unless someone buys me a larger one."

"Your mum should be buying these things for you, not strangers that pass in the night."

"The person who gave the knickers to me is not exactly a stranger – she is the ward sister."

"What! She bought knickers for you?"

"That is right, Gran."

"This is the first thing that needs to be sorted, I'm going to pay the sister back for these knickers. I'm not saying to you two that I am well off, but I can buy you some underwear. After all, I am your gran."

"Thanks very much."

"Whatever happens don't tell your mum or she may come begging for money, I've had that before. When she lived with me she used to take money out of my purse."

"I would never do that, my mum and dad would go mad."

At that the door was pushed open and a breathless social worker appeared. The four of us had a long chat and it was decided that Sam would go and live with her gran until she went to have the baby. I found out that Sam's gran only lived about three quarters of a mile from Sam's parents. The flat that she rented from the council was on the ground floor. It had two double bedrooms; one was larger than the other. The sitting room had French doors out on to the communal garden. The kitchen and the bathroom apparently were not worth talking about as they were both in a state of disrepair.

"Sam, if you had become pregnant a couple of years ago you wouldn't have been able to come and stay with me as I was living in a different block of flats and my flat only had one bedroom."

"Why did you move, Gran?"

"The flat was on the sixth floor. More often than not, the lift was broken. I had an awful job to get up and down the stairs so I was stuck in my flat for weeks on end. Eventually my doctor intervened and got me moved to where I am now."

The four of us looked at one another. Sam continued to ask questions.

"Gran, can you tell me how long your arms and fingers have been bad?"

"A few years now, you don't have to worry about them. One thing I have forgotten to tell you is that I had a mild stroke back along. I can get around okay as long as I'm not rushed, I have difficulty getting in and out of the bath, but I have a home help that comes in to help me with that."

"Does she do your shopping?"

"Yeah, but I try to get out every day. I go to a couple of OAP clubs every week, then once a month I go to WI."

"What does WI stand for?"

"You don't know what that stands for? It's the Women's Institute. Your mother ought to have joined, it might have done her a bit of good and stopped her from going on the bottle. Decent people belong."

"Gran, she's not on the bottle, she's only on the glass."

"Same thing, just a different word."

We all laughed and poor Sam blushed from head to toe.

"Now I'm going to ask you both some questions, I want you to answer me truthfully."

"I don't tell lies, so answering your questions should be easy for me. I can't answer for Sam but I don't think she tells lies either." I stood thinking about what Anne had said about the baby not being mine.

"You know I don't tell lies, Pete."

"I hope you don't, my girl, because if I find out you do, you will go the same way as your mother, out the door, no second chances with me."

"Come on then, let's hear your questions."

I sat on the edge of the bed holding tightly to Sam's hand listening to the questions that came fast and furious. Sam managed to answer them all without hesitating until she was asked if she was quite sure that it was me who had got her pregnant. Sam blushed and sat looking a bit stupid.

"Sam, are you going to tell us all that this baby is not Pete's?" "No, why should I do that?"

"Well, you look as if this is a very awkward question to answer."

"It's not difficult to answer."

"Come on then, answer it."

"Pete is the father of this baby," she replied, still looking embarrassed.

"Why are you looking so embarrassed, Sam?" said Gran, sounding very annoyed.

"Because Anne, that's Pete's sister, has heard rumours at her school about me being pregnant by a black chap in her school."

"I hope it is only gossip. If eventually I find out or see this baby is black, my flat will not be a happy place to visit or to live in."

"Come on, let us look on the bright side," said the social worker, trying to smile.

"Yes, let's. Now, when can Sam come and live at your flat, Gran?" I asked.

"I need to sort the second bedroom out, at the moment it is full of junk. I will have to get the odd job man from one of the other flats to help me out. The only trouble is he isn't as well as he used to be, he's very breathless; his wife told me that he keeps getting chest infections."

"Does he smoke?" asked the social worker.

"Yeah, I think he does. Yes, of course he does, he definitely smokes, I saw him stood outside the flats only the other afternoon with a fag hanging from his mouth."

"That's that, then. I think you should find someone else to help you clear the room."

"What do you mean, that's that?"

"It sounds to me that he may have lung cancer. Fags don't do people any good, they usually finish up digging up the daisies long before they should."

"Oh dear, I never thought of that, he's a friendly bloke."

"Just because he's friendly doesn't mean he isn't ill."

"You are right there, what do you think I should do? You see, the room needs a good clear out before anyone can sleep in it."

"What about you, Pete? Do you think you could clear the room out?" asked Sam, looking as if she was going to start crying once again.

"I don't know, I'm not used to hard work."

"It will do you good, hard work didn't kill anyone," said Gran, smirking to herself.

"It sounds a good idea to me, Pete. When do you think you can start? The thing is we have to get Sam out of here ASAP."

"Tomorrow is my chemistry A-level. After that, I suppose I am free, I leave school Friday and I have to find a job. I suppose clearing out this room is a job, how much will you pay me?"

"Pay you? I'm not going to pay you anything. I'm only having it cleared because my granddaughter has a bun in the oven and hasn't anywhere to live."

"I need a job and I call clearing out your spare room a job."

"I do know that as well, but when Sam comes to stay with me, I will have to feed her for free, so you will have to clear the room for free. You helped to get her in this mess – if it wasn't for you, we wouldn't be sat here together."

"It takes two to tango," said the social worker, trying to calm the situation.

"I know that but I was not involved in any of this mess until you called me. I have told you before that I like to live a peaceful life. Perhaps I better change my mind. Yes, I think I better sleep on this and let you know in the morning whether I will agree to take Sam in."

"Nothing is easy for us, Gran. In fact, it is so hard I will have grey hair before I am eighteen."

"Why should it be easy? I would have thought that you would have had an abortion as they are easy to come by and quite common these days."

"Well if you want to know, Sam wouldn't have one. If it was me having this baby and not Sam, I would have had an abortion. I do realise how difficult it is going to be."

"You can say that again and again son, it won't make any difference. You both have to get used to having a little one around all of the time, the quicker you get used to it the better."

"Mrs Spencer, I think you have said enough. I'm going to get hold of the porter to take you back down to the main hall, I will go to sister's office and ring down for one, once I have done that I'm going back to my office. I will speak to you in the morning, I hope it is going to be good news," said Miss Collins, looking as if she was completely fed up with the situation.

"Thanks, once I am in the main hall I can slowly go on my way. I will ring into the ward tomorrow morning after I have had a think overnight and let you know what I have decided." Miss Collins left the room and went on her way to the office. The three of us just sat looking at one another. The thing is, we didn't have anything in common except the subject of the baby and we had said what we needed to say so we just sat looking at one another until the porter eventually arrived.

"Mrs Spencer?"

"Yeah that's me."

"I've come to take you back down to the hall."

"Thanks, bye then you two. I may see you again or may not, depends whether I feel like taking you in, Sam. I promise you one thing and that is that you will know one way or the other first thing in the morning. Keep your fingers crossed."

I jumped down from the bed. "Bye then, Gran," I said, holding out my hand hoping that she would take hold of it.

"Don't say goodbye by shaking hands, give me a cuddle."

I leant over and put my arm around her shoulder, then gave her a kiss on the check. "Sorry, Gran, to have caused you so much upset."

"You have not caused me much upset, or at least not as much as this baby is going to cause you two. Sam, jump down from the bed and give me a kiss goodbye."

"I didn't think you would want to give either of us a kiss."

"Don't be so silly girl, of course I do, you are my granddaughter."

Sam got down from the bed, taking care not to slip on the lino. The three of us put our arms around one another, while the porter stood at the back of the chair.

"Hurry up and say your goodbyes. I have other patients to collect from different areas of the hospital. If my bleep goes off

I will have to go on my way, then you may have to wait an hour or so for another porter to collect you, he may not have as much patience as me."

Gran pushed us away. "Better go or I'll miss my bus, then it will be a taxi job and I can't afford that." Before we blinked she was being pushed out into the corridor, towards the lift.

"That didn't go too badly, in fact it didn't go badly at all."

"I suppose it was okay. We'll have to wait for the phone call in the morning, it's not as if we have to wait a week, thank goodness."

"Cheer up, Sam, this time tomorrow we should know whether Gran is going to take you in or not. I think you will be living with her and loving every minute of it."

"I hope you are right. If you aren't, I don't know what will happen to me."

"I'm going to say one thing to you, Sam, and that is stop being so negative. You should remember it is a worry for me as well as for you."

"What does negative mean, Pete?"

"The opposite to positive. I'm Mr Positive and you are little Miss Negative."

"I know I'm thick, please tell me what you mean."

"Sam, get yourself a dictionary, it will tell you in there what the words mean."

"I've never had a dictionary, no one has ever given me one."

"Well you could have bought one with your pocket money. Using a dictionary helps you with your English. You not using a dictionary is one of the reasons that you haven't the brains that I'm supposed to have."

"Stop being so horrible."

"Well stop asking me questions that you should know the answers to." I looked down at my wrist to see the time. "I'm fed up with this conversation, I'm going to go on my way. I've been here since twelve and its now four o'clock, time to go." "Go then, I'm going to get back on my bed and have a sleep," "That is the best place for you." I kissed Sam on the forehead. "Bye. I will see you after my exam late tomorrow afternoon, don't you dare phone me before my exam."

"What time is the exam? Why can't I phone you when I hear from Gran?"

"If you phone me with either good or bad news it will put me off my exam, then I will get a poor result. My exam is in the afternoon at one thirty, it finishes at around four. I will then catch the bus straight over to here, I should arrive by five. If I don't arrive by then it will be due to the traffic and I will get here sooner or later."

"Bye, then." Sam put her head on her pillow while I went on my way with my thoughts.

Chapter 20

I wandered out of the hospital and down the hill thinking about my future, which appeared bleak. After walking for about ten minutes or so my head started to spin. Whether it was because I hadn't had anything to eat since breakfast or the worry of always arguing with Sam I don't know, but at last it dawned on me that she was not the brightest star in the universe. How the hell we are going to live together in a flat with a baby, let alone sleep in the same bed every night for the rest of our days, I didn't know. At least I hadn't suggested getting engaged to her, let alone married.

I arrived home only to find everyone as usual sat in the sitting room. "You look like you have seen a ghost."

"Perhaps I have."

"Whatever do you mean, Pete?" said Dad, putting his paper down.

"Well, I've been thinking about Sam. I have decided she's thick."

"I could have told you that weeks ago," said sis, laughing out loud.

"Go to your room, Anne."

"I will when I've heard all of Pete's news."

"My news is nothing to do with you. Do as Dad has just said and go to your room."

"Go now!" shouted Mum.

Anne looked so shocked at us all shouting at her that she left the room immediately.

"Sit down and tell us both what has happened. First of all, have you got a headache?"

"Yeah my head is thumping, it makes me feel sick."

"I'll go and get a headache tablet. Don't start telling Dad what's happened until I return."

"I'll sit here quietly. I hope I'm not going down the same road as you two."

"Whatever do you mean?"

"I don't want high blood pressure like Mum and you." Mum returned carrying two tablets with glass of water.

"Pete, take these two Panadol then tell us what the matter is, I'm sure it can't be as bad as you think."

"To me it's bad."

"Come on, tell us what has happened."

"Give me a second to take these tablets, then I will tell you."

I swallowed them quickly and began:

"Here goes. The boys used to say I shouldn't have got involved with Sam as I had more brains than her, even Mr Down told me this. He even suggested that she should have an abortion. I listened to him, then mentioned it to Sam, but she wouldn't hear of it. If it had been up to me I would have had one, we are both far too young to look after a baby. The stupid thing is I've stood by her and the baby is due soon. It's a bit late, but I've decided that they were right. You know, Dad, Sam doesn't even know what negative means, let alone positive. How the hell can I live with someone as thick as that? Mum, she hasn't even got a dictionary. The way she was talking to me, I doubt if she has ever picked a dictionary up, let alone looked inside one."

"Sorry son. We both thought that this may happen, we didn't like to be the bearer of bad tidings so we kept quiet."

Mum held her arms out and gave me a hug. "I'm sorry as well, Pete."

I pushed her away.

"I'm not going to let either of you down, I will stand by her and hope that suddenly she sprouts a brain."

"You're making me smile, Pete. You make her sound like the scarecrow in *The Wizard of Oz*. He didn't have a brain and he didn't sprout one, so I doubt if Sam will. You must remember brains are not everything, hopefully Sam will make a wonderful mum and you will grow old together."

"I hope you're right but I doubt if spending a lifetime with Sam will come true. What you have said has made me smile, Mum, especially about the scarecrow in *The Wizard of Oz*."

"I think the time has come for us all to find something to smile about, your father and I are fed up with feeling miserable."

"I'm definitely fed up, what with Sam bursting into tears every few minutes. What she will be like if her Gran doesn't take her in, I dread to think."

"Pete, you just concentrate on tomorrow afternoon and this Chemistry exam, your mother and I are behind you and will be thinking of you."

"Thanks. When I leave school on Friday, I am going to look for a job and then a flat/bedsitter in North London. Sam has been talking about having our baby in the mother and baby home in Aylesbury, she can go there in about ten weeks' time if she's lucky."

"Your dad and I have decided that we will buy the cot for our first grandchild along with the bedclothes. Next week I'm going to buy some baby wool and knit a couple of cardigans and booties. I haven't knitted anything for years. Depending on how I get on, I may knit a few more bits."

"Thanks, Mum."

"That's okay, son, everything will come in handy; babies are very expensive to look after and need lots of clothes."

"I am going to promise you two that I am going to try my hardest and stand by Sam and look after her and our baby. There is one thing: when or if she moves in with her gran I won't be visiting her every day, as hopefully I will be working. Also it would cost a fortune to travel to the Old Kent Road. Most probably I will phone her every day, but that is cheaper than visiting."

"Pete, I agree with you over that. What she will think about you not visiting I don't know, but I'm afraid she will have to put up with it. Have you discussed with her who is going to take her to Aylesbury when the time comes?"

"No, she changes the subject when I mention it."

"She will have to talk about it eventually. You could go with her, Pete."

"By the time she goes to Aylesbury, I should be working. I could go with her if it's at the weekend but not if it's midweek as I doubt if the firm will give me time off to take my girlfriend to a mother and baby home. Also it would be the talking point at work for weeks. I'm sure the boss would never keep it to himself."

"I suppose you are right there. Yeah, you are right, Pete. I wouldn't give someone time off to do that. One thing, though, I would keep it to myself. I do know that some wouldn't be able to, let's hope that Sam has to go at a weekend, then nobody will need to know. Yes, let's be positive and think that she will go at a weekend and you can take her," said Mum, standing up on ceremony.

"Yes let's, I think you can catch the train from Baker Street or Marylebone to Aylesbury. How anyone gets to Baker Street from the Elephant and Castle I have no idea. I don't know that area of London," said Dad, looking puzzled.

"I don't know it either. I'm only guessing, but most probably the tube goes to Baker Street. I do know one thing, you can get a free underground map from any station. When you go out, Pete I suggest you call in at Blackheath station and pick one up. Are you listening, Pete?" added Mum.

"Course I am. That sounds a good idea, Mum, I will definitely call in at the station."

248

"With all this upheaval, I have forgotten about food. Have you eaten Pete?"

"No."

"That must be the reason you have a headache, you must be starving. What would you like to eat?"

"I don't feel like eating anything. So much has happened today, I only feel like going to bed."

"Pete, you must eat something. I thought you would be having food at the hospital so I haven't a meal for you. I can make you an egg on toast or I have some cold meat, and I could cook chips to go with it that would be more filling."

"If you insist, I would like egg on toast."

Mum scurried out into the kitchen before I could change my mind.

"Now, son, you still haven't told us what happened at the hospital with Sam's gran."

"It is a very long story. When Mum comes back, I will tell you both all about it."

It wasn't long before Mum returned with the egg on toast.

"Pete is going to tell us about him meeting Sam's gran."

"Give me a chance! If it isn't Mum rushing me when I'm eating, it's you, Dad."

"Oh, sorry, son."

Once I finished eating and had put the plate etc. on the side I explained about Gran and how she's thinking overnight about Sam living with her for a few weeks. Both Mum and Dad sat leaning over with their heads in their hands.

Dad was the first to sit up straight. "I'm beginning to feel sorry for you and Sam. If it isn't one thing, it's another. Now it's Sam's gran who's trying to make things difficult for the pair of you."

"She said we didn't deserve to have it easy."

"I suppose she is right. The thing is, Pete, she is a lot older than us and she comes from the old school. Anyway, how old is she? I'm going to guess sixty plus."

"I'm not sure, let me have a think. She had Sam's mum when she was twenty, Mrs Smithson had Sam at nineteen."

"That made her thirty-nine when Sam was born. Add another sixteen years, that makes her about fifty-five," said Dad with a smile.

"We are both getting on a bit, aren't we, Ernie? It will soon be my birthday – half a century and you will be fifty-three next year, dear," said Mum, looking at Dad as if he should be telling her that she looked young for her age, but he didn't.

"Yes, dear, we will both soon be in our fifties. That makes me feel ancient."

"And me, we can't turn the clock back."

"Mum, you don't look nearly fifty. If I didn't know better, I'd have thought you were in your early forties."

"Thanks, Pete," said Mum, trying to show off by standing up and looking in the mirror. "One thing's for sure, my hair definitely looks fifty plus. I ought to go to the hairdressers, perhaps they could give me a blue rinse, that may cover up the grey."

"You book the hairdressers and I will treat you, Marg."

"Thanks, Ernie, I will sort the hairdressers out. Mind you, Ern, it will cost you a bit. I haven't had it cut for at least six months. Colour, well, I have never had it coloured so I have no idea of the cost."

"I don't mind what it costs, I want you to be a glamorous granny for the birth of your first grandchild."

Mum came over all flushed, then walked over and gave Dad a kiss on the cheek.

"Thanks, dear."

"Anne and I won't recognise you. Tell me, Mum, did your hair start to go grey when you were in your twenties? I've never known it a different colour."

"Yes, Pete, when I was about twenty-two I started getting grey hairs. I used to pull them out until my mum caught me and told me that I would go grey quicker." We all laughed.

"What colour was it before?"

"I can tell you, Pete, it was blonde. Your mother was a blonde bombshell."

"Mum, you must have attracted all the boys."

250

"I suppose I did, but I only had eyes for your dad."

"I'm going to be nosy, how old were you two when you met?"

"That's okay, Pete, be as nosy as you like. I was about nineteen and your father was twenty-three. My parents, your grandparents, thought your dad was far too old for me, they wanted me to go out with someone that was the same age as myself. I don't think they cared what he looked like or what he did for a living as long as he was my age. Where I lived with my parents there was this boy next door but one. He was the one they wanted me to go out with, as he was nineteen, the same age as me. His looks, well, he didn't have any, to me he looked like the back of a bus. He wore black wire-framed National Health specs that made him look thick and dopey. You would have laughed at his hair – it was cut extra short into a pudding-basin style, by his mother, using the kitchen scissors."

"You must have been friends with him to know who cut his hair."

"Yes, we were friends. Well, sort of. He was in the same class as me at school. My desk was behind his so I could have a good look at his hair, I made a comment to him about it. He told me his mother cut it, there were great chunks cut out of it. It's very sad looking back, as you know children can be very cruel and cruel we all were. He left school and got a job down the East End. I used to watch him going to work on his bike, he looked just the same as he did when he went to school. Where he is now after all these years, I don't know, but thinking back on those days makes me smile."

"How did you meet Dad?"

"Your father was a charmer and he charmed me. I used to see him down the local dance hall. He'd stand around the side of the hall with his mates and watch everyone dancing. I thought he had his eye on my girlfriend, then out of the blue he came over to us both and he surprised me by asking me for a dance. Looking back on that makes me grin. Doris my friend said, 'That bloke is coming over to ask me for a dance' and he didn't ask her, it was me you were after wasn't it, Ern? Her face was a picture, I will never forget it."

"Yeah, it was you all right. It was your blonde hair that I fell for in the first instance. Marg, you can have it dyed blonde instead of having a blue rinse, that would remind me of our youth. Yeah, go on, have it dyed blonde."

"No, I'm too old for that silly nonsense, a blue rinse will do me fine. Anyway, Ernie, they are the fashion now, especially for someone my age."

"You're being a spoilsport, Mum. You would look great blonde."

"No I'm not going blonde. In a minute the pair of you will put me off going to the hairdressers altogether, then you will have to put up with me looking my usual boring self."

"You will never be boring to me, dear. If I thought you were boring I would never have popped the question and married you."

"Ernie don't embarrass me, especially in front of Pete; you are making me blush."

"Don't take any notice of me being here, it is nice to see you both happy. I'm pleased to think you can tell me about your younger days."

"Any other questions, Pete, before I go out and do the dishes?"

"Let me have a think. Yeah, what happened to Doris?"

"She was not very happy when I danced with your dad, in fact we fell out because of him dancing with me. If I remember correctly your father walked me home that night and I left her at the dance. When I bumped into her the following week, she wouldn't speak to me so our friendship finished."

"That all seems a long time ago now, Marg. Why Doris should have thought that I would have fancied her, I don't know. I remember she had fat ankles and the boys, including me, used to laugh about them. Your ankles were very shapely and they still are, my mates used to be jealous of me taking you out. It sounds so stupid now, but my mates had a bet on how long we would go out together."

"Ernie, it's the first I've heard of that."

"If I had told you, you would have stopped going out with me."

"You are most probably right there."

"I know I am."

"How many years have you been married?" I asked.

"We have known each other thirty-one years; that sounds like a life time. We didn't get married until I was twenty-three and your father was almost twenty-seven. We have been married twenty-seven years. I didn't have you until I was thirty-three, I had an awful job to get pregnant. In the first instance we used rubbers like the ones we showed you at Grandad's flat. We could not afford for me to get pregnant as we didn't have any money, a bit like now. Eventually we decided to try for a baby and it took a good two years or maybe longer before I got pregnant. Then I lost one baby but soon got pregnant again and had you."

"That was a long time ago, Marg. I remember the day when we thought about trying for a baby, we threw the rubbers in the dustbin. I also remember that I had a pay rise and we had a few pennies left over each week. We decided to put the few pennies away for a rainy day and our rainy day was clothes for when we had a baby – that was seventeen years ago."

The three of us burst out laughing.

"Ernie, I had forgotten all about that. Thinking back on it, makes it seem like only yesterday."

"My dear, it was definitely over seventeen years ago."

"If you haven't any more family history to tell me, I'm going to go to my room. I need a good night's sleep as it is my hardest subject tomorrow, Chemistry. I'll see you both in the morning."

"Good night, son."

Chapter 21

I woke up extra early and lay in bed daydreaming about my Chemistry exam in between worrying about whether Sam's gran was going to take her in and, if she didn't, what the hell were we going to do, me with no job and living at home with no money, Sam homeless. The prospect for us both appeared bleak.

Eventually I got up and went downstairs in my dressing gown to see how everyone was.

"You are up early, Pete I thought you would be having a liein as your exam isn't until this afternoon."

"I haven't had a very good night, Mum. I woke up about five and have been catnapping ever since. I've been worrying about Sam and where she is going to stay if her gran doesn't take her in."

"Please, Pete, don't start that record again. Your mother has got up happy and you are sending both of us on a downward spiral."

"Dad, I'm not meaning to. I will try and forget about Sam and concentrate on my exam."

"Yeah, that is what you should try to do, concentrate on your Chemistry. It is your best subject so you should get good a grade."

"I thought I was better at English than either Chemistry or Biology."

"If that is what you think, son, so be it. We are hoping that you get good grades for all three subjects, then you should be able to get a good job."

"To get into a bank or insurance office I only need a few good O level results and I have them already."

"You seem to have looked into it more than your mother and

I."

"Well I thought I'd better, or I will finish up in queer street. I've found some banks at Finchley Road, you will never believe it but Lloyds are looking for staff. I had a look in the *Evening News* at the jobs available when I was in the paper shop down the town."

"I had a look in the *Evening Standard* the other evening; there wasn't much in that. In fact, there were no adverts for bank jobs. Pete, I did notice that Woolworths were looking for a junior for their branch in Cricklewood. You would start at the bottom, but if you stayed long enough you could become a manager of one of the other branches. I did know someone back along that worked in London, then got transferred to a seaside branch as a manager."

"How much money did it say they started on?"

"I don't know, I think it was only a few pounds, but then they are giving you a training."

"If I managed to get a job in the bank, they would still have to train me, but the money is quite good even at the beginning as a trainee."

"Well, Pete, it is up to you what you do. Just because I work in Woolworths it doesn't mean you should work there."

"Ernie, surely you know which way Pete should go, in a store or a bank?"

"Well, Marg, if I had my time all over again, I would go in a bank... that is, if I had the chance. You have to remember I haven't enough qualifications to work in a bank. I didn't pass enough exams with good results. To work in Woolworths I only needed a couple of O levels. To work in a bank I needed to pass at least five O levels and then take harder exams while working my way up the ladder."

"At least you have enough O levels, Pete, that is something, isn't it, Ern?"

"Yeah, dear it is. Pete, you have to make the decision for yourself."

"I will do that, I'm not helpless. Let us change the subject, I have enough time to sort out a job once I've finished school on

Friday, I'm not going to sit around here wasting time, I'm going to get out and find a job."

"Over the years I have known other people's sons and daughters to sit around wasting time after leaving school until their parents have given them a kick up the you-know-what."

"Bum!" we all laughed. "I can assure you two that I am going to find a job, even if it is as a cleaner until I can get a proper job. I would be bored out of my mind not having anything to do."

"Don't you worry if you can't or won't get a job, I will give you something to do, you can start with painting the walls in this room. I can get the paint at discount price from work."

"You have never told me that, Ern. If I'd known that I would have got you to get the paint months ago to paint this room, it is quite disgusting."

"Dad, if you get the paint I could decorate it for you, decorating it would cheer us all up. I may enjoy it so much that I may decide to become a painter and decorator. Mum, you have always told me how expensive it is if someone has to come in and paint a room for you. If that is the case, the pay must be good."

"I think the pay is very good. It is also good pay in a bank and you don't get messy, in fact you stay clean and go to work in a suit with a shirt and tie, not white overalls that turn brightly coloured with drips of paint over the weeks."

"I will start by painting this room, see how I get on."

"Morning to you all. We are never going to have this room painted by Pete," said Anne, coming through the door as grumpy as ever.

"Yes, I'm going to paint it."

"It needs painting, it is disgusting, but I wouldn't think you would be any good at painting."

"Stop it now, Anne, we are not going to put up with your nonsense. Pete is quite capable of painting this room or any other room for that matter."

"Let him paint it then, if you think he is capable. I think it will look a real mess when he's finished with it."

"Your mum and I are going to let Pete paint it. The only thing is we have to decide on a colour, have you any suggestions?"

"Come on, Anne, let's hear what colour you would like the room to be. Nothing too bright."

"What about boring magnolia?" said Anne, pulling a face.

"I fancy painting the walls pale yellow and the skirting boards bright yellow. What do you think, Mum and Dad?"

"Black and white are the fashion," said Anne, laughing to herself.

"That is not going to happen, black and white is a no go."

"You boring old farts."

"Anne, how dare you speak to us like that?" said Dad, looking as if he was going to explode.

Mum just sat looking at Dad. "Anne, I am fed up with you and your behaviour, you will miss the bus to school if you don't get a move on," said Mum, looking Anne up and down.

"So what? I'm fed up with going to that stupid old dump."

"Get a move on and do what your mother has said. Move!"

"You look a complete mess, you haven't even put on clean clothes. I know, because that blouse had that dirty stain down the front of it yesterday. It seems as if you have taken over from Peter and are determined to upset us like he used to."

"How did you guess?"

"Stop it, Anne, get your shoes on and go to school, now!" shouted Dad, who seemed to be crosser with Anne than he ever seemed to be with me.

"I'm going, I'll go now." She picked up her bag and went out the door.

"I don't know what the matter is with her, she is worse than you ever are, Pete. I must say you have improved beyond belief. The last few months for your mum and I have been a living hell what with Sam and the baby, it has been an awful worry, but it seems to be improving and you seem to be sorting yourself out."

"I'm trying to. Anyway, why are you both still here, aren't you going to work?"

"We both decided to take the day off. We booked it weeks ago. If the weather was good we thought we'd go off for the

257

day. We aren't in any hurry, on the telly last night it said it may rain so we're going to see what happens. If the sun comes out we are thinking of going down to Greenwich for the afternoon. If it doesn't we will potter in the garden. If it rains, well, we don't know what we'll do."

"The pair of you ought to go out together, even if it rains, as you don't have many days off together. I have a good idea if it rains – why don't you go to see a film? You could go up West and treat yourselves to the cinema in Leicester Square, it would do you both good, there should be a film on that you would enjoy."

"We haven't been to the flicks for years, have we, Marg?"

"No, it would make a change."

"I'll have a look in the *Standard* and see what's on." Dad immediately picked up the paper and started to look through.

"Dear, *Thunderball* is on at the Odeon Leicester Square. Sean Connery is James Bond and Claudine Auger plays opposite him as Domino, she was Miss France in 1958."

"Dad, you know more than me! I've heard of Claudine Auger only because some of the boys at school have been talking about her. I'm sure they didn't know she was Miss France back in 1958."

"Pete, I only know all this because it is in this paper. Marg, we should do something completely different on our day off. I'm going to take you to the flicks, rain or shine, to see this James Bond film. We can get ready and go to the matinee, what do you think?"

"Ernie, that will be nice; we haven't been to the cinema in years. It will make a change from staying around here and digging the garden; we can dig the garden any day but to go and see a James Bond film, that's another story."

"After the flicks I'm going to take you for supper in one of the small cafes in Leicester Square. Nothing too flash, but I will make sure you have a nice time."

"Yeah, go on, Dad – spoil Mum. She deserves to be spoilt. In fact, you both deserve to be spoilt – you have had a lot to put up with over the last couple of months."

"You can say that again, son. I'm going to get ready, perhaps the three of us can walk down the road together at lunchtime, then wave you off on the bus for your final exam before we catch the train."

"Mum, I will walk down the road with you both, but you waving me off is another story. I don't want to be embarrassed by you two. After my exam, I'm going up to the hospital hopefully to hear some good news."

"Before we all go out, what are you and Anne going to do for supper?"

"I could get a snack at the hospital."

"That's okay, but what about Anne?"

"What about her? I know, you could always leave her a note telling her to cook herself a meal, there must be eggs in cupboard."

"She can't cook."

"What, Anne can't cook! She must be able to boil an egg."
Mum shook her head.

"I know, I will leave a note with instructions."

"That's a good tease, Anne not being able to cook! I will keep that up my sleeve for when she starts laughing at me about what I can and can't do."

Mum didn't look too happy about my comment. She left the room without saying another word. I followed her and went straight to my room to get my pens and books together before going to the bathroom for a wash.

Eventually the three of us wandered out on to the pavement and strolled down to the station. "I'm going to go on my way now, the bus will arrive in a few minutes."

"We are going to see you off, Pete. This is the last time we can see you get on the bus to school,"

"There is no need to, I'm a big boy now."

"Come on, Pete, your mother is looking forward to seeing you get on the bus."

"I told you both earlier, I'm not a child and I don't want you standing at the bus stop with me and that is that."

"What is the matter with him today?" said a voice from behind me. I turned around and there was Jackie, trying to join in the conversation.

"Who are you?" said Mum looking, Jack up and down.

"I met Pete at the hospital, I'm the part-time receptionist. I guess he is your son, he looks a bit like your old man."

"Yes, he is our son. Enough of the old man, he is my husband and Pete's dad."

"That makes him your old man."

"Jackie, go. I don't want you standing here trying to join in our conversation."

"Why should I go? I thought you and I were friends?"

"You've got that wrong, you are not a friend of mine."

"Well, why did you come up to the hospital with your mates looking for me the other Saturday, if we aren't friends?"

"It is obvious to me that Pete is not friends with you, please go," said Dad, looking as if he'd had enough of me to last him a lifetime.

"I know," I said, "let's go into the station and wait for your train. There's a small café in there where we can get a coffee."

"That sounds a good idea, Pete," said Mum, relieved to be getting out of the way of Jackie.

We managed to find an empty table in the corner. Once seated, Mum suggested that she should go up to the counter for the coffee. Of course, this left Dad to bombard me with questions about Jackie without Mum listening in.

"I don't think you need to ask me anything about Jackie, unless of course, Dad, you are interested in her. I will tell you one thing and that is she is the local tart and she often goes around without any knickers on. At least, that is what she says if anyone gets talking to her."

"Pete, you are the end! Fancy you of all people telling me that!"

"Well, you asked me about her. My mates and I think she's a bit mental."

"You can say that again, son. Now change the subject and hope we don't bump into her again." Mum returned with the coffee.

"I've got about ten minutes before I catch my bus," I said.

"What have you two been talking about?" asked Mum.

"Not a lot. I've been telling Dad about my Chemistry and how I'm hoping for good grades," I replied, going red with embarrassment.

"I wonder when you get the results?"

"I'll ask this afternoon. I think it's sometime in August; if you are wondering because of me getting a job, there no need to worry – I shall try and get work before the results come out. You must remember that I don't need A levels for the jobs I'm applying for."

"The thing is, Pete if you could get a job that needed A levels and if you get good grades, it would mean that you would get more pay and the extra money would come in very handy."

"Dad, you are making me think. If I get a job in a bank with my O levels perhaps when I get the A level results and pass with good grades, they may put my pay up?"

"I have no idea if they will do that. It is worth asking at the interview."

"I must go now. I will smile all the way to school about what you have just said, Dad. It would be wonderful to have a little more than a basic wage. Enjoy the film, I will see you both later this evening, hopefully with good news."

Chapter 22

Arriving in the ward I went to Sam's room only to find the door closed. I looked through the window and saw her asleep, so, instead of going in and disturbing her, I continued along to the ward office, where the senior house officer was sitting, chatting away to the sister. When they saw me approaching their smiles left their faces.

Sister was the first to speak, "Hi, Pete, we have been waiting for you to turn up. There is some good news and there is some not so good."

"I noticed Sam's asleep."

"Yeah, she hasn't had a very good day," said the doctor very seriously.

"Sam's gran rang in this morning as promised, but she can't make her mind up about Sam living with her so nothing much has changed," added the sister, looking directly into my eyes.

"Sam has spent most of the afternoon asleep, this morning she was in some state and I had to get one of the nurses to stay with her to try and calm her down, as you can see it seems to have worked as she is asleep."

"We are giving Gran, as you call her, until Friday to make her mind up. Apparently she has a sister who is a couple of years younger than Gran, who only lives a few miles away. Gran is going to ring her to have a chat about Sam and her pregnancy. By all accounts the sister also lives on her own, in a threebedroom house that she owns; Gran thinks it would be better if Sam could go and live there for a while. The thing is, this sister is much better off than Gran. Apparently, if she is willing, she could easily afford to keep Sam," continued the doctor, looking over the top of his glasses.

"Now, Pete, Gran may look well off but she only has her state pension to live on and she has to pay all her bills and buy her food with a very small amount of money. The story goes that when Mildred lived with her mum, she was in the habit of taking money out of Gran's purse. One day, she took Gran's bank book and managed to take most of her savings. Before Gran realised the money had gone she had kicked Mildred out for being drunk in her flat. Mildred immediately married Keith against Gran's wishes, so it was very difficult for Gran to confront Mildred about the money," added the sister, looking sad.

"Sam has never told me any of this. I understood from Sam that she hadn't seen her gran from when she was three years old until this week. Back along, Sam did tell me that she used to go with her mum and meet Gran behind her dad's back in a coffee bar down the Old Kent. This was when she was very young."

"Yes that's right, Mildred used to take Sam to meet Gran. She didn't tell Keith about the money she had taken. One thing in Mildred's favour is that she did try to pay back some of the money out of her housekeeping but of course, Keith didn't give her enough to be able to do this for more than a couple of weeks. Eventually, Gran and Mildred fell out big time, so they haven't seen each other for over thirteen years."

"How much money did she steal?"

"About five thousand pounds, it was enough to make a great difference to Gran's life."

"I wish Sam and I had that sort of money. Her mum shouldn't have taken that from Gran, it was a terrible thing to do; it's no wonder that they aren't in contact."

"We now have to wait until Friday and hope. The hospital staff think that it would be better if she stayed at Gran's as Sam's doctor is only up the road from the flat and also Sam's friends live down the Old Kent, so she would be able to visit them. The trouble is, Gran seems to think differently."

"I feel like both of you, it would be better for her to live with her gran. I don't think Sam has ever met this aunt, also I don't think it's a good idea to have a change of doctors so late into the pregnancy. Once she gets to the mother and baby home, she will have had three doctors instead of two looking after her – that's if we don't count the hospital doctors."

"We agree with you on that, Pete."

"As you know, I am standing by Sam, but if she goes to stay with this aunt I won't be able to visit her, especially if it's a few miles from the Elephant and Castle. Her living down the Old Kent will cost me an arm and a leg in tube fares, but I think I should be able to visit once a week and again at the weekends. I would phone her every day. You all must remember that I have to get myself a job and also try and find a flat that will take the three of us. From what I have read in the adverts in the *Standard* not many landlords rent to couples with babies or children."

"A job will be quite easy to find as you obviously have passed all your exams, but a flat's another story. I'm sure you will find that more difficult."

"I have to get a well-paid job to keep the three of us, this has to be found long before I look for a flat as I have to save for the deposit. I know for a fact Mum or Dad can't afford to pay it for me, they find it hard enough to pay their own bills let alone help me out."

"I don't know what else to say, Pete, as we keep going over the same old thing. We will have to wait until Friday morning, Gran has promised that she will phone by ten," said sister looking upset.

"Now I have had a chat with you two and you've told me what is going on, I'm going to leave Sam to have a sleep. I don't think it is a good idea to disturb her. When she wakes, please let her know that I came in, also can you tell her that my exam went better than I expected."

"I will," said the sister.

At that I hurried out of the ward and down the corridor to catch the bus to the centre of Blackheath. There were only a few passengers from the hospital on the bus as it was early evening and most of the afternoon visitors, and of course the office staff, had already gone home. I managed to get my favourite seat just inside on the left where I sat with my thoughts. The bus soon arrived in the high street, so, after jumping off, I made a decision to go and get some chips to eat while walking home. Being a Wednesday I assumed there wouldn't be a queue, but of course there was. I chose to stay and wait as I was hungry and all the other shops, where I may have been able to get a snack, were closed. I had to wait a good half-hour as both the fish and the chips were cooked to order. Everyone in the queue seemed to know one another so they were all chatting away, oblivious to the time they were waiting. The boy that was stood behind me was chatting over my head to the boy in front of me. In fact, I finished up joining in the conversation, which was about going up the West End on Saturday night.

"Do you fancy coming with us?"

"I wouldn't mind, it would be a night out, how are you getting there? And where are you going?"

"We are going to a club, if we can get in, we are thinking about going to the Marquee. We went up the West End last Friday to the Marquee but we couldn't get in as the queue was so long. If we can't get in this Saturday we are planning to walk to Oxford Street and go to the 100 Club, jazz is played there most nights, with a bit of luck Humphrey Lyttelton may be playing."

"Who is playing at the Marquee?"

"We don't know, but the other week it was the Stones."

"Can I think about it? Anyway, you haven't told me how you're getting there."

"On the train from the Elephant and Castle to Charing Cross Station, then we are going to walk to Shaftsbury Avenue into Wardour Street to the Marquee Club. If we can't get in, we are going to continue up Wardour Street to Oxford Street; the 100 Club is on the opposite side of the road."

"I don't even know who you both are. I'm Pete Knight." I held out my hand.

"I'm Tom and my friend is Nigel. We come from Lewisham." We shook hands.

"I live just down the road from here. Have you decided what time you will be leaving the Elephant and Castle? I'll have to meet you over there."

"Yeah, we usually catch the train at seven."

"If I don't turn up by ten to seven you know I won't be coming with you."

"You look as if you still go to school," said Tom.

"Actually, it is my last day on Friday."

"You will be throwing out your flannels and white shirt then"

"We had a bonfire for our uniform when we left our dump, didn't we, Nig?"

"Yeah, we did. I'd rather not talk about it as the neighbours called the fire engine. It was a very hot day and we didn't think about everything else catching fire. Of course, it did. My dad's shed went up, I was in terrible trouble."

"Forget about that for a minute. What do you two do for jobs?"

"Whatever comes along, anything. What are you going to do?"

"At the moment I'm thinking of working in an office or bank – that's if they will have me."

"Why shouldn't they? You sound posh enough. I bet you have passed all your exams. You see, Nig and I didn't work at school, if we could get out of going we would. We used to go into school for registration then run, sometimes we stayed but we very rarely went to any of the lessons. We used to go behind the bike shed for a fag then remain there for most of the day, a girl or two would often go along with us."

"I think that was stupid. Look at you both now! If only you had both sat in on the lessons you could both have quite good jobs, instead of that you are, out looking for any job that comes along. That wouldn't suit me."

"Well, that's us. If rubbish needs moving, we'll move it at a cost; if an old bid needs a room painted, we will fleece her." They both burst out laughing.

"I don't agree with that; it's not right to fleece someone just because you didn't work at school."

"That's how we are. There are lots out there like us, you can join us."

"I'm not into that, I think everyone should work hard at school and pass exams."

"There you go, you are definitely not like Tom and me."

"You are next up for your chips, Nig."

"Good, what do you want, Tom?"

"Anything going that is cheap."

"That means batter bits for you. I'm having a large bag of chips."

"What are you having, Pete?" said Tom

"A small bag of chips."

The three of us paid up then left the shop.

"If everything goes according to plan, I will meet you this Saturday at ten to seven outside the Elephant and Castle station."

"We'll be there waiting for you, remember not to come looking like a schoolboy."

"You'll be surprised what I look like out of uniform. Cheers for now," I said, smiling to myself.

"Cheers!" they both shouted.

I went and sat on the wall looking over the park to eat my chips before going home.

Chapter 23

Thursday came and went. Before I realised it, it was Friday and my last day at school. I got up at my normal time and caught the bus down at the station. It was very strange because usually, on a Friday, the bus was full and I had to stand, but today it seemed as if everyone had taken a day's holiday and I had a choice of seats.

My mates were waiting for me at the school gates.

"You're late, Pete!" shouted Dave.

I looked at my watch. "It's my normal time, you lot are early. Whatever has come over you? I've never known you lot early for anything, let alone school."

"We thought we would show the staff how good we can be for once in our lives. You realise, Pete, that we finish here at lunch time. John and I are thinking about going up the West End. You can come with us, if you like."

"Let me have a think. It's too early in the morning to decide on going up to the West End."

"Come on, Pete, it is the first afternoon of real freedom, you can't have anything else to do," said John, laughing at me.

"I know, it's Sam, you have to go and see her. You will be an old man before you know it. The only memories you will have will be about school and going in the girls' lavs for a bit of the other with darling Sam," added Dave.

"Let me have a think, most probably I will come with you."

"Did you hear that, John? Pete is thinking about coming with us!"

"Yeah, I heard. If you do come, it will be a shock to our systems."

"If I don't, it won't be because of Sam; it will be because I haven't any money."

"Poor old Pete hasn't any money. Dave's parents are letting him have fifty pounds a month to spend on whatever he likes."

"You're bloody lucky," I said, not able to hide my surprise.

"Don't get too excited; Dad is only going to pay until I get a job," said Dave, smiling. "I know, Pete, I will treat you to a trip up the West End. That means I will pay your tube fare, it doesn't mean that I'm going to treat you to anything like a coffee."

"Thanks for that, but you two just listen to me. Wednesday night I went and got some chips and met two blokes who have invited me up the West End tomorrow night and I've agreed to go with them. We are going to try and get into the Marquee; if we can't, we are going on to the 100 club in Oxford Street. I'm sure it will be a good night; it will be much better than going up to the West End this afternoon. Fancy coming?"

"What do you think, John?"

"My answer is yes, it sounds better than just going up for the afternoon," said John rubbing his hands.

At that I went on to explain how we were going to get there and the time we were going to meet up.

After spending most of the morning saying my goodbyes to staff and mates I'd known for years, I left school and went straight up to the hospital, hoping for some good news. For once Sam was sat in her room, smiling.

"It's three cheers to me, I left school at lunch time,"

"So what? Anyway, I will say three cheers to you leaving school. I'm pleased to see you. Gran is going to let me live with her until the beginning of October. I'm moving in as soon as the spare bedroom is cleared of all her junk, as she calls it. Gran still has to find someone to clear it out for her; she is hoping you will help."

"I don't know about that, I've got to find a proper job. I'm a young man now, not a school kid, and clearing this room for Gran isn't a proper job. I have met two blokes that do anything for a few bob. After leaving school without passing any exams, they have become odd-job men. The other day I was told by one of them that they were looking for someone to help them out. The one called Tom suggested that I joined them, so I guess they must have a lot of work on. I'll ask them if they have any spare time, if I offer to help with a few jobs they may do me a favour and fit in clearing Gran's spare room. I'm meeting up with them tomorrow night, so I will ask."

"I didn't know you knew anyone other than me that hadn't passed their exams."

"Well, I do."

I went on to explain where I had met them and that we had planned to go up to the West End for the night. Sam wasn't happy about this as she was worried in case I picked someone up for a quickie.

"Who the hell do you think I am? I wouldn't have a bit of how's your father. I wouldn't dream of it, especially without using a johnny so I've bought some to take with me." I laughed out loud at Sam.

"Well, there you go; you are going to pick someone up if you have the chance."

"Sam, I've grown up since I met you in the girls' lavs. I've decided that it's better to be safe than sorry. If I don't use them myself, I will sell them on to my mates."

"What do you mean, Pete? Obviously you don't like the mess you've got yourself in."

"No I don't, I don't think anyone else would either. In fact, most of the time I wish I had never met you. It is my own silly fault, I should have looked the other way when I saw you coming towards me, showing off your tits and wiggling your bum, the thing is I couldn't resist you. Anyway Sam, I have grown fond of you; in fact, I can say I love you and I'm going to stand by you, this should make you smile."

At that, Sam as usual burst out crying.

"Stop the stupid crying or I will go and I won't return until after the weekend."

Sam looked shocked.

"Don't go."

"Well, stop the tears and smile."

Once she realised that I meant what I said, she immediately stopped crying.

"If you start crying again, I will go and then you won't know if my mates will help clear Gran's spare room. Have you any idea what she is going to do with what she calls her junk once it's out of the room?"

"I have not spoken to her. I don't even know which day I can move in. It was the ward sister that gave me the message, saying that I can live with Gran."

At that, the door was pushed open and in walked sister. "I could hear you two in the corridor, it sounded like you were having another quarrel, try and calm down. Yes, it was me that had a chat with your gran. She didn't even say when Sam could move in, only that she would let Sam live with her. Gran seemed more concerned about her junk as she didn't want to throw any of it out. She did mention to me that her sister might take some of it and put it in her roof space, apparently it's quite full with her own belongings but there should be a bit of room for a few more boxes."

"If there is too much junk, Mum and Dad may let Gran put the rest up in our roof as it will only be for a couple of months. My parents only said that Sam couldn't live with us, they didn't say anything about not taking in any bits and bobs belonging to Sam."

"Well, there you go, Sam. Things may turn out okay. I hope you are listening to Pete."

"Yeah, but how the hell Gran will get the boxes over to Blackheath, I don't know."

"You do know, Sam, I told you earlier that I have two mates with a van that may help at a cost of me doing them some favours."

"Yeah, you said something like that. I don't listen or believe things you tell me as you say a lot of rubbish, like telling me you are going to look after me just after saying you wish you hadn't met me."

"Whatever is the matter with you two? I know that you have a lot on your minds, we are all trying to help, please try and calm down and be nice to one another. Sam, you can start by believing what Pete says to you."

"Sister is right, Sam. Start believing what I tell you."

"I will try to."

"Right, I'm going to go and make you both a cup of tea."

"Please can I have a coffee as I never drink tea?"

"There you go again, Pete, that's not true. You do drink tea; you had a cup the other afternoon."

"You know that is not true, you have never seen me drink tea when you're around."

"Well, what were you drinking when Miss Collins got you a drink? I know it was a cup of tea and you drank it."

"For goodness sake, the pair of you, stop arguing! If you go on behaving like you are, your relationship will end before it begins!"

"Do you hear that, Sam? Calm down like sister says and start believing that I am going to look after you and our baby, also remember I can drink whatever I fancy at the time."

Sam sat on her bed looking stupid. Sister turned to go out of the room and, as she did, she looked over at me and smiled as if to say 'Good, at last Pete is trying to drum some sense into Sam'.

"I do realise, Sam, that I am not the type of bloke you thought you would finish up with. You ought to be grateful that I am going to provide a home for you and our baby. If you'd got pregnant by a chap at a factory, you wouldn't know where you would be going to live. Most probably, it would be a flat in a tower block, if you were lucky... or unlucky, whichever way you want to look at it. I can assure you that we won't be living in one of them."

"I'm used to living in a flat, it might suit me to live in a tower block. I'm not sure that I would manage living in a house with a garden like your mum and dad."

"Well, you will have to try and get used to it, as that is where I want to bring our baby up. In the first instance, we will have to live in a flat; however, I can assure you it won't be in a tower block."

"What will it be in, then?"

"Sam, it's possible to rent flats in terrace houses. These houses become too big for the owners once their families have grown up and have left home, so they have to decide whether to sell or get a builder to alter a section of the house into a flat or a few bedsitters. Usually they do the latter and then remain living in part of the house and rent out the other half. I don't fancy living where the landlord lives, as he would know what we got up to. I'm going to try and find a flat without a landlord living on the premises."

"Pete, if you find one with a landlord living in the building, I'd have company when you go to work."

"That's true, but he might not be very nice. Sometimes landlords go out to work; then again he may have a wife who is at home during the day."

"It's up to you, Pete, but I don't fancy being on my own when you go to work."

"Wherever we live, you will be on your own in the daytime unless we are lucky enough to live near your friends. Sam, I'm going to have another look in the paper and see what I can find. I know it won't be a flat in Blackheath as they are far too expensive. Whatever happens I'm going to make sure that the place I find is comfortable. The problem is, Sam, some landlords won't take in couples that have babies, as once a baby starts to cry he or she continues until they get what they want and this could annoy the neighbours so much that they complain to the landlord and we would get kicked out. Anyway, it's first things first: I have to find a job that gives me enough money to keep the three of us."

"You could always get a job down a factory as a machine operator, the money is supposed to be very good. If you work nights you get twenty per cent more pay than on days."

"I can't imagine working in a factory, the people working there are not what I'm used to mixing with."

"All I can say to you, Pete, you can't need or want the money."

"Sam, you know very well I need money."

"Well if you need money, ring a factory and get a job. Mum was always saying they needed extra staff at her factory. I have

273

a feeling it is the same in all factories, as men seem to enjoy moving around to work in different places, especially if they find out that another factory pays a few pennies more an hour."

"I will have a think about doing that while trying to get a job in an office as that will take quite a few weeks to arrange. Also, they may not take me on without my A levels and I don't get the results until August."

"At least you would be working. There is one thing I have to tell you: Mum always said that the women at Christmas tried to rape the young blokes so I suggest you leave before Christmas week. Mum came home laughing one day and told me how the women had chased this bloke that was head of security right through the middle of the factory. He got away by hiding in the men's lavs, though some of the women waited outside the door for quite a while. I have a feeling it was something like an hour or more before they got fed up and went back to work."

"For goodness sake, Sam, I'm not going to have that happen to me. If I take a job in a factory it will only be for a month or so.
Do you know how much notice you have to give?"

"Yeah, only a week."

"That sounds okay. I may sort that out, then again I might help my mates out or just stay home and paint the sitting room for Mum and Dad."

"It's up to you, Pete. I'm not going to be working. I'll just be hanging around getting bigger and bigger with my clothes getting tighter and tighter waiting for the so-called big day."

"Yeah, but what a big day it will be, Sam; a little person is going to pop out from inside you and say, 'Hello, Mummy.'"

Sam did smile; in fact she started to laugh. "I can't laugh much, it makes our baby kick even harder."

"Be boring and don't laugh, whatever else you do don't cry because I will definitely go on my way if you do, as I'm fed up with tears."

"Don't go, I promise I will try not to cry again."

Eventually the ward sister arrived with the tea.

"At last I'm here with your tea. Sorry I've taken so long but the phone kept ringing and I had to answer it, if it rang once it rang ten times."

"Thanks, once I have drunk this I'm going to go on my way as I haven't been home since first thing this morning. If you hear anything from Gran, please can you give me a ring to keep me up to date about what is happening? I doubt if I will be in again until Sunday afternoon."

"Yes, I will ring you straight away."

"Thanks." Sister went on her way as if she was busy and hadn't time to talk.

"Pete, are you coming in tomorrow?" asked Sam, looking as if her world had come to an end once again.

"I just said that I doubt it. I have to start looking for a job and a flat. Mum wants me to paint the sitting room, walls and ceiling. If Dad has bought the paint I shall start it in the morning, it's going to be a big job. At least if I paint the room I may not have to pay anything for my keep for a week or so."

"What! You are going to have to pay to live at home?"

"Yeah, I've left school, my parents won't keep me."

"Will I have to find money to live with Gran?"

"You will have to ask."

"What if she says yes?"

"Sam please don't give me that worry as well."

"I haven't any money. I will be in trouble big time if I have to pay to live with her."

"The other morning you heard what the sister had to say and that was that Gran is not very well off, so don't be surprised if you have to pay for your keep."

"Where the hell will I get money from?"

"I have no idea. If you didn't have bun in the oven. I could make a suggestion, but, as you have, I have no idea."

"What do you mean by that, Pete?"

"You really are thick! I mean you could go on the game, you could sell your body to frustrated men."

"That's terrible, you suggesting that I should do that!"

"Well you have great tits and a great bum. All you would need to do is buy some fancy clothes along with a pair stilettos, you wouldn't need to buy knickers, that would save you a few bob as some women on the game don't wear them, that could be you."

"I don't believe what you're saying, Pete, I don't know anyone that goes out without wearing knickers."

"The thing is, it saves time if you haven't any to take off."

"You get worse and worse, Pete."

"I can tell you something, a mate at school was told by his elder brother that when he went to the pub one night with a friend, they sat opposite two girls that did not have their knickers on, they apparently sat with their legs wide open. I imagine that they'd had quite a bit to drink as they sat smiling at all the men." "That can't be true, it must be one of your stupid jokes."

"Well I can assure you it's true. I can even point the two girls out as they hang around the Elephant and Castle area most nights."

"If I was not up the duff I wouldn't go on the game. I'd rather starve."

"Well, you would starve; just hope that Gran will keep you. With a bit of luck, she will. Once I've finished this tea, I'm off."

"What do you mean you are off? You haven't been here very long."

"I've got to go and see what is happening outside in the big wide world."

"So you'd rather go than stay with me?"

"Yes Sam, I've been here long enough." I was so fed up with Sam sounding so stupid and thick that I decided to leave before I said something that I might regret.

Chapter 24

I slept well Friday night so I was wide awake Saturday morning, ready to pluck up courage to persuade Mum to let me have some money for my trip up to the West End. As usual it was as difficult as getting blood out of a stone; she would not budge.

"Pete, can you give me a good reason for letting you have this money? It was only the other week when I let you have money for the school dance and what did you do? You went out with your mates and got drunk. I don't want my hard-earned cash spent on drink. Once you have a job and live on your own or with

Sam, you can spend your money how you like."

"But Mum…"

"There is no 'but'."

This conversation went on for most of the day, but, at around five o'clock, Mum gave in by giving me enough money for a return ticket into London.

"Whatever you say to your father, don't tell him that I have given you this or I will never hear the last of it."

"Thank you, Mum. You are the best mum in the world." I gave her a hug. "Now, can I have my supper early? I have to get to the Elephant and Castle by quarter to seven."

"I'm getting fed up with you, Pete! You always want something; if it isn't one thing it is another! What's the time now?"

"Ten past five." I must have sounded fed up.

"No need to sound exasperated, think of your father and me." "I do."

"The earliest you can have your supper is in half an hour, that is quarter to six."

"What, you must be joking! How can I get to the Elephant and Castle by quarter to seven if I don't have supper till then?"

"By getting a move on."

"While you get my supper, I will go and get ready."

"Go on then or your supper will be waiting for you."

It took me a while to get organised, especially finding something to wear that made me look older than my age.

"Your supper is on the table, Pete."

"I'll be down, I'm trying to arrange my hair."

"You asked me to hurry, so I have! Get a move on or it will be cold!"

"I'm coming." I hurried down the stairs.

Mum was stood at the bottom. "Pete, looking like you do, before you know it you will be picking up someone else. If I was your age and I was not your mum, I would be looking over my shoulder at you."

"Well, you are not my age but I'm pleased that you approve of how I look."

"You just be careful. Don't do anything that I wouldn't as we don't want another baby on the way."

"That won't happen. I'd better tell you: I have managed to find money for some johnnies, not that I intend using them."

"Well, why waste your money buying them, if they aren't going to be used?"

"You and Dad have said many times that it is better to be safe than sorry. I can always sell them on to my mates, if I don't need them. They're far too shy to go to a chemist to buy any."

"Thank goodness, Pete you aren't that shy."

At that I settled down to eat my supper, then hurriedly went on my way. It didn't take as long as I thought to get to the Elephant and Castle. When I arrived, my mates, Dave and John, were waiting at the entrance to the station, but Nig and Tom were nowhere to be seen.

"Have you been waiting long?"

"No."

"You haven't seen Nig and Tom?"

"We wouldn't know what they looked like if we had."

"That's true, but you would have noticed two chaps standing around as if they were waiting for someone."

"I suppose we would. We haven't seen anyone standing around."

"We better wait a few minutes in case they are late."

"How many minutes do you think we should give them? The thing is, Pete, if we don't hurry we may not get into the Marquee."

"Five."

The three of us stood in silence.

"Times up!" shouted Dave.

"That was a very quick five minutes."

"It had to be or we'll be late."

With that we went and bought our tickets and made our way to the platform and London town.

The three of us managed to get a seat alongside one another and sat quietly with our thoughts all the way to Charing Cross.

"Well, we have arrived; that didn't take long. Which way do we go?" John asked, looking at me as if I should know the direction to the Marquee.

"It's no good looking at me, John, I'm not sure which way to go."

"You invited us, where is your A to Z?" "I don't possess one," I said sheepishly.

"What, you haven't an A to Z?"

"That is what I said; I don't have an A to Z. If you have one, where is it, clever clogs?" I replied, grinning away.

"At home."

"Well, there you go! You are as bad as me, the only difference being that I don't possess one and you do, but you forgot to bring it with you. We'll never find our way unless we have an A to Z."

"We'd better club together and buy one. Once we get up the escalator, we may see a stall that sells papers and A to Zs."

"We'd better get a tube map as well, I think they are free from the ticket office"

"There is a tube map on the back of the A to Z."

"That's true but it's very small; the one that is free is quite large."

"Okay, we will have to get one, let's go up the escalator."

Once at the top we had a look around for the ticket office, but the queue was far too long. We went on our way and found an A to Z in a paper shop.

Dave paid up for the three of us. "This is my treat."

"That's good of you, Dave. If I had to help pay, we would have to go without one."

"I hope you have enough money to get into the club as I'm not paying for everything."

"You don't need to worry about that, Dave, Mum has given me money for that plus the train fare."

"Pete, what are you going to do about buying a beer? Also, if you pick a bird up, how the hell are you going to pay for her drink?"

"I will think about that when the time comes. We have to get into a club first and then I have to pick the bird up; I might find that a bit difficult."

John got into a bit of a flap and started to ask if he could look at the A to Z to find the way to Wardour Street.

"We've got to find our way to Shaftesbury Avenue first," I said, grabbing the A to Z out of Dave's hand.

"You three look as if you have a problem," said a chap that came up from behind, dressed as a rocker.

"Yeah, we do, we are trying to get to the Marquee."

"That's easy enough. Go to Trafalgar Square, then go up Charing Cross Road, turn left once you reach Shaftesbury Avenue and Wardour Street is third on the right. The Marquee is half way up on the right-hand side."

"Are you local?"

"Sort of, I have a bedsitter above the Indian in Old Compton Street."

"You work around here?"

"Yeah, as a waiter in a restaurant at Leicester Square. It is a dead-end job, but it brings in money and pays my rent. Where do you three hang out?"

"Not around here, or at least not at the moment. We have come up to the West End for a good night out."

"You will have a good night if you manage to get into the Marquee. I could come with you, then I can introduce you to some mates of mine. I often go to the Marquee, it only takes about ten minutes to walk there. What do you think? While you three make your minds up, I'm going to go to the lav." He left us stood looking at one another.

"Come on you two, what do you think?" I said, looking John and Dave in the face.

"I say let's go for it," said John, rubbing his hands.

"Yeah, I'm game," added Dave.

"Come on, Pete, what do you think? For goodness sake don't say that you have to think about Sam; if you do, you may as well turn around and go home."

"I'm game."

At that the rocker returned. "Have you made your minds up?" "Yeah, we'll come with you."

"That's good. Before we move off, we'd better introduce ourselves. I'm Robin."

"That name doesn't suit you, especially with you wearing that leather gear."

"I like my name."

"You might like it, but it definitely doesn't go with your looks."

"It might not go with my looks, but that is my name, Rob for short."

"Right, Rob it will be. That's Pete and Dave, I'm John; we have just come over from the Elephant and Castle."

"I've lived in Old Compton Street for the last year, before that I was living at home with Mum and Dad in a boring place called Aylesbury."

"Pete would like to hear all about living in Aylesbury, wouldn't you, Pete?"

"Not really, I'm not going to live there."

"Well Sam is going to live there."

"Who's she?"

"His so-called girlfriend."

"What is the point in you coming to the Marquee if you already have a bird?"

"Sam and I are not serious."

"What!" shouted John and Dave together.

Rob stood looking at the three of us.

"Well, if serious isn't getting some one pregnant and standing
by them, what is serious, Pete?"

"I'm standing by her, but surely I can come to the Marquee for a good time?"

"Depends what you call a good time. My good time is picking up a bird and going back to her place for a bit of how's your father. I was going to introduce the three of you to some birds that I know."

"Well, you can introduce us. We are game, aren't we, Dave?"

"Yeah."

"What is going to happen to you, Pete?"

"I'm going to come with you. You never know, I may pick someone up. Perhaps we will all pick a bird up; this is London and the birds may be game for a one night stand."

"Has something happened to you, Pete?" said John, looking towards Dave.

"It must have, I've never heard you speak like this before, Pete."

"Well you have now. I've decided that I'm game for anything tonight."

"Let's start walking," said Rob, smiling to himself.

I walked ahead with Rob, who kept firing questions at me about Sam going to Aylesbury to the mother and baby home.

"My parents live down the road from the home, on the way to and from school I used to see the naughty girls – as Mum and Dad called them – pushing their prams around and around the garden." He went on to explain how he sometimes had a chat over the fence to the girls. Apparently, they seemed happy enough.

We soon arrived at the Marquee where, as usual, there was a queue.

"Come on, you three, we don't have to wait here, my friend is on the door; he'll let us in, we shouldn't have to pay.. Move over, you lot, we're coming through." With that, we pushed our way to the front, only to find that Rob's friend was having a night off.

"You three, get to the back – you can't just come up to the front and expect to get in without queuing."

"My mate is normally on the door at this time on a Friday night."

"Who's that?"

"Grant."

"He only works midweek,"

"He was here last Friday."

"He may well have been, but the boss was so fed up with him letting people like you lot in for free on a Friday or Saturday night, he is now only allowing him to work here Wednesday nights eight till midnight. I heard Grant say something about giving in his notice and trying to get a full time job at the 100

Club; apparently the pay is better than here."

"Are you trying to tell me that he's left?"

"I can't say one way or the other, he worked here last Wednesday but I haven't seen him since."

"That's that then, we better get to the back of the queue and decide what to do."

"Yeah, move out of my way before I tell you where to go! I don't have patience with kids like you, that want to get in for free."

We turned around and pushed our way back.

"Chaps, what do you think we should do? Stay here or walk over to the 100 and chance my mate is on the door?"

"The thing is, Rob, none of us have been to either club so we don't mind which we go to. If you think we can get in for free at the 100, we better walk over to Oxford Street."

"I can't promise anything, but the one thing I can say is if we stay here we will pay to get in. That's if we manage to get in, look at the queue. If we go over to the 100 we must hurry as it only holds three hundred and fifty people, and it is a Friday night."

"Well, let's go for it! Come on, boys, get a move on!" shouted John.

We hurried up the road. "See that place over there?" said Rob, pointing across the road.

"Yeah, what about it?"

"It's a club, it's the Simson's."

"So? It doesn't look very interesting."

"I suppose it doesn't. To get in, you have to go up the alley way, it brightens up once you go up there."

"Do many people go in there?"

"Depends on the night. The dance floor is very small so only a hundred or so can get in. The drinks are expensive as it is waitress service, you can't just go up to the bar. Every time you want a drink you have to call a waitress over, also you have to give a tip."

"Are you sure about that?"

"Of course I am, I often go there. If we go over now we may all get in for free as it's before ten. You can join for a year for about five bob. There may be a problem about me going in as I went there the other month and picked up a girl that I thought was on her own; then, out of the blue, her so-called boyfriend came over and told me where to go and hit out at me. A couple of the bouncers heard the upset and came running up the stairs and told us both to get out and not return."

"I doubt whether it will be the same blokes on the door," said John.

"I have no idea as I haven't been back since. If the three of you fancy going into Simson's, that is where we will go, I'm game."

With that, we crossed the road and went up the alley. To my surprise the building was lit up with fairy lights and a sign flashing 'Simson's' and another flashing 'open'.

"Looks a bit tat."

"Whatever do you mean, Pete?"

"Well, look at the flashing lights, looks like the local fish and chip shop."

"I can assure you it isn't, once you get in you should be very impressed."

We wandered up to the door; just as we were about to open it Rob called out to the three of us. "Hang on, you three don't go in yet!" With that, he turned his back on us; when he turned around again, he took the three of us by surprise.

"You look just like Buddy Holly."

"That is the idea. Hopefully the doorman won't recognize me; if he does I'm afraid you three will be on your own. Just remember one thing: it's free for you three as it is your first visit." "Don't you worry about that, we won't forget." I pushed open
the door to be greeted by a six-foot-tall man with a balding head in a black suit, a white shirt and a bright-coloured dicky bow.

"You four want to come in?"

"Yeah," I replied as he looked at the four us very strangely.

"What's wrong with that?" said John.

"Nothing, as long as you behave yourselves; any trouble and you four will be out."

"We won't cause any trouble. At least I won't, I'm the quiet type. I walk away from trouble, I never walk towards it."

"That is what I like to hear."

"So we can come in?" said Dave, looking as if he knew everything about life.

"Yeah, you can all come in before I change my mind."

"Cheers."

"Hang on a minute, you have to be stamped on the back of your hands."

"What?"

"It's instead of a ticket that you can lose or hand over to someone else. It's an ink mark on the back of your hand; it will take a few days to wash off."

We were stamped and in we all went, only to find the place lit by candles and deserted.

"What the hell is going on here? The place is empty, we're never going to pick anyone up."

"You'd be surprised. At around ten, the birds will start coming in. If we sit down at one of the low tables with the large sofas, we will soon have company."

"You four find yourselves a seat, then I will come and take your order," said one of the waitresses in one of the shortest skirts I had ever seen. It took us a while to decide where to sit, eventually we plonked ourselves down at the side of the dance floor.

"At least we can see the sights from here, if there are any."

"Have you all decided what you want to drink?"

"Yeah, I'm going to have a G and T. What are you three going to have?" said Dave, getting out his wallet.

"I've only got enough money for half a pint," I said looking a bit stupid.

"I told you lot yesterday that I would buy the first round. Do you all fancy a G and T on me?"

"Yeah, that will do, Dave."

"Right, four G and T's please. Before you go to get them, can I ask you the length of your skirt?"

The waitress grinned. "Yeah, course you can, all the girls in this club have the same length skirt, they are supposed to be the length of the drinks menu."

"That's bloody short! If you bend over we must be able to see your knickers."

"That's right, many a man has had a good look at my knickers," At that she waddled off to get the drinks, but she soon returned.

"What's your name?" asked Dave.

"You can call me anything you like."

"What do you think we should call her, boys?"

"Sweetie is a good name for you as you appear so sweet," said Rob, eyeing her up and down.

"No one has ever called me that except under the bedclothes."

"Well there you go, they say there is a first time for everything and that includes what you're called."

The four of us settled ourselves down on the sofa and quietly drank our G and T's when suddenly, out of the blue, a couple of girls came over. "Hi, Rob, how you doing?"

"Okay. What you up to?"

"Not a lot," said the most slender of the two, looking along at the three of us.

"Oh, these are my mates, Pete, John and Dave; I met up with them at the station. You three, this is Linda – Lin for short – and that's Liz," said Rob with his arm around Lin's waist

"Cheers!" we all shouted, raising our glasses to the pair of them.

"Can we join you?"

"What do you think, boys?" asked Rob.

"I suppose so, but it would be better if there were four of you."

"Don't worry, boys, there are four of us; the other two have gone to the bog."

At that the pair of them plonked themselves down between John and myself.

"Move along a bit," said Liz, looking at me as if she could eat me up.

"Give me a chance."

"Hold your hair on." She squeezed down on to the sofa, leaning over on to my left leg while Lin sat down next to her. It was a tight fit but very cosy.

"You look like Cilla Black."

"That's good, it was my plan to come out as a lookalike."

"In my opinion you have succeeded – well done. There must be something about dressing up, Rob looks like Buddy Holly."

"He often looks like him. Have you noticed Lin? She is trying to look like Sandy Shaw. It's the fashion here to try and look like someone other than yourself."

"We three must look boring to you lot. Anyway, I will say Lin only looks like Sandy because of the dress she has on."

"You wait; when she gets up to dance, she will kick her shoes off and let her hair down." The six of us sat chatting away when one of the girls that went to the lav came hurrying over to our table from the ladies.

"Rob, you will never believe what's happened. Margaret is locked in the loo,"

"What do you mean, locked in the lav?" said Rob, looking as if he didn't believe what he was hearing. "You are always making up things, most people do lock themselves in the lav for privacy."

"Margaret needs help, she can't unlock the door."

"So, what do you expect me to do, Maureen?"

"Help her. She is banking on you coming back to the lavs with me."

"She will have to think again because I'm not getting involved. You'll have to see the doorman."

"How can I go and see him?"

"Just go and see him, he is over by the door! That's him, that large bloke with the bald head."

"Him?" she said, pointing at the doorman.

"Yes, him. Stop pointing towards him – he'll come over here in a minute if you don't stop looking and pointing. Just go and see him," said Rob.

"I'll go over and see what he has to say." Maureen turned to go but before she started to put one foot in front of the other, the doorman was coming towards her.

"I could see you pointing towards me, what's up?"

By this time Maureen was in quite a flap. "It's my friend, she is locked in the loo."

"Tell her to pull the catch down."

"She's tried that, it won't budge."

"When she has been in there for twenty minutes, let me know; then I will come and help."

"You are telling me that you won't help for twenty minutes?"

"That's what I said. I get fed up with girls like you lot saying things have happened and they haven't."

"Well, this is true, my friend is locked in the lav and can't get out!"

"She will have to wait, I'm busy." He then turned and went back to where he was stood.

"One, two, three…" Then, out of the blue, Rob started singing the song about the three old ladies that were locked in the lavatory.

"I've never heard that song before," said Dave.

"I doubt if you would have. Mum and Dad used to sing it. Apparently my gran introduced them to it; when she'd had a few drinks, she would sing it back in the '40s. I will tell you the words:

> *Hey ho the cat's up the apple tree, three old*
> *ladies are locked in the lavatory,*
> *they've been there from Sunday to Saturday*
> *and no one knew they were there."*

While Rob was singing, the juke box was suddenly turned up and we could hardly hear ourselves speak.

Maureen was not happy about the song, let alone the music being turned up. In fact, she was so unhappy that tears arrived – there must be something about girls and crying.

"For goodness sake, stop the tears! It's not you locked in the lav – if it was, there still wouldn't be any need to cry!" I shouted across to her.

"You don't know me or my friends, so you can't comment about any of us and especially about me crying!" shouted Maureen as loud as she dared.

At that I got up and went over to her, I held out my arms to give her a cuddle. "Sorry, I didn't mean to upset you. By the way, I'm Pete Knight from over the river."

"I'm Maureen from down the street in Soho." With that, I kissed her on the cheek and she immediately gave me the most enormous smile.

"You should keep smiling, you've got a lovely smile."

"Thanks, I'm going back to the ladies to let Margaret know what is happening. What she will say or do, I don't know. I do know one thing and that is that there isn't a space at the top of the door, so she can't climb out over, and the space at the bottom is too narrow to crawl under. She will have to wait for help."

"When you come back, I will buy you a drink. I think you will need one, in fact I will get it in now. What would you like?"

"Vodka and lime."

"Right, vodka and lime it is." Maureen

went on her way.

"What you up to, Pete? Earlier you said you only had money for half a pint," said John, looking a bit surprised.

"That's right."

"Well, how the hell are you going you pay for a vodka and lime?"

"I thought perhaps you lot would help me out and then I could pay you back another day."

"You must be joking! Did you hear that, boys? Pete is asking us to help him pay for a vodka and lime!"

"Have you had a funny turn, Pete?" said Dave.

"No."

"If I help you out with this drink, you'll owe me with interest." "How much will that be?"

"Depends how much the drink costs, also whether Maureen will want more than one. My mum has always said to me not to offer to buy anything for anyone if they can't afford to pay for it, because you won't get your money back. I don't think we should help you out."

"Forget about it. If she reminds me, I will just buy her half a bitter."

"You are getting a bit cheeky."

"Have to, I need to remember that I haven't a job and I don't know when I will get the first. Anyway, I don't know her and I'm hardly likely to meet her again after tonight so she is not worth a vodka and lime." I went back to where I was sitting and carried on trying to chat to Liz. There was a problem as we were sitting under a speaker, so I could hardly hear what she had to say. She did manage to tell me that she worked in Boots in Regent Street and her mate Lin worked at Hamley's toy shop; apparently Maureen and Margaret work in a boutique in Carnaby Street.

"Rob, is the music always this loud?"

"Yeah, good, isn't it?"

"If you say so. I thought we'd come to hear live music."

"We have, they're playing in a pub down the road/ they should be here by quarter to eleven. As soon as the group arrives, there will be a loud cheer."

"So we have to listen to this racket till then?"

"You've got it. If you don't like what the doorman puts on, you'll have to go over to the box and pay to put on your favourite."

"This must be some kind of joke."

"I can assure you it isn't."

"I'm going over to see what I can put on. Coming with me, Liz?"

"Yeah, but I'm not spending any of my money on stupid music."

"It's not stupid if you like what you put on. Have you any favourite songs?"

"No."

"You must like some music, what about the Beatles?"

"What about them?"

"Do you like them?"

"I like them, in fact they look quite dishy in their photos, but I'm not so sure about their music."

I did not know how to reply to this, so I said nothing.

"Pete, why have you stopped talking?" Liz asked me after a moment.

"I was having a think."

"What about?"

"About music and you not being very interested in it."

"I am interested, I like Frank Sinatra songs. Mum has all his records. To be honest, I have never heard a Beatles song You see, Mum and Dad won't have pop music in our house."

"You haven't lived! I'm going to put one on; what about Cilla Black's *Anyone Who Has A Heart*? You must have heard that?

You like trying to look like Cilla, so you must like her music."

"Yeah, I suppose I do," she replied, looking a bit stupid.

"Have you any change, Liz?"

"What, you want me to give you money? I thought you were paying. I told you just now that I'm not putting music on. It cost me enough to come into this dive without having to pay for music."

"It cost me nothing to come in. Anyway, getting back to music... if you help me out, I'll have a dance with you."

"Pete, balls to you! I've never been asked to pay to have a dance with anyone!"

"Well, you have now."

Liz stormed back to where we were sitting and stood in front of my mates and her friend Lin.

"Guess what, boys and Lin? If you can all hear me above this racket, Pete has just asked me to pay to put music on the box so we can have a dance. Has anyone ever had to pay for a dance with a boy? I always thought boys paid for girls!" They all sat, looking up at Liz.

"Pete always wants something for nothing," called out Dave.

"That's not true."

"No need to look so embarrassed, Pete, you know very well it is. If we all go out for a drink, someone else pays, it's never you. I'm waiting for the day when you pay for something."

"Well, today may be the day. If you get lucky, I can provide you with a johnny, just ask."

"What, you provide johnnies? I can hardly believe what I'm hearing! You should have brought johnnies when you met Sam and fancied a bit."

"Eh, Pete, have you got someone up the swanny?" said Liz, looking disgusted and pointing at me.

"Fraid so."

"You have a girlfriend with a bun in the oven?"

"I said yes."

"Well, that is the end of you and me, I'm not into one night stands."

"I'm not into them, either."

"Why are you carrying johnnies around if you aren't looking for a bit on the side?"

"Mummy and Daddy said it was better to be safe than sorry and gave me money for them. Would you like one?" I asked, taking the packet out of my trouser pocket and laughing in her face.

"Pete, you are the most disgusting, stupid bloke I have ever met!"

"Well, you can't have met many."

"I'm leaving you lot to it, I'm going to see how Margaret and Maureen are getting on in the loos." With that, Liz put her nose in the air and walked away. Lin followed her.

"That will teach you, Pete! You need to learn to keep your big mouth shut and your eyes open."

I sat down on the sofa with my head in my hands, wondering what to do next, as I knew full well Liz would tell the girls what had happened.

"You have made yourself look completely daft. If I was in your shoes, I would disappear before the four of them come back. You shouldn't have made such a ridiculous statement. If you get a second chance remember that you are in a London club and the girls here are more mature than in Blackheath or at the Elephant and Castle In other words, Pete: grow up," said Dave looking very annoyed with me.

I didn't know what to do, as I was getting more and more embarrassed by the minute.

"Pete, I suggest you go to the lav and wash your face in cold water to cool yourself down," said Rob, looking along at the three of us. "As well as making yourself look a complete fool, Pete, you have made me feel daft. I hope the girls come back and forget what you said. The thing is, Pete, I have my eye on Margaret, so, before you decide to set your sights on her, she's mine."

"Hold your hair on, I will go to the lav and sort myself out, then I'll come back and keep my mouth shut."

"You better. If you don't, you will have lost John's and my friendship."

"Before the girls come back, who would like a Johnny? I'm giving them away."

With that, I hurried on my way before they completely lost their rag with me.

Chapter 25

I stayed in the lav for a good half-hour. The first twenty minutes I spent in a cubicle, sitting on the lid. Once I'd calmed down, I went out into the main area to rinse my face in cold water.

"Who are you?" said a voice from behind me.

I turned around and there stood the doorman. "Why do you want to know who I am?"

"You've just come out of that lav and left it in a disgusting state. There's shit and wee everywhere," he said, pointing at the second door on the left.

"I was in the first cubicle," I replied.

"No, you weren't, I was in the first. I saw you come out of the second cubicle and I've just popped my head round to see the state of it," said the doorman, who was getting ever more annoyed."

"Is this a fucking stitch up? I reckon it is!"

"No, it's not a stitch up. I'm going to get a mop and bucket for you to clean it up."

"Hang on a minute, old man. Let me have a look, because all I've bloody done in there is sit on the lid and pull the flush when
I came out. After that, I've just washed my face and hands."

"So you are saying you didn't use the bog?"

"That's what I said."

"If that is the case, why the hell did you pull the flush?"

"Because I fucking felt like it," I said sarcastically, looking the doorman directly in the face.

"This will teach you a bloody lesson, then. You are going to clean up this bloody mess; there is shit and wee everywhere."

"It's not my bloody fault! The fucking lav must have been blocked!"

"In my opinion, boy, it is your fault because you didn't lift the lid to see what was going on inside."

"How the hell can I clean it up dressed like this?"

"The same way as anyone else with a mop and bucket. Don't you dare go anywhere, just stay put."

"I will, Mr Doorman. Before you go, do you smoke?"

"Yeah, but what is that to do with cleaning?"

"I was wondering if you can let me have a fag. I need one."

"If you smoked, you would have your own fags. I don't want to be the one to give you your first, they're addictive and you may not be able to give them up. I guess you know they cause cancer. I'm addicted to them. Every day I wish I'd never taken my first puff. As soon as I open my eyes in the morning I start coughing, at the same time I'm looking for my fags and I smoke at least three before breakfast. If you could see me, then you wouldn't want to start smoking Sorry, I'm not giving you your first."

"I've had a fag before."

"Well, I'm not going to give you your second, I'll be back in a bit."

With that, he went on his way and it seemed ages before he returned, carrying the bucket and mop.

"Here you are, the cubicle should be as clean as a new pin within half an hour. I'll see you later."

"I'm not going to clean the bloody cubicle for you or anyone else!" I shouted after him.

The doorman immediately turned around to face me. "You'd better clean it – if you don't, you'll get a bill."

"Well, I won't be bloody paying it! I haven't any money!"

"I'll be back in half an hour. If it's not clean by then, you'll be in trouble, big time."

He was gone before I could say any more. I stood there, thinking about how I could get out of this mess, when John and Dave arrived. Their faces were a picture."Thought we'd better come and look for you," said John, looking shocked at seeing me mopping up the mess. "What the hell has happened?"

"Don't ask, there's been an accident and, before you say anything, I have not done anything wrong."

"I don't believe you, Pete. If you didn't make the mess, why the hell are you cleaning it up?"

"Because the doorman caught me coming out of this cubicle after I had flushed the lav and it flooded over."

"Well, you could see it was blocked so you shouldn't have used it or flushed it."

I went on to explain what had happened, Dave suggested that I jumped out of the window and bolted up the road. "You two coming with me?"

"No, we're not."

"If I jump out the window I won't know where to go. I'm going to come back to the table and pretend nothing's the matter. When I see the doorman coming up here, I'll leave by the main door. How I'll get home alone, I don't know."

"Do that then, but don't expect either of us to stand up for you if he comes over."

The three of us rushed back to the table.

"Let me sit between the two of you. Move over, John."

Then, out of the blue, bright spark Dave came out with, "You can always go and hang around in Wardour Street until we come out. You might get picked up by a rent boy or you may be even luckier and find yourself a lady of the night."

"If either happened, it would cost you," said John, laughing out loud. "Rob, have you any ideas?"

"Ideas about what?" called Rob, who was standing across from the sofa, chatting and laughing with his mate.

"Pete is in trouble." Dave went on to explain what had happened. "Have you any suggestions?"

"I can think of one. I could give you the key to my flat or we can all leave with the girls and all of us go back to my place with a bottle or two. Which do you all fancy?"

The three of us looked at one another. "Nothing much is happening here. Also, we didn't have to pay to come in so let's all go back to your place," suggested John.

"We'll have to wait for the girls, twenty minutes must have gone ages ago, they should be here any minute. Pete, you just remember what I told you earlier – I have my eye on Margaret, so don't you dare make a move on her."

"I haven't forgotten, you are welcome to her especially if she's been round the block a few times."

"Enough of that! I will chuck you out of my flat if you dare make a move on Margaret."

"I don't understand why you think I fancy her. I was sitting with Liz before all the upset. As soon as I see the doorman going towards the lavs, I'm off."

"Go then, I saw him going up there five minutes ago. We'll see you outside my flat in Old Compton Street – if you're not there when we arrive, we will think you have been picked up."

"How the hell do I find your flat?"

"Easy! Cross the road outside here, go towards Shaftsbury Avenue, then take the first turning to the left, Stay on the left side of the road. Eventually, you will come across an Indian restaurant where an Indian with a red turban will be standing outside. Now go back ten feet, as you've gone too far. You will see a blue door
– wait outside till we all arrive." I
left.

I soon found the door to the flat. I sat on the step and waited.

"What the hell do you think you are doing sitting here?" said the Indian with the turban, pointing down towards the step.

"Waiting for my mate, he lives here."

"You'd better tell me his name, then I will tell you if he lives here or not."

"Rob."

"Rob what?"

"I don't know his surname, he's never told me."

"He can't be much of a friend. Is Rob short for Robin or Robert?"

"Robin."

"What rubbish, the chap I know that lives here is called Nick! At least, that's what he told me."

"Well, I'm waiting for Rob. We will have to see who turns up; Rob or Nick. What a laugh!"

"I don't think it's a laugh. He pays me rent, I own the flat, both of us have been taken for a ride, regarding his name."

"I suppose we have."

"You can stay sitting on this step till the restaurant closes, which is at eleven. Then you will have to go; I'm not allowing anyone to sleep rough here. Never have and never will."

"Hold your hair on, I understand what you're saying."

"Good, I'm going back to my job, standing guard at the door of the Indian restaurant."

"Before you go, why are you doing a job if you are the owner of the flat and are taking rent?"

"It is none of your bloody business why I work, but, as you've asked, I will tell you. I also own the restaurant and I'm fussy who I allow through the door for a meal. My son is the cook and a very good cook he is. My wife is the waitress."

"You only have one cook and one waitress? That sounds strange to me. All I can say is that you can't be very busy, not like that restaurant at the bottom of Regent Street."

"I've just told you, I'm fussy who we feed. We used to let anyone in, some were tipsy and one night a bloke spewed up in his serviette. That finished me having all and sundry in, as the other guests walked out without paying – I was left out of pocket."

"You should have asked the man who spewed up to pay."

"I did but he legged it. There was no point in phoning for the police; he was gone and his mates had run away with him."

"It would be no good me wanting a meal even though I like the smell that is coming out."

"I would let you in, you seem a nice enough bloke. Are you hungry?"

"Yeah, but I've never eaten Indian food. Also, I'm as poor as a church mouse. The thing is, I've only just left school and I haven't got a job."

"I'll come back in a mo," After a few minutes, Mr Indian returned with a tray. "I've found you some food. Have a taste of this. I can't invite you to eat inside as all the tables are taken."

"Smells good, Mr Indian."

He seemed quite amused to think I had nicknamed him this. "I've been called all sorts over the years, but never Mr Indian. I quite like it, son. What is your name? I mean real name, not nickname." "Pete."

With that, he left me to eat.

The step was quite wide, so I was able to place the tray next to where I sat. I enjoyed every mouthful. The only trouble was Mr Indian hadn't brought me out a glass of water, so the inside of my mouth was burning like hell. Once I'd finished eating, I decided to be helpful and take the empty plate and tray into the restaurant.

"Mrs Indian, please can I have a drink of water?"

"You talking to me, son? I'm not a soft touch like my old man.

I have a name is Mrs Rajiv."

"Mrs Rajiv, please can I have a glass of water?"

"That's better, I'll go and get you one."

While I was drinking the water down in one go, Mr Indian rushed in through the front door to let me know that my friends had arrived in the flat. "There's going to be eight of you in that flat tonight, too many for my liking. Please tell Rob/Nick – whatever you want to call him – not to make a noise. Tell him to remember that parties are not allowed."

"I'll tell him," I replied, smirking to myself. "Thanks for giving me some food. Very nice food, it was, very nice indeed, Mr Indian."

"I didn't think you were the sarcastic type, Pete." "I'm not." I looked across at him strangely.

"I'm sorry to have to say this, but I think you are. I should go before I change my mind about you."

"I'm off. Thanks for the sample of Indian food, Mr Indian, it was very nice."

I hurried out the door and immediately rang the bell of Rob's flat. There was a lot noise coming from inside; it sounded as if someone was falling downstairs.

The door was opened by John. "Come in, come in, sir, you are very welcome."

"Thank you, kind sir." With that, I tripped over the door step and finished up lying on the concrete floor.

"Get up, you stupid idiot! You seem to have come to disturb the peace!" hissed an annoyed John.

"I can assure you, I haven't. I've just come from the restaurant next door, Mr Indian told me to tell Rob that we have to be quiet and that parties are not allowed."

"Don't be so daft, Pete, that can't be true. We are all upstairs; Rob hasn't said anything about not making a noise."

"Perhaps he hasn't got around to telling you all about trying to be quiet."

"Mind you, we have all had quite a lot to drink. When you left, Dave became very generous and got his wallet out to pay for all the drinks. He also paid for the cans and the vodka that we bought at the off-licence, so most probably Rob's forgotten about being quiet."

We both climbed the stairs and found the others standing in the sitting room, sorting out the cans of beer along with the bottle of vodka.

"Have you lot bought enough drink?"

"Yeah, I paid for it all," said Dave. "At the end of the month, I shall be handing you two a bill for your share of it. The girls have paid up for the vodka. Rob is not paying for any of it as he is providing the flat."

"Yeah, that is correct," he said, saluting me.

"Before you go mad and turn the music up, I've met your landlord and he told me that you are called Nick, not Rob. So which is it, Nick or Rob? Also, he said that it states no parties in the contract for this flat."

"He is a stupid old fool, don't take any notice of him. If I want a party I'll have one, he can't do anything about the noise. The other week I had over twelve of us up here. He kept banging on the ceiling, I kept turning the music up, eventually he rang the bell, we all pretended to be deaf, I didn't answer the door. Take note, I'm still here."

"Yeah I do notice that, I'm wondering for how much longer?"

The doorbell rang. "I'll go," said Dave, starting to run down the stairs.

Rob didn't take any notice and carried on talking about his name. "Now, about my name: it depends on the day of the week what I'm called and, of course, who I'm with. Some girls like the name Rob, others hate it, so then I'm called Nick."

I decided in my wisdom to shut up and just enjoy myself. I went over to Liz, who was still trying to look and act as if she was Cilla, but at the same time she looked bored out of her skull.

"What's up with you?"

"Not a lot, I'm just wishing that I could find myself a man like my mates."

"I'm here and I'm lonely, I'll keep you company. Let me pour you a drink."

"I'll have a vodka with a dash."

"Dash of what? We have lime or orange."

Liz looked at me as if I was daft.

"Pete, for goodness sake, lime. Orange doesn't go with vodka, orange goes with gin."

"Well, which is it? Gin and orange or vodka and lime?"

"Vodka to start with, then I will change over to a gin and orange."

I found a tumbler for the vodka and managed to find a coffee mug for my beer.

"Here you are, pour this down your throat, then I'll get you a gin and orange."

Before I blinked, the vodka had gone and Liz was handing back the empty glass.

"I need the G and O now!"

"That was quick."

"Well I've got to catch up with the others. They are miles ahead of me. Margaret has had more drink than any of us," said Liz, sounding quite slurred.

"I'll see if I can find the gin." I went over to the table, only to find there wasn't any. "Rob, got any gin?" I shouted.

"Depends who it's for. If it's for you, no; if it is for Liz, the answer is yeah, it's in the kitchen cupboard behind the plates. Don't you let her drink it all."

We both wandered into the kitchen where we found at least another ten people that Dave had let in.

"Who are you lot?" said Liz, looking round at them all.

"We can ask you the same question. We come here most weekends but we've never seen you lot before," said the bloke that was closest to the pair of us.

"Liz, I think you should sit down before you fall down."

"I'm getting in the swing of things. Hurry up with that gin, then I will sit down on you." She started to pull on my arm, making me very unsteady when pouring the gin.

"Watch it, you silly bitch, the gin is going everywhere but in the glass."

"Don't call me a silly bitch," said Liz, looking around at everyone to see who was going to stand up for her.

"Don't you call her that in front of me."

"Well, that's what she is. Take this, Liz. Drink it, before it goes all over the floor."

"I will drink it, then I will sit down on you."

"You are a lucky boy," laughed one of the girls.

"I'm not taking advantage of her. If she wants to sit on me, she does it when she's sober."

"Pete," screamed Liz, "you are a complete and utter bore."

"You may think that, but there are plenty of birds around that would be pleased that I didn't take advantage of them when they'd had one too many."

"And there are plenty that would like to be taken advantage of," said Rob, peeping around the corner of the door, laughing with the best of them.

"Go back to your woman, Rob. You wanted to pick up Margaret, now you have keep your nose out of my business."

"You remember who you're talking to. This is my flat; behave yourself or you will be out on your neck," said Rob, slurring his words and falling backwards into the sitting room.

"Right, Liz, let us find some where cosy. If you want to take advantage of me, let's start by going out on the landing. Hold on to my arm?"

With a lot of to-ing and fro-ing we eventually arrived on the landing.

"See that door over there?" said Liz, pointing anywhere but at the door.

"Yeah, what about it?"

"The bathroom's behind that door, we could go in there."

"I suppose we could, that's better than staying out here."

We staggered over. Once inside, I locked the door behind us, letting us spend the next couple of hours sat on the floor leaning against the wall having a snog, with me trying to get Liz to take advantage of me without any success.

"I'm going to have to go in a second as it is past two o'clock and I'm not getting any joy with you."

"What do you mean you aren't getting any joy?"

"Exactly what I said, I'm not getting any joy. In other words, you are a waste of time."

"No, I'm not."

"You tell me why you're not, you have had too many drinks, you keep falling asleep, along with saying you are going to spew up. Thank God you haven't, I'm leaving." With that, I attempted to stand up and walk towards the door. Liz held on to my right leg so managed to pull me over. "I've just told you I'm going, so let me go."

I think she realised that I meant what I said and I eventually succeeded in getting out of the bathroom, to be confronted by John who was sitting on the landing.

"Great night, isn't it, Pete?"

"If you like not having any joy when you pick someone up for a one-night stand, it's great."

"Ha, ha, ha."

"Where is your bird?"

"She is looking for more drink. The girls have drunk all the vodka. Lin wants more so she is going around getting the dregs out of the other girls' glasses. I'm not having anything to do with it, that's why I'm sat here."

"You realise it's two o'clock and we have to get home?"

"Don't be such a bore, Pete. If we leave, we can't get home so we may as well stay till morning."

"My mum and dad won't be very happy with me."

"You've left school so they can't say much."

"You'd be surprised what they can say. Surely you can remember what they were like when we went back to my place from the pub, where I got plastered."

"Yeah, I remember. I don't think Dave and I will ever forget."

The bathroom door swung open and Liz was sat in the door way, looking half asleep. "I've been asleep." "So?" I said.

"I woke up and found you missing."

"I told you I was leaving as you're a waste of time."

John sat laughing while Liz got more and more embarrassed by the minute.

"What do you mean, a waste of time? You wanted me to sit on you. Guess what happened, John? Pete couldn't get a hard, so
I went to sleep."

"You know very well that's not true."

"Tell me what really happened, then."

"You had far too much to drink, and every time you tried to get your knickers off you rolled over on the floor. In future, don't drink so much, now piss off."

Liz looked so stupid that she crawled away towards the sitting room.

"You aren't very lucky with birds, Pete."

"You can say that again. One thing I'm pleased about and that is that nothing untoward happened."

John and I fell asleep, but, before we knew it, Rob was kicking us in the bum. "Get up, you two, it's time to go, you can't stay here any longer."

"What?" said John, half asleep.

"Everyone out!" screamed Rob, looking towards the sitting room. "You've all got to go!"

I looked at my watch. "It's only six o'clock."

"That's right, it's six o'clock – everyone out!"

"It's Sunday, surely we can stay a bit longer?"

"No, pick up your rubbish and go," said Rob, standing at the top of the stairs as if he was directing the traffic.

"Where's Dave?"

"I don't know and I don't really care unless he has taken Maureen into my bedroom and they are in my bed. If I find them in there, there'll be trouble, big time. You go and look for them, Pete. If you find them in bed, let them know that they will be going to the launderette before going home."

"What! I will go and look for them, but you can tell them that yourself."

"I will, don't you worry."

The door to Rob's room wouldn't open; it seemed as if Dave had propped the back of a chair under the handle. I banged on the door.

"Can you hear me, Dave?"

"Yeah, we can hear you," replied Dave.

"If you two are in Rob's bed, you are going to be in big trouble."

"We aren't, I wouldn't dream of getting in someone else's bed."

"Well, open the door and come out. We've got to go."

"Give us a chance."

"Hurry up, we all have to go now." The door opened and I went in to see the state of the bed. "You have both been in this bed! Look at it! Rob will be after you. I hope you know how to work a washing machine."

"What do you mean?"

"You are going to have to wash the sheets down the launderette."

"I've never been to a launderette in my life, also I wouldn't know where to go to find one round here."

"I think you should have thought about that before using someone else's bed for a bit of how's your father."

"Don't take any notice of Rob. He always says that about people using his bed, he doesn't mean it. Some Saturday nights, more than one couple have used his bed by morning."

"You're joking!"

"No."

"Maureen, you're telling me that you have been here before and also used this bed before?"

"Yeah, you've got it, Dave. I'm here most weekends. I've used Rob's bed many times. Every weekend Rob says the same old rubbish, he also tries to get everyone out by six but he doesn't succeed. I'll tidy up the bed like I normally do, you go."

305

Dave kissed her goodbye. "I'll ring you, write your number on my hand."

"Do I have to?"

"Yeah you do, I would like to meet up with you. Here's a pen."

"What, even after I've told you I'm here most weekends with different blokes?"

"I expect he thinks he can change you," I said, laughing.

Dave held out his hand. Whether it was her number or not that she wrote, we will have to wait and see.

"Right, we're off. Bye for now."

We left the bedroom and found John waiting where I'd left him, sitting at the top the stairs and chatting to Rob.

"Are you ready, John? We're going!" I called back as I followed Dave down the stairs.

"I'm coming!" shouted John, hurrying after us.

Chapter 26

Once outside, Dave remarked, "I'm in charge of getting us back to the station."

"You don't know how to get to the station any more than we do," replied John.

"One thing I have is the A to Z – that's more than either of you have."

"Suppose you are right there. Which way do you suggest we go, clever clogs?"

"Back to Wardour Street, then we can stop and have a look at the map."

We all walked as quick as we could towards the end of the road. John and Dave seemed to be walking in every direction except in a straight line.

"You two, walk like me in a straight line or we'll never get to the end of the road."

"Pete, are you saying you're walking in a straight line? That's a joke, because you keep going around in circles."

"You two follow me," said John "Let's hold on to one another around the waist, as if we're doing the conga."

This was quite a good idea except we were stopped by a copper in a patrol car.

"What do you three think you are doing?"

"The conga."

"You're in the middle of the road."

"So we are."

"Get over on the path before I book you."

"You are going to book us for dancing up Old Compton Street?"

"I will if you don't get on the path."

"We'll get over on the path immediately, kind sir," said Dave, saluting the police officer.

"Enough of your cheek, my boy, where have you been and where are you going?" asked the police officer.

"We've been above the Indian and we are going back to the Elephant from Charing Cross station."

"Why are you walking this way?" "Don't know," I answered.

"It's quicker if you go the other way. Jump in, I'll take you to Charing Cross."

"Thanks."

"Hurry up, I haven't all day."

I got in the front and Dave and John managed to clamber in the back. Before we knew it we were falling out of the car at the railway station. After saying our goodbyes we went down on to the platform where we found a bench. Two of us had a snooze while the other one acted as a lookout.

"Wake up, you two!" shouted John as the tube rattled into the station.

Dave and I almost fell off the bench.

Once we arrived at the Elephant and Castle we said our goodbyes and I went on my way.

Eventually I arrived home and unlocked the front door, hoping that I could get to my room without disturbing anyone, but Dad was coming down the stairs, looking like thunder.

"What time do you call this, Pete?"

"Don't know and don't really care."

"Go into the kitchen and look up at the clock."

"I don't need to do that, I have a watch."

"Well, look at it then! Tell me what time it is!"

"Why do I have to do that?" I said, becoming more and more annoyed.

"I want you to tell me the time! If you won't look at your watch, I'll tell you the time: it's half eight in the morning. You have been out all night."

"So?"

"If you intend staying out all night, you had better get yourself a job and find yourself a bedsitter to live in. Then you can arrive home whatever time you like. Your mother and I expected you home by midnight."

"I didn't say I was coming home by midnight. I can't remember saying what time I was coming home; I nearly stayed away until tomorrow." I slid down on to the hall floor, laughing at Dad.

"Your mother and I have been worried sick. I mean what I'm saying, you have to get a job, then leave home. It's no good you thinking I will change my mind because I won't, it's obvious to me that you've had far too much to drink once again. I daren't think who paid for the drinks because Mum has told me she only let you have a few bob, definitely not enough money to get drunk."

"Oh, I have a friend called Dave in high places, he has been given money by his dad and he bought all the drinks."

"His father must be stupid."

"You may call it stupid, I call it great. Move out of the way so I can go up to my room."

"When you've got up off the floor, I will move. Until then, I'm staying put." I tried to get up but finished crawling along the hall to the sitting room, where I held on to both arms of one chair and helped myself up.

"Out the way, I'm coming through, you stupid old git."

"I can't imagine who you've been mixing with to talk to me like that."

"Dear friends."

"All I can say to you is your dear friends aren't very suitable. Go up to your room and stay there until you have sobered up."

"I will." With that, I carefully put one foot in front of the other and went up to my room, where I slept for most of the day.

I was woken by Mum knocking on my door at five o'clock. "Pete, get up or you won't sleep tonight."

"Dad told me to stay here till I've sobered up. I can't get straight up, my head is killing me."

309

"That serves you right. Supper will be on the table in half an hour."

"If you get me a couple of Panadol with a glass of water, I'll take them, and try and get up."

"I'm not your servant, get your own tablets. Get dressed and come downstairs."

I managed to get out of bed. Once I'd taken the Panadol I felt a bit better. Mum, Dad and Anne were sat around the table waiting for me. Anne was smirking to herself while Dad and Mum were sat looking like thunder.

"I hope you listened to what your father said when you came home."

"What was that?"

"Don't pretend you didn't hear what I said."

"I didn't."

"Well, your father and I want you out."

"I haven't a job or anywhere to live."

"We are giving you a month to get yourself together, plenty of time. We are prepared to help with the deposit for a bedsitter and moving your things out of here, there's plenty of jobs available."

I looked over at Dad.

"Yeah, that is what we both want. While looking for a job, you can paint this room. You painting it will save us money so it will pay for your keep."

"Your father brought the paint plus brushes home last night, they are out in the shed."

"I might have said that I could paint the room, but I never dreamt you'd take me up on it. What colour paint have you got, Dad?"

"White for the ceiling and cream for the walls."

"Eh, boring colours," said Anne, laughing at me.

"Enough of that, Anne. Tomorrow, we will all help clear the room for painting."

"You must be joking!"

"No this is not a joke, I'm being serious."

"What about seeing Sam?"

"I forgot about Sam," said Mum, winking at Dad.

310

"The ward sister phoned last night. Almost as soon as you went out the door. She rang to say that Sam's moving out on Monday morning to her gran's flat." "That can't be true."

"I can assure you that it is."

"The bedroom's full of Gran's things."

"It isn't any more, her home help has cleared the room."

"What else did the ward sister want?"

"Nothing, Sam isn't expecting you. Apparently, you told her you wouldn't be in over the weekend, so you have plenty of time to get this room arranged for painting on Monday. Also, you will still have time to look through the papers at the jobs; your father has kept a few *Evening Standards* back for you to look at."

"I did tell Sam I wouldn't go in over the weekend, but I could go in tomorrow afternoon."

"This room comes first. We will all get up early and move the furniture out, so no laying in tomorrow for any of us." "I'm not getting up early," shouted Anne.

"'Fraid you will have to help, as your dad and I are getting on and we can't lift everything out."

"I don't see why I should help, I didn't offer any assistance when Pete suggested he would paint the room."

"We are a family and families help each other, so you will be helping," said Dad.

"I will sleep on that, depends how I feel."

"You will be helping, my girl."

"I won't if I have stomach ache."

"You won't have a stomach ache if I have anything to do with it," replied Mum.

Sunday came and went. Before I knew it, it was Monday morning and I was painting the ceiling. I was left to my own devices as Mum and Dad went off to work and Anne went to school.

It only took a couple of hours to put the first coat of white paint on the ceiling, so I had plenty of time to look through the papers at the jobs. I noticed there were part-time jobs at the Elephant and Castle with just a few full-time permanent jobs going in the banks and insurance offices in different areas across London. I used the phone in the first instance to ring for the application forms for the permanent jobs. They promised to send them out immediately, so all I had to do was sit back and wait for the post.

The part-time jobs were a different matter as the employers needed the applicants to call in or phone to arrange for an interview. I spent most of the afternoon ringing around trying to get an interview for any part-time job that I fancied. I was lucky enough to get an interview at McFisheries at the Elephant and Castle, this was for two days a week and also at a bakery further down the Old Kent for three days. They both arranged the interviews for Tuesday afternoon, so I had plenty of time to give the ceiling another coat of paint before leaving.

The men who interviewed me at both jobs asked the same awkward questions, the main one being why did I want to work behind a counter part-time when I seemed to have been well educated. I never dreamt they would ask any questions, let alone this one. I just thought that they would look at me and think 'he's clean and well-spoken', then give me the job without thinking about anything else. In fact, they even needed references.

"Am I hearing right, you need references for me to work behind the counter in a fish shop?"

"That's what I said. I can't take you on unless I have two references, one from your school and one from someone that knows you well, such as a vicar."

"I don't go to church, never have, so that's that. I will have to think of someone else."

"You can always ask your doctor, he must have known you for most of your life."

"Yeah, I suppose he has."

"Well, ask him."

"I will."

At that, the fishmonger handed me a scrap of paper with a biro.

"Now, write down the name of your headmaster and the address of your school along with the other person that I can get a reference from."

"Okay." I did what he asked.

"When will I hear if I've got the job?"

"As soon as I've interviewed everyone and got your references back. Let's think two weeks' time."

He stood up and held out his hand for me to shake it. I then went on my way to the bakery.

The baker, Tom Hall, didn't seem much older than myself but he knew what he was talking about. After showing me around he took me into his tiny office where he offered to make me a coffee. He told me all about the job that he had available and explained the days and hours I would be working if he offered it to me – on Friday from eight thirty a.m. to four thirty p.m. and on Saturday from eight thirty a.m. to two p.m. He went on to tell me that he was also looking for an apprentice baker and asked if I would be interested.

"To be honest with you, I've never thought about becoming a baker."

"I'll explain a bit about being an apprentice. The first thing I need to tell you is that you would have to be here at four in the morning, but you would be going home at around two. What do you feel about that?"

"I don't know. How the hell would I get here from Blackheath, let alone get up before four?"

"I have a couple of rooms upstairs where you could live rent free. All you would have to pay for is your electric and food."

"That sounds okay. Have I got this right, two days working in the bakery and four days working with you as an apprentice with the day off on Sunday?"

"Yeah, you've got it."

"Can you show me where I would be living?"

"Yeah, I'll take you up before you go. Have you got any questions?"

"A few."

"Fire away."

"What about money, how much will I get paid?"

"You will obviously be paid so much an hour for the few days' you work in the shop. For being an apprentice, you will have free rent, also free bread and cakes from the shop."

"That seems quite good, when would you want me to start?"

"As soon as I have received good references."

"Forget about them, when will you want me to start?"

"Well, I'm not able to take you on without any references, so I can't forget them," he said, looking at me as if I was daft.

"If you let me have a bit of paper I'll write down the names and addresses of a couple people you can get in touch with."

"Write down their phone numbers as well, then I'll give them a ring."

"I'm sure you can find the numbers in the phone book, I don't know them."

"Yeah, I'm sure I can if I'm interested enough. Anyway, write down the names and addresses." He gave me a strange look that made me feel awkward and embarrassed.

"Once you've done that, I will take you to the rooms."

The baker went on to tell me about his father and how he used to own the bakery. Apparently he died a few years back, so Tom has been in charge ever since. Until a while ago he had a girl apprentice, but she wasn't any good at baking so he had to let her go.

"I might look a bit young to be in charge, but I can assure you that I won't stand any nonsense. If you start mucking me about,
you will see the door like the girl did."

"I understand."

"Is there anything you need to tell me? If I take you on, I hope
I won't get any nasty surprises."

"You won't get any of those from me." "No
skeletons in the cupboard, then?" "No," I
answered.

"Right then, I will take you upstairs to show you around."

To go upstairs we had to go outside on to the pavement, then along to a filthy green door at the side of the bakery.

"This is where you have to go to get to your rooms. Everyone who works in the bakery has to share your lav and bathroom, the key to this door hangs behind the door in the bakery."

Tom took me up the stairs that made a harsh squeaking sound, every step of the way. The bathroom was situated at the top on the left. The first thing that I could see when the baker opened the door was a very old water heater, which was used to fill both the bath and basin. This was screwed to the wall between the two. The lav, well, this was usable but the seat needed replacing.

We went on into the main room that was to be my bedsitter. The walls were covered in cream paint with dark brown lino on the floor. On top of the lino was a rug that appeared to be handmade.

"Mum made the rug especially for this room, it's old now. At the time, it was her pride and joy. If you come and work here you'll have to make sure you look after it, as I can't afford to replace it."

My face must have looked a picture.

"Sorry about the state of this room, at least you will have an armchair to sit in and a mattress to sleep on. The thing is, Pete, you can't expect much for free. I doubt if you will spend any of your spare time up here."

"I doubt if I will."

The kitchen was through an archway and consisted of a stove and a couple of cupboards. On the floor was yellow lino with holes so that bare floor boards could be seen beneath it.

"Before we leave, where do I wash my dishes as there isn't a sink?"

"In the basin in the bathroom. You'll have to put a bucket underneath as it leaks, someone who worked here a while ago cracked it in temper. I've tried to repair it with elastoplast without success."

"That doesn't work, my dad did that once when ours cracked at home. He finished up buying a new basin."

"Don't you get that sort of idea because I won't be buying one, it would cost a fortune to get a plumber into replace that. If

I take you on, you will have to put up with it – buckets are cheap enough."

"I know that, I can buy one up the market."

"You've got it, Pete, you are my sort of chap."

With that, we went back down the stairs and out on to the pavement where we said our goodbyes.

Chapter 27

Once Tom had gone back into the bakery and was out of sight, I decided to walk further down the road to see if I could find Gran's flat, but I couldn't. Sam had told me that it was just past the surgery on the left-hand side in the Old Kent Road. There were a few flats on the corner, but they didn't look suitable for Gran, so I turned around and went back to the Elephant and home.

I arrived home. This time, it was mum waiting for me. "A man phoned about half an hour ago, saying he wanted to offer you a job at a bakery."

"That was quick."

"What do you mean?"

I went on to explain how I'd been for a couple of interviews.

"That's good because your father and I meant it when we said we wanted you out. I'm very pleased that there is a room with the job."

"Don't get too excited about the room, as it's awful, but it is somewhere to sleep. If you help me to move in, you will see it and wish you hadn't told me to leave home – it's pretty grim."

"Your father and I will never wish that, we are fed up with you and the problems you have brought to this house."

"The other week you told me that I was not that bad."

"We are allowed to change our minds and Sunday morning was the last straw, so the bakery is where you are going to live... that's if you take the job. Are you taking the job?"

"I guess I will have to, Once the baby is born and Sam is living with me, we will have to find a proper flat."

"Can't you stay above the bakery with a baby?"

"No, once you have seen the place, you will understand why."

"Right, I will look forward to seeing it,"

"Good, now I will ask you one question. Have I got to ring the baker back?"

"He didn't say. He asked to speak to you; when I said you were out, he said to tell you the job's yours if you want it."

"I will give him a ring and accept the job when I get around to it; it's obvious to me that you want me out as soon as possible. After that, I'll phone Sam with the good news."

"You may think it's good news, your dad and I would far rather it be you going to university instead of going to a bakery." "At least I'm trying to do the right thing for your grandchild." "Suppose so."

"I haven't chatted to Sam since last Friday at the hospital. She'll be thinking I've done a runner."

"Perhaps you should have."

"Well I haven't, I'm trying to do the right thing and stand by her"

"Calm down, Pete."

"I'm quite calm."

Mum who looked exasperated, got up and walked out of the sitting room and back into her usual place, the kitchen.

I went ahead and made the phone calls. Tom explained how he wanted me to start work at the bakery in two weeks' time, and how I could move into the so-called flat Saturday afternoon after doing the morning shift. Then, the following Monday, I would start as an apprentice.

Sam sounded a bit down when she answered the phone but she cheered up once I told her I had a job in the Old Kent Road. She'd settled in with Gran and was going out and about with friends and was spending a lot of time in the coffee bar with a juke box near Gran's flat. The owner said that he could offer her a job once she'd dropped the baby. "Who is going to look after our baby if you take the job?"

"Gran said she would, for a few hours a day."

"Okay."

"Gran and I are getting on well, she lives in a very nice flat. I've been thinking that we may be able to live with her if we play our cards right. My bedroom is large enough for a double bed and a cot."

"I will have to think about that. To be honest with you, I would far rather live somewhere on our own with our baby."

"It is only a suggestion if we can't afford anywhere of our own."

"Has she mentioned us moving in?"

"No, but she's lovely and I think she'd let us."

"Are you sure Gran isn't being nice so you ask to stay, then she may want you to help look after her? There's got to be a catch and that must be it; yeah, that's it."

"What is the matter with you, Pete? Can't you see anything nice in her? She's my gran and she's lovely."

"Sam, there has got to be a catch."

"No catch, she's just lovely."

With that, bang went Sam's receiver. I was left with the sound of ringing in my ear. I put the receiver down at my end and stood wondering what to do next. After a bit of deliberation, I decided to leave Sam to her own devices, believing that, if she needed me, she would ring.

Tuesday soon became Wednesday and, before I realized, it was the weekend and I was sitting having breakfast in the dining room, with my parents and Anne.

"I like the sitting room, you have made a good job of the painting," said Dad, smiling.

"Good, because if you don't like it I wouldn't be doing it again; I'm still recovering from a painful back and arm ache."

"You get aches and pains once you start doing real work. Your mother has been telling me about the job at the bakery, that can be hard work. I don't know how you will get on with getting up early – Mum says you have to be there at four in the morning." "Yeah I do but I'm going to live for free above the bakery."

"That sounds okay. I want to know how much money you will be earning for food."

"Mum must have told you that I can have food from the bakery for free. I get paid for the days I work in the shop."

"Well, how much is that? I can't see how you'll manage, as you will be paying for electric and that's quite expensive. Also, you will need to buy tea, coffee and milk, along with cereal for breakfast."

"Well, you want me out, so out I'm going. I'll manage somehow. I can always take on a second job down at Piccadilly Circus."

"Doing what?"

"Rent boy."

"I don't know what to answer to that, you're so stupid at times."

"Well, don't answer. You both want me out so out I'm going. Next Saturday is my first day working in the bakery. I move into the room above, Saturday afternoon. If you help me to move in, you will see how I'm living. I wish I'd never set eyes on Sam."

"It's a bit late now to think like that."

"Surely you or Mum have both met people when you were young and done idiotic things?"

"Not as daft as what you've done."

"My pet word to you two is sorry, so sorry again. In a week's time I won't be here, I may never have to say sorry to you again."

Mum had sat and listened to all of our conversation without saying a word and, as soon as I stopped rambling on, she burst into tears.

"Don't start crying, Mum, it's not the end of the world. You'll be able to come and visit me; that's if you can come to terms with where I'm living."

"Pete is right, Marg, stop the crying."

With that, Mum left the room and Anne got up from the table, holding her bowl of cereal.

"I'm going to my room to finish this, I can't stand this conversation."

"That's the best place to go, out the way," I told her. "I'm fed up with it, I'll be going back up in a mo."

"Before you go back upstairs, Pete, I have to tell you I'm prepared to get a van and pay the fee to move your bits over to the bakery on Saturday."

"Thanks, I didn't expect you to pay for that. I hadn't got around to thinking about moving my things out, I only know that I haven't any money. Thank you. Dad, will it be okay for me to take a couple of sheets and a blanket, plus pillows? All I will have is a mattress to sleep on."

"Yeah, of course you can take them. They will be from your bed and no one else is going to sleep there. It's the least your mum and I can do as it is us who want you out. Getting back to food, your mum and I had a chat the other night and we are prepared to buy stuff like milk to tide you over, but you must remember that we won't be able to do the same every week."

"I'm not stupid, I know that you can't afford to buy food for me every week. Thanks for offering to help me out, I'm very grateful that you are going to pay for the use of a van."

"I know a chap at work with a van, he may move you for a few bob. In fact, he owes me so he may move your things for nothing."

"That's even better, Dad. I'm going up to my room."

"Before you go, son, I have something else to say. I'll just go and find Mum." Dad wandered out of the dining room and, before long, they both returned. "Now the three of us are sitting comfortably, your mum and I would like to have a chat about your A levels."

"What about them? As far as I'm concerned it doesn't matter if I pass them or not now I've got a job at the bakers."

"Your mother and I had a chat about your grades the other evening and we need to tell you that if you don't get on with the boss at this bakery, or you don't like it at the bakery, you can still go to university especially if your grades are good."

"I'm going to like it, I have to like it. If I don't I'll have to put up with it, for the sake of your first grandchild."

"It seems that Sam must have settled in with her gran or she would be on the phone. Have you heard from her since she put the receiver down on you?"

"No."

"Well, there you go, I think she has settled in and is enjoying her life with her gran."

"Most probably you are both right; parents are normally right, but I am going to give the bakery a go. If I don't like it or I'm not getting on with Sam, I will think about going to university."

"Your mum has told me that, Gran may take Sam in permanently, as they seem to be getting on well."

"Yeah, she said something about living with her, but I don't think I'd enjoy living in a council flat down the Old Kent Road."

"The thing is, Pete, a flat is what it is – it's a flat. Most don't have any garden; if you're lucky, it may have a balcony."

"The flat is on the ground floor and the back door opens out on to a communal garden, so Sam says. I haven't been there so I haven't seen it."

"A communal garden is better than no garden."

"My idea was to live in a rented flat until we could afford to buy a house similar to this one. I think Sam has other ideas. When we were talking at the hospital she said she was happy living in a flat and didn't seem to think she could live in a house with a garden."

"There you go, that's why she is thinking of living with Gran. You have to remember, Pete, that she was brought up in a flat and doesn't know anything different."

"Suppose you're right, I know you are both right. I will promise you both if I don't get on with the baker, I will leave and go to university. The pair of you should realise that I would prefer to go there, and most probably that is where I'll finish up, and your grandchild will live down the Old Kent Road."

"That is settled then, common sense at last, at least about you going to university."

321

"I'm still going to start the job at the bakery next Saturday. I have to be there at eight thirty; how I will get there I don't know."

"Well, I do – on public transport. You will have to get yourself up and running by about six thirty. If you don't, you'll be late and may have the sack on the first day."

"Tom, that's the baker, said I could move in Saturday afternoon, but I think it may be better to move in on the Sunday so we will have all day to sort things out. I have decided to get the key from him on the Saturday and come back here for the Saturday night. What do you two think?"

"That sounds okay on the surface, son, but we are not having you going out on the tiles again from here. Your mother and I have had enough of your fun and games."

"I'll stay in with you two."

"That's okay with me. What about you, Marg?"

"Yeah, I will give into that as long as you stay in."

"I said I will, so I will."

The week leading up to moving out went very slowly and the nearer I got to Saturday, the more worried I became. I packed most of my things into cardboard boxes. As I didn't have a suitcase, I had the bright idea to tie the ankles of one pair of trousers with string and fill the legs with the few clothes I had. This worked very well.

By Thursday I was ready to leave. Bored out of my mind, but with enough money to get over to the Old Kent Road, I set out to find Sam, as she hadn't contacted me.

Once I arrived at the Elephant I plodded down the Old Kent towards where I thought Gran lived, passing the bakery and the door to my so-called flat, which didn't look too savoury.

On and on I walked until I came to the corner where I thought the flat should be, but, instead of seeing Gran's flat, I saw Sam coming towards me, arm in arm and deep in conversation with Tom. Neither of them saw me walking towards them. I stood in the middle of the path so they couldn't get past without bumping straight into me.

"Hi, Sam, what is going on here?"

Both Sam and Tom looked shocked. Sam let go of Tom's arm immediately.

"What are you doing here, Pete?"

"Looking for you."

"Well, here I am, I think you have met Tom,"

"You know damn well I have, he is going to be my boss… or he was going to be my boss. I think you both need to explain yourselves."

"I'm willing to explain myself," said Tom, looking as if he meant business.

"Sam, you told me that there is a coffee bar near here, so shall we go there and have a chat?"

"Yeah, okay, it's down the road, a bit further on the left. I doubt if you will approve of it."

"Why shouldn't I?"

"Well, you don't seem to like anything that I like."

"You know very well that's not true, it's your hormones talking again." Tom started to smile to himself.

"Why does what I have just said make you smile Tom?"

He couldn't answer me; he just looked embarrassed and carried on walking along beside Sam. Eventually we arrived at Sam's favourite coffee bar. We found a table for three in the window.

"Which one of you is buying the coffee, because I'm not?" I asked.

"I told you, Tom, that Pete always gets someone else to pay up."

"Why should I pay to sit and ask questions about how you two met and what the future holds for you both?"

"This time, Pete is right, I will get three espressos." Tom got up and went to the counter.

While he was away, I fired questions at Sam and found out that she went along to the bakery to see what it was like and found Tom serving behind the counter.

"So you only met a couple of weeks ago? I can hardly believe what you are saying! I can't imagine anyone being picked up when they have a bun in the oven."

"Well, there you go, you were wrong, Pete," said Tom, arriving back with the coffees. "Sam did get picked up by me. She is a lovely girl and I'm very fond of her."

"Tell me what your plans are. I need to know, so I can mark out my future. It's obvious to me that it's not going to be with Sam, so come on, Tom, tell me your plans."

"To be really honest with you, mate, I haven't any. Sam and I get on well but that is as far as it goes at the moment. I'll tell you one thing, she is a damn good screw, so I'll be around for a while."

Sam seemed to like what Tom said and smiled across at him.

"I'm afraid it's over with you, Pete. If it finishes with Tom, I won't be phoning you up. I'm going to stay living with Gran."

"That's that then, I'll finish my coffee, then go on my way." I drank it down as fast as I could and left.

I eventually arrived home, both mum and dad noticed I was upset, I explained what had happened, they suggested I should try and forget Sam and concentrate on my future – which I did.

I finished up going to Birmingham University to study Science. While there mum phoned to say that she had bumped into Sam pushing a black baby in a pram so the baby couldn't possibly be mine. Apparently Sam is still living with her Gran and has nothing to do with her parents.

The End.

Printed in Poland
by Amazon Fulfillment
Poland Sp. z o.o., Wrocław

57906567R00184